A SPY WITHIN

A SPY WITHIN

A Novel

By

Lynnette Baughman

Acknowledgments:

Many people have encouraged me and offered helpful critiques during the gestation of this book. Most important are my husband and my three terrific daughters, to whom this book is dedicated.

I am surrounded by talented and intelligent writers whose help has been beyond measure. First among them is Suzanne Smith, instructor at University of New Mexico-Los Alamos. Thanks also to Shirley-Raye Redmond, Karen Nilsson Brandt, Sharon Lloyd Spence, Jann Arrington Wolcott, Susan Hazen-Hammond, Peggy van Hulsteyn, Dana Evans, Inez Ross, Susan McBride, Diane Gotfryd and Sharon Zukowski. Thanks, as well, to James D. Doss, Michael McGarrity, and Sarah Lovett.

I appreciate the technical advice of Gary DeRosier, Houston Terry Hawkins, Lowell Little, and Neil Zack.

Special thanks to the staffs of Mesa Public Library, the LANL Library, and the Los Alamos Historical Society.

The cover photo of the 1945 Trinity Test is by Jack Aeby and used with permission of the Los Alamos Historical Society.

The author's photo on the back cover is by John McHale who is a terrific professional photographer who came to my place to take the picture.

A SPY WITHIN

A Top Publications Paperback

This edition published 1999
12221 Merit Drive, Suite 750
Dallas, Texas 75251

ISBN#: 0-9666366-4-3
Library of Congress # 99-72829

The characters and events in this novel are fictional and created out of the imagination of the author. Certain real locations and institutions are mentioned, but the characters and events depicted are entirely fictional.

Printed in the United States of America

Chapter One

The day of the first murder began just like any other Monday in Los Alamos. At 8:30 a.m., reporter Patrice Kelsey moved her magnet, a bloodshot eyeball, from OUT to IN on the board behind the receptionist.

Marian looked up from a mound of mail shoved through the door slot over the weekend and tried unsuccessfully to stifle a yawn. "Morning, Patrice. How's it going?"

"Oh, same old cornflakes. How 'bout you?"

"Ummm, same old oatmeal." Surveying the mail, Marian curled her lip. "Here it is Monday, already. Oh well, another day, another dollar."

"What? Did you get a raise?" Patrice rested one hand on her hip. "How come I don't get that much?"

"I was referring to before taxes. Another day, another fifty-seven cents." She noticed Patrice's holly-green crocheted vest. "Did you do that? It's nice, brings out the green in your eyes."

"Thanks." Patrice turned her head to show the matching crocheted elastic band that held her long, ash blond hair in a low ponytail. "No, I don't do handwork. It's an early Christmas present from my mom. Which reminds me, three weeks 'til Christmas."

"You going anywhere?" Marian placed a stack of Sunday papers on the counter by the door and unlocked the cash register.

"You kidding? I can't afford to go anywhere, and I only have about three days of leave accrued anyway." She took a tissue off Marian's desk and wiped a streak of mud off her black pumps. She couldn't help but long for attractive boots to set off the vest and gray wool skirt, but $9.99 Payless pumps would have to do.

"You do anything fun over the weekend?"

"Ah, Marian, I wouldn't know where to start. The laundromat, the frozen pizza, the wink meant just for me from Louis Rukeyser on *Wall Street Week*. It's all a mad blur."

"Girl, you gotta slow down," Marian said with a wry laugh as she picked up the ringing phone. "Good morning, *Guardian*. Yes, Rose, Patrice is right here. Hold on while she staggers to her desk carrying thirty pounds of mail." Marian pointed to a stack so tall it could collapse at any time and said, "Yours! Get it out of here, please." Back into the phone she said, "When will your daughter get home from college?"

Patrice leaned the stack against her chest, then bent way down to pick up a catalog that fell from her grasp. She unloaded the stack of mail on her desk and formed a dike with her hip to keep it from sliding off. Four yellow and three blue Post-It Notes adhered tenuously to her computer screen and waved like butterflies in the breeze from the front door.

"Poor man's e-mail," she'd called it with a slight roll of her eyes when she started working at the paper. Now she participated enthusiastically in the office confetti-graffiti, sticking her own green notes on chairs, monitors, telephones and keyboards, wherever the recipient would most likely see it.

She peeled off the notes and stuck them on the surface of her desk. "How many editors does it take to change a light bulb?" said one of the yellow ones. "See me ASAP--RR" was scribbled on a blue one. Patrice leaned past her desk to see the desk of her boss, managing editor Rick Romero. He was on the phone, his face swivelled away from the newsroom. Two more jokes and three questions from Composition completed the set of mini-missives.

She waved to Marian and waited until she saw her put down the phone, then picked up the receiver and punched the flashing light. "Hi, Rose, what's up?" Her friend Rose was a woman of vast stores of energy and wide-ranging interests, especially history, and in particular the history of Los Alamos. A veritable bulldog when she sank her teeth into a story, Rose had her canines imbedded in a spy tale, a spy who went by the code name Perseus. Although Rose was twenty years older than Patrice, give or take a year, Patrice thought of Rose as her contemporary.

"I got the papers from the FBI in the mail today," Rose said. "The Freedom of Information Act stuff."

"So, hit the high points for me. I'm all yours." Patrice sat down at her terminal and waited impatiently for her computer to boot up. While she listened to Rose she thumbed quickly through the mail for an envelope from Los Alamos National Laboratory, the heart, lungs and brain of the isolated New Mexico town, or at least its main paymaster.

"I can't go into it now," Rose said. "But it gives me more to go on about the 'Last Man.'"

"Does the report mention Doyle Silver?" She ran her tongue over a chapped spot on her lower lip. Pulling open the center drawer of her desk, she found a compact and applied coral lipstick. *Oh, say, that's an improvement! Now I have chapped lips that shine like Day-Glo*. She glanced at her eyes to make sure her mascara wasn't in splotches.

"No, not exactly. It does mention the Soviet courier he saw in Santa Fe in April 1945." Rose cleared her throat, then added, "The courier he *says* he saw."

"Ah, yes, the courier he *allegedly* saw. We'll make a newswoman out of you yet. Does the FBI report use her name? Lona Cohen?" Her computer booted up and she checked e-mail. Nothing urgent there. She filed four messages and swiveled her chair away from the monitor.

"Yes, it names her, but it doesn't say who handed her any secret papers."

"Well, Doyle Silver hasn't named anybody, either. All he

does is dance around like a six year old with a secret."

"I would hardly describe him as dancing. He's bedridden in a nursing home, for heaven's sake."

"I was speaking figuratively," Patrice went on. "He dances around verbally." She mimicked an old crone's voice. "I saw a Russian spy in 1945, and if you're real, real nice I'll tell you his name." She turned back to her computer, brought up the menu of stories she was working on for that day's paper, then continued.

"And speaking of names, yes, Doyle named Lona Cohen as the courier he saw, but let's not forget, in the thrill of the chase, that she was named in papers coast to coast six years ago. He could have picked up her name then. When is he going to name the men, the Big Five? Or the Big Four plus himself?" Patrice was losing patience with the old man and his "big spy story," as he insisted it was. Someday soon he'd tell Rose and her all about the "Last Man bottle" and why the five men toasted each other by the light of the first atomic bomb. It was always "soon," then he'd put off spilling the beans for yet another day, another visit.

"Actually, I have *a lot more* to go on now, a lot more, but I can't go into it now, over the phone."

"Now you're doing it!" Patrice said, exasperated.

"Doing what?"

"Teasing." This time she mimicked a little girl's singsong, "I have a secret, and you don't know it!"

"Look, I'll tell you everything on the way to Española tonight. A whole lot has been happening, but I can't go into it on the phone."

Rose added something, but even with the receiver pressed to her ear Patrice had trouble hearing her. Kent Bolt, publisher of the Los Alamos Guardian and her Boss with a capital B, made a grand and noisy entrance to the newsroom from his office.

Kent bellowed across the room to Rick Romero as if the people at the desks in between were mannequins who had no need of eardrums. "Rick, where are Danny and Patrice?"

The expensive double-breasted suit, accented by a red silk

tie and matching handkerchief in the breast pocket, failed to compensate for Kent's deficit in height and looks. Might as well tape peacock feathers on a bantam rooster.

"What?" Patrice said to Rose. "You'll have to talk louder to compete with this barnyard. Breaking news or something."

"I'll tell you tonight on our way down."

"Down where?" Patrice asked as she bent over her wastebasket to retrieve an envelope that had slipped in from the edge of her desk. "You May Already Be a Winner!" it screamed in red letters. She tossed it back in the basket.

"To Española, to the nursing home." Now it was Rose's turn to sound exasperated. "Don't tell me you forgot!"

"No, I remember." Patrice's shoulders slumped at the thought of the tiring evening ahead. The trip had, in fact, slipped her mind, and she planned to spend the evening with a new James Doss mystery.

Patrice saw the paper's photographer, Danny Carter, stroll in from the darkroom at the same time Kent Bolt spotted her. "I've got to go, Rose," she said. "I'll call you later; I can't promise anything."

Rick Romero closed the distance to his boss and Kent lowered his voice to a humane level, gesturing to Rick by punching the air and pointing in the general direction of the front door. Rick nodded vigorously and Kent strode back into his office.

Rick pointed at Patrice, then Danny, and then toward the coffee break room. Following in Danny's footsteps, she sighed in unison with him and shuffled into the room. Danny was about five-six, muscular, and always needed a haircut. He was the first one to hear the latest jokes and had a gift of telling them for maximum effect. Yes, Danny was one of the few bright spots of working at the *Guardian*, Patrice smiled to herself. One step behind them, Rick shut the door half way.

"Kent heard there's a big anti-nuke demonstration out at the Plutonium Facility. He wants it front page, today, in color."

"How come we gotta give protestors every flippin' thing they want?" Danny shoved his hair back with one hand."We working for them, or what?"

That question had hung in the newsroom like the odor of dirty laundry ever since Kent Bolt bought the failing *Los Alamos Chronicle* from a consortium of losers six months before. Changing the name to "Guardian" signaled a fresh start, but not good news for the staff. Or, Patrice was prepared to argue, for the readers. She pulled the elastic band from her hair and placed it on her wrist, snapping it in annoyance. Why did Kent come to Los Alamos if he hated the place so much, she'd like to know. Or at least hated what it represented, research in nuclear weapons. Nothing would change the history of Los Alamos, that it was the Secret City, the Atomic City, where the first atomic bombs were built during World War II.

"This is not the place or the time for that question," Rick said to Danny without a smile to soften the words. "Just head for Tech Area-55 and do your usual excellent work, in half the usual time."

*****

As Patrice strapped on her seat belt in Danny's Dodge pick-up, he counted the rolls of film in his bag, muttering under his breath. "Rick is right about it being 'not the place for that question,' but he's wrong about the other. It is the time for it."

"I admire your principles," Patrice said, "but this is the world. I'm older, wiser, and I've been unemployed more than you have." At twenty-eight, Patrice was only four years older than Danny, but it felt like more. Losing three jobs in seven years had aged her.

"Sure," she continued, "Kent is a Trojan horse, bought and paid for. But a publisher is just a politician with unlimited ink. Every paper serves its master."

"I can't believe you're saying that!" Danny said. "Why did you become a reporter if you feel that way?" He pulled onto Trinity Drive from the *Guardian's* parking lot.

Patrice thought back to her first jobs. With a degree from University of Missouri School of Journalism and a great portfolio from part-time jobs and internships, she first snagged an excellent job on a Chicago paper, only to lose it when the paper merged with a competitor and both staffs were cut by forty percent. The same thing happened to her twice more on big Midwest papers. She shook her head to banish the clutch of fear such memories always engendered.

"I became a reporter," she answered, choosing her words deliberately, "because I felt like you obviously still do—that Truth is something pure, something worth fighting for, something to give a flip about. I have remained a reporter because..." She shrugged. "Okay, so I'm not sure why."

"Must be the money," Danny said with a snort. On Diamond Drive, the main artery of the town, he headed left across the Omega Canyon Bridge and out Pajarito Road toward the Plutonium Facility.

Each time Patrice lost a job she had picked herself up, got a deferral on her student loans, and flooded the mail with her résumé. A friend from Mizzou who worked for the *Albuquerque Journal* heard about the job at the Los Alamos newspaper and recommended her. She had occasion since that time to wonder how good a friend he really was.

She ran her fingers through her hair to gather it in a tight ponytail and secured it with the elastic band. *Danny will have to make his own mistakes. I'm not even sure I'm through making mine.*

The weather report called for only a slight chance of snow at Los Alamos's altitude, 7,200 feet, but clouds were building in the west and the temperature was dropping precipitously. Patrice hoped Rose Hulle would change her mind about the two of them driving to Española that evening to see Doyle Silver at the nursing home, but she doubted Rose would be deterred.

Rose would probably nag at her again about getting a job that used her skill and talent better. Lately she'd been pushing the idea of the two of them writing a book together, a book about Doyle Silver and spies and stuff. "I don't work well without a net," Patrice had said. Still, the idea of writing a book was intriguing...

"Well, well, well," Danny said when he saw the crowd at Technical Area-55, the Plutonium Facility, "all the world's a stage."

"And all the men and women merely bad actors," Patrice added as she checked the pocket of her blue and gold parka for a pen and a skinny notebook. Danny cut across a curb and parked the Dodge Dakota on a dusty lot with scruffy chamisas. Slinging the strap of his heavy bag over his shoulder, he jumped out of the truck.

Patrice waited a few minutes to survey the demonstrators. She tried to focus her attention on the milling crowd, but the view of the Jemez Mountains to the west and the snow-encrusted Sangre de Cristo Mountains across the Rio Grande valley to the east made her catch her breath. She had lived in northern New Mexico for two years, and the scenery still amazed her.

She hopped down from the high seat and covered her eyes for a minute against the blowing dirt. The wind plastered her gray wool skirt against her legs like a mainsail as she tacked over to Danny.

"Damn wind," Danny said, turning away from the stinging sand as he changed lenses on the Nikon. As usual he had on only a thin nylon jacket.

"You're going to get pneumonia," Patrice said reprovingly.

"Hey, I live with my mother, okay?" he snapped. "I don't need more nagging on the job."

"Sorr-eee!" Patrice said. "I didn't mean to strike a nerve."

Danny glared at her for a couple seconds, then shrugged and smiled. "It's okay. I shouldn't bite your head off, just because I want to see Kent Bolt arrested for impersonating a publisher. You know, that guy, with his pin stripes and his platform shoes, he gives short men a bad name."

"The name Napoleon has crossed my wicked mind from time to time," Patrice said with a laugh of relief. Danny was so happy-go-lucky, she forgot he could get edgy, too. The air at the *Guardian* seemed supercharged with tension lately. Even Rick had been uncharacteristically abrupt when he told them to go to the Plutonium Facility. Patrice sighed and shaded her eyes. *Rick must be under a lot of strain, too.*

She turned her attention to the crowd. "Twenty-nine, thirty, thirty-one," she counted under her breath. Aloud she said, "About forty protesters, and nearly that many waiting at the guard shack to get inside to their jobs."

The Plutonium Facility was certainly not the most representative site for the work that went on at the Laboratory, but it was a popular target of protestors. Dismantling nuclear weapons was more likely taking place there than building bombs. There was also a lot of research at the Lab on medicine, energy, oceanography, weather, and space travel. The time of big bombs was history; the time of giant computers, robotics and cooperation with private industry had arrived. But Kent Bolt didn't want to hear it. He was making the *Guardian* an organ of the Lab's enemies. More than once while shopping at the Farmer's Market or standing in line at Daylight Donuts, Patrice had winced to hear the newspaper called the "Los Alamos Guillotine."

"Does that number sound about right to you? Forty protestors?" Patrice asked.

Danny didn't have time to answer before they heard a guard shout, "Get back! Don't push this fence! Get back!"

The outer gate at the facility opened to allow a pickup truck with a security guard through. The heretofore-quiet protesters took a cue from a tall, skinny man and began to shout. The leather fringe on his jacket and his long, red ponytail lashed his face in the wind. Danny and Patrice could make out the chant then: "No Nukes! No War! No Nukes! No More!" and she saw six or eight additional protesters alight from a van carrying signs with the universal symbol for radiation hazard.

"Let's get closer to the fence," Danny said. He leaned his stocky body into the crowd like a linebacker and Patrice followed, keeping her head down to his height and clutching the strap of the camera bag. She bumped into him when he stopped abruptly. She stood up, then ducked as a sign was passed over their heads. Looking in the wrong direction, she stood back up to her full five feet-eight, just in time to get whacked in the back of her head by the next sign coming over. People closest to the fence snatched the signs and held them aloft like gilt banners in a holy procession. Patrice examined her head with her fingertips. *Good, no blood. It might swell, but there's no cut.*

Then the protesters shoved like elevator doors from both sides at once as the wall-sized chain link gate swung toward them to make room for a security vehicle.

In a split second a pregnant woman spun around the outside of the crowd and broke through the open gate, holding on to the tailgate of the pickup. As the driver leaped from the truck and the shocked guards secured the outer gate, the woman poured red liquid--either blood or something that looked like blood--on herself and screamed as if she were being skewered. At the same time, she handcuffed herself to the inner fence and the crowd cheered wildly.

"Call me crazy," Patrice said as Danny's Nikon fired away, "but I love this town."

Chapter 2

Four hours later the *Guardian*, still damp from the presses, left Danny's hands and sailed to Patrice's desk like a rectangular Frisbee. It landed with a whack that startled her colony of Post-It Notes into flight. At the same time, Danny gave a nearby wheeled chair a kick and it caromed backward into a desk. Since Marian had asked Patrice to answer the phones while she ran an errand, Patrice and Danny had the post-paper newsroom to themselves.

"I feel like a whore." He shoved his hands into his pockets as if he didn't care if he tore holes in them.

His photo of the blood-drenched pregnant woman and the stunned guard with his gun aimed at her made the front page of the *Guardian* and, thanks to Associated Press, would rivet the attention of newspaper readers around the world. That it was chicken blood the woman poured on herself before she snapped the handcuffs to the security fence was noted in the caption at the *Guardian*, but who knows how many papers, saving space, lost the word "chicken."

Patrice knew Danny was torn with elation that his photo was on the wire and disgust at the subject matter. The woman and her fellow protesters had planned the event for maximum exposure and every tiny variable swung their way. The only way "Earth," which the woman insisted was her name, could have done it better would have been to have spontaneously given birth to a hideously deformed baby while handcuffed to the fence. Live on CNN.

"That's it," he said. "I mean that is it. The last straw, the final act; I'm giving notice. Kent can kiss my butt good-bye."

"Can I watch?" Patrice tore the wrapper off a granola bar, settling for a sugar and fiber fix in lieu of lunch. "Want one? I've got two or three more in my drawer."

"No, thanks." He grimaced, one hand on his stomach. "I'm on a strict junk food diet and that looks suspiciously nutritious."

"No way! Rats would die on this stuff." She held out the wrapper. "Read the label: 'This product guaranteed to have no food value.' Would I lie?"

He sighed. "Okay, I'll take one."

"Speaking of rats makes me think of their propensity for leaving sinking ships, which makes me think, readily, of you. Do you have any job prospects lined up?"

"I have some feelers out. My plan is in two weeks I'll either have a good job at a real newspaper or I'll be living out of a shopping cart and showering at a homeless shelter. Either way, it beats working for Kent Bolt and his sinister sister, Catwoman."

Patrice shrugged. They both knew Kent's sister, U.S. Senator Cristal Aragon, had no technical connection, certainly no managerial position, with the paper, but it was a distinction not worth quibbling over, like whether lightning surged up from the ground or down from a cloud. The charred person in the middle had nothing further to say.

"But enough about me," Danny said. "Why do you stay here? Are you hiding from someone? Are you in the Witness Protection Program?"

"You mean, what's a nice girl like me doing in a place like this?"

"Something like that, yeah," he persisted. "I was born here; I grew up here; I live with my mother to save money. But surely you could have done better. And past insanity aside, surely you can do better now."

Patrice sighed, glad Rose wasn't there to rally with Danny

and do a nag duet, both urging her to try something new and better suited to what they insisted was her superior skill and talent. "What you are saying, Dan my man, is not a news bulletin. But right now is not the time." Patrice held up her hand to end the debate. She knew the next words out of his mouth would involve Rick Romero, and she didn't want to have a "Yo, girlfriend" talk about Rick with Danny or anybody else. On cue, the phone on her desk rang. She let it ring twice while Danny took the hint and ambled off toward the darkroom.

"Good afternoon, *Guardian*."

"Patrice!" Rose said. "I've been waiting for you to call."

"I swear I was going to call in fifteen seconds. Just as soon as I swallowed my so-called lunch."

"A lot is going on," Rose said. "I'll tell you on the way to Española to see Doyle Silver."

Patrice coughed, a sliver of granola having lodged in her throat. "Hold on." She put the receiver against her chest while she coughed vigorously and drank her bottled water. "Española?" she rasped into the phone when she thought her throat was clear. "You're sure it has to be tonight?"

"Yes! It's important," Rose said adamantly.

"The weather looks pretty 'iffy,'" Patrice countered, though if pressed on the point, she'd have to admit the weather always looked "iffy" so near the mountains.

"I heard the cold front is going north," Rose said, "probably miss us completely." She paused, then added, "I think Doyle is in trouble. I have a very bad feeling about it." There was a click on the line. "Oh, I...I'll have to call you back."

"Go ahead and take it," Patrice said. "I'll hold on." She doodled on her desk pad, random squiggles that became the common cartoon rendition of an atomic explosion, a mushroom cloud.

She thought about Doyle Silver and wondered what was going on to put Rose in such a state of anxiety. She'd seen the old man around Los Alamos maybe a dozen times during the two years she'd lived there, but didn't know his name until Rose told her.

The two women had been standing at the arc of tinted windows in the library, watching summer lightning dance wickedly through the Jemez Mountains, and automatically counting "five, six, seven" from flash to boom to guess at the distance.

"Look over there," Rose had said, pointing toward a man leaning close over a newspaper spread out on a table, reading it with a magnifying glass. When he leaned back in the chair Patrice could see he was still hunched over, thanks to curvature of the spine. "That's the man who told me about the 'Last Man bottle.' Doyle Silver. Nice old man, lonely. Come on, I'll introduce you."

About a week after the introduction, Rose took Patrice to Doyle Silver's house for coffee. With judicious prodding by Rose, Doyle warmed to his story.

"Lot of people would like to know about this," he said, raising his bushy eyebrows. Then he sat silent as a monk.

Rose set a cup of coffee on the table in front of Doyle, then, from her position behind him, she gestured to Patrice to say something, even crossing her eyes comically.

Patrice saw how the game was to be played; Doyle enjoyed being coaxed. "I'm so interested, Mr. Silver. Rose won't tell me anything, just that you're a man of mystery. Won't you tell me about it?"

"You may call me Doyle," he said, his face softening from the reproach she'd clearly deserved. He sat back and closed his eyes as if gathering his thoughts. Patrice used the opportunity to give Rose a cross-eyed look of her own. Pointedly she looked at her watch to remind Rose she didn't have all day to mollycoddle Doyle Silver.

But two hours later she was spellbound, unaware any time had passed at all.

"We were pioneers," he had begun, in his raspy voice, a product, he admitted, of forty years of smoking. "I came out on the train to Lamy, May of 1943. I always like to say I said yes when Robert Oppenheimer asked me to join the Manhattan Project because I'd always wanted to see Times Square."

He'd been a skinny young man, he said, "as skinny as Robert Oppenheimer, and he didn't even have a shadow if he turned sideways." He'd known all the "big guys," as he referred to Enrico Fermi, Hans Bethe, Richard Feynman, and to Niels Bohr, who visited the project site from time to time.

When he talked of the excitement the scientists felt, out on the frontier of science, discovering secrets known only to God before them, Patrice thought the years fell away from his crinkled face. The light in his brown eyes must have been just like that when he was a twenty-year old college graduate surrounded by giants of physics at Los Alamos.

"I was quite the dancing fool in those days," he said with a throaty laugh that triggered a coughing spell. "Never missed a dance at Fuller Lodge or this other big hall we used. Plenty of pretty Women's Army Corps here then. But it was apparent pretty soon that one had her hat set on me, that was Betty Jean." He sat quiet, lost in reverie. "We were married thirty-six years when she died. No kids."

Rose used any opportunity to steer the conversation toward the "Last Man bottle," but Doyle seemed to know he'd lose his audience if he gave them what they came for too quickly. Instead he detoured to a tale of mischief by Richard Feynman, then segued to the story of the scientist's terminally ill wife, whom Feynman brought to Albuquerque from New Jersey, so he could visit her. She died of tuberculosis toward the end of the war, Doyle said.

Patrice had all but forgotten about the work that waited for her at the newspaper, so enthralled was she by his stories of the famous scientists and the young men like himself who felt like they were in a throne room when Enrico Fermi got up to the blackboard.

At last Doyle got to the Trinity Test, the climax of the

Manhattan Project, the day the frontier of science was penetrated irrevocably.

Patrice had heard the story before and seen it in movies, but she hung on every word. "Truman was in Potsdam, you know, talking to Stalin, waiting for word the test was a success. We packed the plutonium core in Los Alamos in a field carrying case studded with rubber bumpers...put it in a sedan, armed guards ahead of it, us in the pit-assembly crew riding behind."

He continued, warming to his story. "At the McDonald Ranch we spread out the two nickel-plated hemispheres of plutonium on a table, and a beryllium initiator. George Kistiakowsky had a five-foot sphere of high explosives ready."

He told of the bomb's assembly, of raising it to the tower, of the pounding rain in the early hours of July 16, with lightning and thunder, how they feared the test would be canceled. "The one-minute warning rocket fired at 5:29, and at ten seconds a gong sounded..."

He paused, as if hearing the gong sound across the span of time. "The sky flashed brighter than magnesium flares, and the heat hit us like opening a kiln door. The cloud was brilliant purple over us, glowing with radioactivity, then it rose into the air. The sound, like the loudest thunder you can imagine, kept going on and on, echoing back on itself."

He tilted his head back, watching the mushroom cloud rise from the desert floor, then seemed to age again before Patrice's eyes. He lowered his eyes to the floor and pulled his sweater close around him, even though the day was hot and sultry. The charged atmosphere waited for the relief of a thundershower.

A grandfather clock broke the silence with Westminster chimes, then bonged the hour: five.

"There were five of us," he said softly. "We brought two bottles of fine cognac with us from Los Alamos. We said if the bomb worked we'd celebrate by drinking one. If it was a dud, and some people bet it would be, we'd drown our sorrow by drinking two. And so, we passed one bottle round, each man pouring some into a paper cup shaped like a cone. And we held them aloft like crystal snifters, and said, 'To peace, shalom.' And we let the cognac burn all the way down our dry throats to cauterize the fear we had in our bellies. At least, I had the fear."

He took a deep breath and went on. "The other bottle? We signed the label, and wrote on it: 'To be opened by the Last Man and drunk in toast to us all. Trinity Site, New Mexico, July 16, 1945.' Then we packed it in shredded paper in a wooden box."

Doyle would not tell them who the other four were, only that they were all men, and two were already dead. At the same time, he declared the story behind the bottle was a spy story that would "bust Los Alamos wide open," and that he wanted them to write it.

"But not yet," he added. "The time isn't right yet."

Whether he really felt a need to be secretive about his fellows, or whether he used the "Last Man" story to titillate them and assure they'd visit him again, they couldn't be sure.

Patrice had visited him, with Rose, once more at his small house, but he wasn't in the mood, as he put it, "to jaw about history." Rose had gone to see him twice at the nursing home since then. And now she insisted they had to see him at once.

"I'm back," Rose said, "I'm sorry to leave you hanging on like that, but it was an international call for Mel and I had to write down about ten phone numbers."

Just then five people, including Rick Romero, came in the front door together, talking as loud as a pit crew at a Nascar race. Marian hung her coat on a steel tree and mimed picking up a phone receiver to show Patrice she would answer calls. Danny emerged from the darkroom and joined the loud discussion about the Denver Broncos. What with getting the Monday afternoon paper to the pressmen by twelve-thirty, Rick and his entourage had to settle for being Monday-afternoon quarterbacks. Waldo, the sports editor, argued a crucial call in Sunday's game with the pressmen, Dave and Mark.

Patrice was having trouble hearing as a dispute over the

Broncos' collective manhood heated up. "Rose, I've got to go. I've got piles of mail, and calls to return. Oh, and research on those Russians that are coming next week."

"What time shall I pick you up at your apartment?"

The thought of returning to her dismal efficiency apartment was sobering, if not downright depressing. "You can pick me up here at the paper. I'll be ready at six-thirty." She smiled as she hung up. Rose Hulle was nothing if not persistent.

Patrice picked up a press release on the Russian scientists who would visit the Laboratory in nine days, as well as the Russian civilians from Los Alamos's Sister City. The civilians were reciprocating a visit three months before by Los Alamos residents, a "friendship delegation" of fifteen teachers, doctors, politicians and others. Known during the Second World War and until the mid-1990's as Arzamas-16, the city had reclaimed its ancient name, Sarov. At Sarov's heart, just as in Los Alamos, was a nuclear research laboratory.

Over the top of the sheet of paper Patrice watched Rick toss a foam rubber football to Danny, who clutched it to his body and headed for the darkroom.

Rick caught her eye and Patrice blushed to be found staring at him. His provocative smile made her blush even redder.

"I don't think it's a good idea to date people you work with," she'd said to Rose over lunch just a week before.

"I agree," Rose said, "it's not a good idea to date *people* you work with. But it's okay to date *a person* you work with."

"Not if he is my boss. And besides, he hasn't actually asked me out on a date, so the whole subject is pure speculation."

Rose smiled broadly. "Or impure speculation. You're fighting propinquity, Patrice. Just relax and let life happen. Rick is a terrific guy."

Propinquity, she mused as she watched Rick from across the newsroom...the idea that if you stay in proximity with someone of the opposite sex, and you enjoy that proximity, you'll gradually find yourself in love with that person. But would it be the right person, or just an accident--an attraction that could be replaced by attraction to another co-worker in close proximity?

She tried to be uninterested in Rick Romero, or, failing that, to at least be disinterested, cool and detached. None of that resolve was holding, however, as she observed his smile, his dark brown eyes, bordered by crinkly laugh lines, his square jaw.

Yes, Patrice told herself as she lifted the press release high enough to remove Rick from her field of vision, *Danny is right. I should get a better job, somewhere where the cost of living isn't about twenty percent more than I get paid. I should leave Los Alamos.*

But not just yet.

Chapter 3

On the way to Española that evening, Patrice tried without success to get a weather report on Rose's car radio. "All I get is syndicated talk shows and sports."

"I'll give you eyewitness weather," Rose said. "It's raining." She paused. "Now it's not raining." Another pause. "Oops, it's raining again." She turned the windshield wipers from intermittent to regular speed.

"I was hoping for something with a little wider perspective," Patrice said dryly.

"Okay, patchy clouds over northern New Mexico with locally heavy rain over the east side of the Jemez Mountains." They had hugged the hillside on their steep descent down the Main Hill Road, heading east and continuing to drop in elevation as they neared the Rio Grande valley.

Before they reached the river, they turned left and headed north. "Okay, smarty," Patrice said as they took the turnoff, "what's the weather report for the valley?"

"Rain--make that locally heavy rain--in the valley." She turned the wipers to high speed.

"No chance of snow?"

"For Christmas, yes. But the Ouija board says 'not tonight.' Now, tell me about the Russians who are coming next week. At least one teacher, I presume, and at least one doctor."

"Yes, and at least one politician, the mayor of Sarov." Patrice told Rose what she knew of the visitors' schedule so far, and about the anti-nuclear demonstration at the Plutonium

Facility.

"I have to prepare you before you see Doyle," Rose interrupted as they approached Española. "He's lost a lot of his, I don't know, I guess I'd call it spirit or spark."

"Did that happen before he went into a nursing home, or is it a result of the change? And why is he clear down here, anyway, nearly thirty miles from his home? It must have been terribly hard on him to leave his house; he was so crazy about his African violets." The old man had given her a baby violet when she and Rose had visited him in the late summer.

"This was his nephew's idea." Rose moved the heater setting to defrost. "Doyle has no children and his wife died ages ago. His nephew lives in Los Alamos. He talked Doyle into putting his nice house on the market 'just to see what it might get,'--ho, ho, ho--and before Doyle knew what hit him, the nephew slapped a bill of sale in front of him. Doyle thought he'd move into a retirement center or the nursing home in Los Alamos and still be able to see his friends, which is how the nephew talked him into selling the house. But--too late--he found out everything on the Hill was full, and in about three beats of his nephew's so-called heart, Doyle wound up way down here."

"That smells! What do you want to bet the nephew stands to inherit whatever the house sold for?"

"You're a cynical woman, Patrice Kelsey. But in this case, cynicism is probably called for." Again the rain let up and Rose turned off the windshield wipers.

"Speaking of cynical, I'm anxious to find out why we had to come out here tonight, why it couldn't wait? What was it you couldn't talk about on the phone anyway?" She exaggerated Rose's emphasis on the news being mysterious and super-secret.

"All right, Miss Jaded Newswoman, you know how Doyle said he saw a scientist from the Manhattan Project hand over secret papers to a courier for the Soviet Union?"

"Right, to Lona Cohen, at the cocktail lounge of La Fonda Hotel in Santa Fe, in April 1945. Been there, read it in all the papers, waiting for the movie."

"Well, the reason he's so familiar with the incident is--he's the one who handed over secret papers about the development of the atomic bomb."

Patrice's jaw dropped open. "Doyle? Doyle Silver himself was a spy? He told you that?"

"Not only was he a spy, but the other four men in the 'Last Man bottle' pact were also spies. So the spy code-named Perseus that I've been searching for wasn't one man, but a cabal."

Patrice's mouth was still open. "Why that wily old devil! So who are the other spies?"

"That's what I intend to find out tonight." She turned the wipers to high speed again as a deluge like the rinse cycle at a car wash hit them.

Patrice thought that over. "Shocking and intriguing as that is, it doesn't tell why it had to be tonight, come hell or high water. And if this keeps up, high water is the more likely of the two."

"Doyle is afraid someone wants to shut him up, to keep us from finding out about the spies. He insisted we come tonight. Maybe he's being melodramatic about 'danger,' but I believe him."

They threaded their way through very light traffic in Española, crossed the Rio Grande on the old concrete bridge, and drove north on the Taos highway. Rose slowed and leaned forward, looking for their turnoff. Bumping along the shoulder for about a quarter mile, at last she said, "Aha!" and made a sharp right on a dark road. Patrice bit her tongue when one wheel plunged into a chuckhole the size of a grave.

As they pulled into the parking lot of the nursing home, Rose said, "I know this is not the time to go into this, but please be thinking about writing the book on this with me."

"Look, I'm flattered that you think so much of my ability, but you have a husband to support you while you write. I'm always about two weeks from eviction, barely coming up with the rent money in time. I've got to stay at the *Guardian!*"

"Haven't you ever heard of an advance from a publisher? Anyway, don't answer now. Just think about it. I'm sure, absolutely sure, it would be a terrific career move for you."

"So, you've heard the saying around the *Guardian?* 'Nowhere to go but up.'" Patrice laughed.

The rain stopped long enough for them to dart inside without getting wet. Patrice prepared herself for the unpleasant odor she associated with nursing homes as they opened the second set of glass doors of Buena Vista Care Center, but was met instead by such a strong aroma of air freshener she sneezed three times in a row.

Rose said "Good evening" to the nurse at the control center of the institution, a desk with high curved barrier not far from the entrance.

The nurse waved hello and they continued down a central hall. Rose knew where to find Doyle Silver, having visited him at Buena Vista twice before. At a crossroads of wide hallways, a massive bulletin board blazed the message "Happy Thanksgiving" with a border of orange and brown crepe paper. Between the two words, a paper cutout of a tom turkey with blood-red wattles gave them the evil eye. Polaroid photos of diners in wheelchairs and bibs hung from the bulletin board, tacked up with colorful plastic pins. In many of the photos, nurses or aides posed beside the elderly residents, bending awkwardly to lower their heads into the photos.

"Here he is, and here," Rose said, pointing to a gnome-like man with a large paper bib tucked under his neck. His wattles looked suspiciously like those of the turkey on his bib. He was studying his food, oblivious to the camera, with a heavy-set woman aide on his right and a bearded man on his left. Patrice guessed the man was about forty, though his dark beard and glasses made it hard to tell. In the second photo the bearded man was seated beside Doyle, and the beard could not conceal his look of revulsion at the food falling out of the old man's mouth. She thought she saw Doyle in another photo, taken from further away.

In the foreground was a woman in a wheelchair, wearing a blindfold, apparently "it" in some game. Doyle was on the sidelines but his attention was on a balding man who bent low as if to hear what the old man was saying. The camera flash reflected off the top of the visitor's head. He was in street clothes, not the uniforms of the nurses and aides.

"He's down this hall," Rose said, turning from the display.

"Hello, Miz Hulle, how you doin' tonight?" An aide with a voice as silky as a Georgia peach skin was pushing a mobile shelf unit with balky wheels. Her skin was the color of jamoca almond fudge ice cream.

"Hello, Shandra," Rose said warmly. "This is my friend, Patrice."

"Glad to meet you," she said with a nod. "Y'all have any trouble driving down here?" She backed the tall cart full of towels around the corner in three tries, kicking the front wheels back into alignment each time.

"No, it was just rain." Rose followed the cart and Patrice trailed her.

"Well, it's snow now, ma'am. Miz Andrews, you know, that lady they trying to move up to the nursing home up there in Los Alamos? Her daughter called and said it's snowing like crazy up there and the weather report is real bad. She said she's not driving down here in that for anything and we should tell her mama why she can't come. 'Course, that's kind of silly, to go tell the old lady all about it. She doesn't know her daughter from a stranger anymore. But I went into Miz Andrews' room and told her, not expecting anything, you know, and Miz Andrews, she looked at me like I was somebody she was expecting. She told me she was ready to go ice skating, that the pond out behind her home was froze over and there was a big bunch of them, all friends. We was supposed to go skate and then we'd come back for cookies and hot milk with vanilla. Can you believe it? Old woman doesn't say twelve words in twelve weeks, then remembers every detail of something that probably happened sixty years ago."

"I believe it," Rose said. "I love to interview old people about what happened way in the past. Lots of times they remember it better than I remember what happened six months ago."

"And better than they remember what happened six minutes ago!" Shandra added. "Well, y'all have a good visit, now, but if I were y'all, I'd get back up that mountain before they get any more of this weather."

Rose and Patrice stopped at a door with "D. Silver" in red marker on an index card taped to the side of the doorjamb. "Oh, what about the FBI papers?" Patrice asked. They'd talked so much, during their drive to Española, about the anti-nuke demonstration and the Russian visitors, and then Doyle Silver's big revelation, she had forgotten to ask Rose about the Freedom of Information Act material.

"The government used up a vat of black ink covering up the parts they say are still confidential. Out of one hundred twenty-six pages, there's about twenty pages of information, and of that, about ten are worth reading." She shrugged as they entered his room. Doyle's roommate, a shriveled old man, was in the bed closer to the door, his mouth wide and his eyes closed. Doyle was sitting up in the bed by the window.

Patrice had last seen him about three months earlier, but his aging process had accelerated in the interim. Maybe there was a big spy story behind the "Last Man bottle," as he'd claimed, or maybe not. Maybe his life was in danger, as he'd told Rose on the phone. But if he was making it up in order to buy Rose's visits, Patrice couldn't blame him. She took a deep breath and fixed a smile on her face. *If I were seventy-six years old, propped up on pillows, and had nothing to look forward to beyond the next bedpan and "Wheel of Fortune," I'd do a Scheherazade act, too.*

The light beside his bed had a dark green glass cover, which added another tinge of color to his pale skin, already olive from reflecting the walls. His eyes, the same color as his liver spots, were quick and intelligent, as if part of a vital man trapped by some hideous mistake in this disintegrating body. On the sill of the window was a framed photo of the same bearded man she had seen in the snapshots on the bulletin board.

Patrice picked up a chair from the roommate's half of the room and placed it near his bed. Rose scooted the room's other chair beside it and the two women sat like teacher's pets at the front of the class, ready to hang on Doyle Silver's every word.

His story--of five men standing in the desert on July 16, 1945, toasting the day's first of two sunrises with cognac--was interrupted only once, when Rose was called to the front desk to take a phone call.

"Sorry, Miz Hulle," Shandra said from the door, "it won't transfer down here to the room."

Rose shook her head, puzzled. "It must be Mel, but I can't imagine why. I'll be right back."

"Mel is her husband," Patrice told Doyle. "He's a chemist at the Laboratory, and a very, very nice man."

"How come you aren't married?" he asked.

"I haven't met the right man."

"Bet you got a lot of men waiting in line."

"No, no line yet," she laughed.

"Why, if I were forty years younger I'd give it a try myself."

She smiled. "I'm flattered. Thank you."

He asked where she grew up, where she went to college. They were laughing at a caper he'd pulled in college, a story he probably embellished richly, when Rose came back. She was as pale as skim milk, and trembling.

"What's wrong? Who was it?" Patrice asked. "Was it Mel?"

"No, it turned out it wasn't Mel. Nothing's wrong. Let's talk about it later." She turned to the old man and spoke forcefully. "Right now, Doyle, the time has come to name names and get to the bottom line, because it's snowing and we need to leave for home."

"Speak now or forever hold my peace, huh?" he said with a nod. "Okay, I'm ready to talk."

*****

By the time Rose and Patrice left the nursing home, the rain had long since changed to snow. "Hold on a second," Rose said. "I've got to get out my car keys."

While Rose fished in her black leather bag, Patrice leaned close to the plate glass, cupping her hand to the black surface to see out. Miniature ice rinks were forming in the many chuckholes beyond the sheltered sidewalk.

A security guard rose from the vinyl armchair in the vestibule and leaned on the crash bar of the wide metal door to let them out. "Good night, ladies. Take it easy. The roads are getting icy."

Rose said, "Thanks," but her voice was strained. Patrice looked at Rose's reflection in the glass, its surface made into a perfect mirror by the black night beyond, and at her own face above Rose's as if on a totem pole. Rose looked like a doe in headlights.

The tires slung clods of mud into the wheel wells of Rose's Cadillac as they pulled out of the parking lot onto the road. "What's next?" Patrice asked. "I mean with Doyle's story?"

"A lot of work for you and me. This is the first time I ever heard of Douglas Frost, so I've got to pore over Rhodes's books for a start, and contact the Lab archivist. Do you still have Rhodes's books?"

Patrice knew she meant the heavy tomes by Richard Rhodes, the first of which won the Pulitzer Prize. "Yes, I have them, and I'm about one-fourth of the way through *The Making of the Atomic Bomb*. I don't know when I'll be able to start the second one." Her guess was she'd have time to read *Dark Sun: The Making of the Hydrogen Bomb* around the time she checked into some place like Buena Vista herself.

"Can you go to the Historical Museum tomorrow? I mean

the museum's archives, upstairs at the Lodge? We've got to move fast on this, that's my feeling about it."

Patrice felt squeezed on all sides by all the work she had on her desk, and now the "Last Man" project as they called it was taking off like a hot air balloon with no knot in the tether. Rick Romero was counting on her to follow the Russians around and write about them for three, possibly four days, and who knew what Kent Bolt would come up with on ten minutes notice. She suspected he'd known a lot more about the demonstration at the Plutonium Facility than he let on. He might have known it ahead of time, with his ties to the powerful anti-nuke groups in Santa Fe. She didn't like the charade, but he who pays the piper calls the tune.

That reminded her she was "on call" at Kent's pleasure for an interview with his sister, Senator Cristal Aragon. He enjoyed his gatekeeper status with Aragon as much as she enjoyed being the unreachable celebrity. Patrice hoped Aragon would stay away from New Mexico another week, at least until the Russians were gone and Rick could hire someone to shoulder some of the workload at the paper. The lifestyles editor had announced in November she would only stay until Christmas; presumably Danny would be out of there at the same time. And the assistant managing editor, Carolee, had told Rick in the summer she'd be going back to graduate school in January. Even with all that advance notice, no one was in the wings. Rick offered the "promotion" to Patrice but was only authorized to add a pittance to her salary. She'd told him, "Not in this office, not in this lifetime. Any questions?"

The traffic light changed and Rose pulled into the right lane to turn on the old Oñate Street Bridge across the Rio Grande. They would ordinarily be home in Los Alamos in less than half an hour from that corner, but the snow was slowing them down. Already it was spiraling in the headlights, giving the dizzying impression they were driving into a tunnel, no longer level, but falling through space.

Someone honked and Rose swerved right, too fast for the icy conditions on the narrow bridge. Patrice saw a massive car, the kind they call a low-rider, pass on the left just before the back of the Cadillac fishtailed into the left lane. Rose steered into the skid, left, then right, then left, and the car settled back.

They hadn't hit the concrete side of the bridge. "Good job!" Patrice said, her heart pounding.

The streetlights appeared to be surrounded by swarms of yellow wasps, but it was snow falling down and up and sideways in the light. "If it's snowing like this on the Hill, Mel will be worried sick," Rose said.

"I checked the news wire before we left this evening, and there wasn't anything like this on the weather report!" Patrice said. "I thought the low was staying north of us." If Rose's husband was worried, he wasn't the only one. "Speaking of Mel, if that wasn't him on the phone, who was it?"

"It wasn't anyone I know, or at least anyone I know I know."

Patrice stared at Rose. "Excuse me?"

Rose let her breath out slowly. "I've had a death threat. Two death threats to be exact."

Again Patrice waited; Rose said nothing more. "Rose Hulle, if you don't explain to me precisely what you're talking about, you're going to get more than a death threat!"

"Okay, okay. I'm trying to think of how to say it, I mean how to explain it."

"Did you find a dead cat in your mailbox?" Patrice was incredulous. "Or maybe a crude note with words cut out of newspapers, glued together with callous disregard for syntax?"

Rose sighed heavily. "Your reaction explains why I dread going to the police."

"Are you serious about this? You've had death threats?" It was hard for Patrice to say the words without joking. But it was getting through to her at last that Rose was scared.

"The first threat was probably a prank, I thought. Just a

man's voice on the phone. It happened so fast I barely noticed what he sounded like." She pressed a button to lower her power window, brushed snow off the side mirror, and put the window back up.

"What did he say? When did you get the call? Does Mel know?"

"I got a call at home last Tuesday. I remember it was Tuesday night because Mel was due home the next day from the Ukraine, and I was alone. The man with the accent told me I was interfering with a matter that was best left to security experts, that I should stop contacting people and asking questions about spies. He said I wouldn't live to publish my lies. He hung up before I could react."

"Have you told the police?" Patrice followed Rose's example, lowering her window, wiping the side mirror, and raising it again.

"I haven't told anybody. Not even Mel. But I'm going to tell him tonight, and I'll go see the police tomorrow. The voice was so icy...so menacing."

"And the second threat?" Patrice whispered.

Rose looked at her watch. "About an hour ago."

"The call you got at the nursing home?"

Rose nodded. "All he said was, 'You should be home with your husband. You should have listened to me. I hope your affairs are in order.' Then he hung up."

"So he knew you were in Española tonight. He knew you were seeing..." Patrice's voice faded out and she kept her thought to herself. Whoever the caller was, he probably knew Rose wasn't the only person visiting the chatty old gentleman tonight.

The lights of Española disappeared from view behind them as they pulled onto the two-lane highway. All landmarks were invisible in the starless night. They had to rely on their headlights, as ineffective as they were in the snow.

Patrice tried to imagine the valley she knew they were in, with a line of trees paralleling the highway off somewhere to the left about a mile, and beyond them, also parallel to their path, the Rio Grande. The highway, State Road 30, ran about ten miles south, where it intersected with a larger highway, State Road 502.

"We're halfway home," she said when Rose finally turned right at State Road 502 and headed east.

"Yes, but that was the easy half," Rose said ruefully. As they gained elevation, the snow closed in, heavy wet flakes pelting the car and taxing the windshield wipers.

The storm seemed to let up as they got to a relatively flat area, sort of a shelf in the climb, where the highway sign showed the road branching. "This isn't so bad!" Patrice said.

"I wouldn't say I've been nervous," Rose said, her relief apparent in her voice, "but I've been gripping the wheel so tightly I've cut my palms with my fingernails."

Where the road branched Rose stayed left and headed up the steep Main Hill Road. All of a sudden their relief turned to fear. They stared ahead, seeing the road--so clearly visible less than a minute before--vanish beyond a white curtain.

To make matters worse a car that had been behind them for the last few miles was getting uncomfortably close.

"What is he, drunk?" Rose said with a glance in her side mirror. "Now he's turned his brights on!"

An oncoming car popped his brights on, too, and the car behind them dropped back to regular beam, but only until the downhill car passed by. Then he hit his high beams again.

"What is with this guy?" Rose said through clenched teeth. "Oh, Patrice, I should have taken the White Rock turnoff! I'm so sorry!"

"You had no way of knowing," Patrice said quietly. "How's the road?" She looked over at Rose, thinking how for the first time since she'd known her, Rose looked every one of her forty-something years.

"The road's not too bad. I've got decent traction, with the front wheels, anyway. But I can't see a darn thing!"

The lull they'd passed through just a mile or two back was

like the eye of a hurricane. The storm swirled in pillars formed by the wind as it met resistance in the jagged cliffs.

"I'd like to get my hands around that idiot's neck," Patrice said, holding her hand up in front of the rear view mirror to shade Rose's eyes from the blinding glare.

"That helps! Thanks," Rose murmured.

Coming down the steep road with its horseshoe turns, they'd been inside, beside the hill, but going up they were beside the guardrail. Patrice found herself staring at the metal rail, almost hypnotized, trying hard not to think how far down the canyon floor was from there. As they neared the top, though, she was vividly aware: the drop-off was at least four hundred feet to rocks below.

Suddenly the brights from the car behind them filled the interior of the Cadillac like a searchlight. "Oh my God!" Rose screamed.

In half a heartbeat, the time it took them to reach the sharpest turn on the treacherous road, the car behind them closed the distance between them. Rose and Patrice felt a slight bump as the car touched the Cadillac, then felt it accelerate, pushing them straight toward the railing. Rose tried to steer away from the edge, but the road was a launch pad of ice.

Patrice saw the railing coming at them, and heard Rose scream just as she did. There was a wrenching sound of straining metal as the railing held, then a lurch as it gave way. Their screams intensified as they were hurled over the cliff into the blackness swirling with white pinging pellets.

We must have gone airborne, Patrice thought, as the Cadillac slammed against the cliff with a horrendous jolt. "Rose!" she shouted, unable and unwilling to fight her panic. "Rose!"

There was silence for a moment, a long moment, or maybe more time. Patrice shook her head to clear it. It seemed it was the next instant, but maybe it was later. She felt as if she were waking up; she couldn't be sure about time.

Everything was disjointed, and so dark. Pitch black dark,

and bitter cold. The passenger side was on top, Patrice's door above her. She fought at something smothering her, something against her face, too dazed to recognize the airbag.

"Rose!" she shouted again, louder. There was still no answer. Gradually, Patrice got her bearings. *I'm hanging by my seatbelt. Oh, God, I can't move my left arm. What's wrong with it? It doesn't hurt, but it has no strength.*

"Rose! Answer me!" Patrice said. She couldn't see Rose in the darkness. She couldn't even see the dashboard, and the sensation of hanging in her seatbelt made her panic. "Answer me, Rose! Say something! Please say something."

She sensed by the sound of her own voice in the compacted space that the driver's side of the car was way too close to the passenger side. *We must have landed on our side and it's caved in.* She felt awkwardly for Rose with her right hand. She felt skin--the right side of Rose's face!--and held her hand against Rose's neck. There was no pulse.

Her own pulse raced in horror. "Rose! No!" she cried. "Wake up. You've got to wake up! We've got to get out of here!" All of a sudden the car was moving again with a grinding sound. It felt to Patrice as if they were sliding downward, the driver's side against the rocks. She tried to picture the car on the steep hillside and tried to remember the topography--wasn't there a big ledge part of the way to the canyon floor? *Oh my God, are we about to go off the ledge?*

Their slow slide picked up speed, then the car stopped with a lurch that bashed Patrice hard against her seatbelt, away from Rose. It seemed to her she was suspended above the dashboard, her chest compressed by a vise. Then the car rolled in slow motion, righting itself and flinging Patrice against the passenger door.

She called again to Rose; no answer. She rolled to her left slightly and felt again for a pulse. Nothing. The metal creaked, a sign, she thought, that the car would continue to slide.

She tried to force her door open; her heart pounded in

panic that she was trapped. "Stop it!" she said aloud, "you've got to calm down." She noticed then that the headlights were still on, shining into empty space and spotlighting the falling snow. Sobbing, she calmed enough to unlock the door and try the handle again. The door swung open and she felt for the ground with her right foot.

"Oh, no!" she moaned. *There is no ground under my foot.* The car was cantilevered over the canyon. Beneath her side of the car was total darkness.

"Help!" she called, not too loud, afraid sound could be enough to send the car over the edge. She felt an object on the seat beside her and recognized it as a Thermos. She dropped it out the open door and listened. It broke against something rocky not far below her, then bounced away into the distance.

So, there is something solid not terribly far below my side of the car. She exhaled for what seemed like the first time in ten minutes, then released the latch on her seat belt. Holding on to the doorframe, she lowered herself about three feet until one foot touched rocks. She dangled, unable to get a solid footing, and was about to clamber back into the car, when it started to move again.

Patrice lost her grip on the seat belt and fell backward onto jagged rocks, flailing her right arm, trying to grasp anything to stop her fall. Her feet wedged against a boulder and she stiffened them instinctively, coming to an uneasy truce with gravity. From her precarious perch she could see the Cadillac stop as well, its front wheels on a ledge, inches from a black hole that might as well be the very door to hell.

She pawed around with her right hand and felt a woody bush, clinging to the cliff with no more determination than she had. She tugged, gently at first to see if its roots would hold, then more firmly. In the slight light below the headlights, she found a flat rock about three feet square and claimed it with passionate relief.

There she huddled and shivered, staring uphill in the darkness, hooding her eyes from the pelting snow. Until that moment she had been afraid to scream, but as soon as she felt anchored to her stone life raft, the sound of terror burst from her throat and assaulted the silence with a power she never imagined was inside her. *If indeed it is hell below me, I'll do my best to deafen the devil.*

Through the snow she saw a pinpoint of light appear from the road above. She directed her screams in a beacon of sound toward the beacon of light.

"Someone's gone for help!" a man's voice called down to her.

Patrice pulled her knees in toward her body and sat as still as she could, given that her body was wracked with shaking. Her left arm began to throb.

Abhorring a vacuum, nature filled her mind with gushing, exploding, overwhelming images, of Rose, and Doyle Silver, and how Rose had practically begged her to go to the nursing home with her, telling Patrice how worried she was that someone wanted the old man dead. Something about the "Last Man"...that Doyle Silver would not live to be the "Last Man." That was only hours ago, Patrice thought, overcome with grief for her friend. Now I'm perched on the side of a frozen cliff, my mind watching me wait for help, watching myself go into shock.

The sound of sirens seemed to come from across the canyon, but Patrice was lucid enough to recognize it as an echo. *It must be behind and above me, on the Main Hill Road.*

That wasn't all she was lucid enough to recognize. *Rose has been murdered. And I'm supposed to be dead, too.*

Chapter 4

On Thursday morning, Patrice stood at the grave side in Guaje Pines Cemetery, her left arm in a cast and sling. She wore a Velcro corset under her clothes to keep her ribs from hurting so much. After three days she was getting used to taking shallow breaths; the alternative was a piercing pain in her left side. She had a deep, ugly bruise from her right shoulder to her left hip where the seat belt had slammed her. The X-rays showed a slight fracture of three ribs, but that injury was expected to heal quickly. Quickly was a relative term, Patrice was learning, having gone through agonizing contortions to get into a position for sleep and then lying there processing oxygen about as effectively as a salmon on a sandbar.

The official determination was Rose had died instantly of massive head trauma. Getting Patrice up the cliff face in one piece in a snowstorm was a proud moment for the Los Alamos Fire Department plus Rick Romero and four other expert climbers from Search and Rescue. Patrice was at the hospital by the time they retrieved Rose's body, and later the battered Cadillac.

"In my Father's house are many mansions..." the minister from the Methodist Church was saying. Mel Hulle, Rose's husband, and her daughter Allison had the ashen complexions and vacant stares of wax figures.

Patrice stood with them under a canopy, erected against the threat of more snow. So far it was cloudy but dry. The day after the storm, the sun came out and melted most of the snow in town. Now it was cold again, with the scattered islands of snow among the headstones refusing to retreat further, knowing reinforcements were on the way. All around the cluster of mourners were Christmas wreaths on graves, the ribbons and plastic holly berries dressing up the brown grass in a sad parody of welcome.

There was a uniformity to the cemetery that showed its relative newness. The first people were buried there in 1961, four years after the town's gates were opened, allowing people to drive into Los Alamos without scrutiny of their passes by uniformed guards. So it was a real town. Cradle to grave.

Guaje Pines would be a good place to sleep for eternity, Patrice supposed. The small meadow had locust trees and a flagpole at the center, then a ring of Russian olives, then Ponderosa pines, and then an outer ring of hills. It had a sort of center-of-the-universe feel to it, like a place Druids would select for a monument of megalithic posts and lintels. And Rose would never be alone. The meadow was full of elk at night, a breathtaking sight in winter moonlight, people said, and Patrice could hear squirrels and Steller's jays haggling over pineseeds in the Ponderosas.

The ground was spongy with a rime of frost on the dead grass. About fifty yards from Rose's turf-draped grave were four flat rectangles of dirt--winter graves that would not be sodded until spring. Patrice had stopped beside one on her walk over. It was a double headstone, name and two dates for "Loving Husband and Father" on the left, name and one date for "Beloved Wife and Mother" on the right. Loving Husband had been there for twenty years, sodded and settled. Now Beloved Wife was there, beside him for only a month according to the plastic marker skewered in the grass like a croquet wicket. Her sod and the chiseling in stone of her second date, the date of death, were yet to come. It seemed an invasion of their privacy to look.

Across the silver-gray casket, in the throng of friends of Rose and Mel, Patrice saw Danny. He had known Rose Hulle for years, had even taken history from her in high school.

It seemed strange to Patrice to see Danny without a camera around his neck and a massive bag hanging off his shoulder.

Patrice's mother, Karen Meyer, was behind Danny. There's a saying that if a man wants to see what his prospective wife will look like in twenty years, take a good look at her mother. Patrice knew a lot of weddings that advice would cancel, but her mom looked terrific.

Meyer was her stepfather's last name. Her mother and William had been together since Patrice was eleven. Patrice was named after her father, Patrick Kelsey, who died in a car wreck when she was four. Patrice shivered when the thought of her father's car wreck crossed her mind, and wondered if that funeral was what her mom was thinking about when she looked at Mel's face. *Poor Mel. Poor Alli. Hell, poor Rose!*

Mel took Alli by the elbow and followed the funeral director to the limousine. Patrice stayed behind as people drifted to their cars, taking Mel's seat under the canopy and staring at the casket. Her mother and Danny walked over to her.

"Patrice?" Danny said softly. "I'm so sorry about Rose."

She nodded. "She was one of a kind."

"She had a way of making you want to do better, to not disappoint her," Danny said softly.

Patrice smiled, remembering. "She gave me books and articles to read about the history of Los Alamos, and I'd stay up late no matter how tired I was."

"I know what you mean," Danny responded. "More than any teacher I ever had, she made me understand I needed to study so I'd know something, not just to pass a test. That if I knew something, it was mine to keep."

"Yes," Patrice agreed, smiling in spite of her tears. "I think I always feared she'd give me a pop quiz, which is silly, but... Not wanting to disappoint Rose made me learn a lot I would have skipped without her prodding." She stood slowly, as it hurt to use her abdominal muscles at all.

"Captain Bell would like to see you this afternoon if you're up to it," Danny said. "He said he'd be at the police station all day, just to come in anytime."

"First I want to see the car."

"That's likely to be terribly hard on you," her mother said. "The memories..."

"I know it will be painful, but I have to do it. Will you take me to the car lot?" Patrice asked Danny. His shrug was directed more to her mother than to Patrice.

At first neither of them could see a way to get Patrice up and into his pickup without causing more pain than she was in already, but they hit on the idea of setting his toolbox on the ground to boost her up.

"Don't ask me to participate in any 'Say No To Drugs' campaigns for a while," she said. She had broken her arm falling out of a tree when she was ten or eleven, but she didn't remember it hurting so much. *Of course, the memory of pain fades. It has to. Otherwise no one would ever have a second child, or so I've been told.*

Danny pulled behind the auto parts and car repair business where mangled cars were dropped off by the tow truck. "It's Knecht's week to tow," he said. Patrice understood the process. Two towing companies in town alternated being on call for breakdowns or wrecks called in by the police. If the wreck had happened on the other side of the Española turnoff, the car would have been picked up by a tow truck from the valley and taken to Española or Santa Fe. But they were close to home. She tucked her hair behind her ear. *Close, but no kewpie doll.*

"What the hell is it doing out here?" Patrice said, spotting the mashed and misshapen Cadillac in the row of wrecks. "Why isn't it in the impoundment yard? Someone was murdered in this car, damn it! Anybody in this two-bit town ever heard of evidence?"

"Patrice," Danny said in a "Now, now" voice, "the police looked the car over after you made your statement about another car being involved, and they found no evidence of another car."

"In other words, I'm a liar?"

"Don't get excited. I don't doubt you."

"And just who found no evidence? Lieutenant Pauling?" Everyone at the paper privately called him Lieutenant Appalling. "No evidence? Pauling couldn't find rubber on a tire! He couldn't find sugar on a doughnut! Don't tell me they put him in charge?"

"Hey, you're preaching to the choir, here. Save your righteous indignation for Capt. Bell. He's waiting for you."

"Why are the local police investigating, anyway? Or, to be more accurate, not investigating? The State Police should be handling it."

"The spot where you left the road is in Los Alamos County."

"The spot we landed--the spot where Rose died--is out of the county. I'll fight this."

"Let's go see Captain Bell," Danny said.

"Not yet. I have to look at the car." He helped her down, again using the toolbox, and took her right arm. Walking on the muddy gravel was tricky. The last thing she needed was to fall.

Patrice felt bile rising in her throat when she looked at the driver's side of the car, caved in as if it had been T-boned by a Mack truck. The front door on the passenger's side, the door she'd used, was misaligned with the frame, something that must have happened when they recovered the car. Duct tape was wrapped through the open window holding the door to the metal post behind it. The door to the back seat on the passenger side was intact. She opened it and leaned into the vehicle. The plush corduroy seats looked clean and undisturbed, completely out of place in the wreckage, except that there was no foot room; the edges abutted the back of the front seats.

Danny squeezed in and looked under the front seats as she requested, then untied a rope holding the trunk shut.

"Empty," she said, chewing on her lower lip. "Anything they found was probably given to Mel."

"What are you looking for?"

"Her purse. She had a tape recorder in it. She used it that night in Doyle Silver's room. Ironically, she was trying to get a record of what he said because she was fearful for *his* safety. The old geezer will probably live to be a hundred." She felt a wave of grief wash over her. "Oh, no, poor Mr. Silver. He's going to be devastated when he hears Rose is dead."

"Let's go see Capt. Bell, get it over with," Danny said.

"Wait a minute. Do you have a camera with you?"

"Does a squirrel have nuts? What do you need?"

"Would you take some shots of the car, in case the police didn't even bother?"

Patrice waited in the truck while Danny shot a roll of color film.

At the police station Danny waited until Bell came out to the lobby to escort Patrice back to his office.

"Good morning, Captain," Danny said as he shook hands with Bell. Turning to Patrice, he added, "I'll wait out here."

"No, don't wait for me. My mom is right by the phone at the motel. I'll call her to pick me up." Danny started to protest, but she was insistent. "She likes to feel she's helping."

"Well, okay. I've got to run by the paper and see if Rick needs me. Then I want to go over to Mel's and pay my respects."

Capt. Bell was almost courtly, gesturing to Patrice to precede him down the hall. She had to battle her acknowledged bad attitude about the Los Alamos Police Department in order to be cordial. She liked a few of the police officers individually, but collectively she thought they were donkeys. Of course, the feeling was probably mutual.

Patrice had observed the police in New Mexico, as in so many places, as having two goals when it came to a crime: solve it but don't let the media know a damn thing. The enemy, in the minds of the police, had shifted from the criminal to the reporter. The rate of crime solving was poor and getting worse, but police were getting to be masters of "No information at this time." A question about, "Any new developments?" was greeted with the same look Patrice would expect if she'd asked the officer if he remembered to flush the toilet.

"You know Lt. Pauling, don't you?" Bell said as he got to his office.

Pauling stood and adjusted a chair slightly for Patrice at the same time he held out his hand to shake hers. "You're lucky to be alive," he said as Patrice sat down and Bell closed his office door.

"I'm not supposed to be," she said.

"What?" Bell asked as he lowered his bulk into an oversized leather chair the color of paprika. She guessed from the wince on his face that he had hemorrhoids. *How perfect.*

"I said I'm not supposed to be alive. Whoever murdered Rose wanted me dead, too."

Pauling jumped in. "Assuming for the sake of this discussion that Mrs. Hulle was murdered--and I'm not convinced of that--what makes you think you were also a target of this...this madman." He said the word like it was patently ridiculous.

She told them what Rose had said about the two phoned death threats, and that the second showed the caller knew where she was Monday night. "It was probable he knew I was with her, as well, and that whatever Rose heard from Doyle Silver I heard, too."

"Did this Mr. Silver say anything that you think was dangerous information? What were you doing there, by the way?"

The answers Patrice thought of first were Yes, and None of your business, but she took as deep a breath as she could and cleared her throat. "Rose Hulle has been researching the early days of Los Alamos, the war years, for quite some time now. I don't think it would be exaggerating to say she was an expert on what is known about spies who operated here at that time. I was working with her on a story about Mr. Silver."

"I take it he was here during the war?" Bell said.

"Yes, he was a physicist. He told us about a group of five

men who worked on the atomic bomb. One or more of them may have been a spy. Rose and I found it interesting, but we didn't buy it wholesale. We had a lot of cross-referencing to do before we published, if we ever did."

A vision of her desk piled even higher with work than it had been on Monday made Patrice feel hopeless that she'd ever get the research done. To begin with, she didn't have access to Rose's encyclopedic memory, and she'd have to start from scratch to build a relationship with people like the Lab archivist.

She did know about the highly publicized claim by a Soviet spymaster, Anatoli Yatskov, that he'd had another spy inside the Manhattan Project. When the interview with Yatskov was published in the *Washington Post* and reprinted all over the country, he said "Perseus" was still alive. He went on to give details of his courier, Lona Cohen.

Patrice continued, without blabbing everything Doyle had told them. "Mr. Silver told us about seeing a scientist make a hand-off of papers to a woman in April 1945, in Santa Fe. As far as it goes, it matches information about a spy code-named Perseus, a spy never identified and believed by many to still be alive."

"And you think Mr. Silver was in fear for his life because he might tell you this?" Lt. Pauling said with a "Give me a break" tone. "And that you and Rose were in danger? I'm sorry, but that soup's too thin for me."

"Look at it from this perspective," Patrice said. "Imagine I had handed over secrets to the Soviet Union during the war, scientific information that made it possible for them to build their first atomic bomb at least--at the very least--four years earlier than if they'd started from scratch, like we did. And then I went on for the next fifty years with my secret hidden. I could have a security clearance, travel anywhere in the world, teach at any university, maybe amass a fortune in this nasty old capitalistic country, and raise a family with a name they're proud of. Then someone finds out my secret. And that someone is very, very close to publishing it, to holding me up for the shame I so richly deserve. Wouldn't I have a motive for silencing anyone who knew my secret?"

"You're talking about a man who's at least seventy years old, this so-called spy," Pauling said, counting on his fingers. "He could be eighty! I think the whole thing is pretty far-fetched."

"Rose is dead."

"And it's a terrible tragedy. I didn't know her myself, but a lot of people thought very highly of her, as a person and as a writer," Pauling said. "But sometimes coincidences happen."

Patrice was getting angrier by the minute. She tried to count to ten, but only made it to four. "It was no coincidence a car pushed us off the cliff. I saw the headlights. I felt the cars touch lightly and then we picked up speed and Rose lost control. There was another car there!"

"This is where I think we have a communication problem," Pauling said with a nod to Bell. He leaned forward, his fingertips together and his elbows on his knees. "I think there could have been another car close to you on the Main Hill Road that night. You told the officers, I think, that you didn't get a look at it because his brights were on. The snow was heavy, the road was treacherous by then. Black ice! Damn stuff is invisible, and deadly. The question in my mind is why didn't the other car stop if the driver saw you go over the edge?"

At last, Patrice thought, *a question enters his mind. Probably finding it lonely in there, rattling around like a BB in a boxcar.* "Yes, why didn't he?"

"He or she was probably drunk."

"What?"

"The driver was probably drunk to get that close to Mrs. Hulle's car," Pauling said. "And he didn't know she'd lost control, or he knew and he wanted to get out of there before he got a DUI."

"A DUI? Lieutenant, in this state Driving Under the Influence is like jaywalking." It was a topic guaranteed to flare tempers and get total strangers raging together against the system. It seemed everyone was against drunk drivers, everyone was sick and tired of the tragic deaths on New Mexico highways--until they got on a jury, or worse, got elected to a judgeship.

Pauling shrugged and looked at Bell as if to say, "I told you she was like this."

The captain winced and adjusted his butt in his chair. "Why don't you tell us chronologically about your drive home Monday evening?"

The energy Patrice had mustered to get her through the funeral was draining away quickly. "I want to talk about the car that forced us over the cliff. Then I've got to go." Bell nodded for her to continue, and she repeated the pitifully few details she could of the events of Monday night, beginning with Rose being called out of Doyle Silver's room to take a phone call, and finishing with the Cadillac going over the cliff. "I firmly believe if you and the State Police examine Rose's car, you'll find evidence that backs me up. I know there's no paint or glass from another car, but wouldn't it prove something if you find the Cadillac's back bumper was forced in? I mean, that couldn't be caused by a car going forward over a guard rail and landing on the driver's side."

"We'll take another look at it," Bell said, nodding to Pauling. He didn't sound like it was a priority, Patrice noticed, nor did he say anything about the State Police.

"Could I use your phone to call my mother? I need to rest."

"I can drive you," Pauling said.

"Thank you, but no. She's waiting for me to call."

In four minutes Karen Meyer was there in her rental car, and five minutes later Patrice was on a bed at the Hilltop House.

"I got you some ice and soda," her mom said. "Time for your antibiotic."

"I'd better take a pain pill, too. I feel like poop."

While the pill took effect and her body rested, Patrice

recounted for her mother what had been said at the police station.

"Rick Romero called twice since I got back from the funeral," Karen said. "He's very worried about you."

"He's worried about me, yes, but there's a little self-interest in there, too," Patrice said with a wry smile. "We've lost so many people here lately, our office looks like the beach after a shark attack. My absence is bound to make his heart grow fonder."

"I suppose so, but I detected a 'fondness' that goes beyond boss-employee."

Rick had been one of the rescuers who strapped her into a basket out on the side of the cliff, in the snowstorm. She remembered clinging to his hand all the way to the ambulance. She couldn't get over feeling it was a miracle, that her strong will to live had somehow brought him to her side. It could have been another climber, or a fireman, but it was Rick who got to her first and stayed with her through the terrifying ascent in the basket.

She closed her eyes, recalling the ascent, and Rick's hand tight around hers, and the way he kept forcing her to stay conscious, the tug of his voice each time she slipped away. But she was certain her mother was reading too much into Rick's concern. Although he never spoke of his wife to Patrice, she knew from Marian and Danny that Elaine's death from ovarian cancer, at age thirty-one, had left Rick frozen with grief. Three years had passed, and he seemed to have healed, but he told Danny one night, over too many beers, that he wasn't healing, just scabbing over.

Patrice opened her eyes and concentrated on all she needed to do. While she wouldn't cross the street to help Kent Bolt and his "Los Alamos Guillotine," she planned to be back on the job the first minute she could, to help Rick. She tried to sit up, but the stab in her side reminded her that "first minute" was not coming up very soon. There were things she could do, however, even with her handicap. First step would be to get her hovering mother out of Los Alamos.

The phone rang and Karen answered. "Hello? Oh, hello Rick. Yes, she's here, just a minute." She tugged the phone cord free of the bedside table and set the phone beside Patrice.

"Hi, Rick. How are you holding up without me? And don't say, 'Fine.'" She sipped the soda and poured the remainder of the can in her glass.

"The paper is in chaos, crime is rampant in the streets, the free world is at risk of political disaster, and Armageddon looms. We need you back here."

"You always find a way to cheer me up, you silver-tongued devil." She tossed the empty can toward the wastebasket and gave a "thumbs up" when it dropped straight in.

"How do you feel?"

"Like I could make good money dealing painkillers door-to-door by giving my personal testimony to their efficacy."

"Other than that?" he laughed.

"Like ca-ca. I had an unpleasant time at the police station." She twisted the phone cord tight around her finger and watched the end turn white.

"About what I'd expect under the circumstances. I've tried talking to them. Same thing."

The cord uncoiled and her finger turned red again. She wished Rick were there in person instead of on the phone. "Hey, in case I didn't mention it before," she said quietly, "I appreciate you risking your neck out there on the cliff to help rescue me."

"Don't mention it. Now I can write off the cost of my ropes, et cetera, as a business expense. It's an expensive hobby, you know."

"So glad I could help," she said. "Can you come see me later?"

"At the motel? That sounds seedy."

"I'm trying to talk Mom into leaving for Hawaii," she said loudly. Karen shook her head and mouthed "No."

"She's planned this trip for a year," Patrice went on. "It's their anniversary next week. So I expect to be back at my apartment this afternoon. I'll call and let you know." She said good-bye and put the receiver down.

Karen looked at her watch for what must have been the fourth time in a half hour. Patrice seized the opportunity. "Mom, your lips say, 'No, no,' but your eyes say, 'Yes, yes.' I'll be fine, resting in bed and watching TV until my eyelids droop, and you'll be drinking rum punch in the tropical moonlight with a man who adores you. Get out of town."

"You can't even drive a car." Karen had both hands on her hips and a pugnacious look on her face.

"I have friends with cars. I have a telephone. I have a microwave. Please go." She picked up the receiver and handed it to Karen. "Call the toll free number on your printed itinerary and see when the next plane is. I'm getting worn out making pleasant, witty conversation to you all the time. I need some rest."

"Witty conversation, my foot. I've seen better wit on restroom walls."

"Mother!" Patrice did her best to look dismayed.

Karen took the receiver and held down the button with her left hand while she pulled her airline ticket out of her purse. "Your language when you're in pain is nothing to giggle at." Patrice tried not to wince in pain as she swung her legs over the side of the bed and pushed herself upright for a trip to the bathroom. "I saw that! You're in no condition to be staying alone."

"Yes, I am. I'll be fine. Really--I can't stand knowing William will be in Hawaii without you. A lonely man, lying on the beach, surrounded by women in string bikinis..."

"Reading the *Wall Street Journal* and calling his broker on a cell phone." She punched "nine" for an outside line.

"How did you get such a romantic fool to love you? Or even notice you?"

"I have my ways," Karen said archly.

"So call the travel agent. I'm going to run another hot bath and soak for a while."

****

Two hours later Patrice sat propped up on her bed in her apartment with the phone close beside her and the refrigerator stocked with convenience meals. Karen poured her a cup of tea and looked for more to do before she left. She had checked out of the motel earlier, and stowed her bags in her rental car.

Patrice's studio apartment was on the top floor, the third, of an architectural throwback to fallout shelters known as the "concrete caves." The "living room" was comprised of her bed and a dinette set, and the kitchen was compressed into a tiny alcove. The structure in downtown Los Alamos was scheduled for demolition, an event that Patrice conceded could only improve the neighborhood. However, she was one of the people who didn't earn enough to rent something better. With homelessness looming if the wrecking ball did, indeed, swing her way, she had eagerly joined the other occupants in stalling the inevitable at least one more year.

"You'd better go," Patrice said, as Karen set the mug of tea on a TV tray beside the bed. "It takes nearly two hours to get to the airport in Albuquerque--and you have a rental car to turn in."

"Listen to you. You sound like your mother! I have plenty of time to catch the plane. No need to be the first one in line at the check-in."

"Listen to you!" Patrice echoed. "You sound like your daughter!"

"Worse things could happen," she said. "I have a wise daughter. Even if she does have a potty mouth when she's in pain."

"Give William my love. And tell him thanks very much for the flowers."

Karen stalled as long as she could, then kissed Patrice good-bye. "I'm setting the door to lock behind me!"

"Rick will be here in a few minutes," Patrice argued. "I just talked to him. If you lock it I'll just have to get up."

Karen set her jaw as firmly as Patrice set hers, then capitulated. "Well, ask who it is before you say 'Come in.'"

"Okay, okay! Now go!" Patrice laughed. When she was sure Karen was on her way, she got up to get the mail that had accumulated while she was away at the hospital and the motel. Amazing how much mail Resident was entitled to, plus bills addressed to her by name, and solicitations for credit cards at a rate of three a week. She took the mail and the newspapers Karen had bought that morning back to bed with her.

She played the messages on the answering machine again, making a note of two numbers she didn't have. Six messages were from friends in Los Alamos and Santa Fe asking if there were anything they could do to help. Two were from old friends at previous jobs. They must have called the *Guardian*, found out about the accident, and left her messages at home.

Patrice hadn't told her mother the truth when she said she intended to stay in bed all the rest of the day. And she had an ulterior motive in asking Rick to come over. She needed to go somewhere, and she went over in her mind how she would talk him into driving her there.

Ever since she'd talked to Capt. Bell and Lt. Pauling, something she said kept coming back to haunt her. Something she'd said about motive. *Wouldn't the spy, or spies, have a motive for silencing anyone who knew their secret?*

She wanted to go to the nursing home in Española. She had a bad feeling about Doyle Silver's safety.

Chapter 5

"I understand your objections. I would have been disappointed in you if you'd shown less concern for my health. But I've got to go to Española, one way or another. I must talk to Doyle Silver." Patrice had her good right hand on her hip and a resolute look on her face. Her mother had been gone less than an hour.

"All right, I'll take you. Saturday!" Rick stood in front of her apartment door with his arms crossed and his legs apart like a bodyguard. He wore tight Levi pants, washed so many times they were soft as flannel, a leather belt he'd tooled himself, with a silver and turquoise buckle, and a Levi jacket over a Bandelier Marathon T-shirt.

"All I'll be doing is sitting in your car. Less than thirty minutes to get there. I'll walk a hundred yards, talk to the old man, walk back to the car, and ride home. I'll be back in this apartment, the bedcovers up to my little chin, and off to the land of Nod in an hour and a half."

He made a fist. "I could have you off to the land of Nod in no time flat."

"You brute."

"Yeah, right. I see how scared you are."

She bit her lip, quickly rethinking her strategy. In a straightforward tone, no pleading, she asked, "Please drive me down there this afternoon. Please. I have to tell Mr. Silver about

Rose."

"About her accidental death, or her murder?"

"You mean about her accidental death, or the truth?" She felt her calm façade crack, exposing her roiled emotions again. "You don't believe me either, do you? Never mind, I wouldn't go anywhere with you if you asked me."

He held up his hands, palms out, and spoke in a placating tone. "You didn't give me time to answer. I believe you. You're the best eyewitness anybody could want."

"Correction. I'm the worst eyewitness any murderer could want. I don't forget, and I don't give up."

He shook his head in defeat. "All right, then, I give up. Let's go and get it over with. Poor old guy is going to be crushed. Rose was probably the brightest spot in his lonely life. He only has a nephew?"

"I think that's all." Rick held up her parka and she put her right arm in the sleeve; he draped the left side around her sling.

Rick's Dalmatian, Pirate, sat alert in the passenger seat of his Ford Bronco, ready--as befit her fine breeding--for any emergency. She turned her jowly face toward Patrice as she approached the car and showed the large black spot that covered her left eye like a patch. Her spots were spaced around her body fairly evenly except for her rump, which was all white, and her ears, where the black spots ran together. "I suppose this means I have to move?" her big brown doleful eyes seemed to say.

Rick called her out to the sidewalk while he moved her *101 Dalmatians* beach towel to the back seat.

"I bought the video for her," he said, patting the back seat. "Pirate, load up, girl! Atta girl."

"Should I ask why?"

"It was getting too expensive renting it every time she wanted to watch it."

"You're an old softie." Putting her left foot in the car and holding onto a handle in the car's ceiling, Patrice got enough leverage to get into the front seat.

He closed the back door. "Don't let that get around." His words were light-hearted, but his tone and the set of his jaw showed his real mood. He took the seatbelt from her right hand and pulled it across to the latch, then closed her door.

"Bad day at the office?" she said lightly as he got in and started the engine.

"Is there any other kind?" He pulled out of the parking lot by her apartment, waited for an old couple to cross the street, and headed for Central Avenue.

"Well, aren't we in a dark mood?" she said. "Want to talk about it?"

"So much to do, so few reporters." His jaw relaxed a little, and a smile played at the corners of his mouth. "I've had to call in reinforcements. You remember Tiffany?"

Patrice remembered Tiffany, all right. Tall, twenty-one, shapely, tanned from playing tennis on her college team and working as a lifeguard in California. Tiffany had worked at the *Guardian* as an intern in August and half of September. She was the kind of woman that made feminists grind their teeth. She was so gorgeous and so aware of her effect on men that other women hoped she was stupid so they could feel superior. Patrice was not immune to the niggling jealousy. She'd tried, really tried to be fair, kind, unbiased, neutral, unprejudiced and balanced where Tiffany was concerned, but the dirty truth was she couldn't stand her. Tiffany wasn't stupid, though she wasn't what Patrice would call smart, either. Cunning was a better word for her kind of intelligence, cunning as a Persian cat with cream on its whiskers, and just as indolent. Fast on the tennis court and quick to take credit, Tiffany avoided undue exertion in the office.

If Rick had said, "You'll get double your pay to come back soon," he could not have encouraged Patrice's return more than he had by hiring Tiffany.

"What will she be doing?" Keeping a disinterested tone for five words was all she could swing at the moment. Tiffany fished at the top of the gene pool, which meant she liked what she saw in Rick Romero. Patrice saw it as clearly as a two-inch headline, but so far as she could tell, Rick hadn't tumbled.

"Truth is, not much. It was Kent's idea to hire her," he said. "She's home visiting her father for a month before her last semester. Kent heard from her, or from her father, I don't know, and decided she could do some special projects for him and help out in the newsroom, too. It remains to be seen if it will be a net gain or a wash to our workload."

Patrice thought he'd be lucky if it was a wash. Tiffany had a way of distracting people that could be a net loss. She cleared her throat. "Speaking of work, what have I missed?"

"Let's see, on Tuesday, just twelve busloads of cherubic anti-nuke children holding hands around Ashley Pond, news helicopters flying overhead by special permission from the Department of Energy. Made all the networks. Danny's photos were on the wire once again. He was two for two, Monday and Tuesday. The boy's going to get a big head, I tell you. He's not very happy about it, though." He paused. "Did he tell you he gave notice?"

"He told me Monday he was going to, but I tried to talk him out of it."

"Well, thanks for trying, but it didn't work."

She noticed then Rick had chosen an indirect route off "the Hill," as everyone called Los Alamos. Three roads left the Hill: the Main Hill Road, the truck route, and Pajarito Road, which went to White Rock, where about one-third of the town's population lived. The three roads came together again as State Route 502, which widened and spilled on down the canyons to the Rio Grande. Rick was taking the truck route. "I get the impression you don't want to take me past the scene of the crime," Patrice said.

"Have I ever told you how perceptive you are? And how annoying that can be?"

The sun was bright and Patrice closed her eyes and dozed. When she felt the car slow for the turn north toward Española, she opened her eyes, leaned her seat back a few degrees, and observed the valley.

It was a beautiful day for a drive. Close on their left were the Puye Cliffs of Santa Clara Pueblo. The ground sloped away gradually to the right, toward the Rio Grande. They couldn't see the river itself, but bare trees marked its route. Down in the dry arroyos to their right were the stumps of great logs that once held up the track of the Chile Line, the railroad that ran from Santa Fe to Colorado.

Across the valley to the east, Patrice could see the snow-capped Sangre de Cristos, with Santa Fe Baldy and Santa Fe Ski Basin so prominent. North of that she saw Truchas Peaks, and farther north and east, the mountains around Taos. The sky was a shade of blue the state song called azure.

"It really is the Land of Enchantment," Patrice said softly. Tears sprang to her eyes when she thought of Rose, and how her friend would never see it again. Gradually her eyelids shut again.

They came up behind a horse trailer and Pirate barked sharply. Patrice flinched in surprise.

"Looks like you were off to the land of Nod a little earlier than you planned. Sorry Pirate startled you."

The dog continued to bark as they passed the horse trailer, then looked out the back window and growled until it was out of sight.

Patrice told Rick about finding the Cadillac behind Knecht's with the garden-variety fender benders, and about her meeting with Capt. Bell and Lt. Pauling. She gave a quick capsule of what Doyle Silver had told Rose and her Monday night.

"Do you know what a tontine is?" When Rick shook his head, she barged ahead. "Don't feel bad, most people don't. A tontine is an arrangement, a contract actually, where a group of people put money into a pot for investment. The money stays in the pot and grows for years and years. As each investor dies, his share remains, owned by the others, until only one man is left alive. The last man is wealthy."

"That's crazy," Rick said, picking up immediately on the danger in such a contract.

"You're right. It was an annuity scheme thought up by an investment banker in Naples in the late sixteenth century. It became illegal, I don't know when, but my guess is, pretty quickly. The word tontine comes from the banker's name, Lorenzo Tonti, and the word is sometimes used, incorrectly, for 'last man bottles.'"

"Now that I have heard of," he said, "but I thought it was something specific to the First World War--not that I thought about it much at all."

"You probably saw a picture of some wizened old French veteran wheeled out to drink a glass of champagne, or by then it might have been vinegar, to his deceased compatriots," she said. "But it's been done in other wars or disasters by shipmates, or members of a platoon with a lot of esprit d'corps. Especially if they lived through something horrendous like being prisoners of war, they put a bottle of fine bourbon or something aside and swore the last man alive would drink to all of them."

"Sure, I remember some pictures like that. The one I'm thinking of, all the survivors of some god-awful battle signed their names on the label of the bottle."

"Yeah, but it's not a true tontine because the 'last man' doesn't inherit anything of real value."

"Yeah, okay, I see. So did Doyle Silver and his buddies make a tontine, or just agree to one last, solo toast of cognac?"

"That I don't know yet. If what he said is true, their connection had to do with giving information about the Manhattan Project to the Russians. He admitted giving Lona Cohen secret papers himself, papers about the implosion lens, the way to make the bomb go critical and truly be a nuclear bomb. And he felt sure Carl Ellsberg did, too. He saw Ellsberg cheek to jowl with Douglas Frost on several occasions."

"And who was Douglas Frost?"

"One of the five men. I never heard of him before, which

is not significant, but Rose hadn't heard of him, either, and she was a walking encyclopedia of the Manhattan Project. Researching Douglas Frost was the first thing we were going to do."

She looked over at Rick's profile and silently admired how well put together his face was. Then she forced herself to stay on the subject. "Doyle said it was Douglas Frost who talked a lot about the way Jews were being killed by Hitler. He said the American government knew about mass murders of Jews in Poland, Germany and other countries, but was covering it up. He said hundreds of thousands of men, women and children were being gassed. Of course, now we know it was not only true, but worse than that--millions of people were actually killed. But during the war, it was just rumors."

Pirate spotted a cow off toward the river and gave a couple of woofs and a warning growl. "Yes, Pirate," Patrice said, "we feel safe with you to protect us. Good girl." Pirate thrust her face into the front seat and licked Patrice's face.

"Oh, yuck! Dog slobber," she said, wiping it off.

Rick laughed. "Pirate will protect us from cows, but who will protect us from Pirate?"

Patrice made a face and patted Pirate. "Okay, girl, go lie down." Then she turned back to Rick. "Anyway, Douglas Frost said Stalin wanted to save Jews, that Jews were treated well in Russia, and he kept stressing that the Soviet Union was our ally. He talked that up to Doyle, Carl Ellsberg, Gerald Gisle and Henri Sacco. Gisle and Sacco were both Jews, Gisle from Austria and Sacco from Italy. Doyle said they both died of cancer before they were fifty."

"I've read that a lot of people, even in Washington, wanted to do more for Russia. Or, the Soviet Union, as it was then," he said.

"Oh, yeah! They had great propaganda, about how Russia was losing millions of men in the war against Hitler, and how they were our best friend. Well, part of that propaganda was to claim Russia was kind to Jews. Which was a lie just as big as Hitler's, but who knew?"

"Where is the nursing home?" he said.

"Turn at the Oñate Street Bridge, then north and I'll tell you when to turn right."

"So you think Douglas Frost was working for the Russians?"

"Doyle said he's the one that told him where to meet Lona Cohen, though he didn't use her name, just told him how to identify her. And Frost offered him money, but Doyle refused, said he was doing it to help our ally. But, get this, Frost gave him two bottles of cognac. Those were the bottles Doyle took to Trinity Site when they tested the bomb." She watched the street signs. "Slow down, we're close--yes, turn here."

As he pulled into the muddy parking lot, he said, "So you think one of these spies murdered Rose? Or hired someone to do it?" He sounded almost as dubious as the police.

"Not necessarily. There could be other people who stand to lose a lot if the identity of Perseus is exposed."

"Like, what could they lose?"

"Like, I have no idea. But a spy underground in American science for fifty years--maybe in defense work--could leave a lot of toxins."

"But what makes you think Rose was such a threat to Perseus and/or his partners in crime? I mean, she was a bright lady, I know that for a fact, but it just seems too far-fetched."

"I think that's just why she got so close, because the bad guys didn't think she was any threat. Little ol' Rose, with her determination, and a mind as sharp as an editor's tongue, came at them from a direction they weren't watching."

"Is that what you're trying to do?"

"It's definitely too late for that. Once I made the acquaintance of Doyle Silver, any cover I could have had was blown. My only protection is that nobody thinks I'm smart enough to be a threat." To herself she added, "I hope."

He parked and turned off the engine. "I hate to admit I can't remember," he said, "but who was 'Perseus,' anyway?"

"Greek mythology. Perseus killed Medusa, the woman with the worst hair day in history."

"Huh?"

"Medusa was a woman with snakes for hair. Anyone who looked at her was turned to stone. But Perseus managed to cut off her head. He got close enough by using a magic shield that reflected her image. He also saved the beautiful Andromeda from a sea monster. All in all, a brave and righteous hero. Not a name I'd pick for a lying, scheming, spying, sleazebag who'd betray military secrets to another country."

"But, hey, how do you really feel about spies?" Rick laughed. He got out of the car and picked his way through puddles to open Patrice's door. Pirate whimpered as he helped Patrice down from the high seat. "Stay, Pirate. I'll come out and walk you in a few minutes. I'm just going to give Patrice a hand on this muddy parking lot."

A security guard, not the same one Patrice had seen Monday night, saw them coming up the sidewalk and opened the door. "Thanks," Rick said, and to Patrice added, "Will you be okay?"

"Sure. Go walk Pirate. She's been cooped up a long time." She watched him walk back out to his car, noting yet again how broad his shoulders were.

She made a stop at the ladies room, then headed down the corridor to Mr. Silver's room. It was going to be hard to break the news about Rose. She nodded to a nurse walking beside an ancient old lady who was inching down the corridor with her walker. The nurse held on to a harness around the woman's waist, ready to catch her if she stumbled.

As best Patrice could recall, Mr. Silver's room was the third room on the left in the far corridor of the H-shaped building. The door was open, so she gave it a light knock and walked right in.

Doyle Silver's bed, she recalled, was the one by the window. But it was empty. The blanket was pulled taut, no edges left untucked. The sheet was folded precisely back over the satin top of the blanket, and the pillow was fluffy and sterile-looking. There was nothing on the bedside table, no postcards on the wall, no photo of a bearded young man on the windowsill as there had been the other time she was there.

Either this is the wrong room, she thought, or he's moved. She should have stopped at the desk on her way in. To save a trip she might as well ask the roommate. "Excuse me," she said to the elderly gentleman in the other bed. "Excuse me." This time she touched his arm to waken him. His eyes flew open and his leg gave an involuntary jump.

"What? What do you want?" He lifted his bony hand to his face and wiped his mouth.

"I'm sorry to wake you up. I may be in the wrong room. I'm looking for Mr. Silver."

He stared at her, a puzzled expression on his face. Again he wiped at his mouth and tried to wet his lips.

"Water," he said, waving his arm toward his table.

"Sure, here." Patrice held the cup near him and he caught the flexible straw between his lips. He took a sip, then another, then waved the cup away.

"What?" he said again. "Whatcha want?"

"I'm looking for Mr. Silver."

His expression got even more puzzled. "Silver? He passed."

"What? I don't understand. Passed what?"

"Passed."

"I don't understand."

He looked at her as if she were dumber than a stone. "He's dead."

Patrice felt the blood leave her face and had a sensation of all light being sucked out of the room. She reached her good right hand out for something to hold onto, but felt only air.

"Patrice!" It was Rick's voice. He was holding her good elbow. Light seeped back into the room; her face was uncomfortably hot.

"Rick! he said. Mr. Silver is dead."

"I know, Patrice." His arm was around her waist, but his voice seemed to come from a distance. "They told me at the front desk. He died Tuesday. Early Tuesday morning."

Chapter 6

"What do you mean it's too late for an autopsy?" Patrice said to the woman across the desk from her. Virginia Velasquez, Administrator, was the name on the door.

Ms. Velasquez rolled her rump to one side in order to cross her legs before she answered. "Doyle Silver's nephew is his only living relative, or at least his closest living relative," she said. "It was his decision to have Mr. Silver's body cremated."

Patrice's heart sank. "And it's already happened?"

"As far as I know," Velasquez said with a shrug of disinterest. "Pearl Mortuary was handling the arrangements."

"Ms. Velasquez, please call the mortuary and ask. Right away, please."

"What on earth for?" She rearranged two paperweights on a stack of curling fax papers, and examined her fingernails.

"Maybe Mr. Silver didn't die of natural causes. I think there should be an autopsy."

Velasquez uncrossed her legs and leaned forward, resting her massive breasts on her forearms. "Are you trying to make trouble here? You said you visited the man once and now you want to take over and accuse people of killing him? I most certainly won't call the mortuary. Mr. Silver was seventy-six years old, he had a number of health problems, and he died in his sleep. That's all I have to say about it. Now I suggest you leave. I have work to do."

"Ms. Velasquez, wait, please. Okay, never mind what I

said about Mr. Silver," Patrice said to calm her. "I'm just exhausted and upset. I'm not accusing anyone." She took a deep breath to steady her voice. "But there's something else. When I was here with Ms. Hulle Monday night something happened. Someone--Shandra--told her there was a call for her at the front desk. The call was from someone Rose Hulle didn't know, and he threatened her life. Later that same night we were run off a cliff and Rose died. I need to talk to the person who took the phone call. Please help me." She hated groveling, but there were no options.

Velasquez stood up, less angry but still clearly annoyed. "Monday night? I'll have to check the schedule." She lumbered out of the office, which wasn't particularly small, but her bulk made it feel like a closet. Patrice followed her, trying not to count the dimples on her chunky elbows.

Rick was waiting for her in the lobby. "Mr. Silver has probably already been cremated," she said hurriedly, just a shade above a whisper. "Call Pearl Mortuary and ask if it's happened, please. And find out the name and address of his nephew. That's who made the decision."

Rick nodded, dug in his pocket for change, and headed for the pay phone. Patrice stepped over to the four-foot-high curved barrier that screened the nurses and aides from the lobby. Velasquez was behind the barrier, leafing though papers on a clipboard. Out of the corner of her eye Patrice could see Rick thumbing through the phone book that served Santa Fe, Los Alamos and Española.

"About what time was the call?" Velasquez asked.

"We were here from about seven-thirty to nine-thirty. I'd guess it was roughly nine o'clock," Patrice said. She could see Rick punching in a phone number, his eyes on the book.

"Mercy, you worked Monday night, didn't you?" Velasquez addressed the aide Patrice had seen helping the old lady with her walker.

"Did you get a phone call for...?" She looked at Patrice for the answer.

"For Rose Hulle," Patrice told Mercy. "We were in Mr. Silver's room, and Shandra told her there was a call."

Mercy shook her head and in a strong Spanish accent said, "No." She strung the word out as if it had three syllables. "I don't know about any call. Betty was here at the desk most of the time. Maybe she'd know."

"Where's Betty?" Patrice asked, "and Shandra?"

"Betty won't be on until six," Mercy answered.

"Could I call her at home?"

"No," Mercy droned. "She don't have a phone."

"What about Shandra?"

Mercy shuffled through some papers on a clipboard. "She's off sick."

"Does she have a phone?"

Mercy looked at Velasquez for guidance.

"Shandra is hard to reach," the administrator said. She took the clipboard from Mercy and wrote a number on a cube of notepaper and tore off the top square for Patrice. "Leave a message with her grandmother." She shrugged as if she expected it to be a waste of effort.

"Thank you very much. I'll leave a message for Shandra and I'll call Betty here later. Thanks," she said again, and backed away from the space barrier. Rick was off the phone and waiting for her. "Well?"

"It's too late. The nephew wanted it done quickly, no services."

"Did you get his name?"

"Yeah. Lawrence Dreyfus. He lives on Forty-First Street in Los Alamos."

Patrice was surprised, then remembered Rose said the nephew lived in Los Alamos.

Rick gave a sigh of resignation. "I suppose you'll insist on going to see him?"

"I have to do something here first. I want to take another

look around in Mr. Silver's room. I'll just stroll casually toward the restroom and meet you in his room in a few minutes."

The hall was quiet, the only sound a click and whoosh, pause, click and whoosh again from the first room on the left. Patrice recalled the sound was some respiratory device that fed oxygen. She made no sound herself as she walked quickly to Doyle Silver's old room.

The roommate had gone back to sleep, his mouth wide open. Patrice looked at a birthday card displayed on his night stand; above the syrupy machine-generated message was handwritten, "Dear Grandpa Mort."

Rick was as stealthy coming down the hallway as she had been. She gave a little jump of surprise when he appeared. They nodded at each other, and he stationed himself in the doorway to keep an eye on the hallway.

Patrice moved to the far side of what had been Doyle Silver's bed. The wastebasket was empty; the drawer of his night stand was empty. The metal cabinet against the wall had two doors, one for each occupant of the room. She tugged at the door closer to the window, carefully so it wouldn't make noise. Except for a basin with a small box of tissues, a shrink-wrapped plastic drinking cup and a sample box of Polident, the closet was empty.

"Darn," she said under her breath. She pushed the door shut but didn't latch it. Surveying the room, she noticed old tape stuck to the walls where photos and cards had been the night she came; she moved closer to the roommate's bed and looked at the snapshots tacked to a cork board above his night stand. There was a middle-aged couple on a beach, and a boy on a mountain bike, and a photo of Mort in his room, sitting up in a wheelchair, with wrapping paper and socks in his hands. Behind him was Doyle Silver's side of the room, the old gentleman in bed as Patrice had seen him, his few photos and cards displayed on the wall. She studied the picture. There was something different about the night stand. The lamp on it now was a coldly institutional brown thing. In the photo, Silver had the one she'd noticed Monday night and forgotten until she saw the picture. It was a banker's desk lamp with a green glass shade and a polished brass base. A brass chain with a small ball attached made it easy for an old person to turn on and off without a lot of manual dexterity.

"Patrice!" Rick whispered. She nodded and they slipped out of the room and headed back the way they came. Patrice hoped they wouldn't run into Ms. Velasquez, literally or figuratively.

On a bulletin board at the head of the hallway was the Happy Thanksgiving display Rose and Patrice had noticed Monday night. In the photos residents and guests looked at the camera; on the tables were fold-out paper turkey gobblers and cone figures made of black and white paper that vaguely resembled pilgrims.

"Wait!" Patrice said. "Keep your eyes open for any staff people coming this way." She scanned the photos quickly, finding the two she was looking for, Mr. Silver with the bearded man, looking right at the camera, and the one with Silver in the background talking with the balding man. She looked over her shoulder and quickly removed the photos, sliding four or five others over and re-tacking them to cover the bare spots.

Mercy was standing in the lobby. Patrice dabbed at her eyes as they walked past. "Thank you for your help," she said. "We'll call on Mr. Silver's nephew to tell him how sorry we are."

"It's a shame, you know?" Mercy said, bobbing her head up and down. "Mr. Silver used to be so quiet, you know? He'd hardly say a word, but, you know, he cheered up a lot since Mrs. Hulle and his other visitor started coming."

"I wonder if his other visitor was someone I know?" Patrice blew her nose noiselessly.

"A tall man with blond hair, but bald in the front, you know?" Mercy said, bobbing her head again.

"I can't place him. About how old do you think he is?"

"Maybe fifty, you know?" Mercy made every answer sound like a question. "I don't know his name?"

"I hope he knows about Mr. Silver's death. It was a terrible shock to me to find out when I came here."

Mercy nodded sympathetically. "He hasn't been here in a while, since Thanksgiving? You know, I heard him tell Mr. Silver he was going to Mexico?"

Rick patted Patrice in a way meant to show Mercy his concern for her fragile state. "I'd better get you home. You're exhausted."

"Yes, you're right. Thanks again, Mercy. Oh, I suppose Mr. Dreyfus came for Mr. Silver's things, didn't he?"

"Oh, yes, you know? He picked them up Tuesday?"

"Good, good. Well, 'bye now." She leaned on Rick more than she needed to as they walked to the car. Her slow ascent into the high seat was not exaggerated, however. She groaned as she swung her legs in. Pirate leaned her head between the front seats and sniffed Patrice's cheek with her cold, wet nose. "I'm okay, Pirate. You're a good girl."

"Home?" Rick said hopefully.

"Wishful thinking. Let's go right to Lawrence Dreyfus's house."

Chapter 7

By the time Rick and Patrice returned to Los Alamos, midwinter darkness covered the mountains like a black geodesic dome. Patches of feeble light, which started as beams from the brightest lights in town, probed the clouds for a weak spot, but instead tumbled back to earth, washed out and depleted by the effort. The light-trapping clouds kept the day's meager residue of solar heat from radiating back toward the stars, but nonetheless Patrice shivered. The radio announcer said the current temperature was twenty-nine degrees, but she'd bet it was colder.

They stopped at Rick's place to drop off Pirate and feed her, and to pick up Rick's parka. Just after six p.m., they circled a block in North Community, trying to make out numbers on the dark houses. They found Lawrence Dreyfus's place by a process of elimination.

The duplex sat below the level of the street, its front yard studded with towering pine trees. With no porch light and no street light, the yard was dark as a cavern.

Rick and Patrice bumped their way down ten or twelve crumbling concrete steps from the street. On the left hand unit, the one they figured was Dreyfus's half, a sliver of light escaped from the center of a wide downstairs window where the drapes didn't quite meet.

"Damn!" Rick exclaimed as he stumbled over something. "What's that?" He answered his own question. "A tricycle, on the front sidewalk." He rubbed his shin. "Where's a lawyer when you need one?" he muttered.

As their eyes adjusted to the shapes in the yard, they could see another trike and a wagon on the porch of the other side of the duplex.

Feeling his way by the toe-Braille system, tap-tap-step, then tap-tap-step, Rick mounted Dreyfus's porch and punched the bell. Patrice followed in his wake, holding tightly to his sleeve. Even with her parka on, she shivered as they huddled at the door. The wind picked up, delivering a face-slapping reminder that Christmas was coming, ready or not.

"Did it ring?" she asked. "I didn't hear anything." The painkiller she'd taken at Rick's house had not kicked in yet, and she felt worse by the minute.

"Yeah, I heard the bell. Maybe he's not here."

"With my luck, he's probably dead."

With a pop from a tight weather-sealing job, the door swung open. The face Patrice recognized from the framed photo in Mr. Silver's room stared back at her.

She wasn't looking at his face. though. Across his shoulders and down both arms was an undulating snake. The tail was wrapped around one arm and the head leaned out from his other arm, looked from Rick to Patrice, and whipped its forked tongue in and out of mottled green jaws.

"Mr. Dreyfus?" Patrice squeaked. He nodded slightly. "I'm Patrice Kelsey and this is Rick Romero. I'd like to speak with you about your uncle, to say how sorry I am at his death. Could we come in?"

Lawrence Dreyfus wasn't more than five feet ten, probably weighed about one-sixty, but he gave the impression of being larger. His suspenders and bushy beard made her think of a lumberjack. And then there was the snake. Definitely gave him stature, the snake did. Dreyfus looked at them as if they were strange, a judgment that seemed a mite misplaced to Patrice, as she and Rick wore jackets, not reptiles, over their shoulders.

"All right," Dreyfus said at last.

Rick opened the storm door and followed Patrice into the

living room. There were glass cages on the floor along all the walls and on steel shelves. Pegboard tops were held in place by bricks.

Patrice held still but her eyes swept the room. *This gives new meaning to the term "living room." There are more coils in this room than in an orthopedic mattress.* To her right was an aquarium that would have been much improved, to her way of thinking, by water and cute little fishes. Instead, the aquarium (now a terrarium) was the worst thing it could be under the circumstances: empty. She fervently hoped it was the home of the snake she saw atop Lawrence Dreyfus, and not the home of some snake she couldn't see yet, some hungry reptile out for an evening slither, eyeing her juicy ankle from underneath a chair.

A fire blazed in a wood stove that dominated the living room. The place had to be at least eighty-five degrees.

Patrice was at a loss as to which would be more polite to mention first, the live snake or his dead uncle. The snake made up her mind by leaning a good three feet out in front of Dreyfus and a good two and a half feet into the space she thought of as hers. "He's a beauty," she said. "Boa?"

"Red Tailed Boa, from Panama. Her name is Red," Dreyfus said, a proud papa. As if to acknowledge the attention, Red swung her head toward his face and stuck her tongue out at him six or eight times. Her middle formed two coils, one on each side of his neck, and she slid her head up onto the top of his, then looked back at the visitors.

"Is she full grown?" Rick looked completely relaxed.

"Nah. She's about eight feet now. Red Tailed Boas get up to fifteen feet." Responding to Rick's interest, Dreyfus lifted her over his head and spread her out. Red tightened her grip noticeably on his left arm with her tail. "Boas are used to living in trees. As long as they have a good grip with their tails, they feel secure. So the first thing I tell people who want to hold her is, 'Make like a tree.' Let her get a grip on one arm and she won't choke you."

Rick's interest exceeded Patrice's. She had been around only one boa constrictor before, and his name was Heimlich. They were never close.

"We just came by to tell you how sorry we are about your uncle's death. Rick never met him, but I visited him twice last summer, and again the night before he died. He appeared to be pretty healthy. I was shocked when I went to see him today and they told me the dreadful news."

"When did you say you saw him?"

"Monday night. I went with Rose Hulle. She'd been visiting him for several months. We were in a terrible car crash on the way home, and Rose was killed."

"Oh. That's too bad," Dreyfus said, a little too lightly in Patrice's opinion. He unwound the end of Red's red and black tail from his arm and put her in the empty terrarium.

"Yes, it was a shock to get the call about my uncle," with no inflection or emotion. "His death was completely unexpected. I mean, he was terminally ill, you know, with prostate cancer, but we thought he'd hold on another year or two." He made a kissy kissy noise in Red's direction.

"We?" Patrice said.

"What? Oh, uh, my mother is his sister. Myrtle Silver Dreyfus. She lives in Illinois."

"Did she come...?" she almost said "for the funeral."

"No, no. It's too far, and she's not in good health either, so I just took care of what needed to be taken care of."

Patrice wavered a little, unsteady on her feet, and Dreyfus reluctantly took the hint. "Uh, you want to sit down?"

"I would, thank you," she said. A bad taste in her mouth plus a headache made her woozy. She watched Dreyfus take tall stacks of magazines off the wood and wrought iron park bench that served as a couch in the Spartan room.

Rick squeezed in beside her on the bench and Dreyfus pulled up an ottoman for himself. Behind him on the wall was a framed poster that said "Rattlesnakes of New Mexico." Pictures of seven snakes were beside a description of each.

Dreyfus followed Patrice's gaze to the poster. "They're not shown to scale, that's important to know," he said.

"I don't understand," she said. *Furthermore, I don't care.* In spite of her thought process, she managed to look intrigued, or at least curious.

"The pictures show them all the same size. But the Massasauga is tiny compared to the Western Diamondback. This here's a Massasauga." He pointed to a glass cage about six inches from her calf where a skinny sandy-colored snake was climbing the glass and checking out the pegboard top. "And they're just as venomous as a coontail."

"Coontail?" Rick said.

"That's a nickname for the Western Diamondback. The last few inches of their bodies before the rattle are striped black and white. But you didn't come to talk about snakes."

Right you are. Patrice rubbed her neck, feeling the knots of tension under her fingertips. *Just why are we here? To tell him somebody murdered his terminally ill uncle?* Somehow the whole thing seemed more every minute like a figment of her pain-dazed brain.

"It's about my friend Rose," she said slowly and deliberately, locking her eyes on his. "That's really why I'm here. Rose wasn't killed in an accident. Someone threatened her life, and someone forced us off the Main Hill Road Monday night."

Dreyfus snapped the eye contact without showing any sign he'd heard, or cared, what Patrice said. He looked at the floor, then studied a hangnail.

"It's a miracle Patrice is alive," Rick added.

"The police think my murder theory has no foundation. So I'm here on my own, grasping at straws." Sweat dripped between her breasts and poured off her forehead. She had already shed her jacket. *Another fifteen minutes in here, and I'll be molting like the snakes*. "You want to know what this had to do with your uncle, I know. Rose had been visiting with him as part of research she was doing on the atomic spy code-named Perseus. Have you heard of him?"

Dreyfus nodded. "I read about it when the story first came out. Anything new? Anybody know who it was?"

She hedged a little. "I think Rose was getting close. And she was planning to publish her research. Someone called her at the nursing home Monday night, while the two of us were visiting your uncle. She didn't know who it was, but he threatened her. So someone knew we were there. I suppose it shows how paranoid I'm becoming, but I'll tell you, Mr. Dreyfus..."

"Call me Larry."

"...Larry, when I found out your uncle died only hours after talking to Rose, my first thought was that he'd been murdered. I wish there had been an autopsy." There, she'd said it. She was feeling nauseated from the heat and the mental strain and the pain in her arm. "We need to go; I've overdone it. Today started with Rose's funeral. But I wonder if you'd do me a favor?" Larry cocked his head. "Could I see your uncle's things from the nursing home?"

"I guess so. It's just some junk." He went into the kitchen and came back with a cardboard box about three feet square and four feet high, setting it at her feet. He lifted out the banker's desk lamp and set it on the coffee table.

"Shall I just pull things out?" she asked.

"Sure. Here, I'll help you. Do you know what you're looking for?"

"Oh, photos, letters. Maybe a tidy envelope that says, 'Open in the event of my sudden death.'" She was getting punchy. The painkiller had kicked in, and she felt like her scalp was floating six inches above her skull.

The three of them pulled out the old man's denture cup, his glasses, his hemorrhoid ointment, his pajamas. Patrice scratched at her floating scalp. *Ghoulish.*

"The nurse's aide took all the pictures and cards and put them in here," he said, handing Patrice a nine by twelve envelope.

She emptied it into her lap as Larry found the framed photo of himself in the bottom of the box. He made a face at it and placed it face down on the coffee table. It didn't take long to go through the cards; there were only three, signed by Myrtle, Larry, and Rose.

She spread out the eight photos. "That's my mother with Uncle Doyle before I was born," Larry said, "and Uncle Doyle in college, in upstate New York. And then here at Los Alamos during the war."

A skinny man barely recognizable as Doyle squinted as he looked into the camera lens. He was sprawled on the steps of a wooden building, smoking a cigarette. The other pictures were a group photo of eleven men and one woman in front of the old Laboratory cafeteria, circa 1945, according to a notation on the back, and four color snapshots of Doyle as an old man at the nursing home. In one he sat up in bed wearing a birthday hat; in the other three he was in a wheelchair. The last one was from Thanksgiving. Patrice recognized the bib he wore and the old woman with the magenta afghan in the background. In the holiday photo, Doyle looked up at a tall man with thinning blond or light brown hair.

"Do you know who this is?" she asked Larry.

He stared at it a moment. "No, I don't know him."

Patrice looked one more time at the photo of young Doyle Silver on the steps. There was no notation on the back of time or place, but it looked familiar; maybe she'd seen something similar at the Historical Museum. "Do you know if the 'Last Man bottle' of cognac is with Dr. Carl Ellsberg? Or Douglas Frost?"

Dreyfus looked annoyed. "So, you fell for that story, did you?"

Patrice met Rick's look of surprise with one of her own. "Are you saying it wasn't true?"

"My uncle liked attention," he said, as if at-ten-tion were three dirty words. "He didn't always observe the strict boundaries of truth. Oh, there may have been a bottle of cognac once. But as for a five man pact--is that what he told you, that there were five men?"

Patrice nodded, and Dreyfus gave a snort of derision. "Over the years he's named about fifteen men among the five. If I were you, I'd forget it."

She slid the pictures back into the envelope. "Thanks for your help. And thanks for not acting like I'm insane, even if you think I am. Rick, I'm ready to say those three little words you've been wanting to hear for the past three or four hours. 'Take me home.'"

Rick swallowed a yawn. "Gladly."

When they stepped out of the snake sauna they faced a temperature drop of fifty-five degrees. Patrice sat silent in the car.

"You'd better get some food into you," Rick said when they got to her apartment. "You've been taking medicine on an empty stomach. Bad idea." She dropped her parka on a chair and watched without caring as it slid to the floor. Rick squatted in front of the open refrigerator that Karen Meyer had stuffed with microwave entrees early that afternoon.

"Don't go to a lot of trouble. I'd just throw it up anyway. My stomach is the gastrointestinal equivalent of the Love Canal."

He put the teakettle on the burner and looked through the cupboards. "I know you have chamomile tea; I gave it to you."

While Rick bustled and clucked in the closet-sized kitchen, Patrice listened to the single message on her answering machine. Her mother had called from Los Angeles before boarding the plane to Hawaii. "Where are you?" she wanted to know. "I'll call tomorrow," she said. "They're announcing boarding now. I love you."

Patrice looked up the number of the nursing home. "Could I please speak with Betty?" she asked, then untangled the cord while she waited.

"This is Betty," the woman said suspiciously.

"This is Patrice Kelsey. I hope you can help me with something, Betty. I was at the nursing home Monday night with

Rose Hulle to see Mr. Silver. My friend Rose got a phone call at the front desk. Did you take that call?"

"Yeah. I remember I got Shandra to go get her."

"Did the person on the phone tell you his name?"

"Oh, he said he was her husband, that it was important for him to talk to her. That's all I know."

"Did she stand near you when she took the call?"

"Yeah. The cord didn't reach very far over the desk."

Patrice figured as much. "So you could hear what she said? I mean, you couldn't help hearing what she said, right?"

"Well, I had my work to do and it wasn't any of my business. But she was smiling when I handed her the phone. Kind of smiling, you know? Like things were fine. Then she listened to the phone and handed it back to me, and she was white as a ghost. I thought her husband must have told her some terrible news, like somebody in her family died or something. She didn't say anything back to him, just handed me the phone and went back toward Mr. Silver's room."

"Can you remember anything about the voice of the man on the phone?"

"No. Just a man--deep voice, it seems to me."

"Thank you, Betty. I appreciate you taking the time to help me. Have a nice evening, now." She set the receiver down and stared at it, lost in memories of her last night with Rose.

"Hey, you," Rick said, snapping her back to the present. "Your pillow is fluffed up, your tea is hot, and your body craves rest. So get your weary bones over here and let me pamper you."

"Now there's an offer I can't refuse," she said with a smile that was quickly displaced by a yawn.

"Chamomile tea with raw honey," he said, "just what Dr. Romero ordered." He waited until she nestled comfortably against the pillow, then handed her the steaming mug.

"Could you put a mug of tea by my feet?" she said as she sipped it. "They're colder than Eskimo Pies."

In answer he pulled her sneakers and socks off and gently

massaged her feet. "How's that? Warm yet?"

"If I say yes, will you stop?" she said, arching an eyebrow.

"Yes."

"Then, no, they're not warm yet. My guess is you should do that for about an hour."

He rubbed more, pressing his thumb into the arch of each foot and working the muscles toward the toes.

"That's the first pleasant feeling my body has received in days," she sighed. *Truth is, I can't remember how long it's been.*

"I've gotta go," he said, tucking her warm, reddened feet under the afghan that lay across her.

"Couldn't you stay a few minutes? Have a glass of wine? It's in the refrigerator."

He looked at his watch. "Only if you'll let me fix you something to eat."

"It's a deal. I might be able to keep down some soup. Chicken noodle, my favorite."

"Okay. You probably think I can't cook, huh?" He found the soup in the cabinet and the can opener in the top drawer of the kitchenette.

"No, I know you can cook. I ate your green chile stew at the last going-away party. And I've had your chocolate cake. It was great."

"Thank you," he said, giving a slight bow at the waist. "It's one of my better recipes, from scratch. Calls for buttermilk. My brother Luis is a good cook, too. Though it galls me to admit he's better than I am at anything, I'd have to hand him the spatula of honor. Do you have any wine glasses?"

"Just juice glasses and little paper cups. On the right."

He poured the chablis in a three-ounce Dixie cup and made a show of sniffing it before a formal taste. "An insouciant little vintage, piquant, but irascible. North side of the vineyard. September."

She laughed, then moaned. "Laughing makes my ribs hurt."

The microwave beeped that the bowl of ready-to-serve soup was hot. Rick moved her mail off the TV tray and placed the tray beside the bed. "I hope you're going to stay in bed tomorrow."

"Sure," she said without conviction. "What have you got going?" She imagined Tiffany sitting in her chair, giving come-hither looks to Rick over the top of her computer monitor.

"The paper in the morning, a social event in the evening."

"Anybody I know?"

"A voluptuous older woman with lots of money and powerful connections."

"Yes? Go on, you have my attention."

"United States Senator Cristal Aragon. Kent wants me to 'cover' the party in her honor at the Museum of International Folk Art."

"I want to go."

"Sorry. You are confined to quarters. Stay home, take drugs. Which reminds me, aren't you supposed to be on antibiotics?"

"Oh, yeah, I forgot since Mom left. It's one of those plastic containers by the bathroom sink."

He retrieved the pill bottle, read the label and tapped out a capsule into his hand; she swallowed it with tea. "I'd better get my pajamas on or I'll fall asleep in my clothes," she mumbled through a yawn. "But I don't want my feet to get cold again."

"I'll stay long enough to warm them up again." He took her bowl and mug to the sink.

In the bathroom she brushed her teeth and wriggled out of the slacks and gabardine blouse she'd worn all day, one-arm-style. An extra large T-shirt worked as a top with her pajama bottoms. She crawled into bed, aching in what seemed to be every cell of her body. "My feet are okay, but my head is throbbing."

"Can you roll to your left a little?" he asked. Awkwardly, she rotated her body to the left while protecting her broken arm.

He removed the TV tray and placed a dinette chair beside the bed. "Are you comfortable? Can you relax?"

She scooted around a little more and slowly leaned her head on the pillow. "How is that?"

"You tell me," he said. His hands on her shoulders were gentle, warming and kneading the knotted muscles. Rhythmically he massaged her neck, then shoulders, increasing the pressure almost imperceptibly as the muscles gave up some of their tension.

"I think I'm falling in love with your hands," she said. He pressed his thumbs in big circles from her shoulders toward her spine. He said nothing. Then she felt his warm breath against her neck, and one soft kiss on her throat. "I've gotta go."

"I know," she murmured. Slowly she turned her face and watched him put on his parka.

"I'll lock the door behind me." He leaned over and gently brushed her hair off her face. She expected a kiss on her forehead, but instead his lips brushed hers. "If you were aiming for my cheek, you missed," she said.

"Did I? Let me try again." The second time his lips found hers and lingered. For a minute or two she forgot she had regions of throbbing pain in her shoulder, chest, arm and stomach. For a minute she felt good all over, and before that minute was over, she was asleep. As if from a great distance, she heard the door close and the click of the lock.

She tried to hold on to the dream inspired by Rick's kiss, but darker visions crowded in. As she slipped into a deeper state of sleep, her dreams turned to a montage of people in a slow, writhing dance--Rose, and Mel, and Doyle Silver. And slithering through the background of the colorful picture, she recognized a boa constrictor named Red.

Chapter 8

Where is Rose's purse? That question was the second distinct thought Patrice registered on Friday morning as she climbed through vaporous fragments of dreams toward wakefulness. Her first thought had been: Here comes the pain. To her relief, however, the pain seemed less than the day before. She turned her head to see the clock.

"Damn!" she muttered. A stab of pain hit her neck in a spot that hadn't hurt before, though paramedics and doctors kept asking her if it did. So maybe the pain isn't retreating, it's just relocating.

A little after nine, said the clock. She weighed her options, deciding to take a bath first and then call Mel Hulle. Managing a bath by herself would be a giant step toward independence. She ran the water and tossed in two bath oil marbles, then took off her large T-shirt and pajama bottoms. As she stepped gingerly into the hot water, she caught a glimpse of herself in the long mirror on the back of the bathroom door. What her bruises lost in purple and blue they had gained in a ghastly green and yellow motif.

By contortions a circus star would envy, she managed to wash her hair under the tub's spout and keep her cast out of the water. Drying off, then getting jeans and an oversize sweater on with one hand nearly wore her out, though. She plugged in the hair dryer near the bed and rested her right arm in preparation for that task when the phone rang. Danny inquired about her health and offered to bring her a breakfast burrito and coffee.

"My lips want to say, 'Oh, don't go to all that trouble,' but my stomach says, 'Yes, hurry. Extra chile, extra cheese.'" She wanted to see Danny as much for the food he proffered as for news of the outside world. She didn't get a newspaper at her apartment; the *Albuquerque Journal* and the *Santa Fe New Mexican* were both by the door at the *Guardian* when she arrived every morning.

She dialed Mel's number; it rang four times and the answering machine clicked on. Patrice caught her breath, afraid it would be Rose's voice she would hear, still cheerily telling the caller she'd reached the home of Mel and Rose Hulle. Thankfully, she heard Allison's voice instead.

"Mel and Allison, this is Patrice. It's Friday morning about ten..." A click told her someone picked up.

"Patrice, how are you feeling?" Mel asked.

Considering who asked her, she found it a hard question to answer. If she minimized her discomfort, it seemed awry. Would Mel think--Rose is dead, and the other person in the car is fine? Or if she said how much her arm and ribs and neck hurt, would he think--Rose is dead, and you have the nerve to complain about a little pain?

"I'm going to be all right, Mel," she said, choosing her words deliberately. "How are you? I mean, how are you really? And how is Allison?"

"As well as could be expected. You know..." he paused, "you know those cartoons where Sylvester the Cat is run over by a steamroller and he gets up and walks around flat as a playing card? That's as close as I can come to a description of how I feel." His voice was cracking.

"I need to talk to you. There wasn't any way to talk when so many people were around, but I can get a ride over this morning. May I come?"

"Sure." He cleared his throat and steadied his voice. "Allison went to brunch at a friend's house. She's got to study for her finals."

"She's going back for the finals, then?"

"Oh, yes. She'll fly back to Dallas Sunday. She's pretty numb--well, we're both numb, of course. What I really dread, Patrice, is the time reality whacks us right between the eyes. Right now it just doesn't seem real. I know that sounds trite, but that's exactly how it is. Like there's something terribly wrong with Rose, something terribly wrong with our lives, but it will pass. All these people will go away, and Rose will come back. Don't ask me to explain how I can say that. I know it's not true; I know Rose is dead and her body is buried, but I feel as if my brain--and my body, too--is anesthetized."

Without warning, Mel lost control and sobbed, unable to speak. Gradually, he regained his equilibrium. "I'm sorry," he said hoarsely. "I just...I never know in advance when that will happen."

"Mel, don't apologize," Patrice said, wiping tears from her eyes and cheeks. "I'll see you in a little while." She hung up the phone and let the tears fall.

She had gotten to know Rose's husband one day when she hiked a steep trail from White Rock to the Rio Grande with the two of them. Mel told her he'd been married once before, a mismatch that lasted four years in the early 1970s. It was fortunate, he'd said, that he and Bess had not started a family. After Bess decided happiness was Los Alamos in her rear-view mirror, Mel spent all his time and energy on his career as a nuclear chemist. The death of his best friend of a heart attack at age forty-nine had shocked him into a reassessment of his life. And when he woke up, like Rip Van Winkle, he discovered Rose.

He was devoted to her. She teased him that he'd imprinted on her like a baby duck imprints on a mother goose if she's the first creature that waddles by after the egg cracks.

"Lucky for you it was me that answered your car-for-sale ad," she told him. "You could have fallen in love with a lady mud wrestler or a woman with eight children."

Allison had been fourteen when they married. Patrice got

the distinct impression that Mel had done his best to be a good stepfather, a role for which he had no preparation, but all three of them had been relieved when Alli left for college.

Now Mel and Alli would have to help each other through this terrible loss. As much as she hurt over Rose's death, Patrice knew her pain was small compared to theirs.

Chilled by her wet hair, she held the hair dryer in her left hand where it stuck out of the cast, and moved her head around to catch the hot air as she brushed the hair with her right hand. Good thing I have some natural wave. She smiled, remembering how her mother had looked at her hair. Right before she left for the airport, Karen pressed a fifty dollar bill in Patrice's hand. "Do me a favor," she'd said. "Go to a decent hair stylist. It would make me happy."

"Mom," Patrice said indignantly, "I can get a haircut for ten dollars."

"Obviously," Karen said dryly.

Patrice put the hair dryer away, then pulled back the curtains and surveyed the mountains that banked the town on the west. Two ski runs were visible from that angle, both white from Monday's storm. Danny knocked on the door.

"You're a true blue friend," she said, inhaling the aroma of green chile from the bag he carried.

"I've got to go in five minutes flat," he said. "I've got an appointment at the high school."

"If you leave in four flat, could you drop me off at Mel's house?" She cleared space on the dinette table and unwrapped the foil on their food.

He looked at her feet. "You going barefoot? I wouldn't recommend it."

As she ate she put her waterproof boots on over her socks. Sealing the foil on the other half of her burrito, she slid it into the refrigerator and grabbed her parka. "See, I'm ready."

Danny finished his burrito on the way to his truck. "Well, I see you're getting around better," he said as she got in unassisted.

"Tomorrow, tennis."

"And then rock climbing?"

"Never! Cliffs hold no appeal to me." Danny's police scanner crackled and they listened to an officer respond to the call. "Did Rick tell you Rose's friend, Doyle Silver, died a few hours after Rose? Just up and expired without anyone raising an eyebrow, I might add. Don't they need a coroner to look at the body for extra orifices or something?"

"You're such an innocent. For an older woman."

She recalled how Rick described the voluptuous senator. "Speaking of older women, are you going to the party for Senator Aragon in Santa Fe tonight? Rick said he has to go."

"No. I'm going down earlier with Tiffany for Aragon's press conference, then I get the night off."

"What press conference? Tiffany's going?" She was stricken at the thought of all she was missing. She complained as much as the next reporter about the tiring and intrusive nature of her job on her personal life, but now she knew how a starting quarterback felt on the bench. Not only was she out of the game, but that rookie Tiffany was on the field.

"The senator is on the warpath over the plutonium. She's going to get a lot of press over it," he said.

"She hates the Laboratory. She hates this town. Why does she have a house here?"

"I guess she likes the view," he said with a shrug.

"Yeah. So would I." Cristal Aragon's personal business was a pretty well-kept secret, but Patrice knew she owned by far the most expensive house in Los Alamos. Located at the end of North Mesa, a rocky promontory that narrowed like a pointing finger, the mansion had been built on the edge of the cliff, with part of it extending down into the face of the volcanic tuff. It faced away from town, overlooking the mountains across the valley, probably all the way into Colorado. If the valley ever became an inland sea, Cristal Aragon's house would make a perfect lighthouse.

The senator had next to nothing to do with anyone in Los Alamos, just used the house as a "getaway."

She was rich, she had family in Panama--supposedly--and her husband was invisible, said by the senator in an interview to be "a diplomat."

That Cristal Aragon became a senator was about as likely as being struck by lightning. Along with her brother, Kent Bolt, Aragon had backed the right horse in the governor's race, and when New Mexico lost a senator in a plane crash, they had Gov. Ted Somers's ear. Thanks to a quirk in the state constitution, the governor had the power to appoint a senator, but not a congressman; a vacancy in a U.S. Representative district required a special election.

Governor Somers was an outsider, a neophyte in politics who loved to shock the establishment, and selecting a U.S. Senator had been splendid fun for him. He looked at the list presented to him, a list of politicians and experienced public servants, and essentially tossed it over his shoulder. Instead of taking advice from anyone, he plucked Cristal Aragon from obscurity and sent her to Washington.

The coup was alternately applauded and condemned. She had the overwhelming advantage of being Hispanic, and a woman to boot, but the politicos who'd mucked in the party's trenches for years resented her quick climb over their tired bodies.

Patrice half-listened to Danny's description of the anti-nuke children's rally at Ashley Pond as she assessed her odds of getting to Santa Fe that afternoon to cover Sen. Aragon's speech. The cliché, "two chances: slim, and none," was all she could come up with.

Danny pulled up in front of Mel's house and walked around to help Patrice out. "See you later," she smiled. "Thanks for the ride."

Mel and Rose's house was in Western Area. At street level it looked like a one-story house, but it was on a steep slope, accommodating a large daylight basement that looked over the forested canyon behind them. What the north-facing basement lacked in sunlight it gained in privacy. The basement was Rose's work space, with hundreds of books lining the walls and two computers, one she called her old workhorse and a new one with "bells and whistles." Bird feeders hung in the pine trees just beyond the patio, and the birds and squirrels chattered at each other for dominance. A redwood deck off the living room on the main floor served as a receptacle for needles and cones from the tall Ponderosa pines beside it. Construction of the house and deck left the lot as natural as possible. Sitting on the deck in the summer, Patrice had the feeling she was miles from civilization, suspended in the pines.

"When we first moved in here," Rose had told Patrice, "Muffin went crazy chasing birds off the deck." Her fluffy white miniature poodle gave up the anti-bird campaign after the first exhausting summer. Something he would never give up, however, was a battle for Mel's favorite chair. Rose had decorated the room around the burgundy velvet-blend recliner, choosing creamy-white for the couch, with black and burgundy throw pillows, and a pale mauve for the carpet. The material at its edges was a little frayed, but he insisted his old bachelor chair had years of wear left in it.

Muffin barked when Patrice rang the bell, greeted her at the door, and went back to the recliner to curl up for Morning Nap, Part Two.

Patrice followed Mel into the kitchen for a cup of coffee. The kitchen, which was larger than her apartment and had more windows than Macy's, was cluttered with plates of cookies, coffee cakes, homemade bread, jars of jelly and preserves and a couple of layer cakes on pedestal plates. "The refrigerator is full of casseroles with cooking instructions taped to the lids, and salads and cold cuts." He opened the door to show her.

"Wow, Jell-O city," she said. "You may never have to buy groceries again."

"I need to wrap these up," he gestured toward the bounty on the counters, "and fit them into the freezer. Why don't you take some home with you?"

"Thanks," she said as she reached in the refrigerator for the half and half. "I just might do that."

"Would you like a piece of stollen? Sarah Hoffman, a friend from church, brought it over fresh this morning."

"Just a little piece, please." Confectioners' icing dripped down the sides of the German coffeecake, which was garnished with currants and candied fruit.

Mel placed slices on two china plates and set them in the living room. She carried her coffee and sat on the end of the couch nearest the recliner.

Mel returned with his coffee and two forks. "Muffin! Get down!" he ordered. Muffin, who'd looked mighty spry five minutes before, managed to look like he had arthritis and a heart condition as he dragged his weary body out of the warm indentation he'd formed in Mel's chair. He stood in the seat of the chair and looked over the edge as if it were a long way to the floor, a dangerous height. *Rin Tin Tin couldn't jump down from this chair, and you want me to?*

"Muffin! Down!" Muffin boinged from the recliner to the floor and onto the couch, as agile as a puppy, and curled into a ball against Patrice's jeans.

"Hi, Muff," she said. "You miss her, too, don't you?"

"He keeps going downstairs to her office to see if she's there," Mel said. "Yesterday during the funeral we had our neighbor Vera here to watch the house." He sipped his coffee and set it on the table. "And it's a good thing we did, too. Muffin went downstairs and Vera heard him barking ferociously, just going crazy. She ran downstairs and saw a man walking away from the back of the house through the woods. The door was locked, of course."

"Did she call the police?"

"No, she said he was probably a neighbor looking for a

lost dog or something. She didn't want to get written up in the Police Log."

Patrice laughed. The Police Log was the best-read part of the *Guardian*. All the crimes and some of the peccadilloes of the citizenry were printed for the world to see. Most seemed to include the phrase "a 16-year-old male driver."

"I called the police when I got home, though," he added. "Officer Robles came by and took the report."

"Did Vera have a description of the man?"

He scratched his temple, thinking. "Just that he was medium height, medium build, white, and he wore a black parka and a furry hat. She couldn't tell his hair color."

Patrice considered that, looking puzzled. "Did the officer ask any other neighbors if they saw anyone?"

"Not that I know of."

"Did he walk around outside and look for footprints in the snow?" She knew the snow stayed a long time in always-shady spots like the north side of Mel's house.

"No."

"Let's go," she said decisively, setting down her coffee mug. Mel looked surprised, but followed her downstairs. She pulled the drapes back from the patio door and considered where Vera must have stood to see a man in the back yard. She would have had to be pretty close to the door to see more than thirty feet out. Patrice found if she stood ten feet away from the door, over by the computer table, she lost sight of the yard due to the slope of the property. "Where did Vera tell the officer she stood when she saw the man?"

"Right at the glass door. The drapes were open when she came down, and Muffin was at the glass barking furiously."

Patrice unlocked the door and slid it open. The patio outside the door was free of snow, since the deck sheltered it. There was a precise band of snow from the edge of the patio to a line parallel to the back of the house and about ten feet out in the yard, the point the sun reached at its zenith on December days.

Water dripped from the last of the melting snow on the deck above. The patio would be too dangerous to walk across if the temperature dropped below freezing while all that water collected. For the time being it was just messy. Mel and Patrice stepped out and she looked back, seeing again where a prowler (or a neighbor looking for a lost dog) would stand to be seen from the door.

"So the officer didn't come out here to walk across the snow? And you didn't either?" There were unmistakable footprints in the crusty snow--one set.

Mel saw what she was looking at. "Those prints are headed away from the house, don't you think?"

"That would be my guess. Did Alli come out here, or did anyone who came to pay a condolence call?"

"Ah, Patrice, I don't know. There could have been a circus troupe through the house during the past three days and I wouldn't have noticed. Now that you mention it, the officer asked me that, and that's probably why he didn't bother going out to look for footprints. It could have been Alli, or someone else trying to be helpful."

"If that were the case, don't you think he or she would come back in through the same door?"

"What do you mean?"

"The prints only go away from the house," she said. "I could walk from the patio across the snow and wind through the woods to the driveway, or I could walk out and then tiptoe back, using the same holes my feet made on the way out. That's not likely. Another thing--those are big footprints, probably snowboots. Even in boots I doubt Alli's feet are that big."

"So what does it mean?"

Patrice walked across the snow, leaving her prints about three feet to the left of the others. The difference in the size of the prints was easy to see. "Wait here," she said. She walked into the wet but no longer snowy ground beyond the house and looked for more footprints; she couldn't see any. She climbed the embankment, using a few small trees and her good right hand to steady herself on the slippery pine needles. In spite of her caution, her foot slipped and she went down on her knee, getting mud on her jeans. She backed up two steps and looked at the ground. About four feet from where her boot slipped and gouged the mud was another, larger gouge.

She continued onto the driveway and walked back by the side of the house, out of Mel's sight. The driveway, an apron of concrete that ran right next to the house, abutted the neighbor's property line on its other side. Where the house stopped and the driveway continued toward the garage, the inside edge of the driveway was shored up with concrete. She couldn't do it herself, with a cast on one arm and her ribs hurting, but a person with strong legs and good balance could inch down the concrete to the woodpile and work his way toward the patio. Getting back up would be easier, as it would not be a delicate operation to jump from the woodpile to the solid driveway. She brushed her hair off her face. *If I wanted to approach the house without being seen from the kitchen windows, and I wanted to leave no tracks through the snow, I'd come that way. And leave the same way. Unless a dog went crazy and I had to get away faster.*

"I'll have to go back around to the front," she called. "I sort of painted myself into a corner here."

"I'll meet you there," Mel called.

She took off her muddy shoe boots on the porch. "I've got mud on my jeans," she said when he opened the door. She padded into the kitchen in her socks and wiped at her jeans with paper towels. "Boy, you can dress me up, but you can't take me anywhere," she muttered as she washed her hands in the sink.

"There's plenty more coffee, and coffeecake, too," he said. "Would you like to sit in here?"

"Sure. I'll go get my mug."

They sat on stools by the Mexican-tiled cooking island in the middle of the kitchen, facing out to enjoy the view. Patrice told him her theory of a prowler being surprised by Muffin and cutting out across the yard. "I'll talk to Lt. Pauling about it," she said. "Maybe he'll send someone to ask if neighbors saw a man get into a car nearby around that time." She paused, then added, "On second thought, would you talk to Pauling about it? You can get his attention better than I can."

"I think all the neighbors were at the funeral," Mel said.

"Yeah, you're probably right. It's a long shot."

"I presume you're so interested in this because you think the accident was no accident?"

"The police don't think there's anything to what I said."

"All you've told me was at the hospital, that Rose told you she'd had death threats, phone calls, and that someone pushed her car off the cliff. The police seemed to think you were, uh, not completely coherent. And I was in a fog myself. Why don't you tell me all of it? I'm ready to hear it now."

"Before I start, do you have Rose's purse? Did the police find it in the car and give it to you?"

"No. It wasn't in the car when they towed it in."

"Oh, shoot!" she said, shaking her head. "I sure didn't want to hear that."

Chapter 9

She started the story near its end, with the headlights filling the Cadillac and their screams as the guardrail collapsed. Mel's eyes were wide and haunted, focused on a point in the distance, rather than on Patrice.

"Go back," he said at last, sipping his cold coffee. "Go back to the nursing home."

Struggling to maintain enough emotional distance to get through the story, Patrice told of the phone call Rose had received at the nursing home. Mel interrupted to ask a dozen questions, some of them more than once.

His breathing was shallow, tortured; his eyes darted around the room, as if trying to find something to hang on to, something that wasn't as ephemeral as a dust mote in a sunbeam. Then, she had to make it worse.

"I went to the nursing home yesterday afternoon," she said, then paused until Mel seemed to understand what she was saying. "I got Rick Romero to take me to the nursing home yesterday. I went in to tell Mr. Silver what happened to Rose." She took a deep breath. "But he had died early Tuesday morning."

Mel's face contorted in shock and he recoiled as if she'd deliberately burned him. "He died? The day after Rose?"

"Just a few hours later. I think it's suspicious, but his nephew had the body cremated."

"Did he tell you anything? Something worth... What could be worth killing my wife? This is crazy! I'd rather believe it was an accident!" He pounded his fist hard into his other hand.

Patrice sat quietly on the kitchen stool for a moment, then spoke slowly. "The police believe it was an accident. And part of me believes that, too--or wants to believe it. Murder is something in a book, or in headlines from some distant town."

She thought about the implications for herself if Rose was, in fact, murdered. Nervously, she twisted her hair around a finger. *Somebody could still want me dead.*

"As for what Mr. Silver told us," she continued, "it was about five men, two of them dead from cancer twenty-odd years ago. He said he himself handed papers about the implosion lens to a courier working for the Soviet Union. And he said the fourth man, Douglas Frost, was the contact person, the man who gave them the party line, a sob story about how Stalin wanted to make a fine, safe home for Jews."

"What about the fifth man?" Mel asked.

"Doyle said it was Carl Ellsberg. Do you know him?"

"I've certainly heard of him. His work with explosives was legendary. He practically wrote the textbook for a generation of engineers and chemists. He's still alive, isn't he?"

"Yes, he lives in an old house near downtown; that's all I know." She uncrossed her legs and flexed her knees to get more blood circulating. "And, mind you, I don't know if anything Doyle Silver said was false--or if everything he said was the gospel truth. I really need to get my hands on Rose's tape recorder. What he said amounts to a deathbed confession, although he didn't know he was about to cash in his chips."

"Hmmm, if he sat there in his bed thinking he had years to live, he might have made up the story to get attention," Mel said thoughtfully.

"That's exactly what I considered all along. I took his 'Last Man bottle' story and hints about a spy with a grain of salt the size of a gumball. He could have been lying for any of a dozen reasons. Jealousy, a grudge, money, I don't know. But I have a gut feeling that he told us the truth as he understood it. I need to hear again the way he said it. I wasn't even taking notes."

Mel looked up. "But I can't find her purse. I called the police and the fire department rescue guys. It wasn't in the car."

She nodded sadly. "That's what I was afraid of." Her shoulders ached from the tension of sitting on the stool for more than an hour, re-telling the horrifying story. "Let's look around the office for the FBI document. Rose told me it came in the mail Monday. One hundred twenty pages, so it's a substantial package."

Patrice followed Mel downstairs again, with Muffin right on her heels. Together they systematically searched Rose's office, trying to find the Freedom of Information Act material. No luck. They found a box of six diskettes labeled "Perseus" and eight books with bookmarks stacked handy to Rose's work space.

"Could I come over sometime soon and look at these disks on her computer?"

"You can take them with you," he said, getting on his hands and knees to look under the desk. Muffin joined him in the cramped space and gave him a wet dog kiss. Surprised, Mel jerked away from Muffin and hit his head on the underside of the desk. "Darn dog!"

She stifled a laugh. "Unfortunately, I don't have a computer."

"You can take Rose's laptop." He got back to his feet and slipped the laptop, in its black nylon case, out from between the desk and the printer table. "It's got so much more power than her old desktop, it's what she used nearly all the time lately. But that brings up a painful matter. I need to look at her e-mail and tell people she's gone. I just can't do it yet. I planned to ask my sister to do it, but she already left town."

Patrice paused to think how it would be to read e-mail addressed to Rose. Every cheery "Hi!" would seem like a stab. No wonder Mel couldn't do it. With more confidence than she felt, she said, "I can do it."

"No, I can't ask that of you. Not after what you've been through."

Patrice thought about it. "I know she was working on this spy story for weeks, even months, doing research and asking questions. There might be something in her e-mail that would tell me where to look further. Sure, the other part is going to be painful, but I want to do it for her."

Mel looked doubtful. Then his eyes filled to overflowing with tears. "She thought the world of you."

She tried to speak but felt like her throat was tied shut. She just nodded and knelt down to pet Muffin.

"Rose had a Compuserve account," he said, clearing his throat. "The lap top is all set up for it. I won't cancel for a month or two, so use it all you want."

In addition to the books and computer, he loaded the backseat and her lap with plates of coffeecake, miniature muffins, and date-nut bread. He paused before he closed her car door. "How about some sliced ham?"

"I have a small refrigerator," she repeated, "that's small spelled t-i-n-y. No ham. No turkey. No cranberry relish. But I do appreciate the offer."

He wouldn't let her carry anything but her purse and the loaf of date-nut bread up the three flights of stairs to her apartment. He made three trips himself, insisting she sit down, or better yet, lie down and rest.

The hovering attention reminded Patrice of her mother. She smiled to herself. When Mel left, Patrice stood at the window. Idly, she fingered her laminated press badge, which hung around the neck of a stuffed bear on the window sill, as she watched his Ford Taurus pull out of the parking lot and turn west.

In the middle of the day the apartment complex was quiet as a crypt. The parking lot was empty except for her ten-year-old Subaru and three vehicles that had been there so long she suspected they were abandoned. Sadly, the Subaru didn't look that much better than they did. Her car was in need of tires, transmission repair, and brake pads, maybe even a whole new set of brakes. Financially, she felt like Sisyphus: two payments on

MasterCard forward, one rent payment and a car repair bill backward.

She sighed and sat down on the bed. Recounting to Mel the events of Monday night--the visit to Doyle Silver, the trip home in the storm, their car forced off the cliff--left her drained dry of tears. She eyed the laptop computer on the dinette table as if it were a biohazard container. *Tomorrow will be soon enough to face that task*, she thought with a heartfelt sigh.

She decided something else, too. The next day, Saturday, would be soon enough to do the resting she'd promised her mother she would do Thursday and Friday. Right then she had a career to think about. That a U.S. Senator was making war on her town was enough to get her up off a sickbed. That the reporter usurping her beat looked like a young Christie Brinkley was enough to get her up off a deathbed.

She looked down at the press badge and bear, still in her hands. Removing the badge and tapping it against her chin, she ran through a half-dozen scenarios, ways to get herself to Santa Fe and into the press conference. *I have just one ace in the hole. Rick would want his best reporter on a story of this magnitude.* She'd have to pull off a great charade, though, to get past his chivalrous concern for her health.

*****

"Am I going to have to play rough here?" she asked when Rick returned her call and said, as she knew he would, "No! Emphatically, irrevocably, no."

"Am I going to have to bring up the Americans with Disabilities Act?" she went on. "I have a temporary disability, and you're supposed to make reasonable accommodations for me."

Rick applied a string of colorful adverbs to the word "reasonable" and Patrice waited him out.

"I can write with one hand," she said when he wound down. "And my brain is working just fine."

"There's plenty of proof to the contrary! If your brain

were working you'd be in bed. Did you take your antibiotics?"

Her hand shot out and grabbed the pill bottle. "Right on time," she lied. "And I'm about to take another one now." That, at least, was true. "What time shall we leave for Santa Fe?"

"Your hearing is impaired, too! I said no!"

"If the press conference is at four, we should leave at three to make sure we get a parking place. I can use the trip down to tell you about my visit to Mel Hulle." She started to add that she'd be sitting in his car, resting, all the way to and from Santa Fe, but thought better of it. She'd used that old chestnut the day before, to get to Española. Better not remind him how that turned out.

"I'm not coming back right after the press conference. I'm going to have dinner and go to the party at the museum, sponsored by the people who brought us 'Earth' day at Tech Area-55. Citizens Against Nuclear Destruction." Their acronym was CAND, pronounced Can-DEE.

"What's a United States Senator doing hanging out with a bunch of eco-terrorists bent on shutting down our nation's nuclear weapons program?"

"I think you just answered your own question."

"Please take me, Rick. I'll hitchhike if you don't." She stretched the phone cord to the dinette where she'd left her mug of tea, and returned to the bed to sip it as it cooled.

"Next you'll promise to be good if I take you."

She swallowed wrong and coughed. "Those very words were on my lips. Honest, I will. And I won't get out of bed tomorrow."

"Just like you weren't going to get out of bed today?"

"You're weakening; I can tell." He didn't say anything, so she went on. "A prowler tried to get into Rose's office during the funeral. Maybe I'd be in danger here by myself."

"Maybe I'd be in danger if I took you with me."

"Sure, it's risky. Life on the edge, but you're that kind of a guy." She said it like she was joking, but she meant it literally. In her opinion, anybody who climbed mountains was certifiably insane.

"I've got a lot of work to finish before I leave, and I have to go home and change clothes."

That brought up a sticky matter: clothes for a party in Santa Fe. Barring the sudden appearance of a fairy godmother, Patrice knew she'd have a real problem with that one. "I'll be ready at three."

He sighed. "All right, you win. Romero, party of two. And since you're feeling so energetic, or at least lying so effectively about it, there's another story heading for town. With your name on it."

"Tell me, tell me."

"Stefan Ellsberg, son of Carl Ellsberg, is coming next week to give a colloquium at the Laboratory. Thursday, they think, but haven't confirmed it yet."

"What an interesting conjunction," she mused aloud. "Right when I'm intrigued with the father, the son drops in."

"Yeah, made my bell ring right away. Anyway, Stefan is rumored to be getting a presidential appointment for some big overseas job. Maybe an ambassadorship. Announcement could be made here."

Patrice could hear someone in the newsroom calling Rick, so she said again she'd be ready at three and hung up. She took the antibiotic with orange juice and stood in front of her open closet, frowning at the contents.

The phone startled her. It was Axel Pruitt, archivist at the Laboratory. She'd called him from Mel's house and left a message.

"Thank you for calling me back. I'm looking for information on a man named Douglas Frost. Someone told me he was a scientist from England, and that he was here during the war, working on the bomb."

"Ummm, the name doesn't sound familiar," Pruitt said.

"You think he was part of the British delegation?"

"I guess so. Supposedly he was at Trinity Site to watch the first atomic bomb detonate."

"Well, I'll look up the name and see. If he was here, there should be a record."

She thanked him, though she didn't share his confidence in the scope of records from that time. The Manhattan Project had been a rat's nest of secrecy and distrust, with Army intelligence looking over the shoulders of the scientists, and scientists rebelling against the strictures. In spite of all the security measures, David Greenglass, a machinist who happened to be Ethel Rosenberg's brother, smuggled out drawings of implosion lenses to a Soviet courier. It was only the merest of chances that the Soviet spymaster used the same courier for Greenglass and for physicist Klaus Fuchs. When Greenglass fingered the courier, Harry Gold, Gold in turn exposed Fuchs.

If the Army and other organs of security had screwed up and missed other spies--and Patrice had no doubt they had--records of mistakes had a way of disappearing. She knew a spy code-named "Mlad," said to be a Russian word for "youngster", had recently been exposed, alive but old and ill, in England. The FBI admitted, after news of Mlad broke in the press, that they'd suspected him for many years, ever since they decoded wartime messages in the 1950s. Patrice and Rose had wondered if the spy Perseus was a similar case. If the government really sought to identify the spy, would they have to admit what a piss-poor job they'd done all along, with their ultra-tough security and state-of-the-art intelligence?

She rubbed lotion on her dry hands. No wonder the FBI blacked out so much of the Freedom of Information Act report. But where was it?

She'd taken step one to find out who Douglas Frost was. According to Doyle Silver, the last three of the five men in the Last Man compact were Frost, Carl Ellsberg and himself. Larry Dreyfus had been derisive about the group of five, saying he'd heard his uncle name fifteen, but Patrice had such a negative reaction to Dreyfus, she'd give his remarks a mental asterisk for the time being.

Patrice put her coat back on, locked her door behind her, and walked down to the outdoor stairwell at the end of the long hall. Three flights down, she zipped her parka against a west wind and set out for Fuller Lodge, roughly five blocks away.

The Lodge was part of the historical heart of the town, the stone and wood buildings that existed before the war. Like the houses of Bathtub Row and the stone cottage of the Los Alamos Historical Museum, Fuller Lodge was once part of the Ranch School for Boys. Bathtub Row, she knew, got its name during the Manhattan Project, when the original stone houses of the Ranch School, the creme de la creme of housing for scientists working on the bomb, were the only houses with bathtubs.

Inside the Lodge Patrice climbed the rough-hewn pine stairway to the second floor. She opened the door marked Historical Archives, a door that opened not to another room or another hallway, but to another set of stairs, this set steeper, leading to the attic of the Lodge. At the top, through a small window, she could look out on the parking lot and the Jemez Mountains to the west. A half dozen rooms opened off the hallway that paralleled the one beneath it; each was hardly more than a walk-in closet, and all were stuffed with memorabilia.

A low-ceilinged dormer room at the end of the hall contained a large table for viewing items from the file, like folders of photos marked "Trinity Test" or "Oppenheimer, J.R." A staff of three and volunteers catalogued the detritus and helped researchers. The general public never came up here; they went, instead, to the Historical Museum.

Patrice could hear the director, Fran Johnston, on the phone in her office. She walked down the hall to the library/viewing room where Fran's assistant, Sonia Greenway, sat at a computer. She, too, was on the phone.

"No, we don't check photographs out." She smiled at

Patrice and held up one finger to show she'd only be tied up for a minute. "That's right, sir. You can take pictures of them here by prior arrangement, and as long as you credit the Los Alamos Historical Society in your publication." She rattled off their hours and spelled her name. "You're welcome."

Sonia turned her full attention to her visitor. "Patrice! I was so sorry to hear about you being in the accident. How are you feeling? I went to the funeral, of course. We're all just devastated about Rose. How are Mel and..."

"Allison."

"Yes, Allison. How are they doing?"

"I haven't seen Alli since the funeral. She's going to fly back to Dallas Sunday to take her final exams. From what Mel says, she's in shock and just running on autopilot. That's how I'd describe him, too."

"It was a shock to everyone. We're going to miss her. Rose was like a mobile unit of the archives. I keep wanting to call her and ask something she'd know without even looking it up."

Sonia was a small woman, about sixty years old, not over five feet tall and probably one hundred pounds with a book in her hand. She had started as a volunteer and worked into the paid half-time position, still volunteering for anything that needed to be done after her paid time was up. She wore her gray hair brushed back, clipped at the nape of her neck with a black velvet bow on a wide barrette. A hand-knit sweater in Christmas colors livened up her gray wool skirt and black leather dress boots.

Patrice moved the folding chair by the large table over by Sonia's tweed office chair and sat down. "I need a little help," she said, resting her cast on the desk. "Stefan Ellsberg is going to be in town next week to give a colloquium and there's a rumor he might get an important political appointment. To get some background, I'd like to interview his father, Carl. Could you help me with an introduction?"

Sonia looked thoughtful. "Dr. Carl Ellsberg is in what is euphemistically called 'frail health.' I don't know what his mental state is. I could call his daughter, Isobel. She lives with him."

"That would be great."

Sonia tapped her pen on the desk. "So Stefan Ellsberg is coming to town? He was born here, you know."

"No, I didn't. It gives me an even better reason to interview his father and his sister, don't you think? So, can you help me get my foot in the door?" She threaded a finger inside the cast and scratched as best she could. The itch was a new development, one she'd dreaded.

"Well, I know Isobel, as well as anyone can say they know Isobel. She's an old maid, which is a very out-of-fashion expression, but Isobel Ellsberg is a very out-of-fashion woman. She was born a few years after the war, after the Ellsbergs moved back East, so she's about forty-seven. She's lived here with her parents, now just with her father, since, oh, I don't know off-hand. I guess they've actually lived here about twelve years. Could be fifteen."

"Where do they live?"

"They bought one of the houses on Bathtub Row years and years ago, when they were here on sabbatical from Cornell, or was it MIT? Well, whatever. They held on to the house and rented it out part of the year and stayed in it during the summers while Carl worked at the Laboratory. Not every year, though. They spent some years in Europe, and they didn't come here then."

"How long has Mrs. Ellsberg been dead?"

Sonia bit her lip and thought about it. "Five or six years. Carl Ellsberg is over eighty, you know. I've heard he has high blood pressure and maybe he's even had a mini-stroke or two. He was a recluse when he was in good health, so it's no real change to not see him now."

"Do you see Isobel much?"

"Now and then. She's a strange one; not friendly. Spends hours every day in the summer in her garden. I don't know what she does all winter."

"This does not sound promising for a homey interview. But, what the heck, I'll try it. Would you call her to introduce me?"

"Oh, I guess that might work. I've been meaning to ingratiate myself with her in hopes of getting her father's papers or whatever he has from the Manhattan Project for the museum. I'll admit, calling her is not something I look forward to, but I shouldn't be so negative. When do you want to go see Ellsberg, Senior?"

"My time is his time. As soon as possible." She pulled a pocket calendar out of her purse. "Even over the weekend, because I'm going back to work next week and I hate to think how much work is waiting for me, in addition to the Russian visitors Rick wants me to follow around."

"Should you be back to work so soon? I'm going to call your doctor and complain," Sonia said indignantly.

"Oh, don't do that," Patrice blurted, dropping the calendar on the floor.

"Aha! So, you're doing this without your doctor's permission? I suspected as much." Sonia picked up the calendar and gave it back to Patrice.

"Well, I'm only going in part time next week," Patrice countered, "but I'm pretty sure I'll be busy while I'm there."

Sonia pursed her lips in disapproval. "Why should I aid and abet this pursuit?"

"Maybe they'll refuse to see me. Let's just ask. Please?" Sonia gave a "harrumph" noise in disapproval, but picked up the phone book. She wiggled her finger back and forth as she found the name, then picked up the phone and punched the numbers like they deserved tough treatment.

"Isobel," she said cheerily, "this is Sonia Greenway with the Historical Society. How are you?" They chatted back and forth a little. "How is your father?" The room was quiet as Sonia listened, making sympathetic clucking noises from time to time. "Who is his doctor? Oh, that's good. I've heard good things about him." There was another period of silence in the room, a little more small talk, and Sonia moved into the reason for the call.

"...and Patrice would like to interview your father about his career, especially about his time with the Manhattan Project, and she says this would be a perfect time, with your brother coming. Oh, yes, she's planning to interview Stefan next week."

Patrice raised her eyebrows as if to say, "Well? What's she saying?"

"Oh, of course. She understands that. You don't know Stefan's schedule once he gets here. When is he due to arrive? Not 'til Wednesday? I see."

Patrice wrote a note and handed it to Sonia. "Tell her I want to interview her dad before that," the note read. "Tomorrow or Sunday if possible!"

Sonia nodded and asked Isobel what time of day her dad felt best. "That's just what Patrice was thinking, that mid-morning would be best. Could she possibly do it tomorrow?" Sonia made a face like she was getting "No" for an answer, then her face changed and she smiled. "Very good. I'll stop over with her at ten tomorrow, just to introduce her and to say hello. I haven't seen your father in a year. No, she won't stay long. We know how important it is not to tire older people. Thank you so much, Isobel. Good, thanks. We'll see you tomorrow."

"You are magnificent!" Patrice said. "So she says Stefan won't get here until Wednesday?"

"That's what she said."

"Rick said the colloquium is probably Thursday. I guess I just expected he'd come earlier to spend more time with his family."

"Seems strange to me, too. But what do I know? Shall I meet you outside their house tomorrow?"

"Yes, please," Patrice said.

"You know which one?"

"Actually, no."

Sonia sketched the Lodge, the Historical Museum, and the

houses of Bathtub Row on the paper beneath Patrice's note. "This one," she said, circling the house number. "The front faces away from the street. I'll meet you by the back."

There was something else Patrice meant to ask Sonia; she folded the note into a cylinder and tapped it on the desk as she tried to remember what it was. "Oh, yes—do you have anything on Douglas Frost, a British scientist who may have been here during the war?"

"It doesn't sound familiar, but it's easy to check." She pulled a wooden drawer the size of index cards half way out of a cabinet and sorted through the cards with her fingernails. "We'll get these records on the computer some day, but I'll never part with these file cards; they're like old friends. Here's Fermi, Feynman, Frisch... No, I don't see that we have anything on a Douglas Frost. Sorry."

Patrice nodded. "No big deal; thanks for looking. I'll see you in the morning."

When she stepped outside the Lodge, she noticed that the wind had shifted and recalled she hadn't seen a weather report in a good while. Back in her apartment she turned on her radio, set as always to the only local station, and listened to "Silver Bells" while she looked for something to wear to Santa Fe. The weather report followed the song. The announcer said it would be clearing but colder, a real three-dog night.

Chapter 10

On the way to Santa Fe, Patrice read the Friday afternoon *Guardian* Rick brought for her. It was packed with news of a shipment of plutonium to Los Alamos.

"From the Ukraine?" she asked.

"It's very similar to what the Department of Energy did a couple years ago, you know, taking uranium to Oak Ridge," he said. "Get it out of harm's way before somebody sells it to Iraq, or anyone else with hard currency and no questions."

"Nearly 100 kilograms of plutonium 239 it says here, called Project Spectre. That would buy a lot of vodka." She skimmed the reference to the earlier Project Sapphire, in which 600 kilograms of highly enriched uranium was transported from Kazakhstan to Oak Ridge, Tennessee.

She read aloud, "The President and the Secretary of Energy have high praise for the team of scientists from Los Alamos National Laboratory and Oak Ridge National Laboratory who went to the Ukraine under extremely difficult conditions to package the material for safe transport."

"It was already in Los Alamos, locked up, before they released the news," he said. His eye fell on the gas gauge. "Whoa, baby, we're running on fumes. I'd better stop in Pojoaque."

Ten minutes later, while he filled the Bronco with gas, Patrice read how the plutonium was packaged and shipped. "They snuck dawn past a rooster," she said as he got back in the car and dropped his receipt in the glove compartment.

"What rooster? What dawn?"

"The Department of Energy got the plutonium through Santa Fe without CAND finding out and mounting a blockade or something."

"That's not to say they won't go berserk anyway," he sighed.

Half an hour later, Rick parked at El Dorado, the Pueblo Revival-style hotel about three blocks west of the Santa Fe Plaza, and they looked for the meeting room where the conference was scheduled. A sign on the door directed the press to the Plaza at four-thirty.

Patrice had resolved her clothes dilemma with a slim gray skirt, half of her favorite suit, and a magenta and gray oversized sweater. Her right arm fit where it belonged and the other, under the sweater, looked like a large growth on her side. A black wool cape-coat her mother gave her the Christmas before, and which she'd worn only to a concert in Santa Fe and a play in Albuquerque, was perfect for covering both arms. As they threaded their way through crowds outside the hotel and crossed against the light, she was glad she'd worn a wool scarf to fill the gap between her sweater and the cape, but she wished she'd had the foresight to wear a hat, as well.

The sidewalk spilled pedestrians into West San Francisco Street and they moved with the tide of humanity toward the Plaza. Rick moved to her left side and held her gently but firmly against his right side to protect her arm and ribs.

Patrice had seen the plaza even more crowded before, at Southwest Indian Market. But during Indian Market the air crackled with spirit and style, like Mardi Gras without the drunks and transvestites. Now the atmosphere on the plaza was a solstice away by calendar and mood from Indian Market. An acrid smell, like cigar smoke, drifted past, followed by a sweetish odor that might be marijuana. She got a whiff of curry and incense from her left and greasy tacos on her right: dueling cuisines.

Another fume that may have been a Harley-Davidson

overloaded her olfactory system and she resorted to mouth breathing. The press of the crowd spit Rick and Patrice into the plaza in front of the former F.W. Woolworth store, now the Five and Dime General Store. "I see some videocams over toward the bandstand," Rick said. "Hold on to me." Since she was only about four inches shorter than Rick, and taller than most of the people around them, she felt like a gargantuan child holding on to Daddy for dear life.

A mariachi band struck up a polka-type tune, an attempt at musical mood enhancement that worked about as well as Nero's famous fiddle solo. "There's Tiffany," Rick said, adding, "there's Danny, too. Come on, this way."

There was a hideous screech as the microphone feedback overloaded the speakers. "I never thought I'd say this," Patrice said, "but that sound is actually more annoying than mariachi music. Not much, but some."

A state senator she recognized from photos but whose name escaped her said he had the honor to introduce "the Honorable Senator Cristal Aragon, who is getting a lot of attention for New Mexico in the United States Senate."

"New Mexico also got a lot of attention from the hanta virus," Patrice hissed to Rick, "but I wouldn't expect applause."

"Notice who is conspicuous by his absence."

Patrice bobbed her head back and forth to see past the cowboy hats between her and the platform. Ah, the governor wasn't there. Senator Aragon adjusted the microphone lower for her height, a good twelve inches from the man who had introduced her. She wore a hand-painted white Taos coat, a popular fashion take-off on the full-length canvas coat of working cowboys. At her neck was a scarlet scarf. "My fellow New Mexicans..." she began.

"Since when?" Patrice couldn't resist saying, but she got her notepad out and placed it in her left hand, which protruded handily from the bottom of her sweater. She thought of how it must appear to onlookers, like a transplant operation that had gone terribly wrong.

"Shhh," Rick said fiercely. His attempt to admonish her lacked something, though; she saw the corners of his mouth turn up.

"...people who have been a tremendous resource for me, and I want them to come up here now, River Rasmussen and his life-partner, Earth." Patrice recognized the leader of the demonstration at the Plutonium Facility. River was dressed again in his mountain man outfit, fringe a-flying, reddish-blond mustache and goatee like Wild Bill Hickok, but with a red ponytail. In her long, soft leather dress adorned with fringe and beads, a bright headband and braids, Earth looked like his squaw. Her belly was big, all right, and she leaned her shoulders back to thrust it even further out. Some women are pregnant; some are PREGNANT. Earth was of the latter tribe.

Sen. Aragon fought the wind for her notes and spoke of her heavy responsibility in Washington, the responsibility to represent a state of fragile beauty, a state that the U.S. Government wanted to use as a nuclear dumping ground. She would do everything in her power to stop them! The crowd started to get into the spirit of the demonstration, and Patrice saw the radiation hazard signs appear once again.

Aragon began railing specifically against WIPP, the Waste Isolation Pilot Plant, Santa Fe's favorite fear. Set to open years before, the deep man-made salt mine near Carlsbad had recently accepted the first few barrels of low-level nuclear waste. Thousands more barrels of waste were stashed all over the country in railcars, warehouses, and open-air barrel-parking-lots. All over Santa Fe, the "City Different," businesses posted Stop WIPP signs in windows and over cash registers. Buy a blueberry muffin, make a political statement. Planet Earth, love it or leave it.

Aragon continued and Patrice corralled her wayward thoughts. "I'm going to turn the microphone over to River Rasmussen of Citizens Against Nuclear Destruction to tell you about the shipment of deadly plutonium that threatens us all. River?"

He thanked the senator and complimented her profusely for her wisdom in taking up the banner of CAND and fighting the Department of Energy, which was nothing but a tool of the rich and the military.

"The real enemy of this country is the military machine with its multi-billion dollar budget, and the parasites who feed on it," he said. "They don't care if New Mexico is a nuclear wasteland, uninhabitable by human beings. In fact, they would prefer that, because there'd be nobody left to stop them from using thousands of square miles to dump their radioactive garbage." He waited for the cheers to swell and ebb. "They could invite the whole world to send its radioactive garbage and pile it on what used to be Santa Fe. Just so they collect a billion dollars here and there as a commission." More cheers; he waited.

"The Department of Energy is like the real estate agent from hell, and when they see the space on the map between Arizona and Texas, they say 'Location, location, location.'" He waited yet again for the whoops and laughter and cheers to die down, then went on. "There's so much nothing out there in the West, they say, it's already such a wasteland, what's to stop us? But I'll answer that question, my friends. Senator Aragon will stop them! We will stop them!"

Patrice jumped in surprise when the crowd around them suddenly cheered like banshees. She saw Danny Carter climb the bandstand to shoot a half-dozen photos of the crowd, then fire off a series of close-ups of the senator and River.

Tiffany's platinum hair caught the sun and Patrice saw that she wasn't bothering to take notes. Instead she was working her way backward through the crowd toward the Palace of the Governors.

Patrice turned her attention back to the bandstand, where River railed against the shipment of plutonium across sacred Indian lands, and through the streets of Santa Fe, across the Rio Grande.

"Those people on the Hill, in Los Alamos, think plutonium can be handled safely. They don't want to talk about the thousands of years of radioactivity in plutonium. They don't want to listen to us. They don't think their shit stinks! They're so smart, they've got all the answers. I say bull-hocky to that! Last time I looked, this country still had a Constitution! And it says We the People, not We the Helpless." The crowd showed they loved that sound bite.

"There are courts, my friends, and there are ways to stop the military-industrial complex, to bring it to its knees. And by God, we can do it!" His "Thank you, thank you," was drowned out by cheering.

Sen. Aragon continued thanking River and inviting him to bring petitions to Washington, to help her save New Mexico and indeed the whole pristine West from the thugs in the DOE and the rest of the U.S. Government. A final wave for the TV cameras and she nodded to the policeman who stood at the bottom of the stairs to the bandstand. He was instantly joined by two more officers who formed a wedge for her to make it through the crowd at its narrowest point and get into a waiting car. The police car in front of it popped its lights on and led the senator's car away from the plaza.

With the podium empty, the crowd reformed itself, coagulating into clots of mutual interest societies, groups varying in size from two to roughly ten. Danny materialized beside Patrice and Rick, and the three of them oozed toward the outside of the plaza, looking for navigable holes in the wall of people.

"...best thing that ever happened to New Mexico," a man just behind Patrice was saying. She looked back right before a reporter from the *Albuquerque Journal North* bumped into her, en route to jot down whatever River Rasmussen said to the clique around him.

"Yes," River said again, "Senator Aragon is the best thing that ever happened to New Mexico."

Patrice stopped her forward progress and edged closer to

River's now-large circle. He elaborated to the Albuquerque reporter on CAND's plans for a new round of public hearings and lawsuits, but Patrice couldn't hear all the quick questions and answers.

Louder and directed to the entire circle, River said, "Sen. Aragon is what this state needs precisely because she's a political outsider. Anybody who rises through the system belongs to the system." He motioned to Earth to go with him, and she broke off a discussion with a woman with a plume of green hair and a ring in her nostril.

Rick, Danny and Patrice followed in their wake toward the Palace of the Governors.

"Where's Tiffany?" Patrice asked.

"Meeting Kent for drinks," Danny said. "Private reception for Aragon at a home where I would not be good enough to park cars."

"Hey, rich people vote, too," Patrice said.

Rick stopped at the curb and looked at his watch. "My car is at the El Dorado. Let's eat at Garduño's so we don't have to fight for parking somewhere else. It's not expensive." He started to take Patrice's arm, remembered the cast, and put his right hand on her shoulder instead. Danny brought up the rear as they battled toward the corner and headed toward Garduño's. They were ahead of the tourist supper crowd and way ahead of the fashionable supper crowd, so they got in right away.

"Booth, please," Rick said to the hostess, a dark-haired beauty in a black jersey dress and red sash. Patrice followed her across the tiled floor to an oversized booth, raised one step above the floor. The hostess walked with the grace of a dancer, an impression enhanced by her silky black hair, pulled back from her face by a red headband and allowed to sway behind to her waist.

"Enjoy your dinner," she said in a deep, melodic voice, handing each of them a menu, starting with Patrice. "Your waiter will be right with you."

I believe that young woman is underemployed, Patrice

thought as she watched her walk away. That unbidden thought led her to the off-limits issue of her own employment—an issue she'd made off-limits to Danny and Rose, who had both needled her at times about living up to her potential. *Maybe they exaggerated my potential*, one side of her whispered inside her head. *Maybe not!* her other side, the confident side, barked back. *Later! Not now!* her brain told the warring factions. *Right now, look at the menu!*

"This is very nice," Danny said as he perused the menu. "Not at all like the soup kitchen I'll be patronizing if I don't get a job soon."

Rick cleared his throat for dramatic effect and held the large menu up, eclipsing himself from the others. "You'll get a job. Somebody called me about you today, in fact."

"Who? Who called?" Danny snatched the menu from Rick's hands, leaving him to read the air.

"You sound like an owl," Rick said. "What looks good to you, Patrice? I'm hungry."

"You're always hungry," she said. "Who called about Danny?"

"Would you believe the *Washington Post?"*

"No," they said in unison. Patrice added, "Try again."

"And please don't say the *Socorro Defensor-Chieftain*," Danny added, referring to a small town south of Albuquerque.

Rick held up one finger and tugged his ear. "First word," Danny said with a groan, "sounds like..."

Rick pointed at a ceiling fan.

"Sounds like fan," she said. "Tan? Ban? Sudan? You helped Danny get a job in Africa?"

Rick waggled his finger at her and Danny guessed, "Can? San?" Rick nodded Yes vigorously. "San? Lots of cities start with San. San Francisco? San Diego?" Rick urged him to keep the guesses coming.

"East of the Mississippi?" Patrice asked, and Rick shook his head. "Okay, west of the Mississippi. California?" Rick made a drumming motion with his fingers like he couldn't believe it was taking them so long. "Arizona? New Mexico?" He continued to drum and stare at the ceiling. In time with his drumming he hummed, "Da da dum da da da dum dum."

"The Yellow Rose of Texas!" Patrice said, loud enough that a dozen people looked at their table. "San...Antonio?"

Rick bobbed his head and clapped his hands soundlessly. "They're going to call you at home tonight. It's nothing definite, but they are very interested."

"Ooo, sounds like a possible job offer to me," Patrice said. "You know what that means."

"That I'll soon be financially solvent in a town full of women who did not turn me down for the prom?"

"No, that it will soon be time to pee in a cup."

"Uh, excuse me?" Danny said.

"You know, the cup," Patrice said in a stage whisper. Danny still looked perplexed; Rick leaned over close to his ear and whispered, "Urine test." Danny's face reddened and he stuck his tongue out at Patrice.

"And on that note, let's order," Rick said.

*****

"Isn't that Tiffany, fetchingly attired in a short nightgown?" Patrice said while she waited with Rick in the foyer of the museum. Tiffany stood inside with Kent beyond the second set of doors. Technically, she was wearing a cocktail dress of ice blue and violet, but the satin looked alarmingly like lingerie. She was, of course, braless. Her blonde 'do was a seemingly careless clutch of locks atop her head, but tendrils fell hither and yon, too perfectly to be an accident. "I think I've seen that hairdo before," Patrice growled, catlike, into Rick's ear. "But where? Oh yes, that colorful flyer for phone sex!"

"Let's keep our minds on business, shall we?"

"Sure. I just can't help but notice my surroundings."

"Well, why don't you notice the international folk art

more, and Tiffany's taste in clothes less?"

"Tiffany couldn't have less taste in clothes. In fact, she couldn't have less clothes on at all," Patrice said. Rick didn't laugh. "Okay, okay. I will see nothing but art, culture and politicians. My eyes are open and my lips are sealed."

The crowd behind them pressed forward to get inside before the dignitaries, whom Patrice saw alighting from two limousines, but the crowd ahead of them was unbudgeable. She nestled against Rick's side, ostensibly to protect her arm. A state policeman broke the logjam and the crowd spilled through to the open lobby like molten lava from a volcano.

Tiffany spotted them and gave a little wave. Patrice gave a little finger-flurry wave in return and bit back another catty remark.

Senator Aragon entered, behind one and in front of a second state policeman. Patrice heard someone say, "...the governor," and moved further back with the crowd. A scarlet brocade sheath dress set off Aragon's unnaturally dark black hair, which she wore in a tight bun like a flamenco dancer. Over the knee-length dress she wore a matching red coat; on one side of the front was a gold embroidered dragon, the tail of which continued on the back.

A tall, distinguished gentleman in a well-worn tuxedo shook Aragon's hand and gestured toward the wide hallway. She nodded, then turned her attention to the arrival of Governor Ted Somers. A regular butterball, loud, and about six-feet-two, the governor was hard to miss, even in a crowd. He appeared to have been stuffed into his tuxedo; the lapels looked as if they met only in the closet. Patrice thought Ted Somers would look--and feel--more at home at a monster truck rally.

"Senator...Cristal," he boomed, "how wonderful to see you." He leaned forward to hug her and she recoiled, thrusting out her hand instead for a shake.

"I'm sorry Jenette couldn't make it," she said. "Please give her my love."

"Sure, sure," he boomed again. "Fidel! Good to see you!" he said to the gentleman at the senator's elbow.

"Governor, so glad you could come," he said with a handshake. "Would you both follow me, please?"

The guests who lined the entry to the hallway parted and the three moved forward like a procession of bishops to the interior courtyard where a buffet table was set up. Rick and Patrice followed in their wake, behind Kent and Tiffany, who were cheek to cheek in deep conversation.

Patrice wanted to complain about how tired she was and how her arm ached, but she recalled she'd practically held a gun to Rick's head to get him to bring her. Having no audience for her complaints, she searched the area for a chair, gave Rick's arm a squeeze, and headed for a table by a dowager in crushed black velvet. "May I sit down here for a little while?"

The lady looked her over so imperiously Patrice expected her to tuck a lorgnette in front of her eyes, but she nodded her grudging assent. No sooner had Patrice touched the chair than Senator Aragon swept over to "her" table.

"Señora Mondragon," she gushed, dramatically rolling all her R's, "I am so honored you came." The lady in red extended her hand to the lady in black.

"When Señor Portillo asked me to attend, and to help with his museum project, I could not say no. Fidel is very persuasive." Both women beamed at the distinguished gentleman who had followed Aragon to the table. He basked in their attention.

"Señora Mondragon is the museum's greatest friend," he said, "and the new wing will be a magnificent setting for her late husband's collection of folk art."

The governor and the state senator who had introduced Senator Aragon at the rally in the Santa Fe Plaza now joined the luminaries at Mondragon's table. If Patrice could have crawled under it she would have. Instead she sat quietly and imagined that all the people across the room, watching the power guests pay homage to the lady in black, were saying, "Who's that with her?

The tall woman in the unspeakable skirt and sweater? You'd think Señora Mondragon could afford to dress her servants better than that."

Blessedly, the museum director, whose name Patrice recognized when her accidental companion addressed him, steered the senator toward more of his moneyed guests, and the attention of the crowd followed her. The governor, who needed food like a Twinkie needs sugar, waddled over to the buffet table and loaded a plate with rumaki, shrimp, and cocktail shish-ka-bobs.

"I'm going to get some punch. Could I bring you something, some wine or punch?" Patrice asked.

The elegant lady looked pointedly at Patrice's one arm and smiled. "Why don't we sit here and see if some gentleman might get it for both of us?"

Rick spotted Patrice just then and looked puzzled. She motioned him over in what she hoped was a genteel way. Now she knew who her velvet-clad acquaintance was. "Rick," she imagined herself saying, "I'd like you to meet Señora Mondragon. She owns Spain." Instead she turned in her chair so she could hold out her right hand. "I'm Patrice Kelsey, Señora. Thank you for letting me join you for a little while." Fully half the crowd was standing, the small tables and wicker chairs being more a decoration than an invitation to take a load off.

Rick excused himself from a conversation with a reporter Patrice recognized from the *Santa Fe New Mexican*, and made his way toward her.

She noticed how handsome he looked--the best looking man in the place, in fact--but how shabby his clothes looked. And she knew the same could be said for hers.

"Señora Mondragon," Patrice said when Rick reached the table, "I'd like you to meet Rick Romero. We are here as reporters, from the Los Alamos newspaper."

Rick repeated the lady's name, then his own. She offered her hand and he took it in a gentle shake. "I'm pleased to meet you. I was just looking at the model for the Mondragon Wing. It will be an outstanding addition to the museum."

"Rick, we are both so thirsty. Would you get us some wine? Well, punch for me."

"White wine, please, for me," Mondragon said in a kindly voice.

Rick set off in search of liquid refreshment and Patrice resisted the impulse to whip out her notebook and interview the lady, settling instead for small talk about an exhibition of paintings from Spain, which Mondragon had underwritten at the Museum of New Mexico.

Before Rick could snag their drinks and return from the bar, Kent and Tiffany stopped beside their table to greet Mondragon, tossing pleasantries Patrice's way like cheap candy off a homecoming float.

"I didn't catch his name," Mondragon said to Patrice as Kent and Tiffany continued to work the room.

"Kent Bolt. He is the publisher of the *Los Alamos Guardian*, and therefore my boss, and he's also Senator Aragon's brother."

Mondragon returned to the subject of the Spanish painting exhibition and responded with vigor to Patrice's question about a recent Goya controversy. Patrice noticed how much the art patron resembled Rose Hulle, not by appearance, but in her enthusiasm for historical research and accuracy. She felt yet another wave of grief at the loss of her friend.

Rick returned with their drinks just as another man strode up to the table. He looked to be about fifty, with a full head of stark white hair and an unmistakable air of being someone important. Mondragon greeted him warmly and Patrice and Rick moved on, leaving a seat for him.

Away from the table, Patrice swallowed the painkiller she'd extracted from her purse when she saw Rick approach with the drinks. She washed it down with the strawberry punch.

Rick sipped his punch and made a face. "This stuff is

swill. Tastes like Kool-Aid with double the sugar."

"I drank mine straight down without tasting it. The sugar overdose is giving me a headache. Talk about toxic waste!" She hoped he'd say they could leave, but instead he suggested they split up and see what people were saying about the Laboratory and the plutonium.

"There's something going on here besides 'Senator greets art patrons and adds to campaign chest,'" he said. "River Rasmussen and his gravid partner, Earth, are here, and I recognize two other guys from CAND."

"First let's get some water or club soda to dilute the sugar that's coagulating in my delicate stomach," Patrice said.

"The line at the bar is not for the faint of heart or weak of knee. Let's find a drinking fountain."

"I'm right behind you."

She felt a little better, though bloated, after they slaked their thirst. Patrice drifted off to appear engrossed in displays of Guatemalan weaving and Chilean wind instruments, her attention actually on conversations that eddied around her. In the restroom she heard Earth say she was dilated two centimeters. By a bulletin board of Santa Fe events she learned that a war chest for a lawsuit was coming together nicely. Beside a diorama of Columbus she heard snatches of conversation between River and a man she recognized as an aide of the senator. She heard them say "close down," and "block the road," and "TV helicopters."

"Patrice, how are you feeling?" Kent Bolt, without Tiffany at least for the moment, stopped in the hallway. Not waiting for her answer, he went on. "Have you met Senator Aragon?"

"No, I'm sorry to say I haven't. Would you introduce me?"

"Sure, that would be good. I think she's over...yes, she's over there. Follow me."

Patrice looked over Kent's head, noticing with a smile his hair was getting precious on top.

Aragon was speaking in Spanish, one of four languages in

which she was fluent, along with French, Portuguese, and of course, English. Patrice had heard that she spoke and understood enough Russian "to be polite at embassy receptions," and was being tutored in Japanese, at an elementary level, "hardly more than the basic niceties, I'm afraid," Aragon told an Albuquerque television reporter in a rare--very rare--interview.

Kent caught his sister's eye and she excused herself from the Spanish conversation. Kent made a brisk introduction, forgetting for a moment to even say Patrice's last name.

The senator was gracious, able to turn her whole attention to one person like a single spotlight. *She's good*, Patrice thought as they shook hands.

"Kent says you're his best reporter," Aragon said warmly. "Just as soon as I can arrange it, we'll do an interview."

She's very good! Patrice said to herself. "I'm looking forward to it, Senator."

"What do you think of the model of the Mondragon Wing?" Aragon asked brightly. "I think it will be a star in Santa Fe's crown--another star."

"I agree," Patrice said sincerely. Other people were clearing their throats on either side of her, making it clear they wanted an audience with the senator, so Patrice excused herself and backed away, rather like one of the many wives of the King of Siam, who were never to turn their back to the king.

The difference here, Patrice thought, is journalists hate to turn their backs for fear of being knifed.

Cristal Aragon had entered the Senate by a back door, but she had the skill to make it via election, it seemed to Patrice. Of course, no one had looked at her past, at who she really was and where she came from. Patrice would like to do that herself, but it was out of the question with Kent controlling access.

She sighed and looked for Rick. Regrettably, he was in what appeared to be an intense conversation with a man Patrice did not know. And the way her stomach, head, arm, ribs and half a dozen other body parts felt, she didn't want to meet him. She didn't want to "make nice" with anyone else; she just wanted to go home.

In the meantime, she sought privacy in the ladies' room. She chose the farthest stall and sat down on the toilet seat. For about ten minutes she weighed the pros and cons of throwing up against not throwing up. For a moment, she feared she'd faint; she put her forehead against the cold metal side of the stall and held very still.

When she felt a little better, she emerged from the stall, washed her hands and wiped her face with a wet paper towel, and stepped out to face the world again. All she wanted to face, though, was a pillowcase on a soft pillow, on her own bed. With no further pretense of feeling good, she wandered through the lobby until she spotted Rick. This time he was talking in a jocular manner with a shapely auburn-haired woman who looked like she was starving and Rick Romero was a succulent entrée.

"Oh, there you are, honey," Patrice called, striding directly over to the twosome. "Hey, you know, we've gotta go! Remember the babysitter?" She turned briefly to the woman, noting her flawless makeup and eyes so blue they must be tinted contact lenses.

"You know how that is," Patrice said to the now wide-eyed ingénue. "It's so hard to get a good sitter for the twins. We have to be on our way." She took Rick's arm firmly and gave the "Tiffany wave" to Blue Eyes.

In the car she apologized, sounding anything but sincere, and promptly fell asleep. She slept all the way back to Los Alamos, waking just enough at eleven p.m. to climb the stairs of her building, with Rick's help. She found her key by feel in her purse and handed it to him.

"Are you due for a pill?" he asked before she went into the bathroom.

"Yeah, it's in here. I've got a cup." Her big T-shirt and pajama bottoms were in there, too, so she brushed her teeth, changed out of her skirt and sweater, and gave her face a thorough washing.

She listened at the door, then opened it slowly. Rick was leaning against the apartment door, looking almost as tired as she felt.

"Are you mad at me?" she asked.

"Being mad would take more energy than I have right now. Come over here."

She smiled and kissed his cheek. He put his arms around her, watching out for the cast. She tilted her head back slightly and felt his lips brush hers lightly, lightly, then hard. She returned his kiss with the same eagerness. She felt his left hand gently massage her waist and her buttocks, pulling her closer to his hips. With a barely audible moan, he moved his hand up her side in a circular motion. He traced the outline of one breast through the thin T-shirt, then cupped it in his hand and tugged, very gently, on the hardened nipple.

Patrice felt like she was kayaking down the Rio Grande in the spring floods, and a boulder loomed dead ahead. She thought of saying, "Don't! Stop!" but feared it would come out as, "Don't stop!"

Then, to her surprise, she felt him pull away. With a soft kiss on her mouth and one on her forehead, he stood back. "I've got to go."

"I know," she said, not at all sure she meant it.

"Lock the door behind me," he said.

She nodded, shut it tight and checked the lock. Then she crawled into bed. She left the bedside lamp on, not yet willing to face the dark.

If she'd known nothing about Rick's past, of his wife's death, she would have guessed his kisses were mile markers on the road to intimacy. But she couldn't tell what was going on with him, and there was no way to phrase the questions she wanted to ask. He wouldn't be the first man to fool a woman with tender kisses and attention. In fact, Patrice thought with a stab of pain that was under her ribs but had nothing to do with her injuries, he wouldn't be the first man to fool her with kisses. But the most worrisome thing about letting herself want him was her fear that Rick was fooling himself. Even a man who couldn't love a woman—a second woman, after the one love of his life—could respond to physical attraction. And Patrice didn't want Rick to make love to her because she was conveniently available.

The issue, once again, was propinquity, she thought. She recalled a friend in college who had an affair with a married professor. The young woman thought he'd marry her; he refused. Pregnant and desperate, Vicky had gone to the professor's wife, thinking if his wife knew what he'd done, she'd leave him. But the wife had laughed at her. "You're not the first, and you won't be the last to learn the hard way," she said, "that familiarity breeds!"

Patrice turned up the control on her electric blanket and concentrated on relaxing, but the process made her realize how tense and yet how exhausted she was. The more she needed to relax, the less she could. Yet another paradox

I'm going to stay in bed about a week, she told herself. *Or anyway, for a weekend*. But no sooner had she vowed to rest, than she remembered: she had an appointment at ten a.m. Saturday with Dr. Carl Ellsberg and his daughter, Isobel. With a moan, she set her alarm for eight and turned off the light.

She lay in the dark with her eyes open, listening to the wind. Even with her electric blanket on high, she shivered. Gradually she dozed, then slept soundly. She didn't hear the wind increase and sleet pelt her windows sometime after three a.m.

Or, rather, she heard it, but in her dream it seemed to be hitting the windshield of a car, and she was in the car, alone on a road with no guardrail. The car was moving, climbing a hill, but there was no driver, just Patrice in the passenger seat, and she couldn't make a sound or move.

All she could do was watch.

Chapter 11

Saturday morning the alarm went off twice, or so it seemed until Patrice realized the second alarm was the phone. "Hello?"

There was a pause before Mel spoke. "Oops. I woke you up, didn't I? I'm sorry."

"No, honest, you didn't. My alarm went off right before you called." She looked at the clock, on which she'd "killed" the alarm at eight and saw that it was eight-twenty. "What's up?"

"Late last night I found the Freedom of Information Act stuff. Whoever cleaned up the kitchen for the reception after the funeral put it in the phone book drawer."

"That's a relief. But no sign of her purse?"

"No, and I'm sure that if the police or anyone had given it to me, I'd remember," he said.

Patrice sighed, disappointed, but at the same time relieved to hear the tone of Mel's voice. He seemed more focused than he had the day before. "I have an appointment at ten within walking distance of here," she said. "Could I call you later? Then you could bring the FBI material over."

"Sure, that's good. I'll be here all day. Or I could drop it off before you leave."

"If you come a little before ten, I could catch a ride with you over to my appointment."

"I'll see you at quarter to ten," he said.

She poured a big tumbler of orange juice and took her

next-to-last antibiotic capsule. She didn't take a painkiller, although she felt worse rather than better than she had twenty-four hours before.

The message light on her answering machine blinked to show three messages recorded. Her mother left her number at the Maui Westin; a jerky electronic voice said the call was received "Friday, three eighteen p.m."

She yawned and brushed her hair off her forehead. *Three something p.m.? Oh, right after Rick and I left for Santa Fe.*

Axel Pruitt, the Laboratory archivist, at four forty-five p.m. had said, "I haven't found anything to show Douglas Frost was ever in Los Alamos, I mean during the war. He worked on physics in England and Montreal, I did find that. I've got a couple more places to look. Call me Monday or Tuesday if you can. Have a nice weekend."

"Where are you?" her mother demanded in the third message. "You should be there resting! Did you have complications? I was wrong to leave, I can see that. If I don't hear from you tomorrow, I'll call Rick at the paper."

Patrice winced, regretting the worry she'd caused. She quickly calculated the time in Hawaii and knew she couldn't call her mom quite yet. Instead she took another contortionist's bath, minus the hair-washing regimen, and dressed in jeans and a large sweatshirt she'd modified to fit like a normal sleeve over her cast by cutting off one cuff.

She looked out the window and saw the tiny pellets of sleet blowing around on the dry ground. High scudding clouds and brilliant sunshine battled for supremacy. Patrice sighed; the day could go either way. She put on warm socks and her shoe boots. Mel was due in about fifteen minutes, enough time to call her mother, even if she did wake her up.

Karen Meyer brushed aside Patrice's apology about the time. "I can go back to sleep. How are you doing? And where were you last night? You promised me you would rest and let your body heal!"

"I'm sorry I missed your call," she said contritely. "Rick took me out to dinner last night, with Danny Carter." That much was true. She just neglected to say it was in Santa Fe and was part of a busy afternoon and evening of work. "We just got caught up on news so I'll be ready to do a little work this coming week. And I'm feeling much better. Today I'm going out for an hour and then I'll be home in bed. You don't need to worry. So never mind about me, how is Maui? And how is William?" She propped the phone against her ear with her shoulder and bent down to tie her snow boots.

"Hawaii is wonderful and William is having a splendid time, as I am."

Patrice smiled, glad to hear her mother so happy. "Did you go snorkeling out by that old volcano? What's it called?"

"Molokini Island. It was spectacular, but William got seasick. We're going to snorkel more on Oahu. There's an old volcanic cone you just wade into. No boat trip, which William has ruled out in perpetuity."

They talked further of mai tais, hibiscus and guava. Karen described the magnificent lobby and the view from their room. "I'm standing on the balcony now. Listen, I'll hold the phone out and you can hear the waves breaking on the beach." There was a pause. "There, did you hear it?"

"It sounds just like a seashell." She laughed, then noticed the time. "I've got to go, Mom. I slept late and I'm hungry. Probably going to have a bodacious big breakfast."

"Just what your mother would advise, were she there," Karen said, proceeding predictably through a litany of "rest, eat, lock the door, don't go back to work yet," and "say hello to Rick."

Patrice had just hung up the phone when it rang again. "Hello?" No answer. "Hello?" she said again, this time annoyed. "Look, I like heavy breathing as well as the next woman, but I'm not in the mood."

Her smile faded when she heard a man's voice, not one she recognized, say, "You fool." She listened to the dial tone as if it could tell her something, then slammed the receiver down. Her heart pounded in her chest and her hand shook. She wondered how long it would take to get Caller ID put on her phone. *I'll call the phone company Monday.*

With a warmed slice of coffeecake, she drank another tumbler of orange juice. She just had time to put a fresh notepad and backup pen in her purse before Mel arrived.

"I brought you chicken enchiladas, too," he said as he unpacked another abundance of goodies on the dinette table. "And here's the FBI material we were looking for."

"Did you read it yet?"

"Yes, but there's less there than meets the eye. A lot is blacked out by marker. Have you found anything on Rose's laptop?"

Patrice winced again to realize she hadn't touched the computer or books since Mel carried them up to her apartment the day before. "Uh, not yet," she said, looking at her watch. The phone rang and she froze. She felt Mel's eyes on her as she stared at the answering machine. Four rings and it clicked on. Instead of her previous message ("Hi, this is Patrice...") she was glad to hear "Please leave a message." She'd recorded the bland, impersonal message at her mother's insistence, and now was glad of it.

"Patrice? This is Rick. I hope..."

She snatched up the receiver. "Rick, I'm here."

"How are you feeling?"

"Better. Good."

"Are you lying?"

"Yes." She paused. "Mel is here. He found that FBI stuff we were looking for. And he brought over more food. He's giving me a ride right now to Isobel Ellsberg's house."

"Well, call me later. I'll be at the paper from noon on."

Patrice knew that meant "on until midnight" on a Saturday. There was no Saturday *Guardian*, but the Sunday paper went to press Saturday night. On a normal Saturday, Rick wouldn't have to go in until four or five p.m., but with his skeleton staff he'd have to do more jobs than his own.

"If you want a supper break with real food," she said, watching Mel rearrange her small refrigerator to fit in another casserole, "my apartment is full of it, thanks to Mel."

"Sounds good. I'll talk to you later."

"At last those courses in solid geometry come in handy," Mel said as he slid a jar of mayonnaise in sideways like a torpedo into a tube. "Get a spoon, you have to eat the margarine--it won't fit. Well, maybe if I mash the lettuce...ah, there."

In his car Patrice asked, "Did you reach Lt. Pauling about the possible prowler?" Her lip curled ever-so-slightly in annoyance when she said "Pauling."

"Yes, he came by. He was--how shall I say this?--polite but inscrutable. I can't say if he took it seriously or not."

"You mean, you can't--or won't!--say if he takes me seriously or not." She watched his face for a reaction but he gave none. "You are being--how shall I say this?--polite but inscrutable."

He shrugged and laughed a little. "I don't necessarily think Lt. Pauling is a brilliant detective."

"Good call!" she interjected.

"But," he said loudly, "I guess I don't want to jump to conclusions against him, either."

"Fair enough," she said with a rueful smile. "Benefit of the doubt, and all that ladies and gentlemen stuff."

Her attention was drawn to the Santa Fe paper Mel had moved from her seat when she sat down. Out of the corner of her eye she saw "Los Alamos" in a headline. "Lawsuit threatened by anti-nuke coalition" had a byline by the *Santa Fe New Mexican* reporter she'd seen at the museum the night before. It was peppered with quotes from River Rasmussen and Senator Cristal Aragon. Gov. Ted Somers was reported to have said he hoped issues with Los Alamos, meaning the Laboratory, could be resolved without people losing jobs. The thrust of his comments seemed to be, Why can't those folks on the Hill build lawnmowers or something? Rational thought played no part in his diatribe, but it would appeal to a lot of his constituents.

No suggestion of what to do with the plutonium came up, except Earth's plea to "get it out of New Mexico." End quote. Nothing specific was said about the rumored lawsuit, only that their legal action would reinstate a lawsuit started in 1989 and set aside, and that it would be "more" this time.

"More what?" she wondered aloud to Mel as she read him choice chunks of the article. "More stupid? More petulant? More senseless?"

"The situation is bad at the Laboratory," Mel said. "The rumor mill says the DOE is caving in to protestors. I can't believe that, but there are ominous signs, worse than I've seen in thirty years." He shook his head, as if the movement would chase away dark thoughts. "Let's hope I'm wrong. Meanwhile, back to the subject at hand." His voice carried more cheer than his face, which was still tense. "Will you call me tonight after you look over that stuff?"

"Sure. Thanks to your supply train coming in, I can hold out in my apartment for days against the enemy."

He smiled, then his mood darkened again like a cloud passing over the moon. "Patrice, who is the enemy? Who killed Rose?"

She thought of the phone call that had rattled her nerves. The words, "You fool," a man's voice, the tone...of what? Derision. She shivered. "I don't know, Mel. I don't know what the heck is going on."

He stopped behind the house Patrice pointed out. She saw Sonia Greenway coming down the sidewalk and glancing at her watch; they were both right on time. "I'll talk to you later," Mel said before she closed the door. "And Patrice," he added, "be careful."

The front of the Ellsbergs' house faced away from the street, and if a walkway existed it was buried under an amalgam of leftover snow, pine needles and leaves. Sonia knocked at the back door, through which Patrice could see a kitchen counter. Behind them, looking out of place in an old wooden carport, was a gleaming maroon Lexus.

"This part of the house was built on at some point," Sonia said. "The houses didn't have kitchens originally, since everyone ate at a communal dining room."

"What about that house?" Patrice said, motioning with her chin toward the house next door, which appeared to be two or three times the size of the Ellsbergs' house.

"It was a dorm for Ranch School boys. You can't tell now, after all the modification, but it used to have screened sleeping porches all around it where the boys slept year-round. After the Ranch School was evicted, during the war, it was a dorm for WACs, and later subdivided into homes for scientists and their families."

Patrice nodded, but she secretly didn't believe that malarkey about the boys sleeping on porches in the winter. They supposedly wore short pants--actually Boy Scout uniforms--year-round, too. *Yeah, right,* she thought, tugging her coat closer around her and turning her face away from the bitter cold wind as Sonia knocked again, louder.

According to what Sonia had told Patrice the day before, Isobel Ellsberg had lived abroad and on the East Coast most of her life. She had come to Los Alamos as an adult, not counting the three or four summers she'd been there as a girl, and had never fit in.

"Not that she ever tried to fit in," was the way Sonia phrased it. "Whether she has an inferiority complex or a superiority complex I don't pretend to know, but the effect is the same with either one--isolation."

Through the glass of the kitchen door they saw Isobel. "You're certainly prompt," was how she greeted them in a cheerless voice, as if being on time showed some offense, some want of manners. Sonia introduced Patrice, and Isobel extended her hand for a limp shake.

They followed her through the kitchen to the small dining room, which opened into the spacious living room. Inside, as outside, the walls of the house were a jigsaw puzzle of pink, tan and beige stones. A massive fireplace of dark gray stones dominated the central wall, with the bottom of the fireplace atop a slate platform. Instead of radiating heat, the cold stone seemed to make the room even more frigid than their hostess did.

Isobel gestured for them to sit on the couch, facing the barren fireplace. Before she took a seat, Patrice looked out the window behind the couch. Through dirty panes flanked by moth-eaten drapes, in a shade of mustard some catalog writer probably called "harvest gold," she saw the bare stalks of sunflowers and flower beds set off by borders from the now-brown grass.

Isobel Ellsberg stood in the center of the room, her weight on one leg, her arms crossed just beneath her breasts. Her forehead had deep lines that were pinched together in vexation, as if one or both of her visitors had said something boorish. Patrice was puzzled for a moment, then figured it was just the way Isobel looked, no fault of theirs.

Her clothes showed Isobel's European bias. Her cinnamon tweed suit had a mannish cut to the jacket, and the dark brown silk blouse did nothing to soften the severe effect. It looked like something Queen Elizabeth would wear at Balmoral.

"I called your office to cancel this appointment," Isobel said with a trace of haughty superiority, "but you'd just left to come over. My father is not feeling well, and I can't say just when he will feel like having visitors." She didn't sound worried about him, just annoyed. Patrice couldn't guess whether she was annoyed at her father for not feeling well or at them for coming. Or just aggrieved at the universe.

"I'm sorry to hear that," Patrice said, trying to convey empathy. "But perhaps you could help me. I want to get some background on your brother before I hear his colloquium and attend his press conference. It would be so helpful if you could answer a few questions. I won't stay long."

"I doubt I'd be much help in that," Isobel said, but she sat down in an armchair at a right angle to the couch as if they could stay at least a little while.

"I just came over to introduce Patrice," Sonia said, popping up from the couch. "I have to get back to the office. I can let myself out," she added as Isobel started to get back up. "Please give my best to your father. I hope I'll have a chance to see him soon." She shook Isobel's hand and strode out quickly toward the back door with just a half-wave to Patrice.

"Have you heard from your brother about when to expect him?" Patrice asked.

Isobel's pinched face contracted even further for a moment, then she slipped a filter cigarette out of a pack on the end table and sat back. She diddled the cigarette around on the wide arm of the Western-style oak chair, tapping one end and then the other. She leaned forward abruptly and snatched a stainless steel lighter off the coffee table, then lit the cigarette, inhaling deeply and dabbing an imaginary fleck of tobacco off her tongue like Bette Davis in an old movie melodrama. Sonia had said Isobel was about forty-seven, but to Patrice she looked ten years older.

"Stefan had a change of plans. We expected him next Monday, but he was unable to get away from Washington. He won't get here until late Wednesday."

If his colloquium was Thursday, Patrice would have to hustle to get an interview. That made getting background even more desirable. She gave what she hoped was a friendly, you-can-trust-me smile and watched Isobel smoke the cigarette.

The dye job on Isobel's blond hair was two or three weeks overdue, Patrice observed, noting also how that shade of blonde with brassy highlights clashed with her skin tone. The wedge cut with an off-center part wasn't bad, but Isobel would let the hair fall over one eye, then toss it back with a jerk of her head. After about ten times the motion grated on Patrice's nerves. *Get a bobby pin*, she wanted to yell.

"I'm going to have some coffee," Isobel said between puffs. "Would you like some?"

"Yes, thank you."

"Anything in it?"

"A little milk, please." Patrice pulled out her notebook and jotted down a couple questions she didn't want to overlook. A better look around the living room surprised her. The oak furniture looked old, not like antiques, but similar to what one might find in the lobby of a run-down motel on Route 66. The little section of wallpaper she could see in the hall looked as if it had been there forty-plus years. It was hard to imagine Isobel Ellsberg feeling comfortable in the historic but down-at-heels house.

Isobel returned with a teak tray holding two cups on china saucers along with a china creamer. She lowered the tray so Patrice could pour her cream, then take the cup, saucer and spoon.

As she leaned forward to pour the cream, Patrice noticed a vapor of bourbon floating above the coffee. She tasted hers tentatively, hoping the liquor was only in Isobel's, which was the case.

"When my brother is in town, he will stay with a friend," Isobel said as she set the tray on the coffee table and picked up her cup and saucer. "We just have the two bedrooms, you know." She waved toward the hall as if shooing a fly. Her voice drifted off and she took a long drag on her cigarette. "Stefan will see Dad, of course." Patrice noticed she didn't say "Dad and me."

"Stefan and I didn't grow up together, you know," Isobel continued. "He was away at school so much. I'm told--though how would I remember?--that I adored him when I was an infant." She lit a second cigarette, and sipped her coffee, in no hurry to finish the tale.

"He went away to school when I was three and he was ten. I don't remember anything about him as a boy. It seemed I was sent to camp when he had school vacations, or I was left with a nanny in Switzerland while my parents visited him. I don't think I saw him again until I was ten and he was seventeen. Of course I bored him to tears at that age." She laughed, but it wasn't a jolly laugh. "Then he was off to college and our paths rarely crossed again."

"When did your mother die?" Patrice asked.

"Six years ago. She'd been frail for a good eight or nine years before that. I wanted to go back to graduate school, but it looked like her time was short, so I took care of her. She lived longer than any of us expected. Then Dad seemed to go downhill. If I'd gone to grad school I would have had to hire nurses to be with him. And jobs in art history are hard to find, even with a master's degree." She stubbed out the cigarette. "Would you like more coffee?"

"Thank you, no, this is fine."

Isobel left and returned. She sat further back in the sloping chair than she had before, and crossed her legs in a way Patrice felt sure was not approved by finishing schools. She watched Isobel draw circles in the air with one of her cinnamon leather pumps.

"Dad has his good days and his bad days," Isobel said, lighting a third cigarette. "When he heard this morning that Stefan is too busy to come Monday, well, that made it a bad day. Stefan is the apple of Dad's eye. His son--the famous physicist. His son--who has dinner at the White House and golfs with the Secretary of Energy. And gets big, fat awards."

"I heard Stefan might be getting a presidential appointment. Do you know what that might be?"

Isobel looked thoughtful, as if she were having trouble remembering. Her face was getting a little slack, losing that pinched look. "Some job in Russia, I think."

"Isobel!" a husky voice called from down the hall.

"I'll be there in a minute." She drained her coffee cup and took a long drag on her cigarette, then set it in an ashtray. "You'll have to excuse me."

"I have to leave anyway," Patrice said. "Thank you so much for seeing me. I'll call you in a few days and see if I can meet your father, even if he can see me for only fifteen minutes."

Isobel waved the cloud of smoke away as she stood up. "I can't say now. Call me and I'll know what kind of a day he's having. There's some Russian colleague who wants to see him next week, too. I'll have to see how he feels."

"Isobel!" This time his call could be best described as a bellow. Patrice set her coffee cup on the table and waved good-bye.

*****

The wind whipped her hair into her face when she stepped back outside. She pulled her parka close and trudged through the leaves that were blowing across the road and sidewalk, swirling when they met opposition in a fence or house. Until just a week before there had been diehard leaves on most of the trees around town, but the latest windstorm had torn them off and flung them down on the cold ground.

Patrice walked the block to Fuller Lodge, keeping her face down and her eyes open only in slits to keep the blowing dust out. *Snow would be a lot better than this!* she thought.

In the main room of the Lodge, with its high beamed ceiling, rectangular tables were set up in rows, the table tops draped in red, white and green material. When Patrice walked in she heard senior citizens singing along to "Frosty the Snowman." She stepped into the area which opened to the big room and smiled to see the lively, though elderly, crowd having such a good time. There were far more women than men, most of them dressed to the nines in holiday finery.

As Patrice mounted the steps to the narrow gallery that ran the length of the great-room, she noticed a silver-haired lady in a cranberry-red wool suit take the microphone in hand. The motion showed ease in performing, as if she'd done it for years, maybe even professionally. In a voice that showed her age in an almost imperceptible waver, the silver-haired lady led them all in singing

"White Christmas."

She thought of Mel facing Christmas alone and sniffled back some unexpected tears. She continued up the second set of stairs to the Historical Archives in the Lodge's attic.

She found Sonia in the viewing room. "I had an interesting chat with Isobel," she told her. "Seems the old gentleman was in a snit because his adored son couldn't find enough time for him. I'm hoping to talk to him one day next week. What do you have on the Ellsbergs?"

Sonia pointed at the visitors log book and Patrice nodded. Signing in was required whenever someone used materials in the archives. It was the staff's only way to justify their continued employment and requests for improving equipment such as computers. Patrice wrote her name, date and research subject down beneath that of a man from KOAT-TV in Albuquerque, looking for color photos of the first atomic bomb for a news piece on the birth of the atomic age.

"The museum needs to get Carl Ellsberg on videotape for our series about the atomic pioneers--before it's too late," Sonia said. "If you get to see him, would you broach the subject? Tactfully?"

"I can broach the subject, but I don't know how one tactfully reminds an old man he's got one foot in the grave and the other on a banana peel."

Sonia put her hands on her hips. "On second thought..."

Patrice looked further up the page in the visitors log. Students at University of New Mexico-Los Alamos were apparently assigned to watch video-interviews with old timers; five had signed in to see tapes during the past three days. She turned back to the page before and caught her breath. Rose had signed in for the last time the Monday she died. Under "materials used" she'd written "Arzamas-16."

Why would she care about that? Patrice wondered. Rose hadn't mentioned to her she was interested for any reason in Los Alamos's Russian counterpart.

"This is all there is," Sonia said, handing Patrice a nine-by-fifteen inch envelope with "Ellsberg" on a typed label. She undid the clasp and gently emptied the contents onto the pine table. An obituary of Elizabeth Ellsberg was taped to a sheet of typing paper. An eight-by-ten photo showed the couple at a cocktail party next to Kitty and Robert Oppenheimer. From the looks of the background, it was probably taken in Fuller Lodge. The photo was dated on the back, 1944, and numbered for the archive's catalog system. Another eight-by-ten showed Carl Ellsberg, young and skinny, at Trinity Site, the tower holding "the gadget" (as they called the bomb for secrecy's sake) behind him. There were copies of magazine articles with Ellsberg's name highlighted when it appeared, and about ten snapshots. One was Elizabeth and baby Stefan, according to a handwritten notation on the back. She scanned the magazine articles and newspaper clippings. Most were about Carl Ellsberg, but a few featured Stefan Ellsberg, prominent physicist and confidant of liberal politicians.

"Sonia, I'm through with this," she said as she slid the items back in the envelope. "Could I take a look at what you have on Arzamas-16?"

"I'm afraid not."

"What? Why?"

"Because the file is missing. There wasn't much in it; it was an envelope not bigger than the one you just went through. But it's gone. We don't understand how it could have happened."

"But Rose looked at it last week. She signed in."

"Oh, that's what she asked to see. She'd written that down before we found out we didn't have it. It was already gone."

*****

Back outside Fuller Lodge, Patrice could still hear "Jingle Bells" from the senior citizens' party, and the weather was making it seem more apropos by the hour. There was definitely a front moving in. The flag flapped loudly as if snapping at a target just beyond its reach. Patrice shivered and drew her chin down into her coat. The wind-chill factor must be minus-something.

"It's on the way!" a friendly workman in overalls and a sheepskin-lined denim jacket called to her as he walked in from the parking lot. "Radio says it's snowing in Gallup already."

"That's good news for skiers," Patrice said with a smile to match the workman's friendly mien.

"I want it to hold off a week," he said as he passed her. "I got my boy and his wife and my new grandbaby coming in from Farmington."

She pulled her parka as tight as she could without being able to zip it. Four blocks down Central Avenue, she ducked into the Bradbury Science Museum, thankful to get out of the cold. As Sonia had told her, the museum had a special display about Arzamas-16, Sister City of Los Alamos.

One side of a colorful kiosk showed letters from Russian students, residents of the city of eighty thousand, to students in Los Alamos. On a small screen a video prepared in Los Alamos about student life in New Mexico played on a loop. To listen, one picked up a phone receiver.

A second side displayed photos of Andrei Sakharov and other Russian scientists along with group photos of Los Alamos scientists in Russia to conduct a joint experiment using an ultrahigh-current magnetic generator.

A photo of Yuli Khariton, the first scientific director of Arzamas-16, reminded her of his explanation of the Soviet lab's name. The question had been posed to Khariton by his American counterpart, Dr. Siegfried Hecker, the director of the Los Alamos installation. By the time the two men met, American intelligence knew there had been only one Soviet nuclear weapons institute all along.

"Why did you call it 16?" Hecker asked.

"So you would spend so much money to look for the other 15," Khariton replied.

The third side of the kiosk featured pictures and captions about the town of Arzamas-16, including a photo of the Monastery of Sarov. Built on the site of a Tartar fortress that had been abandoned in the fifteenth century, the monastery formed in 1654. Of course, said a note, there had been no religious use of the building from the Russian Revolution until recent years.

Patrice studied the kiosk just long enough to warm up, then walked the last block to her apartment. To her surprise, the wind had actually lessened and the sun put in an appearance. Upstairs, she put on water for tea and made up her mind to face Rose's computer.

But, first, she looked at the FBI material. Dear Ms. Hulle, the cover letter said. Enclosed are copies of documents from FBI records. Aloud Patrice said, "Excisions have been made blah blah blah," but she continued to read: Excisions have been made to protect information exempt from disclosure pursuant to Title 5, United States Code, Section 552 and/or Section 552a. In addition, where excisions were made, the appropriate exempting subsections have been cited opposite the deletions. Where pages have been withheld in their entirety, a deleted page information sheet has been substituted showing the reasons or basis for the deletion. Subsections were marked below, it said, corresponding to Form 4-694a, also enclosed.

Pursuant to your request, 208 page(s) were reviewed and 121 page(s) are being released.

She fluffed up her pillow and turned on the light beside her bed. Stacking the papers on the bed, she poured her tea and phoned Rick.

"So, what did you think of Carl Ellsberg?" he asked.

"He was having what his daughter calls a bad day. Seems Stefan, a.k.a. Golden Boy, can't come to Los Alamos until late Wednesday, and his dad is piqued. I didn't get to meet the old gent yet. Oh, and Isobel is not in Stefan's fan club. In fact, she scarcely knows him. That's all I can tell you."

"Did you say something earlier about a home-cooked

meal?"

"Yes, a home-cooked meal cooked by a real cook. In other words, not me. Would six-thirty be good for a supper break?"

"Perfect, thanks. I'll see you then."

Patrice got comfortable on the bed, leaning up against the pillow. Her eyes grew tired as she plodded through the much-expurgated FBI papers. When she read the same page a third time, her comprehension receding instead of improving, she scrunched the pillow down, tugged an afghan over herself, and slept into the early twilight of the winter afternoon.

*****

While she heated the enchilada casserole in her small oven, she put all the pages of the Freedom of Information Act material back in order. Some pages were so marked up by a censor there were only a few words left to read; other pages were untouched.

Rick arrived, looking haggard. Pirate strolled in beside him and stretched luxuriously. Anytime Rick worked at night he took her with him.

Patrice patted the side of her leg, "Come here, girl. How's the girl?" Pirate sidled up to her and accepted a good rub on the head. Then she circled a throw rug three or four times and curled up on it, her tail tucked tidily beneath her chin.

Rick scratched his jaw line. "Sorry, I skipped shaving to save time."

"Hey, no big deal. The casserole will be hot in a few minutes." She put three puffy dinner rolls on a pie pan and slid it in the oven, then set the table. "How is it going at the paper?"

"Slower than expected. Waldo is in Farmington for a game, and the modem is on the fritz. If it won't work, he'll have to dictate his story to me over the phone. That's the last thing I needed tonight." He recounted his attempt to edit a business story Tiffany had left half done.

She took the casserole and rolls out of the oven and set them on hotpads on the table, tossed the dressing on the salad, and sat down at the table. "I saw the *New Mexican* today, the article about Aragon's rally and the lawsuit."

He nodded, his mouth full. Patrice ate her salad while her enchilada cooled. As usual, Rick ate like a starved man. People said he must have the metabolism of a hummingbird to eat so much and not gain weight.

"Yeah, things are heating up, all right," he said finally. "I'm hearing that thousands of people might show up to protest, coming on buses from all over the country. I don't know how much is true and how much is hype." He dished up a second helping of the casserole and buttered another roll. "This is great! I wish I had more time to enjoy it."

Patrice hesitated, then plunged ahead. "I know my timing is hideous, but I have to ask this anyway. Is there any chance you and your climbing buddies will be practicing soon?"

"I know I'm going to hate myself for asking, but why do you want to know?"

"I've been thinking about Rose's purse, which is missing, and which has a tape in it--a tape recorded Monday night in Doyle Silver's room. Mel doesn't have it, like I told you, and he double-checked with the police and the fire department. They say the purse wasn't in the car when they dragged it up."

"And you think it's still out there on the cliff face."

"Well, in a word, yes."

He set down his fork and clasped his hands over his plate. "Don't tell me you want me to go out there and dangle in space, risking my life and limb, to look for a purse."

"It sounds a lot stupider now that I hear you say it," she conceded. "I was thinking how you and your crazy climbing buddies are always practicing rappelling and belaying. So I thought maybe you could practice over there, I mean instead of somewhere else, and sort of scoop up evidence on your way past."

He said nothing and Patrice couldn't read his expression. "Fresh air," she said.

"Gravity," he countered.

"Exclusive story," she smiled.

"You're fighting dirty. You know my weakest point."

"That's because I share the affliction." She rested her elbows beside her plate and folded her hands to mimic his position.

He turned his attention to the last roll. As he slathered margarine on and took a bite, he shrugged. "All right. You win. I'll call some of the guys tonight. Tomorrow's Sunday, and it might work out." He emphasized "might."

Her smile broadened. "Thanks, Rick."

"I've got to get back to the paper," he said, polishing off the roll. "I have calls in to the Lab's public relations people, at home, about the lawsuit, and about the schedule for the Russian's visit this week."

"When are they supposed to get here?"

"The mayor, along with teachers and students, and a few businesspeople, is to get here Tuesday. Some Russian scientists are coming, too; they just happen to overlap."

Patrice carried the plates to the sink and moved the FBI paperwork back to the table. For the first time she looked at a half sheet of paper attached by something sticky, like gum, to the cover letter. At the top of the smudged photocopy was MEMO in block letters. "Wait a second, this is interesting." She handed it to Rick.

"Rose wasn't the only one who got this?" he said, handing it back.

"So it appears. Two others, a Professor Norman Taggert and Sheldon Libinowitz got it, too. No addresses or other information."

"So of course you want to know what their interest in the case is."

"Of course."

"I don't see offhand how you could find out. The FBI might tell you, then again..."

"If I called someone in the FBI I knew personally, or

rather, someone you knew personally, I might have a better than average chance." She batted her eyelashes like a coquette.

"Hold it right there. My brother is not the most approachable man in the world. Let's put it this way, he fits right in at the FBI. I got most of the personality in my family." He thrust his arms one at a time into his ski parka.

"What did Luis get?" she asked, adjusting the collar of his coat and brushing off a few dog hairs.

"I'd be hard put to say." He stroked his chin and looked from one corner of the room to the other, as if straining to find the answer. "I got the bulk of the brains and good looks, too."

"So maybe he's the humble one."

He gave a snorting laugh. "Not hardly."

"Will you call him, though? Or give me his number?"

"I'll think about it. Come on, Pirate." She awoke, startled from a state of blissful dog dreams.

"And the purse?" Patrice persisted.

"I'll think about that, too. Come on, girl." He opened the apartment door and Pirate darted out and cast left, then right, sniffing at other apartment doors. Rick turned back to Patrice and kissed her lightly on the lips. "Thanks for a great dinner."

Patrice was surprised and more than a little disappointed by the buddy-like kiss, but she made no comment. Instead, she matched his cool-but-affectionate tone. "Call me later tonight, okay?"

"Shouldn't you be getting to bed early?"

"I took a nap this afternoon," she said, giving Pirate a good scratch behind her ears. "And I must, repeat must, use Rose's laptop."

"Come on, Pirate, out in the cold again," Rick said. "Lock the door," he said to Patrice in parting.

Patrice rolled her eyes, but did lock it. She leaned against it, listening as his boots tapped down the hall. She heard the door to the stairwell open and bang shut.

She went over in her mind the way he'd kissed her. Aloud

she said, "Well, that didn't take long!" It had been sexier than a handshake, but not by much. I wonder if he's sorry about what happened—what almost happened—last night? She felt her skin tingle and her nipples hardened to remember the sensation of his hands caressing her. *Stop this!* she ordered herself. *You're acting like a fool. A man takes a drink, you don't think he's an alcoholic! So why do you think if a man kisses you, that he's head over heels in love?*

She shook her head as if the movement would chase away her embarrassment at being so willing—too willing!—the night before. She decided work would banish silly romantic fantasies. Silly groundless romantic fantasies, she added like a footnote.

She finished clearing the table of glasses, salt and pepper, and napkins. By stacking the FBI papers on two of Rose's books, she made a clear workspace for the computer. Lifting the laptop onto the table, she shuddered a little to think: *the last person to touch this was Rose. And now she's dead.*

Could there be something in the computer worth Rose's life? And worth my own?

Chapter 12

Patrice had set her radio alarm for eight Sunday morning, but woke up on her own before it went off. She nudged the little button from Alarm to Radio and heard her all-time favorite Christmas song: José Feliciano singing "Feliz Navidad."

As she had told Danny just a week or so before, "If radio stations played 'Feliz Navidad' ten times more often, and tear-jerkers like 'I'll Be Home for Christmas' about ten times less often, the holiday suicide rate would plummet! I can't believe anybody ever jumped off a bridge singing 'Feliz Navidad.'"

So Sunday started off on the right foot, so to speak. But she had learned to be skeptical.

She felt better, definitely on the road to recovery. "I'm itching to get back to work," she'd told Rick when he called late the night before. "No, wait. That itching is under my cast. But I am eager to get back to work."

He had called to say he and his buddies from search and rescue would do a practice climb Sunday around noon, and that, yes, they'd do it off the mesa where the Main Hill Road came up from the valley. "It will have to be tomorrow," he had said, "because winter is coming in earnest by tomorrow night. We'd best be setting our chestnuts by an open fire."

While the coffee dripped through a filter, she paced in a state of high anxiety about Rose's purse. She was impatient, as well, to pursue some ideas she had about Doyle Silver's nephew. Was Larry Dreyfus telling the truth when he said he didn't recognize the balding man in the nursing home picture?

"...four to six inches possible for the higher elevations by tonight. This is Gary Marshall with the KRSN weather."

Patrice pulled open her drapes and looked west toward the Jemez Mountains and south as best she could from the window. Not a cloud in the sky yet. She knew better than to bet on the weather in Los Alamos, though. They might get nothing, or they might get a major snowstorm at this time of year. The state badly needed snow or it would be a lousy ski season.

She took a leisurely bath, dried her hair, and did a half-good job of curling the ends with a curling iron. Standing in front of the bathroom mirror, she admitted her mother had been right. *I look like I got my hair cut at a barber school. And not by the top student, either.*

Rick called at eleven to say he'd checked and packed his ropes and other equipment. "Actually, I'm glad we're doing this. If I don't get outside and do something 'real' I'm going to go berserk. Oh, I forgot to tell you last night, Danny is taking the job in San Antonio. I plan to wring him dry in his last week here, with the Russians, and God-knows-how-many protests likely, and Stefan Ellsberg, whoever he is and whatever he's up to."

"Well, I'm happy for Danny, but I don't see how we're going to get along without him," she sighed. She sat on the bed and tucked her feet under her to warm them up.

"Uh, that brings up an interesting question," Rick said.

"Don't even think about it. I don't do windows, I don't cover sports, and I don't shoot pictures."

"You do, however, read my mind," he laughed.

"And don't you forget it."

"Say, Pirate misses you," he said. "How about if I drop her off in about an hour? She needs some civilizing after a long night at the paper. Rocco is a bad influence."

"Rocco is a bad influence on you, too, truth be known." Rocco Berini, the twenty-year-old assistant sports editor, was a specialist. He was happy writing sports, and effectively resisted covering anything else. It cost Rick more energy to try to get Rocco to do something than it took to do it himself, which was Rocco's plan. "What did Rocco do this time, teach her how to smoke cigars? Sure, drop her off. We'll do the girl thing. Try on rhinestone collars or something."

"Chew the fat. That's her favorite thing."

"I'm sure. See you in a little while."

She looked up Larry Dreyfus's number but felt hesitant about calling him. She knew she was being a wimp, partly because the snakes made her skin crawl. Maybe he's out, she thought, then chastised herself. What's the worst that could happen? He's there or he's not there. If he's not there, he has an answering machine, or he doesn't. She laughed aloud at the thought of Larry Dreyfus leaving a recording: "Hi, this is Larry--sorry, I can't come to the phone right now—I'm feeding a baby bunny to my python. Your message is important to me..."

She called, but after eight rings there was no answer. She got her pocket calendar out of her purse and wrote herself a note, "Call Dreyfus re: bald guy at nursing home." She noticed she had written "Call phone co. re: Caller I.D." and "Call Axel Pruitt at Lab re: D. Frost" on Monday's To Do space.

Squeezed into the margin by Monday she'd written "Norman Taggert & Sheldon Libinowitz. Ask FBI???"

She'd felt a jolt the night before when she'd finally turned on Rose's laptop computer and checked her Compuserve account for e-mail. Among the twenty-three waiting messages, there was an enigmatic message from a Shel Libinowitz. According to the time and date on the message, it was received by Rose's computer on Monday, about three hours before Rose and Patrice left for Española.

"Sorry, can't help you. Class load too heavy for research this semester. Good luck with your search! Best, Shel Libinowitz." It was from a personal e-mail account, no government agency or university in the address.

Patrice filed it in a message file Rose had named

"Perseus" and pulled up the file "Copy of Sent Messages." She looked for anything sent to Libinowitz. There was just one message, a note introducing herself and a question: had he interviewed Lona Cohen before she died, and if so, could Rose call him with a few questions?

His sprightly "Sorry" didn't answer the question, but maybe he was avoiding it. Patrice wouldn't have noticed the message had she not seen his name on the FBI material. Along with...she looked at the half-sheet again. Along with Prof. Norman Taggert.

She did a search on Copy of Sent Messages for Taggert, then did a slow eyeball search herself in Sent Messages and Perseus. She couldn't find Taggert anywhere. Maybe Rose never heard of him.

She went through the other incoming messages, steeling herself against the pain of "these are messages to Rose, but Rose is dead" by just pretending she was hired help not acquainted with Rose. It wasn't a completely effective ruse, but it helped.

There were messages from Axel Pruitt, the Lab archivist, one suggesting a new source book, one saying he couldn't find anything about Doyle Silver in his records, except that he worked in the Theoretical Division during the Manhattan Project. A third message said, essentially, let's do lunch. Patrice filed them under "Rose, personal."

She did the same with four messages from Sonia Greenway, questions on a video recording coming up with the pilot of the Enola Gay, the B-52 that dropped the bomb on Hiroshima. At least she didn't have to answer those messages; Axel Pruitt and Sonia Greenway knew Rose was dead.

There were several from people who must have known Rose casually, asking if she'd be attending a conference in Boston and a writing conference in San Jose. Patrice wrote them each a brief note of explanation. That was harder.

There was a message from herself at the paper, saying, "Just a quick note—remind me tonight to return your 'Effective

Habits' tape. Thanks! I enjoyed it, but I'm no more effective than I was before. I think it's that 'D' word-Discipline. Yuck. See you at 6:30." Patrice felt a chill throughout her body. She deleted the message.

She called Mel as he'd asked her to. "Before I say one more word," she said, "thank you, thank you for the enchiladas. They were great. Rick sends his best to the cook, too."

"I will tell Maggie Findley her casserole was delicious, but I can't tell her I gave it away," he laughed.

"Well, you wouldn't be lying if you said, 'Those enchiladas were so good, they just disappeared!'"

He laughed heartily; Patrice warmed to the sound, for his sake, for Rose's sake, for life's sake. If she were to die, she hoped her friends would remember her, but she hoped they'd laugh and enjoy themselves at every opportunity.

"I actually called on business," she said.

"Oh, darn. I would rather laugh, but go ahead," Mel said.

"I've looked at the e-mail that came in on Rose's account since last Monday afternoon. Most of it is easy to take care of, just housework sorts of messages. But there's one from a Sheldon Libinowitz that intrigues me. Have you ever heard Rose mention him?"

"I don't think so. In what context would it have been?" he asked.

She read Rose's question to Libinowitz and his "Sorry," reply. "The reason I'm really interested," Patrice said, "is that Libinowitz apparently got a copy of the same Freedom of Information Act material that Rose did." She explained about the note attached to the cover letter.

"What's the other name?" Mel asked.

"It says 'Prof. Norman Taggert.' I didn't find any messages to or from him in Rose's files."

"No, sorry. I've never heard either name. Rose and I were both so busy, me going to the Ukraine and her going ten directions at once, that when we had time together we talked about other things, not work."

"I understand. Well, I'm going to try to find out more about these two guys. Probably nothing there, but I'll poke around."

After she hung up, she pulled the afghan around her shoulders and revised her mental list.

*****

When Rick got to her apartment about thirty minutes later, Patrice had made neat stacks out of the piles of books and papers she'd been working on. She made the bed, which went a long way toward cleaning up the place, and carried the trash down to the Dumpster. She figured she still needed to clean the bathroom before the Board of Health closed her down, but she'd done enough for a while. She was resting on the bed, having unlocked the door, when Rick knocked. "Come on in," she called.

Pirate sauntered in behind Rick. It wasn't her way to appear too eager. *I'm a lady, I'm reserved, so coax me.*

"Hi, Pirate, hi, girl. Come up here by me." Pirate put her front paws up beside Patrice and sort of oozed onto the bed in her unique and comical way.

"The weather report says we will get snow tonight," Rick said, "so it's a good thing we can go today. Say, just in case there are several purses out there, what color is Rose's?"

"Dark, dark green leather, with a long strap."

"Anything else you might want out there?"

"Well, if you see an extra front bumper you might as well pick it up. Maybe then the police would take me seriously. No, that could still be explained as an unfortunate little accident...which brings me, by admittedly circuitous logic, to the subject of the FBI, and, coincidentally, your brother Luis."

He grimaced, but said, "Go ahead, I'm listening."

"I was just thinking your brother might be a good professional ear for the Perseus story. He could find out if Doyle Silver was ever suspected of being a spy. Or Douglas Frost or Carl Ellsberg. Surely they make a note if someone reports a spy."

Rick laughed coldly. "You have a lot more confidence in the FBI than I do, my dear. And having a brother who feels he's in a holy priesthood hasn't increased my regard for 'The Bureau,' as he reverently calls it. But I'll tell you what. I'll call him in a few days and toss the Perseus subject up in the air like a clay pigeon."

"You could call him tonight."

"You're pressing your luck. I'll call him. Period, end of article." He bent over and kissed Patrice, and Pirate whimpered jealously. He scratched her ears and Patrice whimpered, so he scratched her ears, too. "I'll see you girls later. Don't take any Milk-Bones from strangers."

Patrice heard the door lock behind him. She lay still and patted Pirate until the dog was asleep, and thought about sibling rivalry such as seemed to exist between Rick and Luis. From the point of view of an only child, someone who always wanted a brother, the concept was puzzling.

She slowly swung her feet to the floor. Pirate opened one eye, the one with the big black spot over it, to see why Patrice was moving. "Stay, girl, it's all right," she murmured. "I'm going out for a little while."

She brushed her hair and pulled her parka on, then put her driver's license and a twenty-dollar bill in her pocket. She had to empty her purse on the table to find her car keys. She pulled the door tight behind her and made sure it had locked.

Her tan Subaru with the cracked windshield was in the parking lot. "Come on, battery," she said before she turned the key. She needn't have worried; the Subaru started without hesitation. She took it on a test drive, not a test for the car but a test for herself. Could she drive a stick shift with one good hand and the fingertips of her left hand? The verdict, after a dozen turns and backing up in parking lots, was yes, but she'd better not get in any tight spots. Nothing fancy, nothing fast, and no parallel parking.

It felt great to reclaim her independence. She stopped at

Furr's Supermarket to pick up a quart of milk; she also bought a small pack of beef jerky at the checkout stand for Pirate.

She drove up Trinity Drive almost to the pond, then turned left to the *Guardian* office near Los Alamos Inn. She didn't plan to go in, but saw Danny's pickup out front and thought she'd congratulate him on the new job.

She unlocked the front door and went in. "Danny? Yoo-hoo. Honey, I'm home." She locked the door again and surveyed her desk. It had a scent of something cloying. *Tiffany! That vixen Goldilocks has been sitting in my chair.*

She heard the door to the darkroom slam open and called again so Danny would know she was there.

"What are you doing here?" he asked. The portable police scanner on his desk said, "Garble four one, this is garble six two," or something like that.

"I'm feeling much, much better. I came out for a practice drive, and my car headed here out of habit."

"Bad habit! You'd be better off smoking."

"Congratulations on the job."

"Thanks. I'm ecstatic! I was excited to go away to college, then found out about a hundred other people in my high school class were also going to New Mexico State. It was Los Alamos South. Then I planned to go away to work, and instead got a job offer here. 'Better than nothing,' I thought." He held his palms up and made a comical face. "What did I know? Anyway, it's time to get the hell out of Dodge, and San Antonio sounds terrific to me."

"Rick says he's going to work you like a slave this week."

"That's okay. He's got a full plate. What with his ace reporter lying around her apartment eating bonbons and watching soap operas."

"He doesn't know it yet, but I'm planning to be back on the job tomorrow. Part of tomorrow, anyway." She looked at the newest mail in her In box, the stuff tossed there Saturday that Rick hadn't even had time to open and route to the reporters who had sliced up her job like an apple, a wedge here, a wedge there.

The word Personal on a business envelope caught her eye. "Friendship Foundation?" she said, looking at the return address. She slid her steel letter opener in and popped it open. "Congratulations, Your application to Friendship Foundation has been selected..." She read silently.

"I'm going to Russia!" she gasped to Danny. "I told them in my application I want to go to Arzamas-16 to write about our Sister City and they've accepted it. I'm going in April. Then there's a lot of stuff about getting my visa and shots and stuff. I can't believe they said yes."

Getting one of the coveted grants was a feather in her cap. She would do a series of articles from Russia, telling whatever the Russians would let her know of how they built Arzamas-16 to be a secret city just like Los Alamos, and for an identical purpose: to build an atomic bomb.

"Rick will love this news. I'll take this with me and show him when he comes back to my place to get Pirate." She did a little "touchdown dance," but her ribs weren't up to the gyrations.

"Oh, yeah," Danny said, "Rick's out climbing today. He said something about it last night. Well, I've got to head out and shoot a basketball game. You leaving?"

She looked at the mail again and shrugged. "Yes, this can wait. Let's get out of here."

*****

The stairs at her apartment were in concrete stairwells at the north and south ends of the three-story structure. The building was long and narrow, just two apartments wide with a hallway running down the middle of each floor.

As Patrice climbed to the top floor via the south stairwell she could hear Pirate barking like a junk yard dog. She ran up the last stairs and flung open the door from the stairwell to the hallway. At the same moment she saw a man burst through the door to the far stairwell. She didn't get a good look at him. She ran halfway down the hall to her room where Pirate was scratching at the door and barking furiously.

Fumbling with the key in her haste, she unlocked the door. When she'd opened it about six inches, Pirate forced it open and pushed past Patrice into the hall. Ears flapping, she whipped her head left and right and took off full speed ahead for the north end.

Still barking wildly, she pushed against the door, to no avail. It had closed and latched behind the man. Patrice slid the grocery bag inside her apartment, pulled the door tight, and ran after Pirate.

"Get back, Pirate, get back!" She reached over the frantic dog to open the door to the north stairwell. Pirate took off like a shot down the stairs, out of the stairwell and across the parking lot. At the street she stopped and barked even more.

There was no one in sight. Patrice came up behind her, out of breath, and caught sight of a white car rounding the corner at Ninth Street without stopping.

"Stay, Pirate! Stay! Good girl." She snagged her collar and calmed her down. "Come on, let's go home. Good girl." Pirate growled indignantly as she followed Patrice back to the apartment, her way of saying she was prepared to tear somebody limb from limb if he messed with her or her humans.

"It's okay now, girl. You're a good, brave girl. Come on."

Patrice's throat was so dry she could hardly swallow when they got back to the door to her apartment. Her legs felt like she'd worked out at the YMCA. Her heart was pounding. She kept talking in a soothing voice to Pirate, urging her to come inside the apartment. The Dalmatian paced the hallway between the apartment door and the north stairwell four times before she'd follow Patrice inside.

"Sit, girl, that's good," Patrice said. She locked the door behind her and grabbed the phone to call the police non-emergency number. When she got the dispatcher she insisted on speaking with Lt. Pauling.

"He's in a meeting, I'm sorry."

"Then please interrupt him. I have to talk to him or to

Capt. Bell right away."

"If this is an emergency you should have called 911," the woman said.

"It's not that kind of an emergency! Please put me through to Lt. Pauling or Capt. Bell." She almost said "damn it!" but all calls are recorded. The woman put Patrice on hold for what seemed like two minutes.

"Lt. Pauling," he said, clearly annoyed at the interruption.

"Lieutenant, this is Patrice Kelsey. I think someone tried to break into my apartment. He's long gone, so it's not an emergency. Could you please come over?"

Pauling's attitude changed immediately to all-business, Patrice was relieved to note.

"Stay inside, keep the door locked," he said, "I will be there in a few minutes. If you hear anyone outside the door except me, call nine-one-one!"

"Okay, thanks, I will," she agreed, but she had no intention of doing so unless she came up against a certified ax murderer. She knew that if you call 911 in Los Alamos you get police, ambulance and a fire truck, lights and sirens. No either-or. You get it all.

"I'm just glad this town doesn't have a flipping helicopter," she'd said to Rick and Danny on a couple of occasions.

She hung up the phone and coaxed Pirate away from the door and onto the bed. Her legs were shaking as she put the milk away. She made a fresh pot of coffee and cleared space on the table.

"Patrice!" Pauling called out her name and identified himself as he knocked. Pirate went into another barking frenzy at the sound.

Patrice unlocked the door and invited him in. At the same time she put her arm around Pirate's neck and calmed her all over again.

Pauling stood in the open doorway, examining the

doorknob. "No sign of forced entry," he said.

The burden of proof was going to be hers, she could see it coming.

"Tell me what happened." He shut the door and pulled a small pad of paper out of his breast pocket.

She took a deep breath. "I left at about eleven-thirty. No, eleven-forty-five. I drove around a little to practice driving with one hand, then I went to Furr's, and over to the *Guardian* office." She waited while he wrote that down.

"I came straight home, and when I got here Pirate was going crazy. I could hear her from the south stairwell." She told how she caught a glimpse of a man running out the other stairwell door and how Pirate reacted when she opened her door.

"All I could tell was it was a white car that was speeding around the corner onto Ninth Street, toward Central. I don't know anything about the make. It was just a medium-sized, ordinary white car. Not huge, not small." She offered Pauling coffee and poured some for both of them.

"Just black, thanks," he said. "Have you seen anyone hanging around when you've gone out, anyone you don't usually see?"

"No, I stayed cooped up in the apartment most of the weekend. It's been quiet all the time. I don't think I've seen even a neighbor in the hall in a day or two."

"Mel Hulle told me your theory of a prowler coming down off his driveway to the patio door."

She nodded. "I'm wondering if someone wanted to get at Rose's papers or her computer."

"That's a lot of guess work," he said skeptically. "It's a big stretch from three or four footprints in the snow. We're looking into it, though."

"I think if Pirate hadn't been here someone would have broken in. I think I have what someone wants. And it sure isn't silverware and jewelry."

He closed his notebook. "I'll have officers patrol more

often in this area, get out of their cars and walk around, show their presence. And if you see anything suspicious, or you remember anything more about the man you saw this morning, call me at this number." He gave her his card with a number that would ring directly without going through the switchboard.

"Did Mel tell you the man Rose went to see died a few hours after she did?"

"Mister, uh, Silver, I think was the name."

"Yes, Doyle Silver. His nephew lives in Los Alamos. Lawrence Dreyfus made the decision to have his uncle cremated quickly. No medical examiner looked at the body, as far as I've heard."

Pauling again said nothing.

He was really making her angry, but she tried not to show it. She didn't want to give him the satisfaction of looking even a hair out of control.

"So I was wondering if you'd check around about Larry Dreyfus," she went on. "Is he inheriting a lot of money in this situation? It's just a thought."

Pauling opened the notepad again, made a quick note, and put it back in his pocket. Patrice knew he'd never worked as a detective and she didn't trust him to refer to one for advice. The politics inside the local police department were no better than inside any other P.D. Given that set of facts, she had little hope Pauling or anyone else in the department would take a careful look at Larry Dreyfus.

His radio crackled on. "Go ahead."

"We have a report of a climbing accident off the Main Hill Road. Two units responding. Fire and ambulance en route."

"I'm on my way; ten-four."

"A climbing accident?" She sloshed her coffee on her jeans as she stood up. "Rick's out there. I want to go with you."

Pauling said no, but Patrice was determined. She grabbed her parka and keys and locked the door as they went out. He was already halfway down the hall and Patrice had to run to catch up.

She dreaded the moment Pauling found out people were out there climbing to find something she thought was evidence in a case he refused to investigate.

But she dreaded a lot more the thought that anyone was hurt.

It might even be Rick. *Oh, please, God, no. Not Rick!*

Chapter 13

Lt. Pauling carried on a conversation with the dispatcher on his radio as he hustled down the concrete steps. Patrice strained to hear anything about the accident but all she could hear was static and coded cop-talk. She was one stride behind Pauling all the way to his car.

"I'm sorry, you can't go down to the scene," he said briskly. "We're allowing police and rescue personnel only beyond Entrance Park." As he slid into his car he added, "You can wait there and I'll have someone let you know if your friend is injured. What's his name again?"

"Rick Romero."

Pauling slammed his door and popped his lights on as she said "Romero" so she couldn't be sure he heard her.

She drove to Entrance Park, a small picnic area with a spectacular view east across the Rio Grande valley. Traffic had piled up to that point and cars were making U-turns to find another route off the Hill. Patrice spotted Danny beside his pickup at the far end of the park. He was checking his supply of film when she slammed on the Subaru's brakes and enveloped them both in a choking cloud of dust. She leapt from her car and all but assaulted him with her panic about Rick and the other men.

"Danny, I heard it on Lt. Pauling's radio. They said it's a climbing accident. And Rick's down there! They won't let me go!"

Danny's police scanner was continuing the chatter she'd heard on Pauling's radio. She stopped with her mouth still open and listened intently.

"We've got High-Angle here and they're setting up to go over... Did you say one hundred feet?...That's affirmative. One man is stuck one hundred feet down...Ten four... Any word on his condition?... Negative."

"Oh, my gosh!" she said.

"I'm driving down right now," Danny said. "I got permission from the fire chief, as long as I don't get in their way."

"Let me go with you! Please!" she asked frantically.

"No! That wasn't part of my deal with the fire chief. Wait here! I'll let you know as soon as I can." He hefted his camera bag into the truck cab and jumped in. She watched him pull onto the road behind the chief's car and follow as it sped past the police officer stopping unauthorized vehicles.

Patrice walked to the edge of the canyon and looked down. She couldn't see any sign of the accident; it was way around the butte from the park. But she could see down, and it made her sick at her stomach. *How could anyone go over a cliff like this in a car and live? How did I manage to survive?*

All she could figure was that the place the Cadillac went over must have had a substantial ledge somewhere below the road. Well, if it was enough to stop a car, it is enough to stop a climber. *Surely Rick and the other men are all right,* she thought, hugging herself fiercely. *Surely!*

She sat down on the bench of a picnic table and watched a red-tailed hawk ride the air currents in the canyon. The air was cold but the picnic bench was an effective solar collector.

Since Rick had kissed her Friday night, after the art patrons' party in Santa Fe, Patrice had felt a heightened awareness of physical sensation, as if Rick had awakened something stifled and dormant within her. The sun seemed somehow personal, as if its rays were meant to heal her. She concentrated on opening herself to the sun, to welcome its penetrating warmth into her bones. She imagined her cells gathering the sun's rays and using that universal energy to knit the fractures and mend the tissue. Atom by atom her body was healing.

I love him. The thought suffused her body with warmth out of proportion to the weak winter sun. But the warmth could not repel the cold fear that overtook her when she thought again of the cliff and the men in danger.

She breathed as deeply as she could, again and again, trying deliberately to clear her mind. She tried to visualize worries as helium balloons just lifting away from her and floating toward the hawk and beyond, but it didn't work. Instead, a sensation of falling overwhelmed her. *It's my fault Rick and those men are out here.*

Like opening a door to a moldering basement and leaning into the darkness, she forced her mind back one week. *What did Doyle Silver tell us that could set in motion this frightening spiral of events?* Rose was dead, Doyle was dead, a prowler menaced Mel's house and her apartment, and Rick or one of his friends was injured--or worse--right then on the face of a cliff.

Of course, she reasoned, whatever was happening that morning off the edge of the Main Hill Road was an accident, and climbing accidents do happen, even to people without paranoid friends like Patrice Kelsey. About Mel's alleged prowler, all they had was a few footprints in the snow and Mel's friend's statement that she saw a man outside his house. About her alleged prowler she had even less to go on. Her witness was a dog!

Paranoid suspicion was all she had regarding Doyle Silver's death. He was already ashes to ashes, dust to dust. He was history.

History. His story. She had been sifting the ashes all weekend of the history of Los Alamos, and she was still nowhere. It's not the history of Los Alamos, per se, she thought. Los Alamos is a place, just a town. Lots of other places could have been chosen for the amalgamation of brilliant scientists who coalesced to "harness the atom," as atomic research used to be called. But it happened to be Los Alamos, and for better or worse the town and the bomb are inextricably linked.

What she was sifting, she realized with sudden clarity, was the ashes of the history of the day mankind went off a cliff. And the laws of atomic energy are as irrevocable as the laws of gravity. Once you've lunged outward beyond what you see and feel, you can't go back. You can't fall up a cliff.

One small step for man, one giant leap into deep doo-doo for mankind, she thought with a pain in her chest.

She kept coming back to one thought. *There had to be a connection with here and now, or else this whole idea of danger and threats was ridiculous.* If Perseus was still alive, who cared if he--or they, if indeed it was one name for two or more spies--was exposed? Hell, she thought angrily, he'd probably sell his story to the National Enquirer and the highest bidding TV network for a movie of the week. *There is no such thing as shame anymore!*

So maybe nothing sinister is going on here, she considered. Maybe I got a bad bump on the head in that wreck. A very nice but slightly eccentric lady named Rose who had received two prank phone calls happened to die in a car accident on an icy road during a blizzard. Like the bumper sticker says, shit happens.

She heard a siren start up in the distance and turned back toward the road. An ambulance sped up the hill past the park and the line of waiting cars. The high wail dropped in pitch suddenly as it passed. Patrice ran toward her car to follow the ambulance when she heard a honk and saw Danny's Dodge turn off the road onto the dirt parking lot, kicking up a veil of dust behind it. He pulled up beside her car and got out, leaving his motor running.

She said, "Is it Rick?" at the precise moment he shouted, "It's Rick."

"They got him up all right," he went on. "He's got one leg banged up pretty hard. They put a splint on it to move him, and of course a collar to keep his neck immobile, and a back board. They brought him up in a basket."

"Was he conscious?"

"Oh, yeah. Completely. He spotted me and called me over to him right before they slid him into the ambulance. He told me to give this to you." He pulled a dark green purse out from under his jacket. Patrice opened the latch and caught her breath. There was Rose's tape recorder. Tears wet her eyes; she said nothing, just nodded.

"I've got to get back to work and develop the film for tomorrow's paper. You going to the hospital?"

"Of course. Thanks, Danny. God only knows how long I'd have to wait for news if I depended on Pauling." She wiped her eyes on the cuff of her parka and got in her car.

Is it my imagination, she thought as she drove toward the hospital, *or is every second car in town a white, mid-size car all of a sudden?* If it were physically possible, she would have kicked herself for not getting a license number on the car that sped away from her apartment building that morning.

She continually scanned traffic ahead and in her rear-view mirror. She pulled in the west parking lot by the Medical Center, near the emergency entrance, and locked her car doors. She left her purse in the car, on the floor, and carried Rose's purse as if it were her own.

The ambulance was still backed up to the dock; no one was in it. At the sign-in window of the emergency room Patrice asked if she could see Rick Romero. "Take a seat in the waiting room across the hall, please," the nurse said.

Patrice picked up a magazine but didn't know if she even had it right side up. She was listening for any hint she could pick up of Rick's condition.

She spotted the paramedics talking to two police officers in the hall and barged out. "Hi, can you tell me how Rick is?"

"Hey, here's our rescue success story!" a paramedic with the nametag "Garrett" said. "We're hoping to get on Rescue 911.

You want to let us pull you up off the cliff again to re-enact it? We're getting really good at this. Done it once a week so far this winter."

"It's hard to say no, but no. In fact, hell no. I never want to look down farther than one flight of stairs again in my life. But never mind my fall," she said, "how is Rick?"

The four men looked at each other. "He's going to be okay," the second paramedic finally said. He didn't sound convincing, to Patrice's way of thinking.

Just then Lt. Pauling shoved open the door from the parking lot. "Patrice, could I talk to you, please?"

"Sure, yes, what's going on?"

Pauling walked down the hall away from the others and she followed, her heart pumping like a hydrant. "What do you know about Rick's climb?" he asked.

Every time Patrice thought a nightmare was over, it got worse. "He was getting some rock climbing practice with some other guys from search and rescue. He chose that spot because of Rose's wreck. I was hoping to retrieve her purse." It sounded pretty hollow and shabby an explanation there in front of him. She felt like a six-year-old who'd put sugar in the gas tank.

"Who else knew he was going?"

"I don't know the names of the guys climbing with him. Except Dick Kennedy."

"We've talked to all of them. Was there anyone else? Anyone you told about it?"

"I don't understand. What's going on?" she said.

"Rick's fall wasn't an accident. His rope had been sliced through most of the way."

Patrice couldn't have been more shocked if Pauling had hauled off and punched her in the stomach. The rope was sliced? She racked her brain. Had she told anyone Rick was going after the purse? She hadn't told Mel because she hadn't talked to him since before she talked to Rick. *This just came up last night when Rick called me from the Guardian office*. "No," she answered slowly. "Rick made the plans last night and called me late, I'd say nearly eleven. I haven't talked to anyone about it."

"This is confidential information and is not to be released to the media." She nodded that she understood. "I'm going to talk to Rick now. You can go back in the waiting room."

It was another twenty minutes before a nurse opened the door from the emergency room and said Patrice could come in. Lt. Pauling was nowhere in sight, she was relieved to note.

Rick was on an examining table. On the wall was an X-ray display with three angles showing what appeared to be the bones in a lower leg.

"Hey," Rick said with a laugh, "don't look so grim. I'm going to be fine. And how is my dog?"

"Pirate's fine. She's back at my apartment." Patrice decided this wasn't a great time to tell him about the hullabaloo over a possible prowler. "Are you going to have surgery?"

"Yeah, they're going to do a little repair work in there. It's a comminuted fracture of the fibula. Should mend fine." He paused. "Lt. Pauling said he told you about the rope."

"Oh, Rick, I'm so sorry to have dragged you in to this. You could be dead!" She wiped her eyes on her sleeve.

"Well, I'm not, so don't cry."

"Who would have done such a thing?"

"I'm trying to figure out when. Maybe that would be a clue to who. I examined my equipment, including the ropes, this morning before I left home. I went to look at the hill with Dick about nine, then went home and loaded up my gear and Pirate, went by your place, and met the guys at McDonald's for lunch. The gear was locked in the car at your place and at McDonald's. The rest of the time I was in sight of it."

Her eyes were wet again. She leaned over and kissed Rick hard on the lips, then wiped her eyes on her now-soggy cuff. "I got the purse from Danny. Thanks."

"Yeah, I knew he'd give it to you. Don't leave it laying around, okay?"

She held it up. "I won’t let it out of my sight."

He gave a thumbs up and smiled. "Way to go."

She found a tissue in the pocket of her parka and blew her nose. "So, are you going up to surgery soon or what?"

"I don't know. Nobody tells me anything. Listen, this is important. There's something I need you to do."

"Sure. What?"

"In my coat pocket over there is my key ring. Bring it over here, please."

She found it easily and gave it to him. Rick picked one key out to emphasize, then gave her the whole ring. "This is the key to my place. You'll need dog food and stuff. And just as important, my address book is by the phone. Look up my brother's number in Washington and call him. Tell him what's going on, about Rose and you, and about my rope being cut. See if he can come for a visit pronto. It's listed under L for Luis. There are half a dozen addresses and phone numbers crossed out, but I’m sure I circled the new ones."

She nodded, blew her nose, tried to smile, and broke down sobbing. "I shouldn’t have asked you to go out there. I shouldn’t have!"

"Hey, come here." He tugged on her coat to get her close enough to embrace. "I’m going to be okay. And this isn’t your fault." He tightened his grasp on the front of her parka and pulled her down. He kissed her long and urgently, his face bathed by her tears.

"You'll have to excuse us now," the nurse said as she came in through the open accordion doors that defined Rick's examining room. She was carrying a tray of test tubes and other supplies for taking blood.

"I want to know something first," Patrice said. She found a box of tissues and blew her nose.

"What's that?" The nurse pulled out a piece of plastic hose and set the tray down on a metal table. With a practiced motion she examined the veins in his right arm. "Make a fist."

"Are you going to take off all his clothes?"

She grinned. "Maybe. Why?"

"I was just going to offer to help."

The nurse grinned bigger and wrapped the plastic around his right bicep, tapped his veins with her finger, then leaned toward Patrice conspiratorially. "You've seen one, you've seen 'em all."

"That's not what I hear," Patrice said with a laugh.

"Hey!" Rick said. "Do you mind?"

"Oh-oh. I've offended him," Patrice said. She leaned over and kissed him. "'Bye now. I'll call Luis. See you later. Maybe I can sneak Pirate in."

"Dick is getting my car home. He'll get the key to you so Luis can use it," he said.

She kissed him again and smiled at the nurse. "He's all yours."

Patrice wondered if Luis could get away from the FBI on short notice to come help out his brother. *For all I know he could be on an assignment somewhere, maybe even out of the country*. Then she remembered Rick said Luis was stuck in a desk-bound assignment in Washington for a year or so.

She stayed at the hospital until Rick was out of surgery, then drove home around six p.m. It was already dark, but at least the predicted snowstorm wasn't affecting Los Alamos yet.

Pirate recognized her step in the hall, Patrice guessed, because she didn't bark. She was just waiting politely inside the door. "Hi, girl. We're going for a walk in just a minute. Then we'll go to your house and get your food. We're going to be roomies for a while. Won't that be fun?" She patted Pirate's chest and scratched her ears. "We'll stay up late and eat popcorn in bed."

She wrinkled her nose at the burned coffee smell and turned off the coffeemaker. She'd left it on when she raced out after Lt. Pauling hours before. Luckily it had been a full pot.

"I'll just take the messages off the machine and then we'll go," she said to Pirate, who was dancing with excitement at the thought of getting outside. "I know--when a girl's gotta go, a girl's gotta go!"

She pressed the blue Message button and the answering machine hummed and clicked. The red light was blinking three times, then a pause, then three blinks.

"Patrice, this is Mel. It's Sunday about twelve-thirty. I'm taking Allison to the airport. I'll call you later."

"Hello. This is Larry Dreyfus. Uh, you're not there. Uh, I'll call you tomorrow." She wondered with minimal interest what Larry Dreyfus wanted. The electronic voice reported the time of the call, "Four thirty-two p.m." Patrice set down Rose's purse and yawned.

But the third recorded message scared her half to death.

It was Rose's voice!

Chapter 14

Patrice watched the twin-engine Otter approach Los Alamos Airport from the east. She knew its route from memory. From Albuquerque its north-bound shadow had traced the clogged artery of New Mexico, the Rio Grande, to a point at the east end of Frijoles Canyon. Skirting the restricted air space over Bandelier National Monument and Los Alamos National Laboratory, the pilot had continued north across the river, and turned west over the split in the highway called the White Rock Y. It was Monday morning, just after ten.

Pirate stood beside Patrice outside the chain link fence that divided the parking lot from the airport service area. The dog was tense, her eyes locked on the moving light in the sky. From dead ahead, as they were, the landing lights of the fifteen-seat aircraft were as bright as phosphor flares. Pirate strained at the leash and growled, probably hearing more than a human could.

The plane landed and taxied, following its nose and the twin circles carved by its black propellers along the white lines and out of their line of sight. With Pirate heeling obediently, Patrice walked into the lobby and stood by a window.

She had panicked the night before when she heard Rose's voice on her answering machine. It was as if all the fear she'd felt since Rose told her she'd received death threats--all that fear had been building up in her like pressure behind a valve. Then Rose's voice on the answering machine set her off like a gusher.

Her sensible side--which she figured made up about five percent of her by then--listened to the message again. Rose was saying something about Lona Cohen and La Fonda Hotel in Santa Fe. Patrice suddenly recognized where she'd heard those words before, in that order.

She had heard them in Doyle Silver's room at the nursing home, that horrible Monday night, one week before!

With that realization, her knees had buckled. She steadied herself with a hand on a chair and slowly lowered herself into it. She stared, pie-eyed, at the answering machine. "End of messages," the robot voice intoned. The light went on blinking in sets of three.

Rose's voice was recorded during our visit. She felt like a heavyweight fighter had his hand around her heart and was squeezing it. Her skin felt cold and clammy; her rapid, shallow breathing put her on the verge of blacking out. With even more hesitancy than she had replayed the message, Patrice opened Rose's purse.

Slowly, she exhaled, limp as twenty-minute spaghetti. There was the tape recorder. She lifted it out and checked. Yes, the microcassette was inside; another one was at the bottom of the purse. Both had been marked by ever-methodical Rose, in tiny block letters, "D.Silver12/6."

Then, the voice on my phone was not from this tape. The more she thought about it, the weaker and colder she felt. The logical conclusion was inescapable: *Someone else was taping our conversation with Doyle Silver that night! And that vicious, devious person wants to scare the hell out of me.*

She had resisted following the logic any further, but again the conclusion, and the nausea it engendered, were inescapable: *Whoever it is wants me dead! Dead and forever silent, just like Rose.*

Making sure the door was locked, Patrice had tossed a change of clothes and her makeup bag, toothbrush and hairbrush in a plastic bag. She crammed as much as she could of Rose's stuff, starting with the FBI papers, into the case that held the laptop computer. Skirting the answering machine like it might grab her at any moment, she backed out of the apartment with her hands full. Pirate stayed right beside her, the hair on her back straight up in sympathy with Patrice's high anxiety.

From Rick's house she had called his brother Luis in Washington. Luis had taken charge, told her to stay at Rick's, and he'd arrive in a few hours.

She was surprised and relieved to see in the morning that the predicted snowstorm had gone northeast from Gallup and left Los Alamos unscathed. She half-suspected Luis had rerouted the snowstorm, as it would have interfered with his getting a flight to Los Alamos from Albuquerque. He certainly sounded forceful enough to arrange the weather.

Before dawn that morning Luis had called her, from somewhere over Missouri. He said Lt. Pauling would have a police officer escort her to her apartment to get anything she needed, and the officer would retrieve the tape from her answering machine.

She had written down his crisp instructions on what time to be at the Los Alamos Airport to pick him up. As she placed the receiver back on the wall in Rick's kitchen, she knew she should feel better. But instead, she started shaking uncontrollably. She had no choice but to admit: things were getting to her. And there was an abrasive edge to Luis's voice. She was glad on one hand he was taking charge, but at the same time she felt more, rather than less, apprehensive.

Four times on the way to the airport she had to pull over to let police cars pass her. They were headed down the Main Hill Road, just like they had been the day before, when Lt. Pauling got the call about the climbing accident.

The second time she pulled over to make way for police, Patrice turned on the car radio to KRSN and heard Gary Marshall say there was an anti-nuclear weapons demonstration blocking the highway. Demonstrators knew right where to strike, too.

They'd formed some kind of blockade at the bottleneck of the highway that linked Los Alamos to Española and Santa Fe, a wide but vital part of the highway at a place called Totavi.

Commuters were furious at the delay. State Police were said to be backing the demonstrators away from the highway. Patrice knew Danny was there, and he'd taken Jeff Bloom, a capable reporter just out of college, while Carolee Cruz, the assistant managing editor, manned the battlements at the *Guardian*.

Patrice watched the passengers come down the steps and cross the tarmac. Luis Romero was easy to spot. He looked just like Rick would if Rick cut his hair closer and spent half a month's salary on one suit and the other half on a pair of boots. The heather brown wool suit was obviously custom-made. Suits off the rack didn't fit broad shoulders and narrow waists like both the Brothers Romero had.

Over one arm Luis carried a tan Burberry overcoat. Beneath it she could see an eelskin attaché case in soft brown that perfectly matched his cordovan boots. His silk foulard tie with a small precise pattern in blue and gold made her think of Egyptian art.

In a town where the dress code for men is "Zipped Fly and Two Shoes," Luis Romero looked like an apparition from GQ.

Pirate couldn't have been happier to see him if he'd been wearing lamb chops. She danced around beside Patrice and scratched daintily at the carpet with one paw.

"Hello, Pirate! Hi, girl!" Luis gave her a pat on the head before he extended his hand to Patrice.

Pirate placed her rump on Patrice's lace-up boots, leaving her to wonder if the dog wanted to prevent any man but Rick from getting too close to her, or whether the sly dog wanted to keep Luis away from Patrice to have him for herself.

"Hi, I'm Patrice Kelsey." In her jeans and boots, plus an oversize sweater covering her cast, she guessed she must look pretty frumpy. At least she had managed to get her cast inside the sleeve so it looked like she actually did have two arms.

Four other men and one woman, all carrying briefcases, strode in from the tarmac with an air of self-importance. The ground crew carried their suitcases in through another door. One of them answered the ringing phone at the reservation and service desk.

"Dr. Ellsberg?" the employee called, scanning the room. A man just to Patrice's left looked toward the desk. "Over here," he saw gruffly.

"I have a call for you, sir," the employee said. He set the phone on top of the tall desk and held out the receiver to the gentleman.

"Stefan Ellsberg," the passenger said, then listened.

Patrice glanced around the room, trying to look him over without being too obvious. He was medium height, with wide shoulders that supported the neck of a professional wrestler. His full head of hair was jet black, wavy, and unruly in a deliberate, Hollywood way. He looked to be about fifty, maybe fifty-five. His eyes were dark brown, almost black, and cold. His tone of voice on the phone, from what Patrice could hear, was sharp.

"The connections were terrible," he said, raising his voice, then listened. "Chicago!" he barked. "No, you take care of it on your end. I'm very busy!" He handed the phone back to the airport employee without saying good-bye to the caller or thanks to the employee.

It took only a minute to get Luis's suitcase and walk to the Bronco. If Patrice had told Pirate to get in the back seat, she would have crawled in slower than the tide and sulked. But for Luis she leaped in, Miss Congeniality of the canine world.

"I talked to Rick an hour ago," Luis said, "while I was between planes in Albuquerque. He's pretty groggy. We'll go to the police station first."

His tone was not one of suggestions, but of decrees. "You listened to the tape your friend Rose made in Doyle Silver's room, is that right?" Without waiting for her to answer, he barked another question. "What did you learn from that?"

"I listened to two microcassettes this morning at Rick's," she said. "It takes almost two hours to hear the whole conversation, but there was repetition, small talk, and other chatting that doesn't amount to much. The meat of it is about an hour."

"Do you have the microcassettes and recorder with you now?"

"Of course. After Rick risked his neck to get them, I'm not leaving them anywhere."

"You said last night the police don't think you were deliberately forced off the road?" Luis went on.

"That's right. I felt like they weren't taking me seriously. But I think the cut in Rick's rope and the message on my answering machine have changed their mind."

He nodded, all business. "And the message on your machine is Rose's voice? You're sure of that?"

"Yes! I told you that."

"There's no need to get defensive," he said.

She opened her mouth to snap, "I am not defensive!" but fortunately saw the Catch-22 in time. She had been prepared to like Luis, but she was quickly regretting his arrival. Rick was right; he did get all the personality in the family. It wasn't just Luis's choice of words that made her uneasy. He talked like a lawyer cross-examining her.

They pulled into the police station parking lot. Luis turned off the ignition and Pirate put her head forward between the seats; he scratched her ears automatically. "So, you think you've uncovered a spy conspiracy? I think you said last night that Doyle Silver claimed someone he knew as Douglas Frost offered him money to spy for the Soviet Union. Is that what you said?"

"Well, I don't think he used the term 'spy' quite that blatantly."

"A spade's a spade and a spy's a spy," he interrupted.

Why was he being so nasty to her? To demonstrate the

difference in their castes? "Right, I understand, I only meant Frost apparently couched everything in terms of, 'Russia is our ally, millions of Russian men are dying, and our government owes them the truth about this weapon.' There wasn't any thought then that Russia, or rather, the Soviet Union, would be our enemy as soon as Hitler was defeated. Stalin had people visiting the United States, saying he was a friend to Jews."

"Thank you for the lesson," he said icily, "but I took history at Stanford and taught it at Georgetown. I think I'm pretty clear on who our allies were in each of the wars we've fought."

"Why don't we go inside?" she said, trying to force her face into a pleasant expression in spite of her clenched teeth.

Inside the station, Capt. Bell and Lt. Pauling greeted them, their shoes shined and belt buckles gleaming. "Let's go into my office," Bell said.

"I'd like to talk to you alone first, if Patrice doesn't mind," Luis said.

She didn't say she minded, and she didn't say she didn't mind. She just stood there with her mouth open.

"You said you have the microcassettes and recorder?" Luis said, his hand out.

She felt like slapping his hand, but since that was probably a federal crime, she handed over the tapes and recorder. "I'll wait here," she said, stating the obvious.

She leafed through Field and Stream and three indistinguishable journals of law enforcement for what seemed like an hour, but was actually twenty-five minutes by the watch she checked ten times.

What the heck is going on here? She had a vivid recollection of a day when she was in fifth grade. Her mother had been called from work for a conference with her teacher and the principal. Patrice had to sit in the principal's outer office while they talked about her and demanded to know what her mother was "going to do with her." All because she'd hauled off and hit a girl who called her a whore. She had been pretty sure it was a bad insult, though she didn't know what it meant. The girl had been angry because her going-steady boyfriend had asked Patrice to go out behind the elm tree at recess. She hadn't gone, but apparently even being asked made one a "whore."

Her mother, to her credit, kept a straight face through the conference, then took Patrice to the zoo, where they had a lovely time. As they watched monkeys swing from branch to branch in an artificial jungle, her mom said, "Don't hit anybody."

"What if they hit me first?" Patrice asked.

Her mother thought that one over. "Okay, don't hit anybody unless they hit you first. And for heaven's sake, Patrice, make sure you have a reliable witness!"

Patrice tossed the Field and Stream on the corner table and recrossed her legs. She wondered if they'd somehow found out about her fifth-grade assault charge. Luis was, after all, with the FBI. Whoop-de-doo.

"Patrice, would you join us, please?" Lt. Pauling was a very cool customer, she observed.

Again she asked herself, *What the heck is going on here?*

"Have a seat, Patrice," Capt. Bell said, standing as she entered his office. "There are a few questions we'd like to ask you."

She shrugged. "Okay. Sure. Go ahead." She felt a tiny muscle under her left eye twitch, something that only happened when she was under extreme strain. The men were looking at her like three hungry rats, and she was the cheese. "Would you mind telling me what this is all about? You look like you want to hook me up to a polygraph."

"No, no," Bell said soothingly. "Of course not."

Patrice did not feel soothed. She'd thrown out the polygraph remark as an attempt at levity, not a Yes or No question.

"Did you tell anyone Rick would be climbing down the cliff off the Main Hill Road?" Lt. Pauling said.

"No, I told you yesterday. I talked to Mel Hulle Saturday

night, very briefly, but it was before Rick called to say he'd arranged with some of his buddies to go climbing. Rick called from the paper about ten-forty-five Saturday night."

"And whose idea was it for him to go look for the purse on the side of the cliff?" Luis asked.

"Mine." She swallowed hard. "I mean, I asked if he could, or if he would. It was in the context of, 'You guys practice climbing all over the mountains, why not right there where the wreck was?' He thought it over, and talked to his friends, and they said yes. I was right--the purse was there."

"Did you tell anyone Sunday morning that Rick would be stopping at your place?"

"No, I didn't know he would be stopping to drop off Pirate until about an hour before he came. What are these questions about?"

They ignored her question and Pauling asked another one: "What did you do with the microcassettes and recorder from the minute Danny Carter handed them to you?"

"I carried them with me into the hospital to see Rick, then later I carried them to my apartment--they were in Rose's purse all the time. When I hurriedly packed to leave my apartment, I put her purse inside my suitcase for ease of carrying. I only have one good arm, you know."

"So from the time Danny gave them to you, until you say you heard Rose's voice on your answering machine, they were in Rose's purse, but always in your possession?" Luis asked.

"What do you mean, 'until I say I heard Rose's voice?'" She turned to Bell and Pauling. "You've heard the answering machine tape, haven't you?"

"Yes," Bell said heavily. "The problem we have, though, is that you held on to the tapes. You should have left them in our custody. Chain of evidence, you know about that."

She thought about what he'd said. "Okay, I see that might be a problem. But I was in the room with Rose that night, hearing what Doyle Silver said, and I needed to refresh my memory of several details."

"Did you play the microcassettes yesterday afternoon or evening?" Pauling persisted.

She shook her head, unclear on where the question was coming from, or where it was leading. "No. I left them totally untouched, in Rose's purse, until this morning. I've been awake since four a.m. I listened to them then."

The three men exchanged furtive glances. Apparently some silent signal was passed that Luis would speak. Patrice thought fleetingly that they had intended to play "good cop/bad cop," but got their signals crossed, and were instead playing "bad cop/bad cop/bad cop."

Luis cleared his throat. "Are you sure you didn't play part of one tape yesterday between two and six p.m.?"

She paused, a little frightened by the implication that she was lying. Lying about what? And why? What the heck was going on?

Then the realization dawned, making her taste the bile that rises into one's mouth to forewarn one that is time to look for a toilet. The bastards thought she'd called her own number, maybe from the hospital, and played Rose's tape onto her answering machine tape.

And if they thought that, they must think she cut Rick's rope, or got some partner in crime to do it while she kept him busy in her apartment. Suddenly she had total understanding of the women accused of witchcraft in Salem, Massachusetts. If she said, "I'm innocent," they would burn her at the stake.

"No," she said quietly, firmly, not letting anger creep into her voice or demeanor. "I did not take the recorder out of Rose's purse, nor did I play the microcassettes on that recorder or any recorder, until four a.m. today, Monday. And now, gentlemen," she said, rising to her feet, "you'll have to excuse me. I have to get to work at the paper. If you have any more questions, I will be unable to answer until I have an attorney. Excuse me, please."

She left the room, but was further humiliated in the hall.

She could not leave the offices until Pauling or Bell punched in a code to unlock the door to the lobby. She didn't trust herself to ask them to unlock it; she wanted to leave without tears. At least she would deprive them of that satisfaction.

"Oh, let me help you with that," Bell said after she'd stood silently at the door for about thirty long seconds. She said nothing, just walked through the door when he opened it, continued out the front door of the police station, and walked straight down Trinity Drive toward the *Guardian* office. By not looking back, she hoped to salvage what shreds of dignity she could under the circumstances.

The cold air did nothing to cool her temper on her six-block walk to the *Guardian* office.

She went over her exit line in her mind, "And now, gentlemen, you'll have to excuse me." She hoped they were stung by her ironic use of the word "gentlemen."

Ha! Irony is undoubtedly beyond their comprehension, she thought, clenching her teeth until her jaw ached. Gentlemen, be damned, she should have said.

It had always aggravated her to see police on the TV news, calling suspected criminals "gentlemen." That worked if the context was, "We asked the gentleman to step out of the Lincoln Continental." But they used it for wild-eyed bums dripping with blood, an ax or a submachine gun still in their hands when arrested.

"We arrested a gentleman at the residence," went a typical cop report. "Family members say he broke down the door with the ax and proceeded to hack his ex-wife into sections, removing her head first. The gentleman is then alleged to have drunk her blood. The crime is under investigation at this time, and we have no further comment."

Now at last Patrice knew why the police called such animals "gentlemen."

"It takes one to know one," she muttered aloud through her clenched teeth. And to fight them, she'd have to get a lawyer.

She wondered who she could hire for the thirty dollars and fifty cents in her checkbook.

The farther she got from the police station, the harder it was to hold back wet, furious tears that made it tough to see where she was going.

Chapter 15

Luis had said Rick was groggy when he'd called him from the airplane, but that was no longer the case by the time Patrice walked into the newspaper office.

"Patrice! Come over here," someone called from the far side of the newsroom. "Rick's on the phone."

Patrice headed slowly toward the voice she'd heard, wishing, too late, that she'd gone to her apartment instead of the newspaper office. Her cheeks were red, stung by the cold and wind on her walk from the police station, but her racing pulse and icy hands had more to do with shock and anger than with the brisk walk.

Carolee Cruz, serving as managing editor of the *Guardian* for the time being, sat at Rick's desk in his cramped cubicle. With the phone propped against her shoulder, she read a menu of wire stories aloud.

"Okay, here comes Patrice." Carolee rolled her eyes and held the receiver out at arm's length before Patrice could even put her purse down. "It's Rick. He wants to talk to you."

"Did Luis get here?" He launched into his questions without waiting for Patrice to say hello. "Are you all right? Why didn't you call me this morning? Didn't you know I'd be worried about you?"

"Why would you be worried?" She hadn't told him about the frightening message on her answering machine, the sound of Rose's voice that seemed to be from the grave. Nor had she told him about the man she believed was trying to get into her apartment the day before while she was out driving and Rick was out climbing.

"Think about it," he said with an uncharacteristic snap in his voice. "Somebody tried to kill me yesterday! I'm entitled to be paranoid about your safety. Is Luis here?" he demanded again.

"Yes, I picked him up at the airport. He wanted to go talk to the police first thing. He should be walking into your room any minute now." She was afraid she'd blurt out her worries, and her anger at his brother, so she abruptly said, "Here's Carolee again," and darted toward the ladies' room.

She was shocked at her face in the mirror. The last week, especially the past twenty-four hours, had sapped the color from her skin. Her lips were pale, almost translucent, and badly chapped. She had circles under her eyes. Even her hair had lost luster from the stress that buffeted her from every direction.

She heard someone coming and stepped quickly into one of the two stalls. It gave her privacy, which she wanted, but it also gave her time to think, which she didn't want. *How did I get into this mess?*

The night before, from Rick's house, she'd called Luis in Washington. Next she'd called Danny and Carolee. The two of them raced over to Rick's house to trouble-shoot the coming week at the newspaper. The week would be a nightmare at best and a disaster at worst with the managing editor suddenly out of commission.

The three of them had tossed ideas around, trying to figure out first, how to cover the news and second, how to put it in readable form on newsprint by one o'clock every afternoon. They agreed they could do either one well, but doing both with a skeleton crew was a grim prospect.

"How long do you think Rick's going to be in the hospital?" Danny had asked, scratching Pirate under her chin.

"Only a few days," Patrice answered, "but he's going to be in a cast to the middle of his thigh. He'll have to stay home for weeks is my guess."

Danny, Carolee and Patrice agreed that Danny would take reporter Jeff Bloom everywhere with him to cover the news. Carolee and Patrice would stay at the paper and work with wire copy, phone work, writing, and layout. Waldo, the sports editor, and Rocco Berini, his assistant, could be pressed to help, and Tiffany might pitch in, if they were lucky.

If Carolee had to go to a scene to interview and report on something, Patrice would stay at the office and assemble the paper.

"That accident couldn't have happened to a nicer guy," Carolee had said of Rick's broken leg.

"Yeah, and it couldn't happen at a worse time," Danny added. "When will his brother get here?"

"He didn't have his flight times for certain when we talked, but he's hoping to be here before noon tomorrow. He said he'd call me en route to let me know."

Carolee and Danny insisted they could put out the Monday paper without Patrice, since she was not up to full speed yet, and she had to pick up Luis Romero at the airport.

Observing the chaos in the newsroom as she passed through, on a fast track to the ladies' room, she wondered if Danny's and Carolee's confidence was eroding, but she was too distraught to care.

When the other person left the restroom, Patrice emerged from her steel cubicle and faced the mirror again. She washed her face and applied lipstick and mascara. Using a trick she hadn't tried since high school, she dabbed lipstick on each cheek and rubbed it in wide circles. *Now I look like a cadaver with cheap rouge*, she had to admit, and washed her face again.

In the break room she poured a cup of coffee, added creamer, and dunked a stale doughnut in it. Her batteries--or at least her blood sugar--thus re-charged, she ventured into the fray, jumping on a rewrite of a story about the demonstrators who had closed down State Road 502 below the point where the three roads to and from the Hill merge. The State Police moved the demonstrators back and re-opened the highway after two hours, but the publicity war was won by CAND. Danny had gotten great shots, and the comments from furious commuters made for lively copy. Patrice wrote a quick sidebar on the press conference by Senator Aragon that she and Rick had attended in Santa Fe.

"Five minutes, people," Carolee yelled above the din. "Five minutes to deadline. Anything not on my screen in five minutes will wrap tomorrow's fish, not today's!"

Patrice proofed the sidebar and called out "Twelve inches on Aragon, slug is Witchy Woman, coming to you now." She pressed Send on her keyboard and headed for the darkroom.

Danny was leaning on a light table in the advertising room, telling a cute intern about his job at the San Antonio paper. Patrice was in no mood for manners. "I've got to talk to you, now."

"Duty calls," he said with a shrug to the intern, and followed Patrice into the darkroom. She closed the door tight behind her.

"I'm in trouble," she said.

Danny stared at her, speechless. "What did you say?"

"Oh, for pity's sake, not that kind of trouble! It's a thousand times worse than that. You won't believe this."

"Try me."

"Rick's brother, Luis Romero of the Federal Bureau of Investigation, has come in a big bird from the sky to save us all, and as his first decree, he has convinced the local gendarmes that I, Patrice Kelsey, a woman of sound mind and badly banged-up body, played Rose's tape into my own message machine and pretended to be scared. And that's not all. I'm also being accused of tampering with Rick's rope and trying to kill him." She paused.

"Okay, this time you're right. I don't believe it."

She paced, two steps each way--all there was room for, and that was only if Danny pressed himself against the sink. "I wish I had a cigarette," she said.

"Patrice," Danny said, "you don't smoke. In fact, you have never smoked."

"Well, it's high time I started then. Cigarettes are just like money in the Big House."

"You're not going to the Big House," he said. "Unless you mean Cristal Aragon's mansion."

"Oh, shit!"

"Patrice, at the risk of sounding like Pollyanna, swearing does not become you. I've never heard you swear before. Is this another part of getting ready for the Big House?"

She stopped pacing and looked for a Kleenex to blow her nose and wipe her eyes. "How could Rick's brother think I could be a sneaky, violent person? I want to kill him!"

"He just doesn't know the real you." He put his hand on her shoulders. "Now, why don't we talk about this like reasonable people, over a reasonably good cup of coffee."

She thought about it for a minute, as if weighing the pros and cons. "All right, my apartment, thirty minutes. Be there. And if you know a good, cheap lawyer, bring him or her. Preferably her, because I hate men."

"Even me?"

"Don't press your luck."

"Okay, okay. I'll be there. Now please, calm down. We'll get this all straightened out."

*****

"What time did Rick go over to your apartment yesterday morning?" Danny said. He'd talked Patrice into lying down with a warm, damp washcloth on her forehead. While they talked, he scrubbed out her burned Pyrex coffeepot and made fresh coffee.

"About ten-thirty. He told me last night at the hospital he'd gone to look at the hillside with Dick Kennedy about nine, then went home and got his gear, and brought Pirate over here. Then he met the guys at McDonald's for lunch before they went on the climb."

"And when did you have a possible prowler?"

"Let's see. I didn't leave right away. When I went out I drove around for a little while getting used to driving with one hand, and I went to the grocery store and the *Guardian*. You saw me there, what time was that? Almost noon?" He nodded. "I guess it was about noon when I got back and Pirate was barking her chops off."

"So yesterday at ten-thirty Rick came over to your apartment, and his gear was in his car..."

"He said the car was locked here and at McDonald's," Patrice added.

"Who else knew he was climbing?"

"I didn't tell anyone. He told the guys he was climbing with and whoever was working at the paper Saturday night probably heard him say it. Did you?"

"Yeah. Now, let's see, Saturday night there was Rick, me, Carolee, and Rocco, but Rocco left early. Waldo was on the phone from Farmington about ten times." He tapped his forehead. "Oh, and Kent Bolt came in for an hour or so, mostly making calls in his office."

She took the washcloth off her face and started to sit up. "I've got to go back..."

"Lie down! That's an order. The coffee isn't even ready yet."

"May I make a phone call?" He didn't object, so she sat up and pulled her calendar out of her purse. A minute later she reached Axel Pruitt, the Lab archivist. "Thanks for calling me on Friday," she said. "Did you find anything about Douglas Frost?"

"I have looked and looked. No sign he was ever here. He worked in Montreal, and in England. His work was apparently connected with the Manhattan Project, at least loosely. So there is a chance he could have been brought over for a secret consultation or something, but I can't find it in black and white. Why are you looking for him?"

"I'm sorry, Axel, I can't go into it until I have some proof of certain things. I appreciate your help, and I promise to fill you in soon."

"Oh, a mystery in progress?"

She thought about Rose; to herself she said, *Yeah, a murder mystery*. To Axel she said, "Either a great story or a big fizzle. I'll call you soon."

Danny poured their coffee, adding milk to hers. "Thanks," she murmured, distracted. She found the number in her calendar for Public Affairs at the Laboratory and called.

"Craig Smith, please. Oh, hi, Craig. This is Patrice Kelsey. Marian said you returned Rick Romero's call? Yes, it's terrible about his leg." She hurried through the small talk and asked what he knew about Stefan Ellsberg.

"Stefan Ellsberg is a physicist in the Department of Energy," he said. "He's going to give a colloquium Thursday morning, ten a.m., in the Physics Auditorium about 'Politics of the New Atomic Partnership.' Then he'll hold a press conference where the DOE will announce his appointment to something or other in Russia. They didn't send me the details of that yet."

"When can I interview him?"

"He's not coming into town until Wednesday," Craig said.

She opened her mouth to say she'd seen him arrive that morning, but decided to leave it alone. "Thanks, Craig. You'll let me know? And when can I expect to interview the mayor of Arzamas-16?"

"Mayor Kozar will arrive tomorrow. I'll have to get back to you about his schedule."

"Thanks, Craig. Talk to you soon." She hung up and sipped her coffee, deep in thought. "Danny, I need your nice, logical mind to help me on this."

"Well, that's a change," he said. "Most women are interested in my body." He struck a bodybuilder's pose.

Patrice didn't even focus her eyes on him, nor did she react to his attempt at levity. "Someone knew Rose would be at Buena Vista Nursing Home Monday night. He, she or they knew she would be talking to Doyle Silver. They had to know it in advance, and they were ready to tape the conversation. How could that happen?"

Danny set his coffee on the TV tray and pulled a dinette chair over by her bed. "Well, I think there are two questions here. One, how did he, she or they know she'd be going? And two, how did they tape the conversation in Mr. Silver's room?"

"She could have told someone, or," her eyes widened and she snapped her fingers, "or her phone was bugged! I think that's the answer to number one. And there had to be a tape recorder or some kind of bug in Doyle's room." She fluffed up her pillow, propped it against the wall, and got comfortable.

"What about your phone?" he asked.

"Mine? No, she called me at work to remind me about going to see Doyle. We never spoke of it while I was at home."

"Oh, and I suppose this spook who is vicious enough to kill Rose, and try to kill you, just went away and doesn't care to whom you spill the frijoles? Not mighty darn likely, in my opinion." He drained his coffee and poured himself more.

Patrice held her mug between her hands as if to warm them, oblivious to the coffee as a beverage. She'd written an article about the latest developments in phone taps and bugs, so she knew what to look for, but she felt paralyzed. Was some third party listening every time she picked up the receiver? Was someone listening to her and Danny right now?

Reluctantly, she set down her mug and picked up the receiver of her phone. She gave the mouthpiece cover two turns and removed it.

Well, look what the phone company did not install, she thought. She gestured to Danny to come get a closer look. She held a finger to her lips to say "Shhh." Then with a fingernail she popped a carbon button transmitter into her hand. It had been modified, with a soldered ring, making it a little thicker than a normal phone microphone.

Patrice set it on the TV tray and pointed at the door. Danny nodded and followed her into the hall.

"It's probably dead without leeching off the phone's power supply, but I don't like talking near any kind of microphone," she said.

"That's the evidence you've been looking for, or at least part of it." Danny spoke in a whisper.

"You forget, I'm a target of the Federal Bureau of Insinuation. Luis the Lion Heart will claim I put it there and made sure you were available to see me claim to be finding it." She shook her head. "This is sickening!"

Danny did a Humphrey Bogart imitation. "So, sweetheart, where'd you hide the receiver?"

Patrice thought a minute. "It's probably not inside my apartment. It has to be easily accessible for changing batteries and tapes. But it's probably somewhere in the building."

"What about the prowler?" Danny whispered.

"Huh?"

"Maybe the prowler Pirate chased away was here to pick up a tape in your apartment. Lord knows your lock is probably one they teach how to pick in burglar kindergarten."

She considered what he said, frowning at the doorknob in her hand. "It's possible, but it's far more likely the listening post is out of the room."

"So, watcha gonna do?"

"Will you testify at my trial, that you saw me take the tap out of my phone?"

"I'll do better than that. I'll testify, and I'll visit you at the Big House. I'll even bring you cigarettes."

She ignored him, deep in thought. "I'm going to take the tap to Luis and throw myself on him. I mean, throw myself on his mercy." She made a face like she was gagging. "I will politely ask him to look for the receiver. It's probably something sophisticated enough he'll never believe I could have rigged it."

Danny nodded. "Yeah, rigging phone taps is a guy thing. Hey, be sure to put the tap in a plastic Baggie. They do that on all the cop shows, so it must be *de riguer*."

"What would I do without you?" she said facetiously.

"Well, little lady, you won't have to find out."

"I killed the last man who called me little lady."

"I'll keep that in mind." He smiled. "You want a ride to the police station?"

"No, I've got my car here. I left it when I came over this morning to let the police officer in to get the answering machine tape. Luis is probably at the hospital anyway. I'm going over there."

"Tell Rick I'll bring him a paper as soon as it's off the press, okay?"

"Sure. And Danny, sincerely, thank you for being here." She kissed him on the cheek.

"Aw, shucks. Anytime."

*****

She knocked once as she entered Rick's hospital room. As she expected, Luis was sitting in a chair by Rick's bed. "Good afternoon, Agent Romero." She walked to the other side of the bed and kissed Rick on the cheek.

"Whoa," Rick said, "what's this Agent Romero stuff? You two have met, why isn't it 'Luis'?"

"Our relationship is strictly adversarial," she said with a cold smile at Luis. "Have you told Rick about our little run-in at the police station?"

Luis put his hands behind his head, placed one expensive boot on the knee of his expensive slacks, and leaned his chair back on two legs. "I didn't see any need to at this point," he said, with a look Patrice would call a smirk.

She stifled the urge to slap his face and smiled. "I've been thinking a lot since I left the police station--about how anyone knew when and where Rose was going Monday night, and how anyone knew Rick was going after her purse." She pulled the Baggie with the carbon button out of her purse. "At Danny Carter's suggestion, I unscrewed the mouthpiece of my phone, and this little bugger dropped out."

She handed it to Luis and went on. "I don't know a lot about phone taps and room bugs, but I know there has to be a receiver for the signal from this button somewhere in or near my apartment."

The smirk evaporated from his face and he set the chair down. He took the Baggie and looked at the button. "How long ago did you find this?"

She looked at her watch. "Twenty minutes ago."

"I'd better get over there in case removing this triggers some kind of alarm signal to the listener." He took his suitcoat from a hanger in Rick's metal cabinet and shot his cuffs out of the sleeves. "Do I have your permission to look inside your apartment?"

Without a word she handed him a key. "I strongly suspect there's a tap on one or more phones at Rose's house as well." She gave him Mel's address, which he wrote in his pocket notebook. "Uh, you want the phone number so you can call and tell him the phone might be tapped?" she said.

"Umm, okay." He looked up, his pencil poised to write it down. She said nothing, just gave him a cold, "gotcha" smile. With a faint blush of embarrassment that showed on his neck and ears, he put the notebook away. "Is this your only key?" He snapped.

"No, it's my spare. My lock is probably pretty easy to pick, so I'm going to get my landlord to install a deadbolt today."

She knew from experience that Mr. Ruffaus took two weeks to do any one day task, but she also knew that in her present mood she could convince him of his liability should anyone break into her apartment and cause her harm. *As if I haven't been harmed already!*

Mr. Ruffaus was used to dealing with poor, sweet Patrice, girl reporter, always a week late with the rent, and she's so sorry, but she has to give him a post-dated check until payday, again.

Not anymore he wasn't dealing with "poor Patrice!" she told herself. *From now on, Mr. Ruffaus was dealing with Xena, the Warrior Princess.*

Luis seemed to sense the change in Patrice, but he wasn't about to apologize for his high-handed attitude and accusations. Not yet, anyway. He directed his attention to Rick. "I'll be busy this afternoon, looks like, but I'll be back to see you this evening."

"Don't forget to walk Pirate!" Rick called as Luis strode from the room. Patrice thought she saw a few shreds of dignity dragging from the heels of his expensive boots.

"What the hell is going on?" Rick said to Patrice.

She closed the door to the hall and sat down in Luis's chair. She wished she could put two hands behind her head, prop her cheap boot on her cheap jeans, and lean the chair back on two legs, but her broken arm made that impossible. "So much to tell, so little time," she said. *Where should I start?*

"Remember on the way to Santa Fe Friday, I told you I thought a prowler came to the door of Rose's office during her funeral?" she said. "And her poodle went off like a Doberman on steroids? Well, Pirate did the same for me yesterday while you were out climbing."

Rick raised his eyebrows. "Go on. I'm not going anywhere."

She took a deep breath and exhaled slowly, blowing out her cheeks. "I didn't tell you yet, but while you were in the recovery room last night, and I went home to get Pirate, I played the messages on my answering machine. I had a nasty shock..." She stopped suddenly. Something was nagging at the back of her mind. Something about the messages. Mel called, said he was taking Allison to the airport. And Larry Dreyfus called. Why? What business could he possibly have with her?

"You had a nasty shock," Rick prompted. "What happened?"

She held up her hand as if she were getting messages from a spaceship and didn't want him to drown them out. She formed a picture in her mind of sitting at Larry Dreyfus's herpetarium.

She had felt sick at her stomach and wanted to leave, but she'd asked him something. *Now I remember! I asked to see his uncle's personal effects.*

"When we went to Larry Dreyfus's house, and he brought out the box of his uncle's things, what was in it?"

The furrows in Rick's brow mirrored hers. "An envelope with cards and photos. A denture cup. A picture of Dreyfus in a cheap frame."

Patrice closed her eyes and concentrated, seeing the old man's pajamas and then the bottom of the cardboard box. Holding up her hand again for silence, or maybe it served as an antennae, she scrolled the picture back in her mind to where Larry Dreyfus brought the box out of the kitchen and set it in front of her. Before he lifted out the envelope and toiletry items, he set the green banker's lamp on the coffee table.

"The lamp!" she said aloud. "He had the lamp from Doyle Silver's bedside table." She opened her eyes to find Rick staring at her, a worried expression on his face. She smiled. "Want me to read your palm, mister?"

"Thanks, no. I just had it done in the operating room. They said I have a short life line."

"They said the same about mine, but I have a plan." She bit her lip, gnawing by habit at the chapped spot.

"Tell me what's going on. That's an order. I am still your boss."

She looked at him and gave him a wide smile. "Well, boss, having cheated death on the side of a cliff in a blizzard, I don't salute quite as readily as I used to. My job at the paper is just a job. One of many jobs available. That was something Rose kept telling me, but I didn't believe her."

"Funny, but I have had the same epiphany, and on the same cliff side." He wriggled around, trying to scratch an itch on his backside. "Come here, please. I've got a killer itch between my shoulder blades." He turned his torso as much as he could without jarring his broken leg.

She scratched his back, noticing as she did that she'd chewed all her fingernails down to the quick. "How does your leg feel?"

"Do you want the macho answer, or the truth?"

"Ummm, never mind. I think I can guess."

"That feels great. Don't stop." She stopped and he looked up. "I mean, please don't stop." She continued scratching, gradually changing her touch to a one-handed massage.

"Oh, baby, baby," he said, and she stopped again. "I didn't mean that literally!" he said. "I just mean, oh, that feels good." She continued the massage.

"Now," he went on, "I would like to know what the nasty shock was on your answering machine, and I'm dying to know what's going on between you and my brother. I thought the two of you were going to pull out light-sabers and fight a duel right over my hospital bed." He held up one hand to forestall any clash with her. "And I'm asking not as your boss, but as your friend and ardent admirer."

She smiled and massaged him harder. "How ardent?"

"Ow! Let's discuss that later. What was on your answering machine?"

She gave his back a parting scratch and sat down in the chair. "Okay. There was a message from Mel, and one from Larry Dreyfus. And the third message was Rose's voice."

"What? How the...? Go on." He waited. "I mean, please go on."

Chapter 16

"You were right," Luis said casually to Patrice when he returned to the hospital at three o'clock. "I found the receiver and tape recorder in a maintenance closet on the first floor. I bagged it and took it to Capt. Bell."

Met by stony silence and an unwavering stare, he cleared his throat and crossed his hands behind his butt like a soldier at parade rest. "I owe you an apology." He cleared his throat in a "well, so much for that little task" tone, and asked Rick how he felt.

"Didn't I just hear you say you owed Patrice an apology?" Rick prompted. "I agree."

Luis looked distinctly uncomfortable. "Patrice, I'm sorry I was so abrupt in my questioning this morning. Sometimes in law enforcement we don't have time for the social niceties."

"Social niceties!" she exploded. "You led the police to think I had faked the message on my answering machine. And all this time I thought they were dime store cowboys who could learn something from real cops like the FBI. Well, you can take the FBI and shove it!"

"Well, I...I mean," Luis sputtered, looking to Rick for support.

"Don't look at me, bro. You're the 'agent in charge' here. I'm just a fallen hero."

Luis held up his hands as if to calm down a hysterical

woman, which made Patrice even more angry. Luckily for Luis, who didn't have a clue what to say next, except, "I *said* I was sorry," which he had a pretty good idea would not help, Danny walked in.

"You must be Luis Romero," Danny said, extending his hand to shake. "I've heard so much about you." He smiled at Patrice as he said it. "I'm Danny Carter, photographer for the *Guardian* for three more days—that's seventy-two hours, but who's counting?"

"Three days?" Rick barked. "You're supposed to work through Friday."

"Ain't life a bitch? Hey, I gotta pack and start driving."

"Is my whole staff in mutiny, or what?" Rick asked, to no one in particular.

"It's post-traumatic stress syndrome. We've all got it," Patrice said, taking the newspaper from Danny's outstretched hand. He gave one to Rick, too.

"All but me," Rick said. "I've got current-traumatic stress syndrome."

"When are you going home?" Danny asked, pulling out a felt-tipped pen to sign Rick's cast.

"Tomorrow. In the morning I hope, in the afternoon, I expect. But I want to know what's going on. What about the bugs, Luis? Have you been to Mel Hulle's house yet?"

"No, I'm on my way right now. I just stopped to tell you about the receiver I found at Patrice's apartment building, and to apologize." He turned to Patrice. "Look, I'm not very good at apologies, but I'm sincerely sorry." He held out his hand. After a moment's hesitation, she shook it.

"Will you come with me over to Mr. Hulle's house?" Luis added. "I would appreciate hearing any ideas you have about who tried to kill my brother."

"Well...okay," she said at last, still hesitant to trust him. "But I think we have to make another stop, too. I remembered a little while ago that Larry Dreyfus left a message on my machine yesterday afternoon and said he'd call back. I can't see any reason he'd call me, but I'm going to call him back and quickly think of a reason to go to his house and look again at his uncle's belongings, the junk Larry brought up from the nursing home. In fact, I'll call him right now."

"Tell him you're buying a boa constrictor and you want to see Red again," Rick suggested with a wink.

She made a face to show her utter disgust of Dreyfus's snakes, pulled her pocket calendar out and got his number. Rick read the *Guardian* and Danny and Luis went to the window to look down at the canyon behind the hospital.

"Hello, Larry?" she said. "Patrice Kelsey, returning your call. What can I do for you?"

"Oh, it's nothing, I mean it's probably not important," he stammered. "Uh, I just happened to remember who that was in the picture you showed me."

Patrice thought back. "The balding man with your uncle at the nursing home?" she asked.

"Yes, uh-huh, yes. He's a social worker, a guy who likes to listen to old people and, I don't know, handle insurance for them or something. His name is Erik something."

"Erik? But you don't know his last name? Does he work at Buena Vista?"

"No, no. He's a volunteer or something. I never talked to him myself. My uncle just mentioned him, that's all."

"Do you have any idea how I can reach him to ask him a couple questions?" she said.

"Uh, no. He was going to Mexico for a while is what I heard. I don't know when he'll come back."

"I see. That's disappointing, but, oh well. I sure appreciate you calling to tell me that. But say, while I have you on the line, I need to ask a favor. Is there any way I could stop by your place for five minutes to look at your uncle's things again?" she asked. Rick looked up from the paper and she shrugged her shoulders to show she hadn't gotten an answer yet.

"What for?"

"Um, those old pictures in the box? I was so sick the other night when Rick Romero and I went to your house, I hardly saw them. It would just take a minute." Like a salesman eager to close the deal before the customer can think of a reason to say No, she barged ahead. "I can be there in ten minutes. I won't stay but five minutes, ten minutes tops."

"Well, I guess..." he started.

"Good!" she interrupted. "I'll be right over. Um, Rick's brother will be with me. He's giving me a ride; I'm not supposed to drive yet." That much was true. But "not supposed to drive" was one thing; not driving was another.

I'm getting pretty good at situational honesty, she thought as she hung up the phone and winked at Rick.

*****

While Patrice opened Doyle Silver's denture holder, examined each item in his toilet kit, and took the tube of hemorrhoid ointment out of the box, Luis examined the framed photo and studied the green banker's lamp. He set it down gently on the coffee table, near his knee.

"I heard from my brother about your Panama Red. Would you show him to me?"

"Sure, be glad to." He walked to a glass cage the size of a coffin against the wall between the living room and the kitchen. "Wake up, Red. You've got company." He lifted the lid and leaned in, both arms extended. "There, that's my big boy." While he sorted out the coils and made little clucking noises to his "big boy," Luis quickly lifted the lamp and palmed a black electronic device the size of a spool of thread from the hollow brass bottom. Slipping the device into his pocket, he strolled over to the snake cage. "Boy, Rick was right. He is a beauty!"

*****

"Why didn't you ask him anything about the bug?" Patrice asked as soon as they got in the Bronco. "And shouldn't you disable it or something before we talk?"

Luis took the bug out of his pocket and popped it open with his Swiss Army knife, removed the battery, and put the pieces in a Baggie he had in his vest pocket. Patrice thought of Danny's description of what real cops do, and smiled.

"Now, why didn't you ask Larry Dreyfus anything about the bug?" she said again.

"If he knew it was there, he would sure as hell have removed it before he let us look at it. And if he didn't know it was there, what could he tell us? However, he might blab our business to hostile ears, knowingly or unknowingly."

She thought that over. "Very clever, Dr. Watson. Now then, take a left here and a right on Diamond Drive. I'll tell you when to turn right again."

"This kind of crystal controlled device has a pretty decent battery," he said, "enough to transmit voices in a room about fifty yards, even through glass. It transmits on narrow band FM and is picked up by a parabolic microphone. While you and Rose talked to Doyle Silver, someone was nearby with the microphone and tape recorder."

"Take a right here," she said. "His house is on the right. No, not yet, keep going."

"Tell me what you remember of the layout of the nursing home, if you would," Luis said.

"It's in a very dark part of town, only a couple lights in the parking lot and one streetlight where the driveway abuts the road," she said. "Here's Mel's house, where the Taurus is parked."

Rick pulled into the driveway and turned off the engine. "Go on about the nursing home."

"Well, there is a parking lot in front, which was very muddy that night. The office is near the door, and the rooms are in an 'H' off that main hall. Doyle Silver's room was in the far corridor..."

"So it was by an outside wall?"

"Oh, yes. He had a window to what must have been the

very back of the facility. Darker than the inside of a cow."

Luis nodded. "How convenient. Well, let's go see Mel."

*****

Finding the tap in Rose's downstairs phone, the one in her office, was as easy as locating Patrice's had been. Mel and Patrice described the incident of a prowler during the funeral, and Luis searched the patio area thoroughly, but couldn't find a recorder.

"He's had plenty of time to retrieve it by now," he said, "but I'll ask Capt. Bell to send some officers over to do a better search. There are other places he could have put a recorder, but he would have to find someplace with easy access to change tapes and batteries."

"How long could it run?" Patrice asked.

"Oh, it's voice activated, so it only operates when the phone is in use. With slow speed on the tape, probably two hours of conversation. But there are a lot of models, a lot of variables. We'll figure it all out, no question of that."

"We?"

"I mean the Bureau. The local P.D. is eager to have Bureau expertise on these bugs and taps."

While the three of them searched Rose's office, Patrice took a good look at her Rolodex. "Aha! Here it is, Sheldon Libinowitz. Palo Alto, California."

"And he is...?" Luis asked.

Patrice gave him a quick rundown on the FBI Freedom of Information packet and how an internal memo was attached to the cover letter, stating that the packet was also going to Sheldon Libinowitz and Prof. Norman Taggert. She checked the Rolodex again for Norman and Taggert, but found nothing.

*****

Luis dropped her at her car in the hospital parking lot before he drove to the police station. "Here's your apartment key back," he said, "and a spare key to Rick's. That doofus admitted he only locks it about half the time. From now on, it's locked all the time, whether any of us are there or gone." His tone left no room for argument.

Besides, Patrice thought ruefully, the standard Los Alamos comeback, "Oh crime is so low here, we don't even think about locking our doors," was pretty thin soup in light of Rose's grave, the cast on her arm, and the cast on Rick's leg. Not to mention two prowlers--two she'd heard of--in a week.

She needed to make a half dozen phone calls, and she just couldn't bring herself to use her phone, not so soon after the discovery of the tap. How many calls had "he, she or they" listened to? The thought made her shiver with disgust. Who had she talked to? What had she said?

Before she drove to Rick's house to use his phone and rest, she drove to the management office that oversaw her apartment building and three others. Mincing no words, and making liberal use of the words "legally liable" and "potential lawsuit," she convinced Mr. Ruffaus that, yes, he could pick up the phone, dial the number for Los Alamos Lock and Key, a number he had on his desk calendar, and that, yes, he could pay John McHale extra to come right away and install a deadbolt.

"Thank you." She was about to turn on her heel when Mr. Ruffaus asked if her mother and father were still in town.

"My mother and...what did you say?"

"Your mother and father. I didn't meet your mother, I just saw her from a distance, very nice looking lady, but the first day after your car wreck your father came to get something for you, in your apartment, and he didn't have your key. I think he said it was pajamas and a robe you needed. So I let him in."

"What did he look like?"

"Huh?"

"This man who said he was my father, what did he look like?" she said coldly.

Sweat broke out on chubby Mr. Ruffaus's forehead. "Uh, let me see, kind of tall, like you, fair skin, kind of pale, with a receding hairline. Light brown hair around the sides, you know?"

He gestured to show hair on the sides and back of his head.

"May I use your phone?" she said, freezing him with a look. He nodded his head vigorously, yes, and slid it across the desk toward her. She dialed the hospital. "Room two twenty-four, please." She listened to a series of clicks, then one ring.

"Rick Romero."

"Rick, this is Patrice. I am in the office of Mr. Ruffaus," she held the phone away from her mouth and spoke to the now heavily perspiring man, "What is your first name?"

"Jules," he croaked, cleared his throat, and repeated it.

"I am in the office of Jules Ruffaus, who manages my apartment, and I have discovered, to my shock and dismay, that he let some stranger into my apartment while I was in the hospital. Which means that's probably when the tap was put on my phone, and which also means the man has a key to my apartment."

Jules Ruffaus was quick to say, "No, he brought it back, I got it back."

Patrice gave him a withering look. "I'm going over to your house to make some calls. I'll call you from there." She handed the receiver back to Ruffaus and left.

Even with a deadbolt she wasn't sure she could ever sleep in that apartment again. Maybe with a deadbolt, and Pirate the killer watchdog, and a gun. But she had to go back sooner or later. Her wardrobe, such as it was, was all there.

She decided to put off a visit to her violated home until evening. Maybe Danny could go with her, or Luis.

The whole stinking situation made it even more imperative that they figure out who killed Rose. And to figure that out, they had to discover why. So far, Patrice hadn't a ghost of a guess on that enigma.

*****

She slept an hour in a recliner chair and awoke in the early evening darkness. She turned on lights around the silent house and sat down again by the phone. The Monday list in her pocket calendar said:

Craig Smith at Pub. Aff. Re: Stefan Ellsberg & Mayor Kozar

Axel Pruitt at Lab Archives Re: Frost, Libinowitz & Taggert

Isobel Ellsberg Re: meeting her father and finding Stefan

In the margin she'd written the phone number for Sheldon Libinowitz that she'd found on Rose's Rolodex.

She was lucky on the two calls to the Laboratory. Both times she got a human instead of voice mail, something of a record. Craig in Public Affairs said that he wasn't able to firm anything up for her with either Stefan Ellsberg or Mayor Kozar. As best Patrice could tell, Craig still didn't know Stefan had arrived more than six hours earlier. What was the prodigal son up to? she wondered.

Pirate had been scratching at the back door ever since Patrice came in the front. She let her in, commiserating with her about the cold and how heartless and undeserving of her devotion humans were. Pirate curled up at her feet while she continued making phone calls. She lay close, knowing, as all dogs do, that she might get her belly scratched if she placed herself strategically and looked cute. It worked, as usual.

Axel Pruitt at the Laboratory archives had nothing to add to the little he knew of Douglas Frost, and he'd never heard of Sheldon Libinowitz, but the name Norman Taggert was a hit.

"Yes, he called me, oh, sometime before the first of November," Axel said. "He's a professor of history at Berkeley. Not a real mellow fellow, pretty much 'I need information and I expect you to drop everything and get it' kind of guy. Naturally, I blew him off."

"Was he asking about Douglas Frost, too?"

"No, he was asking about Carl Ellsberg and something else. Now, what was it?" He thought a few seconds, then snapped his fingers. "I know, Arzamas-16."

"Did he say why he was interested in either Ellsberg or

Arzamas-16?"

"Well, he didn't say so on the phone, but when he came in to the office..."

"He came here? To Los Alamos?"

"Yes, I remember it was the day before Thanksgiving, because I was trying to get away early. So naturally it's the busiest day of the year, you know?"

"Boy, do I! In order to get Thanksgiving off, we have to put out the Wednesday paper by one p.m. and then get a Thursday paper out by midnight."

"I hear you. Anyway, he came in and wanted to see what I had, and looked around, but I didn't find much. He was annoyed and left. Okay by me. You know the saying, don't go away mad, just go away. That's the way I felt about it. Now, are you going to tell me anything about what you're working on?"

"I'm trying to find out why Sheldon Libinowitz and Norman Taggert got the same FBI Freedom of Information material that Rose received the day she died," Patrice said, rubbing her forehead. "That car wreck was no accident, Axel, and I intend to prove it. I'll talk to you tomorrow. Or more likely the next day. Tomorrow I have to pretend I'm Rick and put the paper out. What a nightmare that will be."

"How is Rick?"

"Well, he's got a broken leg. They operated on it and put two pins in. He's in the hospital now, but he hopes to get out tomorrow." She almost added, "That was no accident either," but remembered in time that Lt. Pauling had warned her to keep it quiet.

Isobel was vague about when her father could see Patrice, but she repeated that some Russian politician was coming to meet him Wednesday morning. "I'll call you early tomorrow afternoon," Patrice said, knowing she would be lucky to survive the morning at the *Guardian*, much less have time for calling Isobel until the paper was on the street.

"I've got to go," Isobel said.

"Wait, one more question, please," Patrice said. "Have you heard any more about when Stefan will arrive?"

Isobel was clearly annoyed. "I told you he's coming Wednesday afternoon."

Patrice sputtered, "Sorry, thanks, 'bye," and hung up. Before she made any more calls, she took four ibuprofen with a glass of orange juice.

Next she phoned the Los Alamos Inn and the Hilltop House and asked for Stefan Ellsberg. He was not registered at either motel, nor was he listed at the Holiday Inn Express or the Bandelier Inn. She thought about that. *Where else could he be? He's not a bed and breakfast kind of guy.*

At Sheldon Libinowitz's number, in Palo Alto, a woman answered the phone. "History Department, Shirley speaking."

"Ah, Shirley, I hope you can help me. I'm looking for Sheldon Libinowitz. A friend gave me his number." Patrice heard a sharp intake of breath, then nothing. "Excuse me?"

"I'm sorry. This is hard when someone calls for Shel--for Dr. Libinowitz, but I know it will go on for quite some time until people find out."

Patrice had that sick feeling in the pit of her stomach again. The feeling she got when the old man in Doyle Silver's room said, "He passed."

"Is he ill? Or injured?" she asked, not even wanting to phrase the question.

"He died in a tragic accident. He was swimming in the pool here at Stanford and had an attack of exercise-induced asthma. They couldn't get to him in time."

Now it was Patrice's turn to be silent. "When did it happen?" she finally asked.

"Last Tuesday. The funeral was Friday. Do you want the address for memorial donations?"

To be polite, Patrice said yes, but she didn't write it down. "Thank you very much."

"What did you say your name is?" Shirley asked, probably

poised to write it in a message list.

"I didn't say. That's all right, just an interested friend."

She didn't feel like calling anybody else, not one more call, but a look at her watch told her she might catch Professor Taggert if she called right away. It was five-thirty and pitch dark in Los Alamos, but of course it was an hour earlier in California. She dialed information for the university, then university information for the history department, then Taggert's number. A student intern informed her that Dr. Taggert was not in his campus office today. "Could you give me his home number?" Patrice said. She was so tired by then it was hard to get the words out.

"I'm sorry, I'm not allowed to do that. But the professor calls in for messages every day when he's not here, so if you leave your name and number, I'll write it in his log."

Patrice sighed. "Actually, I'd better do that tomorrow. I would be hard to reach tonight. Thanks anyway."

She let Pirate out to pee and inspect the back yard for intruders, then let her back in and fed her. "You're such a good girl," she said, patting her thin flanks. "A good, brave girl. An excellent companion for Xena, the reporter princess."

She called Mr. Ruffaus and asked him to wait at his office to give her the keys to her new deadbolt, and he fell all over himself to "be available, help you out, your convenience," etc. She locked Rick's door behind her, drove to Ruffaus's office, and picked up her new keys. She called the *Guardian* office, hoping to catch Danny, but no one answered.

She thought of calling Rick's room to see if Luis was there, but the whole process of getting someone to walk up and down a few stairs with her just seemed too much trouble. Instead she drove the two blocks to her apartment and parked her Subaru as close as she could get to the building. Too tired to care whether she ate supper or not, wanting only to take a hot bath and go to bed, she trudged up the dark stairwell to the third floor. *The sooner I get my stuff, the sooner I'll be floating in fragrant bath water.* She shivered in the bitter cold and amended her fantasy. *The sooner I'll be floating in fragrant* ***hot*** *bath water.*

As she climbed, she made a mental list of clothes to pack. She had agreed with Rick and Luis that it made sense for her to stay at Rick's place for a few days. She could use the fold-out couch.

To carry her clothes, shoes, toiletries, and her extra coat, she'd probably have to make two or three trips, what with having only one usable arm. *Maybe I'll bring the coffeecake Mel gave me; Rick and Luis would like it.*

She'd better get enough stuff for two days; she could wash her clothes at Rick's place. Oh, and she had to remember this time to find her mother's phone number at the Westin Maui. If she didn't call her she'd have, uh, apo something, apo...apoplexy. That was the word she was searching for. Apoplexy.

If Patrice hadn't been so fatigued and so caught up in the list she was writing in her mind, she would have heard the steps behind her in the stairwell.

Chapter 17

She felt him before she heard him. Someone had come up beside her in the stairwell as if in such a hurry he had to pass her. In a hurry, yet silent. He bumped her left side--hard--throwing her against the concrete wall. In the same movement, he slapped his hand over her mouth. She hadn't had time to make a sound, and now she couldn't yell, couldn't breathe. His big hand pressed on her nostrils as well as her mouth, cutting off all air.

With all the strength in her body focused like a laser on her mouth, she stretched her jaws as wide as she could and bit down hard on the leather glove against her. She must have bitten through, because he jerked just enough for her to get one breath before he smothered her again.

She grabbed a railing with her right hand and gained enough leverage to kick out at his legs. She was aiming for the back of his knees to get him off balance. If he fell, he would probably pull her down with him, but she'd get air to breathe and, just as important, a chance to scream.

She twisted her neck, trying to get a look at his face, but saw instead a black ski mask. Using her cast as a battering ram and pushing off the railing with her strong right arm, she shoved him toward the outside wall. At the same time her left boot hit his right knee with enough force to buckle it. Either movement alone would have been useless, and on flat ground even timing wouldn't be enough to break his grip, but gravity was her ally.

His hand came away from her mouth as he stumbled backward to regain his balance. At the same instant she screamed a powerful, piercing shriek that reverberated in the stairwell like a fire alarm. She hurled herself against him. Taking advantage of his imbalance, she managed to knock him down the stairs backwards. She fell, too, but at least she wasn't hitting concrete as he was. Again and again she screamed, twisting her head left then right to keep her mouth free of his powerful hands.

"What's going on?" a man's voice said from the next floor down. Patrice could tell he was in the stairwell. Before she could yell again, her attacker had clamped his hand over her face and again cut off all air. This time she felt herself losing consciousness. She knew she was smothering, dying. She thought of Rick for a split second, but it was too late to tell him anything. Too late to tell anybody anything.

Just when she thought she'd drift away peacefully, the bastard whacked her head like a melon against the edge of a concrete stair. Everything went red, then black and silent.

*****

She heard voices, and tried to open her eyes, but they were stuck. Must be glued shut. Pain shot through her head like high voltage arcing from ear to ear. This must be what a baseball feels like, she thought. Going a hundred miles an hour to a soft home in the catcher's mitt, no worries, then THWACK, some guy with a weapon hits it a hundred miles an hour in the other direction.

"Patrice." She thought she heard Rick's voice. She tried again to open her eyes. She couldn't swallow. Her throat hurt like the worst strep throat in the world.

I must be alive, she thought. Nobody dead could hurt this much.

"Patrice." This time she opened her eyes the width of a sharp knife and made out a shape, a head silhouetted against a brilliant, blinding light. Interrogation, she thought, torture. She was pretty sure she'd seen this movie before. Or was it real?

I will tell you anything you want to know, she thought, but she couldn't make a sound. Her eyes were glued shut, her lips were glued shut, and her throat was on fire. She could move her eyes beneath the lids, but the slightest movement set off the blue arcs of electricity from ear to ear. She wondered if Rick was there, and if he could see the blue arcs outside her body, or if all that was inside.

"Patrice, you're in the hospital," the voice said. It wasn't Rick's voice. That made her sad. She tried again to open her eyes. This time one opened enough that she got a good look at the face in front of her.

She recognized him, or rather, she knew she knew him, but from where? No name came with the face. She felt a horrible throbbing in her arm, her left arm, but she couldn't move it. It was tied down or something.

They must have strapped me down for the torture. I don't like this movie. I want to go home. I want a drink of water.

"Patrice, it's me, Jules Ruffaus," the man said. "You're in the hospital."

This time her eyes shot open, wide with disbelief. Why was Mr. Ruffaus here? She had a shadow of a memory of hearing his voice. Was that in the stairwell? Why was she in the stairwell? Or was that in the movie? She let her eyes fall shut again.

"Somebody attacked you outside your apartment," he said. "I was on my way to make sure your new keys worked. I heard you scream."

That part she remembered. Ah, that scream had been a wonderful sound. She had taken a breath, and screamed her lungs out. Just like she'd screamed in the snowstorm. *Why did I scream in a snowstorm? This is all very confusing. Why have they tied me down if Mr. Ruffaus is here? He wouldn't let them tie me down.*

"The man in a ski mask got away. I called an ambulance." Flashing lights. She remembered seeing red, then black. Everything was black. Then it was red again, then black.

The man in the ski mask--is that what Mr. Ruffaus said?

I hate that man in the ski mask! He hurt me.

"Patrice." This time the voice was farther away. It sounded like Rick. *Wasn't he in the snowstorm dream, too? He wouldn't let them tie me down like Mr. Ruffaus did. When I wake up I'm going to tell Rick I love him.*

"Patrice, I'm over here. No, don't try to turn your head. They have your neck immobilized. I got Luis to bring me down to the emergency room in a wheelchair."

Now, that was a new puzzle. Who was Luis? And why was Rick in a wheelchair? He was in the snowstorm dream. She was sure of it. She remembered the ambulance, and Rick rode with her. No, that was Mr. Ruffaus. Flashing lights, red lights. Blue arcs of high voltage in her head. And Rick holding her hand.

"Luis is in the hall, talking to the police. They want to talk to you when you can remember what happened," Rick said.

How can I remember what happened when I can't even remember who Luis is? I was in a snowstorm, that's all I remember. And someone was driving. That's all I can remember. I want to sleep now. Leave me alone. I have a headache. I have a bad headache. And I'm thirsty. Go away.

*****

The night passed, but time was not linear to Patrice. It seemed people paraded in and out of her room, hour after hour, loud as a marching band. She kept her eyes shut, but sometimes she was awake, really awake, then she'd just drift and be gone again. She heard someone say, "Yes, she's got a pretty bad concussion. She'll be all right, but she has to stay here at least today." Another time she heard someone say, "When can she talk to us?" but she didn't hear the answer. She didn't want to talk to anyone. *Go away. Just go away.*

*****

"Lift her on three," a woman said. Patrice wanted to say no, for them to leave her alone, but she heard the woman again. "One, two, three."

Panic overtook her as she felt her body lift and drop again, this time on a frigid slab.

"No, no!" she managed to moan aloud. She wanted to shout that she was not dead, but she couldn't form the words. "No, don't" was all she could say, and it was garbled.

"It's all right, honey," the woman said, her mouth inches from Patrice's ear. She felt the woman's hands on her shoulders, jiggling her from side to side, jarring her head. She felt her body move, a sliding motion, head first.

She was terrified. She clutched at the woman and grabbed cloth in her fist. "Don't!" she cried.

"It's all right now, honey," the woman said gently. "Hold real still, there's nothing to be afraid of. We're just going to take some pictures of your head. You got a bad bump. It's going to be all right."

"My head hurts," Patrice said. Her voice echoed back to her, like she was in a tunnel. She forced her eyes open and saw a curved roof over her face, like a bandshell.

"You're going to hear some clicks, now," a man said from far away. "Hold very still."

The table vibrated and the tunnel hummed. She tried to count the clicks but there were too many. She slept again.

*****

When she was undeniably, unavoidably awake, it was full daylight. She was in a bed beside a window. She looked out at softly falling snow. When did that start? How long have I been here? Then she remembered, it was snowing on their way home. Rose was driving, and they could hardly see the road. Then something happened. They must have been in an accident, because she was in a hospital. "Ohhh!" she moaned when she moved her eyes too quickly toward the voice that said her name.

"Patrice. How do you feel?"

The man looked like Rick, but it wasn't Rick. She stared at him, confused. "What day is it?" she managed to say. Her lips were chapped and cracked; she tasted blood. Her throat felt like she'd swallowed scouring powder. "I'm thirsty."

"You can have some chipped ice," he said, "but they don't want you to drink yet." Gently, he placed shavings of ice on her lips. She sucked them, grateful for the moisture in her parched throat.

"More. More ice."

"Here's a little more. The nurse said not to overdo it."

He wore a sweatshirt from Stanford. She didn't know anybody at Stanford. But she had phoned Stanford, she remembered that. Why would she call Stanford if she didn't know anyone? When the last molecule of water had been wrung from the ice, she said, "Who are you?"

"I'm Luis Romero, Rick's brother. I'm a special agent with the FBI."

Rose got something from the FBI. Why didn't Rose show it to me? "Where is Rick?"

"He's here in the hospital, in his room."

"Was he hurt in the accident? Was Rose hurt?"

The man named Luis looked very sad. *Maybe Rick was hurt real bad. That's why they won't let me see him. Poor Rick. I love him. I want to tell him I love him.*

I don't want to talk any more. Go away. I have a headache.

*****

When she awoke again, the snow had stopped and the sun was out. She remembered who Luis was, that he had come from Washington when Rick was hurt. Rick was climbing, looking for something. For a green purse. Rose's purse? *This doesn't make sense.* Rick wouldn't care about a purse. But he was hurt, she was sure of that. He had a broken leg.

Gradually she surveyed the room and looked down at her own body. She had a cast on her left arm and lots of people had written their names on it. She was glad to hear voices coming closer. Someone had to tell her what happened. Where was Rose?

"Watch out!" a man said. "Don't bump my leg!"

Out of the corner of her eye she saw a leg, then a wheelchair enter the room. "Rick!" she said. "I'm so sorry you were hurt."

Luis maneuvered the chair next to her bed so Rick was facing her and could hold her hand. "Patrice, the police need you to remember something. Do you know who grabbed you in the stairwell of your apartment? Jules Ruffaus saw a man in a ski mask. Do you know who it was?"

There was something familiar about what he said, but she thought that was a movie. She hadn't ever been in a movie. "No," she said at last. "Where is Rose?"

He patted her hand. "Listen to me. You have a concussion, and you've forgotten some things. The doctor says your memory will come back, but we should help you remember so you get oriented. A week ago you went to Española with Rose, and you went off a cliff in the snowstorm. Rose died, Patrice. You went to the funeral."

Her face reddened as she started to cry. "Funeral? Oh God, I remember now." A keening noise rose from her throat.

"And I broke my leg trying to get Rose's purse out on the cliff. Because her tape recorder was in it. A tape recording of Doyle Silver at the nursing home. Do you remember that?" He scratched at his two-day beard.

She sighed deeply. "I remember. And he's dead, too."

"That's right! And you were going to your apartment last night to get some clothes, and you were going to stay at my house for a few days, with me and my brother. But someone attacked you in the stairwell."

She thought about it. "I don't know who it was. He had on a mask. I'm sorry." She started to cry again.

"Hush now, don't cry. It's okay. You're doing really well, and you might think of more about him later." He squeezed her hand and she squeezed back.

"I'm glad you came to see me," she said. Then she looked

puzzled. "What day is it?"

"Tuesday. Luis got here yesterday, and you picked him up at the airport." She looked at the ceiling while her brain processed the new information and opened up the dormant connections in her brain. Snatches of all sorts of things were coming to her, some things clear, and yet without context. She remembered calling Stanford University, and she remembered that Sheldon Libinowitz was dead. But who was he?

"The doctor said Luis can take both of us home today, but you have to stay in bed and rest. Will you be a good girl?"

"Pirate," she said. "Pirate's a good girl. Chased the prowler away." Sheldon Libinowitz got the stuff from the FBI, like Rose did. And someone else; there were three people. The name wouldn't come to her though. "I'll be a good girl. Pirate will sleep with me." She smiled. "Girl-time."

"Okay, you rest now until the doctor comes. I have to get back to my room."

"Good boy," she said. "You be a good boy."

Putting all his weight on his good leg, he lifted himself far enough out of the chair to put his face near hers. She turned her head, ready for the kiss she hoped was coming. He kissed her cheek and then her dry, chapped lips. "See you in a little while," he said. "Rest now."

*****

Three hours later Patrice rested her back and her head against a pile of pillows on the fold-out bed at Rick's house. He was comfortable in a recliner near by, with his leg elevated. Pirate was stretched out on the bed, her head in Patrice's lap.

"You look like a bum," Patrice said in her still-raspy voice. The trip from the hospital had tired her, but it was a body-ache kind of fatigue, not the dopey sleepiness she'd felt all the while she was in the hospital.

Rick scratched his beard. "I'm going to shave soon. Or maybe I should let it grow."

Patrice shook her head slightly from side to side as if she

had a glass of water balanced on her head. "Um-umm. Too scratchy."

She fumbled in her lap without looking down for the pocket calendar she'd extracted from her purse. She held it up in front of her face, concentrating on the notes in her handwriting, trying to get the events of the past eight days lined up in her mind. She saw the list she'd made the day before, to call Public Affairs at the Laboratory about Stefan Ellsberg and Mayor Kozar, to call the Lab archivist, to call Isobel Ellsberg. She remembered calling Stanford, and trying to call Professor Taggert at Berkeley.

"I was supposed to put out the paper today," she said. "Who's doing it?"

"Carolee Cruz, the assistant managing editor." Rick used the first and last names of everyone he mentioned, to help her get oriented. "Danny Carter is taking pictures of the Russians who are visiting." She looked puzzled, so he added, "the visitors from Arzamas-16."

"Oh, yes. I remember now. That file is missing at the Historical Archives."

Luis came into the room with a tray of tea in a teapot, sugar, cups, and coffeecake. "Where did this come from?" Patrice asked as she set a slice beside her teacup.

"From Mel Hulle's freezer," Luis said.

Luis leaned across her to pet Pirate. Impulsively, Patrice touched his face and stroked his cheek. "Nice and smooth," she said. "Feels good."

"That settles it. I'm shaving," Rick said. "Help me get into the bathroom."

"Pretty soon," Luis laughed. "Drink your tea." To Patrice he said, "Have you remembered yet about the phone taps?"

"Bugs?" she said.

"Phone taps are the devices we found in your phone and Mel Hulle's phones. Those were transmitters. We didn't find a receiver at Mel's house, but I found a receiver downstairs at your apartment building." She nodded, yes, that she remembered.

Luis went on. "Bugs are different from phone taps. A bug picks up all the noise in a room, and transmits it to a listening post, probably in a van or somewhere with a good receiver. It was a bug that was used in Doyle Silver's room. Do you remember where the bug was?"

She thought about it, scrunching her forehead, then smiled, "Yes! It was in the green lamp!"

Luis smiled wide to show how pleased he was at the return of her memory. "You're doing great. If you remember anything about the man who attacked you, tell me right away."

"Is Lt. Pauling coming over?" Rick said.

"No, I told him Patrice couldn't remember enough to help yet, and she needs to rest."

"I don't want to rest anymore," she said. "I want to work."

"What a woman!" Rick said. "If only all my staff were as devoted as you are."

"Bring me the phone, please. I can talk on the phone while I rest, can't I?"

Pirate stood and stretched, then gently stepped off the bed and headed for the back door where she waited patiently until Luis got the message and let her out. On his way back he brought Patrice the phone, stretching the cord as far as it would go from the kitchen. She had her finger on the number and started punching, and punching.

"What are you doing, calling Hong Kong?" Rick said.

"Berkeley," she said, "plus a long extension number. Hello, yes, is Professor Taggert in? I see. How may I reach him? Is he at home, do you know? All right, I see. Let me leave my number, then, and you can get it to him." She gave Rick's number and thanked the history department secretary for her help."

She sat with her thumb on the phone's off button. "I need to call my mother. But the number is in my apartment. And I still need clothes."

"I'll pick up some things," Luis said. "Where do I look for the phone number?"

"I want to go with you." She batted her eyes like a coquette. "Pleeease? I feel lots better."

"No. You're supposed to stay quiet. That's how I got you out of the hospital," Luis said firmly.

"I have an idea!" she said.

"I don't like the sound of this," Rick interjected.

"If you take me over to my apartment," she went on, "I could walk up the stairwell, and maybe my memory would improve."

Luis looked dubious; Rick was completely against it.

"How about I get up and walk around the house for a while, to prove I'm steady on my feet?"

"Are you admitting, then, that you've been a dizzy blond?" Rick said.

"I wouldn't put it that way," she huffed, "but yes, I've had a balance problem." She swung her legs to the floor and rocked herself to a standing position.

Luis put out his hand to steady her, but she waved him off. "I can do this." She tied the belt of her bathrobe tighter and walked slowly and steadily toward the bathroom. "Look, ma, no hands!"

She made a detour to the bedroom to snatch her torn and dirty clothes, the only clothes she had, off the bed, and went into the bathroom. When she emerged, she was dressed. She also wore a look of steely determination.

"It will only take a few minutes," she said, "and I might remember something critically important."

"All right," Luis said at last. "Just to get you some clothes." He patted his gun. "And my best friend goes with us."

*****

Her memory of the night before was not improved by their laborious ascent of the stairs. She kept her teeth clenched to hide the pain she felt in her broken arm, re-damaged ribs, and tail bone. In the apartment Luis got her suitcase down and she handed him jeans, a sweater, a sweatshirt, pajama bottoms, and a plastic bag of shampoo and other toiletries. "Will this fit?" she asked, holding out her hair dryer.

He took that suitcase and some food from her refrigerator down to the Bronco while she packed her lingerie and odds and ends, her checkbook and a few bills in a smaller suitcase. For good measure, she tossed in a new red dress she hadn't worn yet, and high heels that made her almost five feet eleven inches.

When he came back to the apartment to get her, she asked him to play the four messages on her answering machine. The memory of hearing Rose's voice had returned in nauseating detail, and she couldn't bring herself to press Play. While the machine rewound, she found her mother's number in Hawaii and slipped it into her pocket.

The first message on the new cassette, which the police had placed in her machine when they took the frightening one as evidence, was from Larry Dreyfus, calling again Monday as he'd said he would. She recalled the visit she and Luis had made to Larry's house but was confused about the time frame. They went inside, and Luis found the bug in the base of the lamp. Was that only yesterday? she puzzled.

The second message was from Sonia Greenway at the Historical Archives, asking Patrice to please call her back or stop by. That also came in Monday.

The third call was a hang up, just enough noise to activate the recorder, but nothing she or Luis could make out. And the fourth call was Mel Hulle, also asking Patrice to call back. "No rush," he'd added.

Patrice carried her gray skirt and crocheted vest over her arm while Luis carried the second suitcase down the stairs.

He opened the car door for her, but she hesitated. "Wait a minute," she said brightly. "I have another idea!"

Chapter 18

"In the immortal words of my brother, who knows you very well, 'I don't like the sound of this,'" Luis said.

He stood with one hand on the car door, and his sports coat fell away enough that Patrice could see a little of the harness that held his weapon. "Since we're only a few blocks from the *Guardian*, why don't we stop and see if there are any messages?" she said. "Today's paper will be off the presses soon and we can take a copy to Rick." She saw his face cloud up and sensed a big, angry "No!" coming, so she rushed ahead. "I feel so much better, Luis, honest. We'll just be there a few minutes."

He grumpily conceded that they were close to the newspaper office, and Rick had asked him to pick up his paycheck. "All right, for five minutes."

Patrice got into the Bronco and smiled as Luis walked around to the driver's side. He had sounded just like her mother used to when Patrice was a little girl. "You may have one candy bar and one comic book. No more!" Patrice had learned the Art of the Deal before she could read.

"Welcome home!" Marian said when Patrice and Luis walked in.

"Now there's a scary thought," Patrice said. "Have you met Rick's brother? FBI Special Agent Luis Romero, this is Marian Beal, receptionist in charge."

"So glad to meet you," Marian said. "How's Rick?"

"I got Rick and Patrice out of the hospital today. He's home resting. She's supposed to be home resting," he said.

"Oh, Patrice! I'm so glad--and surprised—to see you out," Marian said, her relief evident. "I thought you'd be in the hospital a week, the way Danny talked this morning."

Patrice didn't remember Danny coming to see her at the hospital, but there was probably a lot she didn't remember about her time there. "Well, they say it was a bad concussion, and I'll admit I was pretty goofy for a while."

"Pretty goofy?" Luis interjected. "Ha!"

Patrice pointedly ignored him and asked Marian about mail and messages. Behind them the newsroom looked like the floor of the New York Stock Exchange during a market crash. Half of Patrice wanted to wade in and mud-wrestle with the news but half of her had better sense. She couldn't turn her head fast without feeling slightly out of kilter. The doctor was right: she needed rest.

"You got a call about fifteen minutes ago from Craig Smith," Marian said, handing her a pink message slip. "I was going to give it to Carolee, but I didn't want to venture into the lion's den so close to deadline."

On cue, behind them, Carolee bellowed, "I need copy, people! I need copy to edit. The Send key is the one on the top row, left hand side."

Danny yelled, "Photos in five minutes, or you can have my first born child."

"No deal!" Carolee yelled back. "I raised five of my own. You can keep the little pisser."

"Ah, the sound of professionals, happy in their work," Patrice smiled at Luis.

"I hope none of these people has a gun permit." Turning to Marian, he said, "Before I forget, Rick asked me to pick up his paycheck."

Marian nodded. "Sure, I have it locked up. Wait here just a minute, please."

"Do I have one? Look in Petty Cash," Patrice called as Marian walked away. "Uh, you want some coffee? The break room is back there, and our coffee is good. That's Kent Bolt's idea of lavish employee incentive." She looked at the pink slip in her hand. "I need to return this call to Public Affairs."

"Coffee sounds good."

While Luis headed for the break room, Patrice called Craig Smith from an available phone in classified advertising. "Craig, hi, it's Patrice."

"Patrice! I thought you were killed or something. Where are you?"

"At the *Guardian*. I'm only here for five minutes, though. I got a limited dispensation from Rick's brother, the FBI agent who accompanied me. He has a gun, which he's threatening to use on me if I try to stay longer. So, what have you got?"

"Two things, Mayor Kozar is staying at the Hilltop House with the other Russians. They arrived today, on schedule. I don't have his room number. And Stefan Ellsberg arrived today, too--I have a phone number for him. It's not the same as his father's number, so I don't know where he's staying. Anyway, whoever is going to interview him can track him down at this number."

Patrice copied it down. "Thanks, Craig. I'll talk to you soon. Oh, what time is Stefan Ellsberg's colloquium?"

"Thursday, ten a.m. at the Physics Building Auditorium. It's not classified, so somebody from the paper should have no trouble getting in. Who's going to cover it, do you know?"

Me! I'm going to cover it, she thought, but said, "That's up to the assistant managing editor, Carolee Cruz. She's in charge for the time being."

She thanked Craig again and headed for her desk where she kept a copy of the specialized phone directory. To her dismay, Goldilocks was sitting in her chair--again.

"Good morning, Tiffany. Could I lean over you here and get something?"

"Sure. How are you Patrice? Kent said some mugger beat

you black and blue last night."

"Yeah, it was awful. I'm getting better, though." She pulled the directory off the shelf above her computer monitor and sat down in the waiting area near Marian's desk.

She looked at the number Craig had given her for Stefan Ellsberg and looked it up in the reverse directory. For each phone number, there was an address listed. She scanned the page with her finger and stopped at the right number, then moved her finger across to the address. Fifteen forty nine Santa Barbara. Son of a gun! Stefan Ellsberg was staying at Senator Aragon's mansion, a.k.a. The Big House.

Well, that wasn't so remarkable, really, she conceded. He was pals with the president, and about to get a presidential appointment. Stefan Ellsberg and Senator Aragon probably knew each other well in Washington, so she invited him to be her houseguest. As far as she knew, Aragon wasn't even in town.

She leaned across Tiffany again to put the directory back. On a whim she said, "I've been wondering, who does your hair? It's always so pretty." She hated to say that, but it was an undeniable fact.

"Ruby Maes, over by the Amberly Restaurant." Tiffany barely glanced at Patrice, her eyes on the sheaf of club notes she'd attached to the paper holder by the computer screen. Her fingers were flying over the keyboard.

Dadburn it, Patrice thought ruefully. She even types faster than I do. "Uh, do you think she'd work me in if you asked?"

Tiffany stopped and looked around at Patrice, staring unabashedly at her hair. *I've seen that look before*, Patrice admitted to herself, with chagrin. *From my mother*.

"I'll call her," Tiffany said at last. "Anytime this afternoon?"

Patrice considered briefly what Luis would say. Oh well, in for a dime, in for a dollar. "I'm free now or anytime, yes."

Tiffany picked up the phone and Patrice stepped a polite distance away. She didn't want to hear Tiffany's description of her "hair emergency." *I have my pride. Not much, but some.*

"She can take you now." Tiffany smiled.

"I thank you and my mother thanks you," she said with a slight bow at the waist.

"What?"

"Nothing. I'll go right on over there. Thanks."

Luis was standing at Marian's desk, tucking an envelope into the vest pocket of his sport coat. "You were right, it is good coffee." He took a last swallow and tossed the cup in the wastebasket.

"Here's your check, Patrice," Marian said, then turned her attention to the ringing phone.

"Luis, I've got to get my hair fixed, and I managed to get an appointment right now, while I'm already out. I can't even wash it easily by myself thanks to this." She looked down at her broken arm."

"You shouldn't even be out of bed. I have half a mind to take you back to the hospital!"

"I will feel worlds better with clean hair. Please? It's just a few blocks from here, and it'll be the perfect therapy. Or," she added brightly, "you could help me wash it!"

"I guess another half hour wouldn't hurt," he said with a shrug.

She wisely did not correct him and say it would certainly take more than a half hour. Instead she smiled and waved a cheery good-bye to Marian.

*****

"While you get your hair fixed, I'm going to the supermarket to get groceries," Luis said as he turned onto Trinity Drive. "I'm fixing a special chicken dish tonight. I don't suppose my brother mentioned that I'm a great cook?"

"In fact, he did. He's avocado green with envy," she smiled.

The light near her apartment building turned red. She looked down the street and saw her Subaru in the lot. "You know, if we picked up my car, I could go straight back to Rick's place the minute I finish at the beauty salon."

He said nothing, but she noticed his eyebrows pulled together in a dark look.

"Of course, I would drive straight to Rick's, no detours."

To her amazement, he agreed, apparently thinking she'd be through with her hair appointment before he finished at the grocery store. She let him continue in that misapprehension.

They parted company in the parking lot of her apartment building. In her rearview mirror, she saw Luis watch until she was out of sight.

*****

Ruby's Beauty Salon, owned by Ruby Maes, was about a football field length from the Ellsbergs' "real" front door, the one they didn't use. The proximity was scarcely noticeable, though, because most of Bathtub Row was set off by a fence from the commercial area so close by.

If Patrice had walked in a minute sooner, she would have bumped right into Isobel Ellsberg coming out. Instead, she sat in her car and watched Isobel settle into her Lexus and light a cigarette. Just seeing it made Patrice want to roll down her window and inhale fresh air. She wondered why Isobel wouldn't just walk over from her house, but, of course, she probably had other errands. The liquor store for one, she mused.

Well, if Tiffany and Isobel were representative of Ruby's work, she sighed, she was in the right place. Isobel looked terrific with her new dye job and a trim.

When Patrice left an hour later, she knew she looked better than anyone around her would be able to remember. And she did feel better, just like she'd told Luis she would.

She caught sight of her reflection in the shop's window and laughed out loud. *Mom was right*, she conceded. *Again.*

Since it would not be a strict violation of her pact with Luis, she strolled over to Central Avenue. She'd told him she would drive straight home, and she would. When she got in the car, she would do exactly that. But she could walk around town, couldn't she?

The music system at CB Fox, one of two department stores in town, was playing "Silver Bells" when Patrice walked in the door. She admired the decorations, not having had the time or the inclination to shop yet. The fancy-schmancy chocolates in the front display case would be a good gift for Danny and Marian. She looked at scarves and purses and ties, and found a sweater that would look very good on Rick. She sighed heavily, calculating how much money she didn't have in her checkbook, and figuring she'd have to wait for the payday right before Christmas before she bought anything for her mom and William, and the others.

"Nice hair!" Dave Fox, owner of the store, called. He was ringing up a ski sweater in the men's department.

"Merry Christmas!" Mr. Benner, the previous owner, must be seventy-five, Patrice figured, but he still came in to work every day. "New hairdo?" he asked.

"Yes, thanks," she said with a wave at both of them.

She continued ambling through the store, checking out the sales rack in the women's clothing section. Then she walked back to her car in front of Ruby's Salon.

Some kinds of fatigue come on gradually, and some kinds hit a person like a bright idea. Patrice felt overwhelmingly tired, and her bright idea was to drive straight to Rick's house and get some rest. She kept an eye on the rearview mirror, though. To her relief, no one seemed to be following her.

*****

She returned to Rick's place before Luis did. She tip-toed in, relieved to see Rick asleep in the stretched-out recliner.

He stirred slightly, barely opening one eye. "Luis went to get some prescriptions filled."

"Pirate and I are going to take a nap," she said softly.

"She got a head start..."

Patrice waited a moment, smiling as she realized he had

gone back to sleep in mid-sentence. "Pirate, come here girl," she whispered.

The dog, like Rick, opened one eye and yawned. With a shake of her collar and a pause to scratch her own chin with a hind leg, she moved stiffly to Patrice's side and sniffed her kneecaps.

Patrice tossed her coat over the back of the couch, which was still opened up as a sofabed, and lay down as stiffly as Pirate had gotten up. "We're a pair, aren't we, girlfriend?" She patted the bed beside her and Pirate oozed onto it.

*****

When Patrice awoke, the room was in semi-darkness. She tilted her chin to see Rick. He was still asleep in the recliner. Outside the front window she saw the glow of sunset between the black mountains and the still-blue sky. She could hear Luis in the kitchen, muttering under his breath.

"...don't see how anybody can cook with these cheap pans," he said, then continued, "...need my own pans, and when was the last time you sharpened a knife?"

She smiled and scratched Pirate. She was pretty sure she knew what Rick would get for Christmas from Luis.

Quietly, she gathered up clean clothes and bath oil and took possession of one of the two bathrooms for a luxurious hour. She soaked, keeping her hair out of the water, and shaved her legs. They hadn't been visible since the day of Rose's death, when Patrice wore her gray skirt and crocheted vest, so she took her time shaving, drying, and applying lotion. If she didn't use lotion all winter, her skin was like the sands of the Kalahari.

She wriggled into sheer black pantyhose, no mean feat with one arm, and then tried something just as hard--getting a turtleneck sweater dress over her head and maneuvering her cast through the stretchy armhole. She had been saving the red dress--the store called the color "claret"--for a holiday party or parties, but dinner at Rick's was as close to a party as she was likely to get. And there was no one she'd rather dress up for than Rick, anyway.

She turned her back to the long mirror and tried to look over her shoulder. *Good grief, but this dress is short. Either I'm getting taller, or I didn't take a good look in the mirror at the store. This is what Rick calls a "Pretty Woman" dress,* she thought with a smile. *Oh, what the heck. Live, live, live.*

She got out the still-new makeup Rose had given her the previous Christmas and gave herself the works--foundation, blush, taupe eye shadow, and dark brown mascara. She even lined her lips with "Primrose" and filled in with "Antique Rose."

She set down the red high heels she'd had since college, the ones she called the ruby slippers, hoping she could still walk in them. It was possession of the shoes, after all, that nudged her to buy the dress, which was a perfect match. In the high heels, she was as tall as Rick and about an inch taller than Luis.

The sound of Rick and Luis laughing in the living room made her wish she had grown up with a brother or sister. She took one final look in the long mirror, fluffed her shoulder-length hair, and smiled nervously.

She emerged in the middle of their heated discussion of the failing Russian economy. Luis, in an apron, waved a spatula toward Rick to emphasize some point of contention. He froze in mid-wave when he saw her enter the room.

Both men stared at her without saying a word.

"Rick, you sly fox," Luis said at last. "You didn't tell me she had legs."

"You're making my artificial blush redundant," she said.

A heavenly aroma of garlic, basil and oregano greeted her. Pirate, she could see, was in dog heaven: two men who loved her and something meaty sizzling in the kitchen. She licked her chops, wagged her tail, and stretched her neck toward the kitchen. *It just doesn't get any better than this,* she seemed to be saying.

Maybe she has something there, Patrice thought as her own stomach growled.

Rick sat on the bed in the living room, his crutches propped against the arm of the sofa. She kissed him hello, wobbling a little on her heels. "How do you feel?"

"Like I've been rode hard and put up wet," he said. "Maybe we could save money on painkillers by buying a gross for the two of us."

Patrice sniffed the aroma wafting from the kitchen about as indelicately as Pirate did. "What's cooking?" she called to Luis.

"Chicken Marengo. Come see." He tossed her an apron that said, "I'd rather be climbing," which she recognized as Rick's. "Would you wash those fresh mushrooms and remove the stems?" He pointed with a cleaver. "They go in whole with the green olives for the last five minutes."

The counter and sink, buried with pans, lids, and two cutting boards, held enough knives to stage a coup d'etat. "Why do men always cook like Mom is cleaning up the kitchen?" she asked as she dug an olive out of the jar.

"Why don't more women cook like Mom?" Luis countered.

"Touché. Got me there." She popped the olive in her mouth.

She washed her hands, then shoved enough utensils aside to wash the mushrooms while Luis sautéed fresh garlic in butter. Next he slid cut-up chicken breasts from a Pyrex pie pan into the garlic and butter in the electric frypan and stirred them with a wooden spoon.

"Rick!" he called. "Where's your corkscrew?"

"I don't have one. I can only afford wine with screw-on lids."

"Lucky for us I have my versatile pocket knife." With a smile, he pulled a small corkscrew tool from the side of his knife and opened the Lancer's Vin Rosé. "This is the kind of emergency we prepare for at FBI school. The training is a bitch."

He carried the open bottle into the living room. "I almost

hate to ask, but what do you use for wine glasses? Peanut butter jars?"

Rick scowled and crossed his arms. "I happen to have wine glasses on the top shelf over the stove. Real crystal, I'll have you know."

Luis got down three glasses, washed them, and poured each of them a glass of wine. He added tomatoes to the chicken and garlic, tossed in half a cup of the wine, and turned the frypan down to simmer. "Let's go put our feet up." He turned a dining chair toward the living room and sat down, stretching his long legs in front of him.

Patrice picked up the *Guardian* from the coffee table and settled into the recliner. Although she tugged at the bottom of her dress, it wriggled up and left a lot of her shapely thigh exposed.

"Senator Aragon calls for Lab closure," she read aloud as she skimmed the article. "Ah, the slings and arrows of outrageous rhetoric." She lowered the paper to look at Rick and blushed to see he was staring unabashedly at her legs.

"Very nice," he sighed. "Great hair, great dress. No, make that 'sensational' dress."

"Thank you. Now, about Senator Aragon's tirade, as reported in the *Guardian*?"

"Yeah, poor Carolee. She called to tell me Kent was on her like a bad toupee to make sure she didn't leave out one word of Aragon's statement."

Luis stood and caught Patrice's eye. "I need to cook the noodles and finish the chicken. Would you see if you can find three matching plates? Preferably not paper!"

"Hey!" Rick called indignantly. "You're just saying that because I can't chase you out of here."

Patrice set the table and Rick pulled himself up on crutches to get to a chair. Luis brought in a serving platter with chicken, tomatoes, mushrooms and green olives nestled in wide egg noodles, and a tossed salad. Pirate sat by Luis's chair and gazed at him with her big brown eyes.

"Pirate!" Rick said sharply. "Go lie down!" She walked away from the table with her head lowered and curled into a ball on the living room rug. "You can spoil my girlfriend, but I'll be damned if I'll let you spoil my dog."

"Why do I not feel flattered?" Patrice dished noodles and chicken onto her plate as Luis held it.

"So, tell me what you do for fun in this tiny town." He took Rick's plate from him and dished up chicken for Rick, then for himself, then moved the large walnut salad bowl closer to Patrice.

She took some salad. "I don't know. What do people do for fun here, Rick?"

"I think the secret to happiness is low expectations." He took a bite of the chicken and favored Luis with an ecstatic look. "Delicious, as always. You're going to make some woman very happy, brother mine."

"I'm going to make lots of women happy by staying single," he said with a wicked grin.

"I know not being married to you would make me happier." Patrice batted her eyes and smiled sweetly.

Rick burst out laughing. Luis scowled and passed the wood bowl to Rick. "More salad anyone?"

Patrice speared an olive with her fork and examined it in mid-air. "All kidding aside, I can't remember when I've eaten anything so scrumptious. Thank you, Luis!"

The shared stories of great restaurants and memorable meals. Rick heaved a big sigh. "Gosh, I'd love to help with the dishes, bro, but you know what the doctor said." He poured the last of the wine into the three glasses. "He said I have to stay off my feet."

"Funny, that's the first time today you've quoted the doctor," Luis said.

"I'll help." Patrice stood and placed Rick's empty plate on top of hers, all the utensils on top of the stack.

"No, you won't," Luis said, firmly taking the plates from

her hands. "I'll do it later. I never go to sleep before midnight anyway."

"Well, if you're looking for something to do in Los Alamos after ten p.m., washing dishes is probably as good as it gets," Rick laughed.

Luis added his plate to the stack and carried them toward the kitchen. In the living room, Rick lowered himself gingerly into the recliner and Pirate put her head on his knee, contrite about having begged at the table, an absolute no-no.

"Can she have a t-r-e-a-t?" Patrice asked.

"Yeah. The Milk-Bones are on top of the refrigerator."

Patrice got a bone and Pirate sat up and shook hands for it. "Good girl!"

"I really like your hair." Rick smiled at Patrice and patted the dog on her flanks to show she was forgiven for her lapse in manners.

"I wondered if you'd notice."

"Just because I don't say much doesn't mean I'm not staring at you like a boa constrictor eyes a sluggish rodent."

"You say the sweetest things." She sat on the edge of the sofabed, trying without success to tug the hem of her dress down.

"Hard to believe I make my living with words, huh?"

"You're making a living?" Her eyes went wide with surprise.

He shrugged. "Loosely defined."

"Speaking of making a living, I've got to make a couple of phone calls." First she called Isobel Ellsberg.

"Well," Isobel answered reluctantly when Patrice asked for a few minutes with Carl Ellsberg, "I guess you can come by tomorrow morning. My father will be up and dressed as he's expecting an old colleague to stop in at ten."

"Thank you, Isobel. I'll be there at nine-thirty."

Next she looked up the Hilltop House in the phone book, dialed, and asked for Mr. Kozar.

The motel operator rang the room six or seven times and

came back on the line. "He's not in his room. Is he one of the Russians?"

"Yes, he is."

"Well, they're all in the cocktail lounge. I don't have a way to page him."

"That's okay, thanks very much." She hung the phone back up in the kitchen and frowned.

"What's up," Luis asked as he followed her into the living room.

"The Russians are all in the cocktail lounge, including Mayor Kozar whom I absolutely must interview." She considered her options. "Luis, I have an idea. Never mind the smart remarks, buster," she said to Rick, then turned back to Luis. "Why don't I show you the nightlife of Los Alamos?"

"That couldn't take more than fifteen minutes," Rick said.

"Are you sure you're up to it?" Luis asked. She nodded. His expression showed his reluctance to agree. At last he shrugged. "Well, all right. What red-blooded man would pass up an opportunity like this?"

"A red-blooded man who doesn't want to see his red blood all over the carpet," Rick said dryly.

"What, jealous, little brother?" Luis taunted. "Don't worry, I'll have her home and in bed before eleven."

"That's what worries me."

"Rick Romero!" Patrice said in mock horror. "Shame on you!"

*****

The Loft at the Hilltop House was livelier than Patrice expected. The work crew from the ski hill was there, celebrating the snow. And eight men in almost identical suits were nursing drinks, having pulled three small tables together.

"It looks like six pallbearers and two spares," Patrice said. The waitress set two napkins on the table. "I'll have a glass of chablis."

"Seven and seven." As the waitress walked away, Luis leaned closer to Patrice. "There are your Russians, as obvious to me as Indians in loin cloths."

"Probably drinking all the vodka in the place, huh?"

"No, no. In America they want only good American whiskey. They're probably giving a shot in the arm to the Tennessee economy right now."

The waitress returned with their drinks. "Do you want to run a tab?"

"No, thanks." Luis pulled out his wallet.

Patrice noticed that the eight men, besides sharing similar taste in clothes, all had bushy eyebrows, and six of them were smoking.

"Bunch of Russians," the waitress said, noticing Patrice's interest. "The one on the far end is the mayor of some place in Russia." Luis waved off his change. "Thank you."

"My friend in Public Affairs says Kozar is fluent in English." She lifted a small notebook out of her purse. "If he doesn't want to talk now at least I can set up an appointment for tomorrow." She sipped her wine and set it down. "I'll be back in a few minutes."

"Has anyone ever said you're a fun date?" Luis said. "No? Did you ever wonder why?"

She wasn't listening to him; her thoughts were on the questions she had for the mayor. "Nothing ventured, nothing gained. Here goes."

She walked over to the thin, sallow-faced man the waitress had pointed out. His suit was a little shabby, but his shirt and tie were obviously new and probably American. He was smoking a Marlboro, and Luis was right: he was drinking something amber-colored.

"Excuse me, please." To her embarrassment they all stood up. "No, please sit down. I didn't mean to disturb you." She turned to the man at the end of the table. "Are you Mr. Kozar?"

"Yes, I'm Vladimir Kozar."

"Oh, good." She held out her hand. "I’m Patrice Kelsey." He shook her hand and then the others all shook her hand. It was like greeting a genial octopus.

"Mr. Kozar, I'm a newspaper reporter, and I'm going to Arzamas-16 in April to write some articles about your city. I'm very happy to meet you here."

"Please, sit down," he said. The man on her right brought another chair and the group moved all their chairs a little to fit her in.

The waitress came to the conjoined tables with a full tray. "Jack Daniels," she said as she placed a drink in front of the mayor, and went down the line dispensing Vat 69, Chivas Regal and more J.D.

"You will join us in a drink, of course," Kozar said, leaving no room for demurral.

"Umm, yes, all right. A glass of chablis, please."

"You say you’re coming to Arzamas-16?" Kozar offered her a cigarette.

"No, thank you; I don’t smoke." She gave him a brief description of her planned trip to Russia, who the sponsor was and their expectations of her as a reporter. "But I’m eager to know your impressions of Los Alamos," she prompted, her pen poised above her notepad.

He exhaled smoke through both nostrils and nodded. "I have fallen love with your grocer--I think you call it a supermarket. Sadly, there is nothing like it in Russia..."

He compared the Sister Cities in several ways, then responded to her question about his professional background.

"A chemist. Yes, I am a chemist by professional training. I worked for a time in Leningrad," he interrupted himself with a laugh. "Leningrad is once again St. Petersburg, as you know." He went on with a few details of his education and his work in Arzamas-16. Kozar’s English was excellent, as the man in Public Affairs had told Patrice it was.

"Where did you learn to speak English so well?" she

asked.
He paused thoughtfully. "My parents were able to send me to a private school. I learned English as a young boy." He gestured toward her wine glass. "You will have some more wine, I hope?"

"Thank you, no. I really shouldn't; in fact, I have some wine at the other table. Before I go, though, I wonder when I'll see you and your fellow travelers again."

He tossed down the last of his whiskey and held up the empty highball glass to show the waitress he wanted another Jack Daniels. To Patrice he said, "I have some business to take care of in the morning, an appointment at ten o'clock with an old man who can't have visitors for very long. Then we are lunching with members of your County Council, but I might be able to visit with you late tomorrow afternoon. That is, if you have more questions...?"

"Yes, I'd like that very much. I'll call the Laboratory tomorrow and see if we can get together." She stood up and all eight men rushed to their feet. She shook hands with Kozar and the two men nearest him, gave a little wave to the others, and rejoined Luis.

She picked up her original glass of wine. "Did you ever, in your wildest dreams, think you'd be sitting in a cocktail lounge in Los Alamos, New Mexico, with a van-full of half-loaded Russians?"

"No." Luis held up his glass and clinked it against hers. "But then, I never dreamed we'd have an FBI liaison office in Moscow, either."

Chapter 19

Patrice had a full grid of activities planned for Wednesday, starting with a trip to Cristal Aragon's neighborhood, but she knew it wouldn't be easy to get away from Rick and Luis without a big long explanation. Dressed warmly in jeans and snow boots, she lifted Pirate's leash from a nail in the kitchen. While Rick and Luis were in the bathroom, trying to give Rick a shower with a plastic garbage bag tied around his cast, she whistled to Pirate and headed for her car. She'd left a scribbled note: Took Pirate for a walk.

"This is true," she said to Pirate as she unlocked her car door. "We're going for a walk. I just neglected to say where."

She parked five long blocks back from the end of North Mesa and snapped Pirate's leash to her collar. "Maybe later I can let you run loose, girl."

Pirate answered with an ear-flapping shake of her head and a pant that sounded like, "Yeah, yeah!"

The Dalmatian was a spotted stepsister to the greyhound and a distant cousin to the cheetah, built to fly at ground level. For the time being, though, Pirate followed Patrice's lead, heeling perfectly, knees high, royalty on parade.

"If you were a woman, you'd never go out without your hair done and your makeup on, would you?" She picked up her pace to something like a racewalk.

Pirate gave her a haughty look and increased her pace to a graceful canter.

"Oh, I see, you think I could learn something about keeping up appearances myself. You may be right, you and Tiffany both."

The chance she would see anything of her quarry, Stefan Ellsberg, was so slim as to be a vapor, but Patrice figured she had nothing to lose.

On two legs and four legs, they jogged to the end of the street where they paused to look across the valley toward Taos. The sky was a dazzling blue, making the snow she'd watched the day before from her hospital bed seem like part of a dismal movie, rated "R" for violence.

"Now that's a view to die for, isn't it, girl?" Patrice had difficulty catching her breath after the exercise in the cold air. The pounding motion had jarred her head, too, giving her a sharp headache at the base of her skull. Placing her hand on the back of her neck and standing stock-still, she added, "I didn't mean I want to die for it."

Pirate spotted a ground squirrel and tugged fiercely at the leash.

"No, girl, not here. You'd run after that squirrel and your last leap would be about four hundred feet, straight down. I don't think they teach 'gravity' at puppy school."

In deference to her sore neck, Patrice turned her whole body to better observe the house at the end of Santa Barbara Street. Three cars were parked on the driveway leading to the rock-top aerie: a silver Porsche Turbo Carrera, so new she believed she could smell the interior from where she stood, a baby blue Volvo 850 sedan, and, looking like a poor relative, a white U.S. Government van. The Porsche had a temporary tag in the back window; the Volvo had New Mexico plates.

She was in luck, which she noted was a wild aberration in her recent fortunes. Two men walked down the driveway from the house. Patrice recognized Stefan from the airport. He wore black running tights and a jade pullover with a hood. When she had seen him in a dark suit at the airport she thought his stocky physique looked a little heavy, but in tights she could see he was muscular like a weightlifter.

The man beside him was dressed in a navy blue suit; under the unbuttoned jacket Patrice could see the leather straps of a holster. He was taller than Ellsberg and thin, giving the duo a Mutt and Jeff appearance. Ellsberg pushed the hood off his head, and his thick black hair blew back from his face. She noticed, again, that he had the neck of a bull.

They seemed to be arguing about something, but she couldn't hear. "Jeff" got in the Volvo and backed up without looking, then spun around and shot up the road like an renegade teenager. So thoughtless. *What a pig*, she thought..

Ellsberg looked around to assess the weather. The snow was three or four inches deep on the yards and sidewalks, but the road was clear of snow and dry. The wind whipping the point of land emphasized the frigid air temperature. He stopped at the bottom of the driveway and spread his legs, leaning over to stretch out his hamstrings.

Patrice approached, shadowed by Pirate, and called out a cheery, "Good morning."

He stayed perpendicular at his waist and turned only his head sideways to see her. "Good morning." The vapor from his mouth looked as frosty as he sounded.

"Excuse me, are you Stefan Ellsberg?"

He turned his head more sharply this time to get a better look at her and slowly stood erect. "Yes." His eyes reminded Patrice of Red, the boa constrictor. All Ellsberg lacked was a tongue whipping in and out.

A man of few words, she thought: so far, three. "I'm Patrice Kelsey. I'm with the *Los Alamos Guardian*. I have a request in with the Laboratory to speak with you, but they haven't been able to firm it up yet. So since I'm here, could I ask you just a couple of questions?"

He looked annoyed, but he didn't tell her to butt out or buzz off, so she charged ahead. "I understand you were born here, and that your father and sister live here now. Will they be at the press conference Thursday?"

"Unfortunately, my father is not in robust health, and my sister looks after him. They will be unable to attend." He did some slow high steps in place to warm up his leg muscles. It was clear he wasn't going to stand still very long.

"What is the purpose of the press conference? I've heard a rumor you're to be appointed to a position with the U.S. Government inside Russia. Is that true?" Pirate moved directly in front of her and sat, her shoulders square to the man. Patrice heard a faint growl in the dog's throat and patted her reassuringly.

Ellsberg heard the growl, too, and glared at the dog, then shifted his glare to the woman as he spit out an answer. "Any announcement about my future employment with the Department of Energy will have to wait until Thursday."

"Did you know the late Doyle Silver?"

"I never heard the name. Now you'll have to excuse me. I have a busy schedule today and I need to get some exercise." He loped off up the road without a backward glance.

She watched him for a minute, then took a closer look at the dealer's tag in the back window of the Porsche. It was leased in Santa Fe the day before. She wished she could think of some excuse to ring the doorbell. Aha! I have it.

She strode up to the door and rang the bell. Thinking no one was going to answer, she was about to walk along the side to get a limited look at the balconies that jutted over the canyon, when the large wooden door swung open.

"Yes?" Even wearing a bathrobe and a towel wrapped around her head, Sen. Cristal Aragon was a disdainfully proud woman.

"I'm sorry to bother you, Senator Aragon..."

"It's very cold standing here in the doorway with wet hair," she said in a combative tone matched by her icy stare.

"I just spoke with Stefan Ellsberg as he left for his run, and I wanted to leave him my card." She gave the senator a weak smile. "So if you'd just give him this, I'll be on my way. Thanks."

Aragon glanced at the card and closed the door quickly. While the door was open Patrice got a look at a marble floor so shiny she could see a painting reflected as if in a pool of black water. The room beyond, a vast open arena, had windows so immense she could see the view straight to Taos over Aragon's shoulder. *So*, she thought with a twinge of virulent jealousy, *so that's how the other one percent lives.*

Sighing as she turned to go, she said aloud to Pirate, "I guess it's more like the other one-tenth of one percent, girlfriend."

She took Pirate back to Rick's house and changed into her gray skirt, white blouse and green vest. By nine-thirty she parked at Fuller Lodge and walked toward the home of Carl and Isobel Ellsberg.

Patrice pretended not to notice the chill in Isobel's greeting. Instead she gushed, "I'm looking forward so much to meeting your father. And I promise not to tire him out."

Isobel backed up and let Patrice inside. "I haven't finished dressing my father, and his guest is coming at ten."

If Isobel expected Patrice to back out the door in deference and say politely that she'd call some other time, she was destined to be disappointed. *I'm not that easy to get rid of,* Patrice thought. *Not like I used to be.* Aloud she said, "Do you need any help with coffee or anything?"

Isobel hesitated. "Well, I guess you could make the coffee. The coffeemaker is over here and the coffee and filters are in the cabinet above it. I'll get Dad dressed and into the living room."

"I won't stay long," Patrice lied. It would be impolite of her to stay if Dr. Ellsberg's guest came, but she counted on it being too awkward for Isobel to throw her out in front of the honored guest. *I'll just play it by ear.*

To counterbalance her lie about not staying long, she smiled at Isobel and said truthfully, "I love what you've done with your hair." She'd really perked up her appearance with a softer shade of blond and a decent layered cut. Her light blue suit did a lot, too, to palliate her cold demeanor.

"Thanks." She looked at Patrice's hair, noticing what had to be a tremendous improvement. "Yours looks good, too."

Patrice resisted the urge to fluff it as she had been doing ever since she came out of Ruby's. "Thanks. It's easier to take care of."

Isobel turned to go but Patrice spoke quickly. "Oh, before you go help your father, I wonder if I could ask you one question." Isobel looked back, so she rushed on, "I've been working on a story unrelated to your brother's visit, and I came across an odd coincidence. Did you know an old gentleman named Doyle Silver?"

"I know of him. I know he passed away last week. I haven't seen him in years."

"Was he a friend of your father's?"

"A passing acquaintance, that's all." Isobel shrugged to show her lack on interest in the subject.

"The acquaintance between your father and Mr. Silver goes back fifty years, doesn't it?"

"My father has known his barber since the war, too, but that doesn't qualify him as a 'friend.'" Her tone was scathing. Patrice was tiptoeing through a minefield and not missing many mines.

Quickly, Patrice held out a photo of Doyle Silver taken at the nursing home at Thanksgiving. "Do you happen to know who the balding man beside him is?"

Isobel took it from her hand and turned it toward the window to get better light on it. "Yes; it's Erik Griegson." She slapped the photo back in Patrice's hand. "He's visited my father two or three times. I don't know anything about him. I tried to put him off when he called but my father insisted on seeing him." Her words demonstrated disinterest in the man, but Patrice sensed anger as well.

"Now if you'll excuse me, I have to hurry if I'm going to get my father settled before company comes." She turned smartly on her heel and marched toward the bedroom.

Patrice put the photo away and quickly made the coffee. She looked around in the kitchen for nice cups, then remembered the china cabinet in the dining room. Carefully, she removed five English bone china cups and saucers. She set the matching sugar bowl in the living room, put cream in the creamer, and took five sterling silver spoons from a drawer. In another drawer of the cabinet she found linen napkins in the palest pink, embroidered with an "E."

She also found a china coffee pot for serving; no Mr. Coffee and chunky mugs for this occasion.

Having seen photos of Carl Ellsberg as a young man partying with the Oppenheimers, Patrice never would have recognized the gargoyle Isobel helped out of the bedroom. Hunchbacked, probably a result of severe osteoporosis, he walked with the aid of a cane on one side and Isobel on the other. He stopped and cocked his head to look Patrice over, as if one eye were better than the other. He did the same when Isobel spoke to him, cocking one ear toward her.

"This is Patrice Kelsey," she said, "from the newspaper, the *Guardian*."

"What?" he said loudly, clearly puzzled.

"She's from the newspaper. The old *Chronicle*."

"Oh, yes, the paper," he nodded.

"He doesn't remember the paper's new name," Isobel explained as she held his arm and lowered him very slowly into a soft armchair. "She wants to ask you some questions about the old days, about the Manhattan Project," she said, enunciating right into his good ear.

As the last of his weight transferred to the chair from Isobel's arm, she pulled the lever on the side of the chair and gently raised the footrest.

A silver and turquoise bolo tie topped his white shirt. He'd buttoned two buttons of the warm cardigan sweater, leaving the bottom two open, and the sweater spread over his stomach.

Patrice eased into the conversation with a little small talk, commenting on Bathtub Row, what a pleasure it was to be there.

"Of course we didn't live here during the war, no sir." His mouth appeared to be dry, and he ran his tongue all around his lips every other sentence or so. "The bigwigs like Hans Bethe had these houses then." Bethe, Patrice knew, was one of the Nobel laureates who worked on the Manhattan Project.

She asked him about the Trinity Test in the desert north of Alamogordo, in 1945. "Damn thing nearly didn't happen, you know. Big lightning storm about the time it was supposed to go off. Storm cleared just in time to get the shot off before dawn."

Patrice stole a peek at her watch: ten-fifteen. Mayor Kozar would probably be there any minute. She hoped for a delay as the old man warmed to his story.

"The bomb was up in a tower, like those oil things...?" He looked at Isobel.

"Like an oil derrick," she filled in for him.

"Yes, that's it. And we heard the countdown: Ten, Nine, Eight..." He counted off the fingers of one hand twice with a single finger of the other hand, "Seven, Six, Five, Four, Three, Two, One." He slowly raised his spindly arms out and into an arc above him. "There was the flash, brighter than the sun, that's the only way to describe it, brighter than the sun, and colors of green and purple, and of course yellow and orange." He looked up at his wrinkled hands and gradually lowered them to his lap.

"The mushroom cloud went up way into the atmosphere, and the sound wave hit us like a freight train. You wanna know what I said when I saw it?"

"Sure, yes, I do," Patrice said with a vigorous nod.

He smiled. "I said, "Oh shit!" Yes, that's all I said. Big important moment, and everybody was saying smart things, like Oppie quoted from the Bag-dad-vita or whatever that Indian thing was called, and all I could think of to say was, 'Oh shit.'" His laugh segued into a coughing spell.

"I think that's enough tale telling," Isobel said firmly.

"Dr. Ellsberg, I enjoyed meeting you and I appreciate hearing your story. Sonia Greenway at the Historical Archives asked me to see if you would talk to her for their oral history program."

"Well, I could probably be persuaded." He favored her with a kindly smile and ignored Isobel, who stood in preparation to show Patrice out.

Patrice, too, ignored Isobel. "I'm hoping to interview your son sometime this week. I understand he was born in Los Alamos during the war."

"Oh, yes," he chuckled, "born in Box 1663. It's on his birth certificate." It was a charming piece of local history, that babies born in the secret town of Los Alamos during the war were said to have been born at "Box 1663, Rural, Santa Fe County."

"Oh, yes," he repeated. "Stefan was..." His voice trailed off and he seemed saddened by mention of his son's name. "He'll be here today."

They heard a loud knock at the kitchen door. "Excuse me," Isobel said. Carl Ellsberg didn't notice she'd said anything.

To Patrice he seemed lost in thought, his bushy white eyebrows drawn tight. His lips moved as if in conversation, but she couldn't make out what he said. She listened for voices in the kitchen. It was apparently two men talking with Isobel.

"I'm sorry, I can never be sure just how alert he'll be," she said as she returned to the living room. "Dad?" He studied his buttons and continued his lip movements. "Dad!"

He looked up, annoyed, as someone would be to have his train of thought interrupted. "Dad, Dr. Sudoplatov is here to see you."

"My dear friend." The guest extended both his hands toward Carl Ellsberg but stopped short of the chair. "You remember me, I hope?" His deeply lined face, topped by wild black eyebrows, rested on his chest as if he had no neck. The olive skin and broad cheeks hinted at Mongols in his family tree. The wide grin seemed a little too forced to Patrice, like a stoic auditioning as Santa Claus.

Ellsberg was fixated on Sudoplatov's face as he held out one bony hand, allowing the guest to take it in his meaty paws.

"I have looked forward to seeing you again," Sudoplatov said.

"My father and Dr. Sudoplatov were students in college together before the war," Isobel said to Patrice.

"My dear friend," the guest went on, "I have brought with me a colleague from Russia who says it is one of his dearest wishes to meet you. He is here on business. I'll bring him in to meet you in just a moment; but first, I have a gift for you."

He stepped back to the dining table and picked up a wrapped box he had set there on his way in.

"Our trip has been wonderful," he said as he set the gift on Carl Ellsberg's lap. Ellsberg tore at the paper and found a wooden box. To be helpful, Sudoplatov cut the tape on the sides of the box and jiggled the cover a little so Ellsberg could remove it easily. Even leaning to see around Isobel, Patrice couldn't see what was inside.

"Yes, our trip has been wonderful. Everyone is so open and helpful in the West." He stepped toward the kitchen again and called, "Vladimir Nikolayevich, Dr. Ellsberg can see you now."

The second guest walked into the room slowly, looking around at the details, then faced the recliner. Carl Ellsberg was still staring at the open box on his lap.

"Vladimir Nikolayevich Kozar is the mayor of Arzamas-16," Sudoplatov said, pride evident in both his voice and his manner. "It is a great day in the history of our two nations when he can travel here, don't you agree, Dr. Ellsberg?"

Ellsberg raised his eyes to see the guest. The Russian mayor stood almost at attention in front of Ellsberg, who stared at Kozar with his mouth open. "I'm honored to meet you, Dr. Ellsberg," Kozar said.

Ellsberg's eyes widened, but his mouth fell slack. At the same time his body gave a jerk, then seemed to melt back into the chair, losing whatever starch held him in place. His head fell to one side.

"Dad!" Isobel shrieked. "Somebody call 911!"

Patrice jumped for the portable phone on the coffee table and dialed, giving the name and address. "I think he might have had a stroke," she told the operator.

Isobel and the two men were hovering over him, taking off his bolo tie and lifting him to the couch where he could lie flatter and presumably breathe better. Patrice ran out behind the house to wave the paramedics to the right place.

About twenty minutes later the ambulance pulled away from the back door with Carl Ellsberg inside. Isobel followed the ambulance in her Lexus. Sudoplatov and Kozar left.

Patrice carried the cream into the kitchen and turned off the coffee maker. Then she went back into the living room and picked up the gift box Carl Ellsberg had opened. Inside, nestled in shredded paper, was a bottle of cognac. Delicately, she lifted it out so she could see the label in the light.

Five signatures were scrawled on the label. She made out one that began with a "G" and one that began with a squiggle that might be an "S." Probably Gisle and Sacco, the men who died of cancer many years ago. Tiny numbers beside their names said 3-30-59 and 8-3-64. By the signature that clearly said "Douglas Frost," was a date just seven months before. And by "Doyle Silver" was the date of his death, eight days in the past.

Written beneath the winery name on the label were the words, carefully printed: 'To be opened by the Last Man and drunk in toast to us all. Trinity Site, New Mexico, July 16, 1945.'

Patrice shook her head. Whatever Carl Ellsberg was in his life, whatever the nature of his association with Gisle, Sacco, Frost and Silver, one thing was certain. Carl Ellsberg was the Last Man. She set the bottle back in its paper nest and picked up her purse to leave.

Lt. Pauling arrived at the back door just as she stepped outside. He lowered his car window. "I might have known I'd find *you* here," was all he said.

Chapter 20

Feeling like Typhoid Mary, yet again, Patrice drove to the *Guardian* office. She half-hoped the lifestyles editor would ask her for assistance. She'd love to slide into a seat and concentrate on news of the 4-H Club, and the title of the sermon at White Rock Baptist Church, and the date of auditions for the next light opera production--all the trivial pursuits of a town that, underneath its reputation as the birthplace of the Atomic Age, was just an ordinary town.

Carolee was in a state of comparative nirvana, deadline being more than an hour away. "Have you lined up an interview with Kozar yet?" Carolee said as she walked to the break room with Patrice for coffee.

"I talked to him last night at The Loft. I think I'll see him again this afternoon." She picked up the Pyrex coffee pot, examined the black liquid as if she couldn't identify it, and set it back on the hot plate.

Carolee looked from Patrice to the coffeepot and back again. Picking it up, she peered inside suspiciously. "What's the matter? You see something floating in it?"

Patrice shrugged. "No, I just don't know what I want. Not coffee. I'm sure it's fine." She turned to a poster taped to the wall as if the cartoon bears' message about safety on stairs required careful study.

Carolee poured herself a cup of coffee and returned to the subject at hand. "Danny's getting some pictures of Mayor Kozar and the Russkies this afternoon at the science museum. I need an article for tomorrow for sure." She waited; Patrice said nothing.

"Patrice, will you have an article about Kozar for tomorrow?"

Patrice turned back around. "Yes, sure. That'll be fine."

"Are you going to cover Ellsberg's colloquium tomorrow? If not, I need to know."

"Yes, I feel well enough to go." Seeing that Carolee looked doubtful, she added, "I'm definitely going to the colloquium."

"You want to tell me what's wrong? You're not your usual feisty self." Carolee sipped her coffee, added creamer, and sipped it again.

Patrice sat in a folding chair and leaned heavily on her good elbow. "Just a little while ago, while I was at the home of Stefan's father and sister, the old man had a stroke or something and had to be rushed to the hospital."

"Holy cow! I wonder if Stefan's colloquium or press conference will be canceled?"

"I'll stay on top of it," Patrice said with no enthusiasm.

"Is anything else bothering you?" Carolee asked.

"Oh, nothing is bothering me except that everyone connected with me is struck with terrible disasters. I'm getting a complex."

"Well, no offense, but I'm not going for any rides with you, or any walks down dark alleys, either," Carolee said. Patrice looked so morose, Carolee added, "Hey, I'm kidding! All right?"

"Patrice?" Kent Bolt was standing in the door of his office. The rigid planes of his face were even more stiff and cold than usual. "Could you come in my office, please?"

Tiffany, typing at Carolee's regular terminal, glanced over her shoulder with what Patrice would swear was a triumphal look.

Two waves of feelings washed over Patrice, first the old clutch of fear that she'd done something wrong, that she'd be on the street, unemployed.

Then a warm feeling cascaded over her, blocking the fear. It was a sensation of power. I didn't survive on that cliff in a blizzard to be cowed by the ilk of Kent Bolt. With her step a little lighter, she followed him into his office.

"Close the door, please. How are things coming along?" He gestured toward the chair closest to the front of his desk for her and seated himself in the imposing leather chair behind it. "Is your arm healing properly?"

She sat down, her back stiff and her head high. "Yes, thank you. An X-ray of my arm and ribs shows I'm on the mend."

"Has your doctor given you a signed release to be back at work full time?"

"No, part time. He wants me to get more rest." She fought the urge to look away from his eyes, fixing him instead with a steely gaze.

"And yet you can go for an early-morning hike in freezing weather to pursue an interview with Stefan Ellsberg?"

Of course, she thought. I left my card with Senator Aragon, Kent's sister. That's why he's ticked.

Her gaze still steadfast, she responded calmly to his goading question. "Stefan Ellsberg's colloquium is tomorrow, Kent, and as the Laboratory has been unable to arrange an interview for me, I contacted him on my own. I was doing no more than I expect reporters from other papers are doing. I'd hate to read an exclusive interview with Stefan Ellsberg in the *Albuquerque Journal.*" She noted with a touch of cheer that Kent looked away from her stare. She'd taken the wind out of his sails--for the moment, anyway.

"Uh, yes, well. I wanted to tell you--Senator Aragon will probably serve as intermediary, to arrange an interview with uh, Dr. Stefan Ellsberg."

"I will appreciate that. I need to do it this afternoon so it can be in tomorrow's paper."

"Uh, what's this about Stefan Ellsberg's father having a stroke?" he asked.

"I was at his home, to interview him about the Manhattan Project, when it happened. It appeared to be some kind of seizure or heart attack, or stroke. The ambulance took him to the hospital," she answered. "Do you know Carl Ellsberg?"

"No!" he said, a little too strongly. "Why do you ask?"

"Just making conversation."

"Oh. All right then. Well, if you hear anything about his condition I'd like to hear about it."

"Sure, okay."

When Patrice emerged from the office, Tiffany stood and lifted a few papers from a stack beside her terminal. Smoothing her short skirt, she strolled in Kent's open door.

Patrice sat down in her own seat, reveling in the feeling of being home, of reclaiming her territory. She fingered the stacks of press releases and photo contact sheets reporter Jeff Bloom had assembled for some after-deadline work.

She retrieved her pocket calendar from her purse and tried again to reach Prof. Norman Taggert at University of California, Berkeley. The receptionist in the history department said he was there but would have to call her back. She gave her number and doodled on the desk pad. About ten minutes later Marian said, "Patrice, you have a call on line two."

"Thanks." She set down her coffee and picked up the receiver. "This is Patrice Kelsey."

"Dr. Norman Taggert, returning your call." Patrice had a knee-jerk negative reaction to the use of "doctor," but of course, she quickly told herself, on a university campus that would be standard. It was just that there were so many people with doctorates in Los Alamos, it was considered gauche to refer to oneself that way.

"Thank you for calling me, Dr. Taggert. I'm working on a story about Lona Cohen, the American woman who served as a spy courier for the Soviet Union during the war. My friend Rose Hulle received a packet of information from the FBI under the Freedom of Information Act. A memo said the information was sent to you and to a gentleman at Stanford named Sheldon Libinowitz."

"I request quite a lot of information for my historical research," he said. "I don't know if that has come or not."

"I see. Do you do any of your research here in Los Alamos?" She continued doodling, writing his name and boxing it inside rectangles and ovals.

"I don't see that it's any of your business where I do research, young lady, but yes, I have been in Los Alamos. I was there right before Thanksgiving, then I had business in Chicago. Ever since Thanksgiving weekend, I have been in sunny California."

"If you don't care for snow, this would be a bad time to visit Los Alamos," she said.

"Oh, you have snow so early in the winter? I didn't know that. Well, I have to be going..."

"Wait, please let me ask you one more thing. Did you know Rose Hulle or Sheldon Libinowitz?"

"No, I've never made their acquaintance. Are they historians?"

"They were historians. As I said, they are the two people beside yourself who received the FBI material. They both died in the past two weeks." Danny Carter and Jeff Bloom burst in the front door, Danny on a beeline to the darkroom and Jeff beating a path to the desk where Patrice sat. She stood immediately and stretched the phone cord.

"Well, of course I'm sorry to hear it," Taggert said. "How did they die?"

"Rose was in a car wreck and Mr. Libinowitz drowned; they said he had an asthma attack while swimming."

"How sad," he said, sounding more bored than sad. "Well, it just goes to show, none of us know what the future holds. Good luck with your search. Good-bye, Miss...?"

"Kelsey. Patrice Kelsey." She was about to spell it when she heard the dial tone.

"Sorry about needing your desk," Jeff said. He was already typing his story.

"No problem. I'll move out of your way."

"Patrice!" Carolee yelled from across the room. "Are you still here?"

"No!"

"Just as I thought!" Carolee said. "Could you please help here for a little while? I'm backed up on editing and two front page stories aren't even written yet."

Patrice walked over to Carolee's desk, tired of the two of them yelling like prison inmates who can't see each other. "Okay, what do you want me to edit?"

On a piece of paper she tore off a news release. Carolee jotted down the column inches and story slugs, the short, pithy name given to a story in order to find it on a list. "These three, please, and stand by to check the stories Jeff and Tiffany are working on." Since Tiffany was still in Kent's office, Patrice hoped she wasn't working on a story anybody cared to read. Oh well, she shrugged, not my problem.

*****

In the break room with Danny, she ate a late lunch--a green chile cheeseburger from Sonic and a large cherry lime. They split an order of onion rings.

"You know, don't you, that everywhere we go today people are going to go 'sniff, sniff,' like Pirate does for steak," Patrice laughed. "After I eat onion rings I feel like a plane that flies over the beach trailing a banner, 'Eat at Sonic.'"

"As soon as I get to San Antonio, *after* I locate a Sonic Drive-In, I will start looking for jobs for you and Rick. You gotta get out of here before Kent ruins you."

"Well, it wouldn't hurt if you'd look around, I guess." She wadded up the foil wrapper and tossed it in the wastebasket.

Back at her terminal to type up her notes on her quick interview with Mayor Kozar at The Loft, she heard the front door of the *Guardian* open so hard it slammed against the wall. She stood to see what or who blew in, and saw Carolee in a light jacket, her hair and all the rest of her covered with a layer of snow.

"Ho, ho, ho, Merry Christmas, boys and girls." She stomped her feet and shook snow all over the entryway. "Time to wax your skis, Danny."

"Not this year. I'll be deep in the heart of Texas, remember?"

"Oh, yeah." Carolee hung up her sopping jacket and hugged her arms around her. "I'd like to be deep in the heart of anywhere warm. There's three or four inches on the ground, and it's coming down heavier all the time."

Half an hour later, Patrice stepped gingerly through the snow, filling her pumps with the stuff before she got to her car. She slid in, emptied her shoes, and tugged on her snow boots. Before she drove to Rick's house to rest, she drove to Fuller Lodge and walked up to the Historical Archives. Sonia Greenway was in her usual milieu--on the phone once again.

She looked at Patrice and whispered 'Hi." Into the phone she said, "Someone came in. I'll have to call you back, Edna."

Turning her full attention to Patrice, she said, "What on earth happened to you? I heard you got mugged by some crazy man in a ski mask."

"You heard right. If my landlord hadn't shown up when he did, I wouldn't be standing here. But I came to ask about a man you may have met. Has Norman Taggert ever come here to do research?"

"Yes, I remember the name. He's from UC Berkeley I seem to recall. I'll just take a look in the infallible log." She looked at several pages, then said, "Ah, here it is, the Wednesday before Thanksgiving."

"What did he want?"

"He looked up a dozen people and looked at the file on the Trinity Test."

"What did he look like?"

"Look like? Oh, medium height, pale complexion, light brown, wavy hair. Kind of pompous."

"That would be Normie all right," Patrice said. "In kindergarten he was written up as 'not willing to share toys.'"

Sonia put the log back on the table by the file cabinet. "How is Carl Ellsberg? Were you able to see him this morning?"

Patrice told her what had happened that morning. "I don't know what his condition is. In fact, I'm just about to walk over to his house. If Isobel's not there, I'll stop by the hospital."

*****

She walked over to the Ellsbergs' house, trying to whistle "Winter Wonderland," finally giving up and humming. Although the time was only three p.m., the lead-colored clouds made it seem later. She kicked through the snow, not even guessing where a sidewalk was.

For the second time that day, she was lucky. First she'd met and spoken with--well, spoken to--Stefan Ellsberg. Now she saw a light on at the Ellsberg home. There was no sign of Stefan, but Isobel's Lexus was there. Patrice knocked loudly on the back door. After a minute she saw Isobel walk into the kitchen.

"Yes?"

"Hi, Isobel. I was at the Lodge to see Sonia Greenway, and I just walked over. How is your father?"

She didn't answer the question. "Come in."

Patrice stomped her feet outside and brushed the snow off her parka and ski hat. Isobel didn't offer to take them, so she set them on the kitchen cabinet near the door.

Isobel unscrewed the top of a half gallon of Glenlivet Scotch and poured two tumblers full. She handed one to Patrice, sloshing a little over the top.

"Come on in. Let's have a drink. I want to drink to

something." She held the glass up like a toast.

"To what, Isobel?" Patrice wiped her damp hand on her skirt and held her glass up just a little, in imitation of Isobel's pose. Isobel took a big swallow and held her glass aloft again.

"To my brother. The asshole!"

Chapter 21

The dining room was in shambles. Sloppy stacks of papers, boxes with papers pulled halfway out, and plastic file boxes nearly obscured the dark wood of the dining table. At the center of the jumble Patrice noticed an open metal fireproof box. A dozen or so fat envelopes of various sizes jutted out the top at odd angles.

"I should have done this years ago." Isobel stared unblinking at the metal filebox. "But that wouldn't have made any difference, looking in here years ago." She shook her head slowly from side to side, then adjusted her stance for better balance. She set her wet glass on the wood table, which looked to Patrice like an antique, and sat down hard in a carved captain's chair.

The powder blue wool suit Isobel had on since that morning was creased in all the wrong places, and a lipstick smear marred the left sleeve. The zipper of the skirt had migrated to her left hip from the center of the back.

Patrice set her glass of scotch on an empty envelope and moved a stack of papers from a chair to the floor so she, too, could sit down. She faced the large hutch and china cabinet filled with English china and Italian glassware. Isobel--or her mother--had selected lovely things when they lived and traveled in Europe.

Isobel reached into a cardboard box on the floor next to her and pulled out a large sheet of white paper rolled in at the edges. "Isn't this sweet?" She formed a pucker with her lips and exaggerated the word sweet. "Mother saved my early attempts at art. She thought I had talent. Maybe it was only desperate hope. Once they found out Stefan got all the brains, they just hoped I had talent. But instead," she patted her hair like a Hollywood starlet and laughed hoarsely, "I got the looks in the family."

She unrolled the paper and stared at the bumpy red and blue patterns on the paper. "This was a joint effort. A duet in fingerpaint, so to speak. The little red handprints are mine and the bigger blue prints are my precious elder brother's. I don't remember doing this. I couldn't have been more than three, because that's when Stefan went away to school, when he was ten." The paper snapped back into a tube-shape and she tossed it to Patrice. She caught it and delicately unrolled the fragile old paper to examine the patternless jumble of small red hand and finger marks, and bigger blue ones.

"We don't even have pictures of us together," Isobel went on, in a sort of manic intimacy that made Patrice distinctly uncomfortable. As she talked she moved and restacked papers, searching for something. "Ah, here they are! Come to mama." She retrieved a pack of cigarettes from a pyramid of envelopes, tapped it, and pulled one cigarette out with her lips. She patted herself down, found her lighter, used it, and sat back.

"It seemed like it was always just me and my parents," she went on. "I was the child who spilled the milk and lost my lunch money and talked back to my mother. Stefan was the perfect god-like son they talked about all the time."

Patrice let the paper roll back up and set it on the table. Isobel snatched it like a baton and made a show of dropping it into the wastebasket.

Isobel was clearly smashed. Patrice considered sipping the scotch to be polite, but Isobel was beyond noticing her manners or lack of them.

"How is your father?" Patrice asked again.

"He can't talk." Isobel exhaled a cloud of smoke and watched it rise. In a flat, emotionless voice she said, "The doctor says his mind is the same but he can't communicate, which is terrifying for a stroke victim. I say what's the difference? He never communicated when he was..." She seemed to lose her train of thought momentarily, then remembered. "I almost said 'alive.' I mean when he was 'well.'" She took a swallow of scotch that would have made an Irish longshoreman's eyes bug out, but she had no trouble getting it down.

"In case you're wondering what this mess is," Isobel went on, "I was looking for his will. His Last Will and Testament. I knew what it said, that he left me the house and two-thirds of his money. Not that I want this cruddy dump, you understand. But it's worth about four hundred thousand dollars. I'd sell it so fast the ink wouldn't dry before I was gone. I hate this town." She paused to suck on her scotch.

"But guess what he did!" She started speaking before she had completely swallowed, and scotch dribbled out of the side of her mouth. She wiped it with her other hand, appearing to be puzzled about how her face got wet. "No, really, guess!"

Her eyes were bright, almost feverish. She wiped the side of her mouth with the cuff of her sleeve and went on. "Guess what I found when I went to get out the will he 'executed,' that's the right word, the will he 'executed' after Mother died and I agreed to stay here and take care of him? That sly son of a bitch made another will without telling me. He's trying to leave everything to my brother. Listen to this."

Patrice saw an ashtray on the chair seat beside her and quickly slid it in front of Isobel. She was too late; the ash fell on the hardwood floor.

Isobel took a long drag on the cigarette and rested it in the ashtray. Leaning awkwardly across the table, she plucked a bulging envelope from the metal box and pulled out a sheaf of papers with a blue paper cover, the sheaf apparently attached at the top. She read the first page and roughly pushed it over the top, and the second, looking for something. "Here it is: 'My daughter, Isobel J. Ellsberg, can live in my house,' da-da-da, address and legal description, 'for the remainder of her life. I specifically leave her a bequest of twenty thousand dollars. The remainder of my estate, and my house after Isobel's death, I leave to my son, Stefan C. Ellsberg.'" She closed her eyes and rubbed her forehead.

With a shaking hand, Isobel placed the stubby cigarette between her lips and took a final drag, then ground it out. "I can live in this dump for the rest of my life. Or I can go be a goddam bag woman on the street. Do you know how long twenty thousand dollars lasts?"

Patrice nodded. Isobel was right; it was a cruel will.

"I'll fight this thing in court. This will never stand up. Stefan C. Ellsberg can kiss my shiny heiney!"

"Could I see the will for a minute?" Patrice asked.

"Sure, help yourself." Isobel sailed it to her across the table.

Patrice caught it in midair and scanned the document, looking for the date it was signed and the witnesses. It had been executed six months before, handled by the lawyer Patrice respected least of any she knew, which was saying a lot. The will was witnessed by Erik Griegson and...

This is too weird, just too weird! Patrice thought. *The other witness was Cristal Aragon!*

Griegson, Patrice recalled, was the man Isobel identified in the picture of old Doyle Silver at the nursing home. She had said Griegson came to see her father a couple of times. She'd said the old man insisted on seeing him. What had Larry Dreyfus said about the man in the picture? Something like he was a volunteer named Erik who helped old people with their insurance or something.

"You see who witnessed it, huh?" Isobel stood unsteadily and went to the kitchen to pour another drink. "Cristal's been married about ten times and came out with money every time. That house on the end of North Mesa, where Stefan is staying, that was her payoff from one marriage." She leaned on the doorjamb between the kitchen and dining room and held up her full glass in mock toast. "Nice work if you can get it, I say."

Patrice watched her take a long pull at her new glass of scotch.

Isobel savored the scotch, closing her eyes as if she were in ecstasy. When she opened them, she said decisively, "I'm tired. I'm going to take a nap." She took another swallow, then reached her arm out stiffly, setting the glass down too near the edge of the table. It wobbled and crashed to the floor.

"Shit!" Isobel said, looking at the broken glass. "Waste of good scotch."

"I'll clean it up," Patrice said, afraid Isobel would sever an artery if she tried to do it herself. "Why don't you get some rest?"

Isobel continued to stare at the broken glass and yawned. "I think I'll take a nap." She bumped down the hall toward what Patrice presumed was her bedroom.

Patrice found paper towels plus a broom and dustpan and cleaned up the shards of glass. She folded up the will, squeezed it back into its envelope, and set it in the open metal box. She got a clean piece of typing paper, wrote her name and Rick's phone number on it, and put it like a tent over the box, so Isobel couldn't miss it. Letting herself out the back door, she walked back to her car at Fuller Lodge.

Maybe Isobel has a good idea, she thought with a smile. *I feel like taking a nap, too.*

*****

That evening she awoke to the aroma of baked Rock Cornish Game Hens. "Uh, say, Luis, any chance you could get an FBI job in Los Alamos?" she asked when he came into the living room.

He gave Rick a wrapped package, which turned out to be a corkscrew so he could open the Mateus. The table was already set, with a wine glass at each place.

Luis poured the wine and turned back to Rick. "Now, let me help you get on your feet." He stood close to the recliner and held out one arm, stiff as a rod. Rick hooked an elbow over it and scooted forward in the chair.

"Actually," Patrice said, "you can only help him to his foot."

She held his crutches out, but Rick shook his head. Instead of using them, he hopped to the table, causing Pirate to curl closer to the couch and tuck her tail under her.

"Smells great," he said to Luis as he gently lowered himself into his chair. "Mom would be proud."

Luis shook out his linen napkin and sniffed with disdain. "Mom," he said, "would be jealous."

Between heartfelt compliments on the dinner, Patrice told them about seeing Isobel that afternoon.

"She had looked in a fireproof box to get out her father's will, which she said she's known for years what it said. She was to get the house, which is worth a lot, maybe four hundred thousand, and most of his money. I get the feeling it was a quid pro quo for her staying to nurse her mother for years, then turn around and have to do the same for her father."

She paused to savor a bit of tender, butter-basted breast from her Rock Cornish game hen. "This is delicious, Luis!"

"You're welcome. Now, go on about Isobel."

"Well, my friends, you won't believe what appeared to Isobel's wondering eyes. The old coot executed a new will six months ago and didn't tell her."

"Something tells me this is the 'now the bad news' part," Rick said.

"You've got it. The new will reverses the inheritance. Stefan gets almost everything. Isobel gets twenty thousand dollars and she can live in the house until her death, then Stefan can have it or sell it. And knowing how Isobel feels about Los Alamos, 'living' in that house is like a prison sentence." She pulled a drumstick off the miniature chicken and held it between her fingers to get the meat off with her teeth.

"And as far as you could tell it is a valid will?" Rick asked.

"Looked mighty legal to me. And I haven't told you the best part yet. It was witnessed by Erik Griegson and Cristal Aragon!"

Luis whistled. "And I thought small towns were boring!"

"Did you tell me who Erik Griegson is?" Rick asked. "I don't remember." He tried to eat the hen with a knife and fork, then gave up. With his hands he dismembered the fowl and ate with his fingers. "Umm, delicious," he echoed.

"Remember the snapshot I took off the bulletin board at the nursing home? There was a man bent over, listening to Doyle Silver, and the light reflected off his shiny dome. I showed it to Larry Dreyfus the night you and I went to the snake pit. He said he didn't know who it was, but I spoke to him Monday and he remembered it's a social worker named Erik. He was vague about who Erik worked for, just said it wasn't the nursing home. When I tried to find out how to track down this kindly soul who visits the elderly, he quickly said, oh, I think he went to Mexico."

"And you think 'Erik' is Erik Griegson?" Luis asked.

"Better than that. Isobel recognized his picture when I showed it to her this morning. She said he came at least twice to see her father, who insisted on seeing him."

"Hmmm," Rick said, "curiouser and curiouser."

"Of course Isobel is in a blind rage about the will. If I were her brother I don't think I'd walk down any dark alleys."

"Yes," Rick said, holding his knife out in front of him and thumbing the blade theatrically, "sibling rivalry can be a frightening thing."

"It's not my fault Mother always loved me best!" Luis said. He started to pour each of them a second glass of Mateus.

Patrice held her hand over her glass. "I can't carouse until all hours tonight, guys," she said. "I'm going back to work tomorrow."

"What do you call what you've been doing all week?" Rick asked.

"I mean work where my byline is there for all the world

to see, or at least for the tiny portion of the world reached by the *Guardian*."

"Speaking of work, I talked to FBI headquarters today," Luis said. "They're delighted I happen to be here just now. So I'll be going to work tomorrow, too. Sitting in the audience at Ellsberg's colloquium and just listening."

"Yeah, well, I'll be doing more than just listening. The minute it's over I'll have to race back over to the paper to write it up. My boss is a slavedriver."

"Why don't you help the old slavedriver to the couch?" Rick said. He winced as he accidentally bumped his cast against the table leg, then stood, centered his weight over his good foot, and used her shoulder to maintain his balance while he hopped back to the recliner.

"Speaking of the FBI," Patrice mused aloud to Luis, "do you have a way to see where Prof. Norman Taggert was the night Rose was killed? He told me, in a sanctimonious tone, that he was here the day before Thanksgiving, then went to Chicago, and has been in California ever since."

Luis shrugged noncommittally. Changing the subject, he asked, "Why don't I give you a ride to the colloquium tomorrow? I have a friend who can arrange special parking."

"Handicapped?" she said, looking at her cast and sling.

"Something even better; government license plates. What time shall I pick you up at the paper?"

"Nine should be good. Thanks." Luis held up the wine bottle and she shrugged. "Well, just half a glass. I don't want to get too wild and giddy." Again she offered to help with the dishes, but again Luis insisted he'd do it later.

"I had time today to read that book you brought me at the hospital," Rick said.

"Talk louder," Luis called from the kitchen. "I'm making coffee."

"I said I read one of the books Rose was using for research. There's a whole chapter on Lona and Morris Cohen."

"What's the book?" Luis called. "I've probably read it."

Rick took the book off the TV tray beside his recliner. "*Red Spies in the U.S.* by George Carpozi, Jr."

"Oh yeah, that's a good one. Tells about sleepers and spy schools. Patrice, you want cream in your coffee, right?"

"Yes, thank you. So tell me about the book," she said to Rick. "I haven't read it."

"The Cohens were born in New York," Rick said. "They were suspected by the FBI of being spies in some way connected to the Rosenbergs. By the time Julius and Ethel Rosenberg were executed, the Cohens had disappeared."

"They turned up ten years later in England," Luis said as he handed Patrice a mug of coffee.

"I'm telling this story," Rick said, peeved. "They were living under the name 'Kroger' and collecting secret information on nuclear powered ships."

"Tell her about Gordon Lonsdale," Luis passed Rick a mug of coffee and sat down with his.

"I'm getting to that! Would you put a towel in your mouth or something?"

Luis rolled his eyes and sat back in his chair, sipping his coffee.

Rick went on. "While they were pretending to be the Krogers, a nice couple from New Zealand, this guy Gordon Lonsdale would come to their house and give them NATO secrets he'd gotten from a British shipyard. The Cohens sent some of it in microdots in books, but most of it they sent direct to Moscow by a superfast radio transmitter in their back yard. Well, this guy Lonsdale was pretending to be a Canadian citizen working in England, but he was really Russian."

He opened the book, looking for the chapter on the Cohens. "Yeah, here it is. There really was a boy in Canada named Gordon Lonsdale, born in a little mining town, but his mother left his father and went to Finland, never to be heard of again. Meanwhile, the guy who was going to pretend to be

Lonsdale was going to a special spy school in Moscow. Listen to this." He read:

"'He attended classes in English, geography, the theater, and the capitalistic system. He learned to dress, talk and order food in the manner of the West...and he received courses in spy techniques, photography, microfilming and radio communications.' It says he went to a special town where everything was like America and England and Canada. He spoke only English, saw American and British movies, listened to pop records, and learned to look at home in the West. And he wasn't the only one they trained like that, of course. They sent these specialists all over the world and they would just lie low until they were activated."

"They're called 'sleepers,'" Luis said.

"You just can't help yourself, can you?" Rick said with an exaggerated sigh.

"Do you think Perseus was a sleeper?" she asked. "Or 'sleepers,' plural?"

"It's possible," Luis said. "He could have been sent well before the war, educated here, then put himself in line to be recruited to the Manhattan Project. More likely, though, he was an idealist who just happened to work here on the bomb, like Klaus Fuchs, someone with a huge ego who thought he should bridge the gap between Russia and the West." Oblivious to the irony, Rick yawned loudly.

"My brother, however, is definitely a sleeper."

"I just want to be a sleeper. Man, will this week ever end?" In answer Patrice walked over and kissed him on the forehead. He smiled wickedly. "How would you like to run away with me?"

"If we pooled our money, how far do you think we could get?"

"Hmm, I see your point."

Luis chimed in. "What has two heads, three legs, three arms..."

"And fifty dollars," Rick finished.

*****

Patrice answered the phone on one ring so Rick could sleep. He had fallen asleep in the recliner and she'd covered him with a quilt.

"Patrice, I was hoping you were there. This is Isobel Ellsberg."

"Isobel, how are you? And how is your father?"

"He's about the same. They just say 'stable.' But I found some pictures..." She seemed to have trouble talking. Patrice thought she might be crying. "Could you come over?"

Patrice almost said, "Now?" like it was a crazy idea, which in fact it was. Instead she said smoothly, "I'd be glad to. It'll just take me a few minutes." Luckily she hadn't gotten ready for bed yet. She thought about what Luis would say (and Rick, if he were sentient) about her going out alone at night. It wasn't something she wanted to risk, either. "Uh, Isobel, I do have one problem. I'll have to get Rick's brother to come with me. Do you still want me to come?"

Isobel hesitated for a few seconds. "All right."

She tapped lightly on the bedroom door and heard, "Come in."

Luis had his laptop computer set up on Rick's desk and was tapping at the keys. Saving his work to the disk, he turned toward Patrice. "What's up?"

She explained Isobel's request and asked if he'd go with her. "Sure. I want to see this woman for myself. Why should you have all the fun?"

The windshields of the Bronco and her Subaru were covered with wet snow. Luis helped her into the Bronco and cleared the windshield.

"If there's a hard freeze tonight with this wet snow coating all the trees and power lines, we could be in for a utility man's nightmare," he said, as he got in and turned on the defroster.

He parked a block from Isobel's in order to be under the only streetlight in the neighborhood. The snow made it look like an orange fuzzy ball.

Isobel must have been watching for them; she opened the door as they trudged up the walk. She'd changed to silvery leggings and a green sweater with silver threads. She was smoking a cigarette, and she had a drink in her hand, but she seemed alert and sober. Patrice introduced Luis, saying he was an agent with the FBI, and added, "How is your father?"

Isobel cocked her head to one side and studied her glass, rubbing lipstick off the edge with her thumb. "He's stable. That's all they say about it. I don't think they know one way or the other." She took a sip of the amber liquid. "I took a nap after you left, and when I woke up and showered I did some thinking. And then I did some detective work around here."

They followed her into the living room. The clutter in the dining room had increased, if such a thing was possible, and it had spilled over into the living room. Canceled checks and bank statements covered the coffee table. Three brick-red folders the size of passports were fanned out like playing cards on the chair where Carl Ellsberg had been sitting some twelve hours earlier.

Isobel scooped them up and returned to the dining room to slip the red folders in the top drawer of the china cabinet. Then she looked around for her glass; it was nearly empty. "Would you like something? Scotch? Bourbon? I have some white wine, too." They hesitated. "Coffee? I could easily make some coffee."

Patrice said, "I believe I'd like a glass of wine."

"I'll have a small scotch, neat," Luis added.

While Isobel puttered in the kitchen, Patrice moved a stack of manila folders to the floor beside the dining chair she'd used before. Luis stayed on his feet.

Isobel came back with three glasses. Luis and Patrice removed theirs carefully from the triangle. Taking a sip of her scotch, Isobel said, "I apologize for the way I was this afternoon. I'd been through such a shock."

"Yes, your father's stroke..."

Isobel's head jerked. "I wasn't referring to that. I was referring to finding his new will dumping me at the door of the poorhouse." She invited them to the living room where she took a seat in the recliner and Patrice lowered herself into an oak armchair. Luis turned the dining chair around and moved it just barely across the imaginary line into the living room.

Patrice took a deep breath, relieved to find she could breathe deeper than she could a few days before, and sipped her wine.

Isobel struck a match with a dramatic flourish and lit her cigarette. She took a deep drag and set it in the clean malachite ashtray beside her.

"You probably think finding out Dad was leaving everything to Stefan would make me feel even more depressed, and I guess it did, for a while. You saw me this afternoon." She spoke to Patrice with an edge of "us girls gotta stick together" intimacy.

Patrice saw how Luis's seating himself outside their space was intentional. Isobel seemed to forget he was there.

"Yes, I was lower than I've ever been, but now I feel energized. Now I'm ready to fight. Stefan will get that money over my dead body." She paused and waved the cigarette in the air. "Figuratively speaking, of course."

Good grief, Patrice thought, *this is better than pay television*. "Isobel, I'll admit I'm spellbound by this drama, but why are you telling me?"

She looked thoughtful. "I don't have anyone else to tell." Patrice thought she detected a note of sadness, but maybe not. *Isobel is a hard woman to read.*

Isobel concentrated on her cigarette and her scotch. Patrice cleared her throat. "You know, this morning when I showed you the picture of Doyle Silver and the other man, the man you said was Erik Griegson? I forgot to ask if you know Mr. Silver's nephew, Lawrence Dreyfus."

"Quite well. We're going to be married."

Much better than pay television! "Well...that's certainly a...I mean, congratulations."

"I found something else you'll find intensely interesting, something besides Dad's new will," she said, blowing a smoke ring.

Patrice's jaw dropped open. *If I could do that, I think I'd smoke, too.* Isobel tapped the cigarette on the edge of the ashtray, took a fortifying gulp of scotch, and went down the hall. She came back with a small blue envelope.

"I found these pictures under the lining of my mother's sewing basket." She handed them to Patrice.

They were pictures of a family--a father, mother, son and daughter. From their clothes Patrice guessed the pictures were taken in the 1950s, and all on the same day. The father was easy to recognize after all the photos she'd seen of a young, vigorous Carl Ellsberg. The woman was definitely the same woman in the photos of the Ellsbergs with the Oppenheimers. The little girl was about three, with blond braids on top of her head. Patrice looked from the pictures to Isobel and back. It was, as they say, the spitting image.

But the boy? She turned the picture over. "Carl, Elizabeth, Isobel and Stefan. Syracuse, NY." Another picture was a closer view of Isobel and Stefan in front of a rose trellis. "This doesn't look anything like the Stefan Ellsberg I met this morning on North Mesa," Patrice said.

Isobel smiled a cold smile. "Bingo! You see it, too. I was afraid it was just me, that I was seeing it wrong. But I've always had a good eye for faces. When I was in art school I showed a flair for portraits. Someone is masquerading as Stefan Ellsberg."

Patrice stared at the pictures. "You've never seen these pictures until today?"

"No. There are no pictures of Stefan in any family albums until, well, I think in the first pictures he's about twelve. He was at school in England."

"Could I see that?"

"It's on a shelf in the hall closet. I can get it down."

While she was gone, Luis moved his chair beside Patrice and looked at the pictures.

"Here it is," Isobel said. "Let me clean it off a little." She went into the kitchen and came back with a damp washcloth.

Patrice opened the scrapbook and looked at a clear shot of a boy in a rugby outfit. He had thick, unruly black hair and penetrating eyes, and his strong jaw thrust out in a challenge. It was without a doubt the same person she had seen at the airport and in front of the house on North Mesa--the man called Stefan Ellsberg.

She put the long-hidden photo of Isobel and her big brother beside it. The two photos were most assuredly not of the same boy.

Luis asked Isobel, "Why would anyone substitute another boy for your real brother? And the most important question: Why would your parents allow it?"

"Oh, I don't think they knew!" Isobel said, confused.

"They had to," Luis said. "You were kept away from him, but you said they visited Stefan at school and he joined them in Switzerland when you were away. They knew all along. And they destroyed their pictures of the old Stefan."

"Except these," Isobel said.

"And where did you say you found them? Your mother hid them like a treasure where no one else ever looked. I'll bet even your father didn't know these pictures still existed."

"Well then, where's my real brother? Maybe he's been dead for years! And who the hell is the big shot who's giving a talk at the Laboratory tomorrow?"

Thoughts of recent revelations of babies switched at birth by accident came into Patrice's mind. "It's possible he's your real brother, and not this boy in the Syracuse photo. Both scenarios are unlikely, but, yes, something happened."

"For one thing," Luis said, "Puberty happened. I've seen

people change so much I myself wouldn't believe it was the same person. As for the hair, hair grows and darkens or lightens, with or without chemical help. So don't pay any attention to the hair."

Patrice thought about it. Turning to Luis she said, "Stefan Ellsberg has all kinds of clearance doesn't he?

"Sure. He has a rare Department of Energy badge with a nuclear symbol on the back; you've probably never seen one. It gets him into any nuclear installation in the country. I was looking into his clearance because of the nature of his possible appointment to work in Russia."

"Would some security agency somewhere have his fingerprints?"

"Sure. Why?"

"Because Isobel has the fingerprints of the boy she thought was her brother."

"I do?"

Patrice walked over to the dining room and pulled the duet in fingerpaints, lovingly saved by Isobel's mother, out of the wastebasket. "How long would it take to get this to an expert in Washington?" Patrice asked Luis.

"We don't need to. The Bureau contracts with a scientist here at the Laboratory for consultation on fingerprints. He developed the new method, using gold. I'll get Stefan's prints from the Bureau, have them here in a few hours."

Isobel laughed. "Just in case you don't have Mr. Big Shot's prints handy, they're all over that present he brought for Dad." She pointed to a crystal vase at the center of the dining room table. "You're welcome to it."

"Are you coming to the colloquium tomorrow?" Patrice asked Isobel.

"Oh, yes. The Director of the Laboratory invited me, and now I wouldn't miss it for the world." She held up her glass of scotch in a toast. "To Stefan Ellsberg. Whoever the hell he is." She drained the glass and made her way toward the kitchen as if the floor was moving ever so slightly.

Luis picked up the crystal vase with his handkerchief. On an impulse, Patrice asked if she could borrow the old family photos Isobel had found in her mother's sewing basket, "just for a day."

"Sure," Isobel said. "Thass okay." The scotch was taking effect, as it inevitably would.

"Good night," Luis said as he held Patrice's coat for her.

Holding his arm as she stepped down the icy back steps, Patrice called back to Isobel. "Good night. We'll see you at the colloquium."

*****

The sound of Rachmaninoff's *Second Piano Concerto* resonated from Rick's living room as Patrice and Luis came up the snowy sidewalk and Luis unlocked the door. Rick was sitting in the recliner, reading another of Rose's source books on Soviet espionage. He wore absurdly large sweat pants Luis had bought to go over his cast, and an Atomic City Roadrunners T-shirt. He was freshly shaved.

"I thought you said he was a sleeper," Patrice said, looking at her watch.

"What did you do," Luis nodded to Rick as he took off his overcoat, "get a second wind?"

"Something like that. I have a lot on my mind, couldn't sleep. Might as well improve my mind. Sure can't do anything about my body."

Patrice detected a dark tone to what he said. Thinking it might be some friction between brothers, she excused herself and took a bath. Listening to Rachmaninoff, she lay in the tub and gradually relaxed. She toweled dry and rubbed lotion on her arms and legs, brushed her teeth, put on her pajamas and robe, and emerged. The door to Luis's room was closed.

Rick was alone in the living room. He'd turned off his reading light and moved to the sofabed, where he leaned against the couch back and pillows. The candles Luis had used at dinner were flickering on an end table beside the couch. Three fat

Christmas candles burned on the coffee table, which had been pushed out of the way to make room for the couch to open into a bed for Patrice. The candles provided the only light in the room. Beside the dinner candles was an open bottle of Lancer's Vin Rosé and two stemmed glasses. "I'm letting the wine breathe," he said. "My cosmopolitan brother tells me that's how it's done in fine restaurants."

That wine is breathing more than I am right now, Patrice thought. "I've been enjoying the music," she said softly. She noticed the concerto had finished. "What is this piece?"

"It's by Rachmaninoff, too. *Rhapsody on a Theme by Paganini.*"

"Oh, yes. Now I recognize it. I love the 'Eighteenth Variation' best."

"Me too. Would you like some wine?" He patted the bed beside him and poured two glasses.

She scooted over beside him and took one glass, hypnotized by the candlelight reflected in the pale wine.

"We need to talk," he said, wrapping his left arm around her shoulders. She could smell his aftershave--her favorite, Obsession.

"You make talking sound a little ominous." She sipped the wine, feeling its warmth travel down her throat. Her skin was still warm and flushed from her hot bath, and now she felt her internal temperature going up. And it wasn't only because of the wine.

"I don't mean to. It's so hard for me, that I guess it is ominous. I have to get ready and plan just what to say and how to say it." He drank some wine and seemed to be looking for words.

"I've always found you to be articulate," she said. "Articulate to a fault, in fact."

"How many times have you heard me talk about my feelings? Never. And now I want to, but I've blocked it so long, I can't get words to come out of my mouth." He shrugged.

"Words about your wife, and how much you miss her?" She leaned her head on his shoulder to avoid meeting his eyes.

He said nothing for a painfully long time. "Yes, about Elaine, and how much I miss her. But I almost lost you, too, and that hurt just as much. I guess I'd gone from caring about you to being in love with you without knowing it, then when I realized how close I came to losing you--twice! in the car wreck, and to that bastard who beat you up--I had to recognize the pain for what it was."

"And what was it?" she asked, holding her breath without meaning to.

"Proof that I not only could love another woman after losing Elaine, but that I did, in fact, love you." He turned enough to reach her with his lips and she returned his tentative kiss with a passion that embarrassed her.

"Luis!" she said when she took a breath. "He could walk out here any minute."

Rick grinned. "My brother won't come out of that room for anything. Maybe if the house is on fire, but I doubt even then." He kissed her again. "But don't worry, I'm not going to ravish you. Not right now, anyway. Not until the cast is off." He kissed her again, with increasing urgency.

She pulled her lips away long enough to say, "Your cast, or mine?"

"Which one comes off first?" He pressed his lips hard against hers.

She kissed him again, then giggled and had to pull away. "Air! I need air!" She was helpless with laughter.

"I don't know when I've been so insulted," he said, crossing his arms in front of him.

"I'm sorry, really I'm sorry. But I just had such a lascivious thought." He waited. "Okay, I'll tell you. What has three legs, three arms, and three heads and drinks wine from two glasses?"

"Patrice Kelsey, I'm shocked at you!" He started laughing, too. "So much for romance."

She took another sip of wine and set the glass back by the

candles. Tucking her knees under her, she rotated so she was facing him. Protecting her cast, she lay down with her head in his lap.

"Remember when I was gradually waking up at the hospital after getting a concussion? And I said, 'I love you.' Well, I was out of it, but not that far out of it. I meant it. I love you."

He bent his head over and kissed her mouth and her eyes, and her forehead.

She spoke again. "Rick, I've been thinking about something Isobel Ellsberg said today, that her brother was away at school all the time and had a god-like status with her parents. But she was there on the scene. She said, 'I was the one who spilled the milk and lost my lunch money.' And I guess since then I've been thinking about how your wife, Elaine, is gone, and there's no way she'll ever be unkind, or short-tempered, or get a speeding ticket. So she'll always be perfect to you. But I'm the one who's likely to spill the milk or spill the beans or bite your brother's head off when he acts like an ass. And I don't know if I can live with the comparison."

He opened his mouth to say something, closed it, then opened it again. She placed two fingers on his lips. "I don't want you to search for words and try to make me feel one way or another. We have time to get used to this. Let's just take one step at a time."

She gave him a light kiss and scooted back off the bed. She blew out the Christmas candles and put the cork back in the wine bottle.

"I can take a hint!" he said, blowing out the two dinner candles and shoving himself to a standing position. Hopping around the sofabed, he stopped long enough to kiss her once more, holding her close and whispering again, "I love you."

Then he hopped on to his bedroom and she crawled under the covers on the sofabed. Alone, but not really alone. Not anymore.

Chapter 22

Patrice woke up at least once an hour during what remained of Wednesday night. She knew she had because she kept looking at the red numbers on the radio alarm clock. When it said 5:56 she turned off the alarm and turned on the radio. She was four minutes ahead of the news, just in time for a commercial from Metzger's Hardware. She recognized Gary Marshall's voice doing the commercial, accompanied by sleighbells.

"Yes, that's right, it's time for the white stuff, and it's piling up in your driveway right now. Lucky for you, Metzger's Hardware has snow shovels and snowblowers and salt-free ice melting compounds. Yes, you woulda, coulda, shoulda bought it yesterday, but don't feel bad..."

She peeked out the living room drapes to see. *Holy Mother Russia! There must be a foot and a half of snow on top of what fell by the time Luis and I got home.* Pirate stretched, got off the bed, and nuzzled the back of Patrice's knee. "You want to go out girl? Well, just wait 'til you see what's all over the yard."

Patrice unlocked and opened the front door and Pirate bounded out into a snow bank. The Dalmatian loved to play in the snow, especially if there were frolicking humans throwing snowballs, but with her short hair and thin body she couldn't take the cold for long.

Patrice closed the door to about the width of her face while she waited for Pirate. Her Subaru was a blob of white, no metal showing.

"Coming up in thirty seconds, all the national news from CBS followed by state and local news. Los Alamos Schools are on a one-hour delay, Pojoaque and Española schools are on a two-hour delay. Los Alamos National Laboratory is on time, however, I repeat, the Lab is on time. No delays at the Lab. Stay tuned for a complete list of delays and cancellations following CBS News. This is Gary Marshall, KRSN."

Pirate came back in and made a miniature snowstorm in the living room by shaking head to tail. Patrice found her slippers, and went into the kitchen. She put coffee beans in the grinder and was about to turn it on when she heard a name on the radio news that stopped her in her tracks.

"Dr. Stefan Ellsberg, a consultant on nuclear security matters with the Department of Energy, has been selected for a new job by the President," the announcer for CBS said. "Word that Dr. Ellsberg will be the new Science Advisor inside the U.S. Embassy in Moscow, Russia, was confirmed this morning by the office of the Secretary of Energy. While technically an employee of the DOE, Ellsberg will be attached to the State Department during his two-year foreign assignment. It had been rumored last week that Dr. Parker Bowles, chairman of the physics department at University of Illinois, would be appointed, but that was not the case. Ellsberg is said to be in Los Alamos, New Mexico for consultations on nuclear issues with officials of Los Alamos National Laboratory.

"New figures released today on spending for Medicare..."

Patrice turned on the coffee grinder, set up the coffeemaker to do its thing, and headed for the bathroom.

When she emerged, dressed in black wool slacks and a bulky sweater, Luis was in the kitchen. Rick, in his sweatpants from hell and T-shirt, was in the recliner again. She winked and blew him a kiss.

"The cat is out of the bag about Ellsberg's new job," she said. "It was on the radio. I'm sure by now Luis has told you about our visit to Isobel. I have the pictures she found; you're going to love them." She looked under the sofabed for her snow boots. "Oh, by the way, have you guys looked out the window?" She sang, "Sleighbells ring, are you list'nin'?"

Luis looked out the front door and turned on the porch light. "There's about two feet on the ground and it's still snowing hard," he told Rick.

"Look at my car," she said.

"I don't see your car. I guess that's your point, huh?" He closed the door and shivered. "Brrr. Nice weather, for Siberia."

"Could you give me a ride to the paper in the Bronco? Very soon?"

"I'm going, too," Rick said. "I figured out how I can prop up my cast in the aisle by my terminal and do an honest day's work for a criminal wage. Give me a hand, will you?"

Luis folded his arms and said emphatically, "And I say if you can't get out of the chair by yourself, you're not going anywhere."

Rick looked hopefully at Patrice.

"Don't look at me, buster. I'm not going to aid and abet this insane idea."

"Et tu, Brute?" he said. In a swift movement, he propelled himself out of the chair at the same time that he folded down the leg rest. Balanced surprisingly well on one foot, he gave them a look of triumph and a regal "Hummph." Without a word he hopped past them into the bedroom.

"Well," Luis said, "there goes Peter Cottontail, hopping down the bunny trail. I guess I'd better get dressed or the two of you--the halt and the lame--will leave me behind."

*****

At the *Guardian*, Luis made coffee while Rick and Patrice revved up their computer terminals for what promised to be a bitch of a day. She laid the Ellsberg family photos on the table in the break room and explained to Rick how Isobel had never seen a picture of her brother under age ten until she found those. "He doesn't look anything like the Stefan Ellsberg I saw," she concluded.

"Describe the man you saw. No, wait!" Rick snapped his fingers like he'd just remembered something. She followed him as he hopped to his desk and watched him sort through a morass of paperwork. "Here it is!" He pulled a five-by-seven black and white photo out of an envelope. It was a formal news photo of Stefan Ellsberg, put out by the Department of Energy to publicize his colloquium.

"That's the man I saw--whoever he is," she said.

"What's the phone number here that bypasses the answering machine?" Luis said. "I'm going to get somebody in Washington to work on where Carl Ellsberg got his money, and whether he traveled behind the Iron Curtain before it came down." He looked at his watch. "I also have to get in touch with the scientist here who does fingerprints for the Bureau."

"Patrice," Rick said, "please get Luis set up in the business manager's office. And please call Danny and ask him to come in as soon as he can. Or sooner."

At eight Marian unlocked the front door and came in. When she saw all the lights on she stopped stock-still and looked comically at her watch. She held it up to her ear like she thought it had stopped.

Rick laughed. "No, you're fine, Marian. We're workaholics."

She shook the snow off her wool coat and hung it up to dry. "It's really coming down," she called to Rick. "Now the schools are on a two-hour delay and the Laboratory is on a one-hour delay."

Patrice and Luis stepped out of the business manager's semi-private cubicle. "Marian," Patrice said, "you know Rick's brother Luis. He'll be getting some phone calls here this morning."

"Yes, hello again," Marian said with a warm smile. "Let me know if you need anything."

Rick pulled up the news story about Stefan Ellsberg's

appointment on the wire service. "Give me what you can about his being born here, Patrice. I want an excuse to run the photo of him as a child next to the new one. We won't comment; we'll just plunk it in there and let it raise questions by itself. Do you have the press release from the Lab about his graduate degrees, et cetera? Work that in, too. Get as much done as you can before the colloquium so I can do a tentative layout." She didn't answer and he looked up. "Please," he added with chagrin.

Danny arrived and headed to the darkroom. "I got some good shots of Mayor Kozar at the science museum yesterday," he said to Rick as he flew by. Then he stopped and reversed his steps. "What the hey are you doing here?" he said to Rick.

*****

An hour later the newsroom was filled with reporters, and the coat rack was full as well, with wet parkas, scarves and hats. Each person who came in gave his or her eyewitness weather report, calling loudly that the snow looked like at least two feet so far, and it was still snowing like crazy.

Patrice called across the newsroom to Rick. "I've written in everything I can about Stefan Ellsberg ahead of time. I slugged it FRAUD," she added, referring to the word he'd need to look for in his computer menu. "It's twenty-seven inches, but there's some fat. Depending on what is worth saying about the colloquium, I'll try to stop at forty. Will we have enough room for that?"

Rick grinned, happy to be back in the thick of things. "You know the answer to that. You get the story, I worry about the room."

Luis had been on the phone since before the coffee was ready; then he'd gone to meet someone at the Laboratory. He came back into the newsroom, muttering expletives about the snow and roads. He caught Patrice's eye and said, "We'd better leave soon. Traffic on Diamond looks like the Beltway."

"Let's talk a minute before you go," Rick said. With difficulty, he extricated himself from his chair and the adjoining chair where he rested his broken leg. "Let's go into Kent's office."

Kent was not there, no surprise to Patrice, with the weather what it was. She guessed the highway to Santa Fe was probably clogged worse than a Pentagon elevator at quitting time.

"Now, the colloquium is at ten," Rick said. "And I have your write up on . . ."

He was interrupted by a knock on the door. "I'm sorry to interrupt," Danny said, "but I thought you'd want to see this right away. When I went to put the picture of Mayor Kozar at the science museum down on your desk, I happened to set it next to the picture of Stefan Ellsberg as a boy. Look at this." He held out the photo of Isobel and Stefan in one hand and a good, clear photo of the Russian mayor in the other. Patrice and Luis crowded close to get a good look.

"Son of a bitch!" Rick said. "Son of a bitch!"

Chapter 23

Patrice and Luis settled into the third row on the right-hand side of the Physics Auditorium.

"So, you are sure two of the men with Mayor Kozar Tuesday night were KGB agents?" She was dubious.

"KGB or its equivalent in the new Russia, yes."

"How can you tell?"

Luis shrugged. "I can't explain how I know. It's just something you learn to detect. It's like how women detect a jerk. It's a combination of instinct and learning."

She looked incredulous. "You mean to tell me there are women who can detect a jerk? Now I know you're making it up."

The auditorium was only about a third full, probably a combination of the snowstorm and lack of interest. A well-groomed man from Public Affairs introduced Stefan Ellsberg.

The only man in the room better groomed than the Public Affairs guy and Stefan Ellsberg was Luis, Patrice noted with a smile. She knew that in some sort of Los Alamos corollary to "real men" jokes, "real scientists" didn't dress up for anybody. There were more faded flannel shirts in the audience than in a lumber camp. Ellsberg didn't look anything like a real scientist. He looked like a politician.

The host said flattering things and the Lab photographer shot about eighteen photos of Ellsberg speaking earnestly about the importance of nuclear accountability, non-proliferation and safe dismantling of the thirty thousand weapons in Russia's nuclear arsenal.

"What do you think?" Luis said.

"I like his tie," Patrice answered wryly. She caught Isobel's glance from one row up, in the center section and waved. Isobel smiled and nodded to the two of them.

When Ellsberg finished, Patrice and Luis left by a side door and drove back to the newspaper office.

Back at her terminal, Patrice rubbed her hands to warm them up enough to type. Sitting forward in her chair so her left hand could reach the keyboard, she whipped out a quick article on what Ellsberg had said.

As she walked by Rick's desk en route to the composition room, she said quietly, "Is it okay if I just put 'blah-blah-blah' for what Ellsberg said?" She picked up the dummy of the front page to see how much space Rick had assigned for the Ellsberg story. The photos had been sized and their placement noted on the dummy. A story about the county utilities budget spread across six columns on the bottom of the page.

"I don't care what you put as long as you don't say anything about his identification problem. Kent is paranoid about anything that flirts with libel. And here he comes now."

She saw Kent approaching Rick's desk. "The colloquium story is filed under COLLO," she said quickly and kept walking.

Patrice walked into Composition to see the front page before the pressmen took it. On the right an article with photo detailed the visit to Los Alamos by a delegation from the Sister City, Arzamas-16. The picture showed Kozar examining a display at the Bradbury Science Museum. Beside him were two Russian students. On the left, a news/feature article described Stefan Ellsberg's plum job. Beside it was the photo of Ellsberg sent in by the DOE. A sidebar, written by Patrice, about Ellsberg having been born in Los Alamos and being the son of famous particle physicist Carl Ellsberg began beside that and both said "continued on page 7." The photo of ten-year-old Stefan Ellsberg (with Isobel cropped out) was enlarged and placed prominently on the page, not far from Kozar's photo. It looked like they had made a mistake and put the childhood photo by the wrong man. It will be interesting to see the reaction, Patrice mused. It occurred to her at that moment that Isobel had probably not thought of the possible Kozar connection.

"Patrice, line two," Marian said on the intercom.

"Thank you. This is Patrice."

"Patrice! Oh, my God!" Patrice could barely make out the words through the sobs from Isobel Ellsberg. "Come over here quick. Please, help me! I've been robbed!" Isobel's tears and ragged breathing underscored her distress. "Someone broke into the house while I was at the colloquium and stole something."

"Call the police. I'll be right over," Patrice said. She found Luis in the business manager's office; he was just hanging up the phone. "Isobel just called and begged me to come over. She was robbed--actually, burgled--while she was at the colloquium."

"I've got to wait here for a call," he said.

"I can go alone. She's calling the police." Luis looked concerned but Patrice insisted, so he tossed her the keys to the Bronco.

"Okay. If I get this call before you get back, I'll come over there." She opened her mouth to point out that since she now had the car, getting there would be a long walk for him, but she decided to skedaddle instead.

The police had arrived before Patrice got to Isobel's house. When she walked in through the kitchen she heard Isobel sobbing.

Patrice continued into the dining room. The home had, indeed, been ransacked. The floor was speckled with broken pieces of china from the cabinet. Isobel sat in the dining room between two police officers. She had her face buried in a linen napkin which muffled her sobs.

Isobel lifted her face and shouted, "I can't just 'notify the bank,' about the loss! Aren't you listening to me? The goddam bank is in Liechtenstein!"

"Hello, officer, I'm Patrice Kelsey. Ms. Ellsberg asked me to come." She pulled a chair close to Isobel and sat down, their knees touching. "Isobel, what was stolen?"

"The passbooks!" Isobel continued to shout. "The three passbooks to bank accounts. I found them yesterday. They're red, about this big." She formed a rectangle with her fingers.

Patrice recalled seeing three books about the size of passports the night before. Isobel had scooped them off the recliner and placed them in the center drawer of the china cabinet before she and Luis sat down.

The young police officer wasn't catching on. He continued to write notes about the scene and ask her if she was missing any jewelry, silverware, or cash.

The phone rang and, as Isobel was in no condition to talk, Patrice answered it.

"Isobel Ellsberg, please. This is Los Alamos Medical Center."

"Ms. Ellsberg has had a shock and can't come to the phone. Could I help you? This is a friend."

"Her father has suffered a coronary and it's important she come to the hospital. I haven't been able to reach her brother," the woman said.

"Did you try Public Affairs at the Laboratory?" Patrice asked. "Dr. Stefan Ellsberg gave a talk there this morning."

"Thank you. I'll try that. In the meantime, could you bring Ms. Ellsberg here?"

"I'll try," she said, then hung up the phone. She placed her hand gently on Isobel's shoulder. "Isobel, listen to me, please. I have to tell you something."

Her shoulders gradually stopped heaving and she took a deep, quivering breath. "What is it?"

Patrice knelt in front of her so she was looking up at Isobel's red, swollen face. "That call was from the hospital. They say your father is worse. They need you to go there right away."

Isobel looked at her and sniffed loudly, wiping her nose with the napkin. She didn't say anything, so Patrice repeated the message. This time Isobel nodded and got to her feet. Lt. Pauling arrived to see about the burglary report and Patrice told him about the hospital call.

"Come with me, Ms. Ellsberg," Pauling said. "I'll take you to the hospital." Isobel followed him out, forgetting her coat. Patrice hurried behind her and gave it to Pauling. "I'll see you at the hospital," she said to Isobel.

"Call Larry!" she sniffed. "Please."

"Sure, I'll call him right away."

By the time Patrice parked and found the cardiac care unit, Isobel had calmed down and Pauling had left to find Stefan. Patrice called Luis from a pay phone to tell him where she was.

"Marian said I could use her car," he said. "I'll be there in ten minutes."

Patrice leafed through a magazine article titled "Can Women Have It All?" without seeing the words while they waited for word about Isobel's father.

A doctor came into the waiting room. He apparently thought the two women were related; his explanation of the procedure used on Carl Ellsberg was directed more to Patrice than to Isobel. The bottom line was, old Dr. Ellsberg was fading, and the family was being allowed in to say farewell. Isobel followed him, the napkin still twisted in her hands.

Luis found Patrice after Isobel went into the CCU. "Well, I got the call I'd been expecting," he said in a low voice. "Carl Ellsberg has a long history of making cash deposits and withdrawals in very large sums, far more than he could ever have received from salary and investments. And before his health failed he traveled frequently to Eastern Bloc countries, especially to Budapest. On a half dozen of those trips he was watched, but he managed to lose the tail. There's no record of where he went. At least we have no record of where he went."

"How did he keep a security clearance?"

"Good question. It appears the routine personnel security checks he underwent made a curious bypass. A bureaucratic bypass that defies all reason."

"What's that?"

"He was certified A-OK by a young federal servant, Aldrich Ames, whose address is now a federal prison."

Isobel came back out, supported by the doctor. He helped her into a seat. "Dr. Ellsberg passed away just now. Has anyone found his son yet?"

"No," Patrice said. "Several people are trying to locate him. I spoke to Ms. Ellsberg's fiancé before I came. He's on his way to take care of her."

Isobel was vigorously twisting the napkin and muttering something through clenched teeth. Patrice sat close enough to pat her hands. "I've got to get those passbooks back!" Isobel said fiercely.

"Who else do you suppose knew about them?"

"I didn't know until yesterday myself!" Isobel wiped her eyes and continued in a raspy voice. "Larry knew. I told him last night; he saw the passbooks and the new will, and the pictures I found in Mother's sewing basket. And I'm sure Stefan knew. Maybe those people who signed the will. Maybe the lawyer. It certainly wasn't Larry that took them. He wouldn't gain anything by that. He was going to marry me, and anything I inherited we'd share. That's how I wanted it." She blew her nose and started to cry all over again. "We were going to live in Italy. That's my favorite place."

A nurse came out to express her condolences and asked Isobel to go with her to take care of some important paperwork. Patrice borrowed Luis's cellular phone to call Public Affairs at the Laboratory. "Craig? Have you located Stefan Ellsberg yet?" She was pretty sure that if anyone could find him it would be Craig. After all, it was Craig who gave her the phone number that turned out to be Senator Aragon's home number.

"Yes," he answered in a weary voice. "The hospital has called about five times to say his father is worse."

"Carl Ellsberg died a few minutes ago," she said.

"Oh." He paused. "I reached Stefan about five minutes ago and he said he'd drive to the hospital." He added, as an afterthought, "As you might guess, the press conference is postponed."

"Thanks, Craig. Here's to better days," she said.

Just then Larry Dreyfus showed up dressed in what the irreverent wags at the paper called "Labbie uniform": ill-fitting chinos, frayed flannel shirt with two pockets, both with plastic pocket protectors, and a chain around his neck from which dangled and clattered his Lab badge, radiation film badge, and ten or twelve keys.

No wonder the men to women ratio is so high in Los Alamos, Patrice said to herself. Isobel returned with the nurse and hugged Larry, snuffling softly into his shirt.

"Isobel, I'm so sorry about your father. We've got to go, now, but I'll call you later," Patrice said. "Please let me know if there's anything I can do."

"Thank you for coming," Isobel said, wiping her nose on an already soggy tissue.

Patrice called Rick from the lobby and told him about Ellsberg's death. It was too late to get it in Thursday's paper, so it would have to keep until Friday.

"How about I call in an order for a couple of pizzas and you pick them up on your way back?" he said. "We need to sit down and comb through this rat's nest. I've gotten calls from the *Washington Post* and *The New York Times* this morning. They heard the FBI is digging fast for information on Stefan Ellsberg and his father, and they smell blood. We're sitting in the center of a huge story, and they want it before we get it for ourselves."

*****

Twenty-five minutes later Rick, Luis and Patrice

commandeered the break room. Rick tossed all the newspapers off the table into a pile in the corner and Luis spread the pizza boxes and salad containers out to share. All three of them had their mouths full when the intercom buzzed on the wall phone. Rick picked it up and listened. "For Agent Romero," he said, handing it to Luis.

"This is Special Agent Luis Romero. Yes, Dr. Malone. What did you find out?"

"That's the fingerprint expert," Patrice said for Rick's benefit. They set their pizza slices down and stared at Luis's face.

"They don't match? Thanks. Hold on." He took the receiver away from his mouth and turned to Rick. "Dr. Malone says the boy's clear fingerprints on the edge of the fingerpainting do not match the fingerprints on the vase Stefan Ellsberg gave to Carl Ellsberg two days ago. The boy's prints also do not match the fingerprints sent this morning from the FBI. The prints on the vase do match the FBI's prints for the man who says he's Stefan Ellsberg, however."

"Ask him if this is something he can make a copy of, like a blowup we can reproduce," Rick said with a big smile.

Luis repeated the question. "Easy, can do, he says, just like a poster for the post office." Rick gestured that he wanted the receiver. "Here's my brother Rick, the paper's managing editor."

"Dr. Malone? Thanks for the good work. We're all toasting you with Pepsi." They held up their cans to confirm the salute. "Here's Luis back."

"What's that?" Luis said, his smile fading. "Who else asked? Did Agent Watters tell you? No, I don't know the name. Just a minute." He nodded toward Rick. "Does the name Lowell Carswell mean anything to you?"

Rick almost choked. "It sure as hell does. He's with the *Washington Post*."

Luis mouthed "Oh," and held the receiver back to his mouth. "Did Watters tell him anything yet? Good. Yeah, I'll call Watters and ask him to keep the lid on. He can just take a long,

long lunch hour and then leave early." He laughed at something Malone said. "You're a hell of a guy. Thanks again."

Luis hung up the phone and grabbed the last slice of sausage pizza right before Rick did. "Malone had to talk to my friend Agent Watters at the Bureau--that's who sent the fingerprints for comparison--and Watters said Lowell Carswell has been calling every hour to see if there's more on the Ellsberg story. Carswell is just fishing, Watters told Malone, but he can't be put off forever. I think the *Post* will have the story by Saturday at the latest. Tomorrow is even possible."

"Yeah, Lowell Carswell never takes 'no comment' for an answer," Rick said.

"Under other circumstances, I'd wish him well. But not on *my story!*" Patrice said vehemently.

There was a quick knock at the door, it opened a crack, and a young man from the back room handed in three copies of the Thursday *Guardian*. The three of them stared at the page one photos.

"Well," Patrice said, "now we know why Carl Ellsberg had a stroke when he saw Kozar walk in! Isobel will have a stroke when she sees this." They sat quietly munching the pizza. Patrice's mind raced with the implications of the powder keg/story they were sitting on.

She wiped her hands on a napkin. "You know, Isobel said the passbooks were to a bank in Liechtenstein, and at the hospital she told me Larry Dreyfus wouldn't have taken them, because, as she put it, 'Anything I inherited we'd share.' Well, I don't think Isobel is playing with all the dots on her dominoes today, because I'll bet Larry was thinking about the measly twenty thousand dollars Daddy Big Bucks was leaving her."

"Are you sure Larry knew about the new will?" Rick asked.

Patrice thought about it. "I remember now--yes, she said she'd shown it to him. The will and the passbooks and the pictures of Stefan as a boy."

"Anyway," she went on, "what I'm thinking is, once Ellsberg senior died and Ellsberg junior picked up the passbooks, checkbooks, stocks and bonds, along with authorization from a probate court to own it all, Larry and Isobel would be living on love. My guess is, love wasn't enough for Larry and the other snakes."

"So you think Larry took the passbooks?" Luis asked.

"Not necessarily, but I wouldn't rule him out like Isobel so quickly did. Isobel thinks she could 'take Stefan to court' over the will, but she's living in a dream world. Stefan soon will be in Moscow, the money sits in numbered accounts in Liechtenstein, to which he alone should have the passbooks under the will, and Isobel will be out of luck." She took another bite of pizza. "Larry Dreyfus's only chance to get those passbooks with Carl Ellsberg's account numbers was today," she said in conclusion.

"You're assuming," Luis said, "that Stefan was absolutely sure nothing would prevent him from getting them. He had good reason to take them, too."

"What about the lawyer and the people who signed the will?" Rick added.

"True," Luis said. "And whoever gave Carl Ellsberg the payoffs all these years would have known he was rich as Croesus. To repatriate that money would be the perfect crime. A sting! What's the family going to do? Declare publicly that he was a Russian spy and sue the former Soviet Union?"

"Luis," Rick said, "you have a truly devious, criminal mind. I'm proud to be your brother."

"What I want to know," Patrice said, "is where does Vladimir Kozar fit into this? And Senator Aragon?"

"What I want to know is, whose idea was it to order anchovies?" Luis said, picking them off his piece and laying them on another slice.

Rick opened the door and called. "Danny! We need you."

Danny sauntered in like he owned the joint. "Nice sentiment, but I'm packing to leave. This was my last day at the

Guardian. It's time for *Adios, Compadres*, as they say in San Antonio. *Vaya con Dios*."

"You can vaya all you want after midnight. For now, you're still on this team. Have some pizza," Rick added to soften the blow.

"Who ordered anchovies?" Danny asked. "I love anchovies!"

"Oh, heck, who are we fooling?" Patrice said. "We're going to get scooped every which way but loose on this story!"

"Not so fast!" Rick said. "As you put it, it's your story."

"Only until the *Washington Post* prints it," she sighed.

"Do the words 'Extra! Extra! Read all about it!' mean anything to you?" Rick said.

"You mean...?"

"Yes. A special edition!" He picked up the intercom. "Marian, do me a favor please. Go in the pressroom and ask Dave and Mark to come in here the minute they're through with today's run. Thanks." To Luis he said, "Can you get Dr. Malone over here with the fingerprints?"

Luis said, "I'm sure he'll come, or I can pick them up."

Rick opened the door. "Patrice, please start writing. Write it long, put in everything. We'll trim later. And call Sonia Greenway at the archives. We need more pictures. Kent will be back from lunch in about half an hour, and I'll have to present the story and try to talk him into letting us put out a special edition."

"I'll start writing," she said with a rueful smile, "but I have a bad feeling about asking Senator Aragon's brother if we can expose a big scandal on her very doorstep."

Chapter 24

By seven o'clock Patrice had the story. She felt like Woodward and Bernstein, Joan of Arc, and Xena the Warrior Princess all rolled into one. Her physical state and her mental state were polar opposites, exhaustion battling with euphoria.

And it was all for nothing. As the incriminating lava crept closer to Cristal Aragon, Kent Bolt crept closer to the far edge of rationality.

"You have no proof!" he shouted, his face as red as a pomegranate. He was deaf and blind to Rick's insistence that the story would break in two or three days anyway, but another paper would get all the glory. When Rick used the word "glory," Patrice thought Kent would grab him by the neck and choke him.

Luis also saw the rage in Kent's face and stepped in between them. "Other papers are calling the Bureau now," he said. "It won't stay secret for long."

"I own this paper! I and...uh, my partners." He stuck his finger in Rick's face and sputtered in anger. "You don't print a word--a word!--unless I say so!" He turned on his heel and burst into his office, slamming the door behind him.

The newsroom looked like an action film on freeze-frame. So near, and yet so far! In about eighteen hours, when the *Washington Post* printed a copyrighted story about the identity of Perseus and the perverse replacement of Carl Ellsberg's son with--with whom? Patrice wondered as she picked lint and Pirate's white fur off her black slacks.

To Rick, an hour before, Patrice had merrily called out, "I'd like to know who the man who calls himself Stefan Ellsberg was before he assumed that identity! What's the Russian equivalent of John Doe?"

"Ivan Doesky?" Rick called back.

The *Post's* story would have a skeletal feel. They were outsiders. Patrice's story had flesh and blood and bones! But they'd be across the line first. You don't have to win pretty; you just have to win.

She quickly scanned the story on her monitor and saved a copy on a disk. She wasn't willing to give up. Yes, there were holes in the story, but she was pretty sure how to fill them in. The big hole was that no one had confronted the man who called himself Stefan Ellsberg, or Senator Aragon. Kent was probably on the phone with them at that very moment, telling them to get out of town. The storm that would make it extremely difficult for any outside reporter to get into Patrice's town and steal her story would also make it hard for Stefan and Aragon to slip away.

She left her computer monitor on and pulled her parka out from under her desk where she'd tossed it. The keys to Rick's Bronco were still in the pocket.

The streets were all but deserted. Patrice followed a snowplow down Diamond Drive until she had a chance to pass it. By the time she reached the municipal golf course the road felt icy, so she put the Bronco in four-wheel drive. She was glad she had halfway up the steep hill to North Mesa.

The distance to the tip of the mesa had never seemed so long before. Out there the elegant houses grabbed the rocky mesa on one side and flaunted gravity with their jutting decks on the other. The owners had each borrowed a king's ransom for thirty years to pay for the view, but that night the dismal visibility made it worthless. The snow was an equalizer, in more ways than one.

Few cars sat at the curb on such a night in that

neighborhood of two- and three-car garages. Patrice parked two blocks away, leaving the door unlocked in case she needed to get in fast, and kicked her way through the snow to Senator Aragon's door. Through the open garage door she could see the Porsche and the Volvo 850, as well as a white Saturn in the driveway. The dark garage contrasted sharply with the house, lit up like the headquarters of an investor-owned utility.

Patrice triggered a movement-sensitive spotlight as she walked up the driveway. To forestall any defensive action, which might happen if she tried to be sneaky, she walked quickly to the door and rang the bell.

She expected to be interrogated over the intercom, so she was surprised when Senator Cristal Aragon opened the door wide.

Aragon's words were the antithesis of welcome, however. "What are you doing here? We are very busy."

Patrice saw four red leather-trimmed suitcases in the entryway and a full-length fur coat draped over them. *Mink, schmink*, she thought, *I don't know the difference, but I recognize "expensive" when I see it.*

"I won't be long," Patrice said as she shoved the door with her shoulder and strode past Aragon into the entryway. "It's urgent that I speak with Dr. Ellsberg, just for a moment."

Aragon's eyes narrowed and she opened the door wider instead of closing it. Her bee-stung lips, her talon nails and her high heels were all the same identical shade of blood red. Her black cashmere suit was tight, with a long skirt. "Get out!" she ordered, clearly not one to mince words.

Stefan Ellsberg--or so Patrice had to think of him for lack of another name--came down the polished wood staircase and set his beige leather garment bag on the marble floor before he saw her. "What's going on? What do you want?"

"My paper is printing a story about Carl Ellsberg spying for the Soviet Union during World War II. I came to get your comment. If you wish to deny the story, I will include your statement." She saw Aragon's eagle talons flex as she took a step closer to her. Patrice edged farther into the foyer.

"I'm not in a position to deny the rumor with any authority," Stefan said. "I personally have no knowledge of my father's daily life during my childhood, and before I was born. But I know why you're moving so fast to spread the filth across your paper. You have an ideal situation, an opportunity to tarnish the reputation of a respected scientist--myself--by blackening the name of my father." He opened a small closet and took a wool scarf off the shelf and set it on a suitcase.

"And how can you lose?" he went on. "My father's protection from libel ended with his death. You can drag his corpse through slime with no fear of legal action, can't you?"

"I don't think..." Patrice said, trying not to back up and show weakness. Ellsberg's face was so close to hers she looked cross-eyed at his nose.

"Well, you have no idea what you're talking about," he interrupted forcefully. "Dozens--no, hundreds--of great American and European scientists have worked to improve relations between the U.S. and the Soviet republics." He brushed some invisible lint off his sport coat and took an overcoat out of the closet, still on a wooden hanger.

"My father and the others who believed in world peace through cooperation were courageous to face the opposition of the power-mad politicians like Senator Joe McCarthy," Ellsberg said confidently. "And when you print your rumors and call them facts, scientists of the world will rally to defend my father's reputation. You will look like the lying fools you are, you journalists." He spat the last word with a sneer of disgust.

Patrice looked him in the eye. "Your name plays a much bigger part in the story than you seem to recognize."

"What are you talking about?" He removed the hanger, placed it back in the closet, and draped the black wool coat with fur collar over his garment bag.

"About your false identity as Stefan Ellsberg. About how you and the real Stefan were switched when he was about ten."

He moved toward Patrice like a panther, ready to pounce. She held her ground, aware that Aragon was close behind her, probably smelling her fear.

His face contorted with rage. "You should be jailed for such a lie. If you print such a thing, I'll sue for millions."

"Don't worry, Stefan, she's lying." Kent Bolt walked in the still open door and quietly shut it behind him. "My paper isn't printing a word of these allegations. And this bitch no longer works for my paper, anyway."

A car door slammed and Stefan motioned Aragon, Kent and Patrice into the living room. Patrice stalled, watching the door. He opened it a crack and turned back to Aragon. "It's Isobel and her lover boy."

"I thought maybe it was Mayor Kozar," Patrice said, "coming to claim the millions of dollars old Dr. Ellsberg salted away for his only son." She was ready to duck if Kent punched her, but the open-hand slap that nearly dislocated her jaw came from Cristal Aragon.

"Take her into the bedroom." Stefan's bushy eyebrows lowered and his eyes narrowed into slits. "Now!"

In a heartbeat, a balding man of medium height stepped into the entryway from the living room, and with the speed and ferocity of a wolverine, he pulled Patrice's right arm behind her in a torturous position that brought her to her knees.

She recognized Erik Griegson from his photo with Doyle Silver. It made sense he knew Cristal Aragon, Patrice thought, though she couldn't imagine how. Together they'd witnessed the very-very-last will and testament of Carl Ellsberg.

"Move or I'll do this with your broken arm!" he hissed. Patrice almost vomited from the pain in her heretofore "good" arm. She tried to get her feet under her when he said again, "Move! And I mean now!"

The doorbell rang and Stefan delayed opening it, glaring at Griegson and Patrice. Though she was nearly doubled over at the waist, she got to her feet and went where Griegson shoved her, toward the living room. Some social worker! she thought.

Straight ahead Patrice saw carpeted steps down to a sunken living room. The enormous windows and sliding glass doors reflected the room back to itself. Just before the steps Griegson shoved Patrice to the right, down a hallway with thick ivory carpeting. About halfway down the hall he hurled her into what she felt sure was the master bedroom. The bed was bigger than king size and three walls were mirrored, reflecting the light of a pink crystal chandelier. Patrice thought the place looked like a suite at Caesar's Palace.

Cristal Aragon followed them into the bedroom and closed the door behind her. "In here," she said, leading the way across the room, past a bathroom twice the size of Patrice's apartment, and into a massive closet.

Griegson loosened his hold and Patrice started to stand up straight, but Aragon wrenched her arm up again to bring her to her knees. Above Patrice, Aragon leaned into the wall of clothes, shoved a dozen evening gowns back, and exposed the wall behind them. A hidden door with a large outside latch was flush with the wall. About five feet long and three feet high, it opened downward like the slot on a mailbox. In the dim light in the walk-in closet Patrice couldn't see anything inside the gaping space.

"Erik, put her in," Aragon said, backing out of the evening gowns.

He shoved Patrice forward and she hit her head against the wall at the back of the space. It was only about three feet deep. She rolled in, trying to protect her broken left arm from further damage, and the wood door slammed upward beside her. She heard the latch lock into place inches from her ear.

Patrice lay like a rag doll in the dark, fighting the nausea from the pain in her right arm. *It must have every kind of muscle damage arms can have*, she thought. She moved it slightly and flexed it, trying to assess the damage. *Jeez, but that man is strong!*

As the pain ebbed she felt around her prison. It must have been five feet long exactly; she had to keep her knees drawn up a little to fit. It had virtually no air. It was a good place to hide fairly large valuable objects, like paintings or Indian pottery, but was no place for living human beings.

She went over in her mind how many turns they had made to get where she was. It seemed to her they'd gone in sort of a "U," and that the foyer wasn't far away as the rat crawls. Silly though the thought of a rat in a house like this was, she wished she hadn't thought of it.

She was pretty sure she heard a door slam and someone yelling. She tried cupping her hand around her ear against each wall until she found where the sound was louder.

She recognized Isobel's voice. She was yelling, all right. Patrice could make out the word "passbooks" and "mine." Stefan was yelling back, calling her a lazy bitch.

Voices close by surprised Patrice, and she put her ear against the wooden door to the hiding place. She tried not to think of the word *coffin* to describe it.

"Leave her in the hidden closet," Griegson was saying to someone. "I'm going to give her a shot of..." She couldn't understand what he said next. He must have been in the bathroom when he started talking and gone back into the bedroom. Another voice was too muffled to make out.

Patrice could tell by the change in pressure in her box that the door to the walk-in closet opened. Just then she heard Isobel scream, "You lying bastard!" followed by a gunshot.

"Shit!" Aragon said, not far from the door to Patrice's cell. "Go on, Erik, see what's happening. Shoot that bitch if you have to. I'll take care of Nancy Drew here and meet you in the garage."

"Where are the passbooks?"

"Where do you think they are? Stefan has them. We'll all go together. Quit worrying and do what you have to do! Go help Stefan!"

Patrice heard the hangers slide back and the key in the

lock. She leaned her right shoulder against the door and pressed her feet hard against the opposite wall. When the lock gave way, she torpedoed the door into Aragon and scrambled past her.

One step into the bedroom, Patrice grabbed a pottery lamp and ran back into the closet before Aragon had regained her balance and gotten her breath back to scream. She crashed it on her head with every ounce of her strength plus the advantage of standing over her, and Aragon slumped onto the carpet.

This lamp must have a stone core, Patrice thought for an instant. It didn't even break. In Aragon's hand was a needle with God-knew-what in it. Patrice was sorely tempted to inject her with it, but she settled for rolling her into the hidden vault and locking it.

She put the syringe, with a cap on the needle, into her inside zippered pocket, and set the heavy lamp back on the table. Things looked normal.

Back in the bedroom she quietly closed the door to the hall and took a quick look around. Beside the bed rested the holder for a portable phone, but no phone. A laptop computer in a leather case lay open on the bed. Beside it were the airline ticket folders. She looked inside the folders--they were empty.

She reached down on the right side of the computer, released the disk inside, and dropped it in her coat pocket. She rifled through the tight pocket in the top of the computer case for any other disks. She found three more and pocketed them, too.

She pulled out the bedside table drawer--nothing but magazines. She pulled out the center drawer of the dresser. Lingerie, a jewelry box, and--eureka!--a dainty little gun. She shoved the gun into the inside right pocket of her ski parka. Feeling farther back in the drawer, she extricated a small box of bullets and jammed them into her left inside pocket.

She listened at the door. Isobel was screaming, "Leave him alone! That's my gun! Give me my gun, you bastard!"

Patrice knew from what she'd seen of the house that she couldn't make it to the garage without going past the foyer, where the circus was going on. She could make it to the staircase, but getting upstairs was probably a mistake, and she couldn't afford any mistakes.

She pressed the lock button beside the doorknob of the bedroom door, then opened the French door to the deck, stepped out into the bitter cold, and slid it shut behind her. She was startled to hear a click as it automatically locked.

In the dark she couldn't tell how far down the ground was under the deck, but she crawled under the bottom railing, on her stomach, feet first, and felt for a foothold on the wooden crossbars. It would have been a lot easier with two arms, but she guessed she had enough adrenaline for a platoon. If she had to crawl down a hundred-foot tower over a vat of alligators, she could do it. She wanted out of there, at any price.

She lost track of height as she concentrated on her footholds, brushing off the snow each time before she put her weight on the next spot. It was pitch black, but she had developed a sense of where the cliff edge was. She was on a three-sided point of rock, like the bow of a ship. When she felt the ground, she kept hold of the deck supports and moved sideways toward the wall of the house. Like a spider, she flattened her belly against the concrete and moved across the wall of what must be the basement. She had about forty feet to go when light flooded the deck above her, the deck that rimmed the living room in a fan shape.

She held perfectly still, afraid of dislodging a rock and making a sound. She couldn't tell which was colder--her front, against the icy concrete, or her back, being whipped by the wind on this rocky snag. At least she was sheltered by the deck from the snow, which was still falling at a horrific rate.

Someone landed hard on the deck right over her head. Patrice again heard Isobel yell, "You bastard!" presumably at Stefan, though Erik Griegson was a bastard, too. "Leave me alone."

Patrice could hear Dreyfus from inside the house saying,

"Leave her alone." She heard the glass door slide shut, and the sound of his voice was muffled suddenly.

"The good news," Stefan was saying, only a few feet from where Patrice clung to the wall, "is the Pope will make you a saint. You've been such a perfect martyr."

"What are you... What are you doing? Let go! Let go of me!" The confidence and anger in Isobel's voice were supplanted by fear. There was a scuffle. Snow fell between the cracks of the deck onto the back of Patrice's neck. The sound of their voices moved outward, toward the edge of the deck.

"Let go!" Isobel said. "I'm not going over there by the edge. I'm going to scream."

"Go ahead and scream," he said, as if the idea amused him. "People always scream around here--when they fall off cliffs!"

The next sound Patrice heard was a sound she would not forget as long as she lived. Isobel Ellsberg's scream of utter terror died away into the black hole of the canyon beneath Patrice's feet.

She placed her forehead against the concrete and held tight to steady herself. Trying to overcome the waves of nausea made her grip even more precarious.

The sliding door opened and Griegson emerged with Dreyfus. He must be holding Dreyfus in a hammerlock, Patrice guessed, from the groaning and scuffling above her. "Your turn, lover boy," Stefan said.

"Get his other arm," Griegson said. The scuffle again moved away from Patrice, toward the railing of the deck. "You know," Stefan said in a voice icier than the snow and wind, "you really should mind your own business."

Again there was the terrifying scream of a human falling, and falling, and falling.

Someone stepped out of the living room onto the deck. "I don't want any part of this!" Kent Bolt spat out the words. "Where's Patrice?"

"She's taking a nap," Stefan said. "The sooner you get out

of here the less you'll have to deny." In a different tone, a command voice, he barked, "Tell Cristal to finish packing. We're leaving. After you," he said. Patrice was pretty sure he addressed the last comment to Kent.

All three went back in and Patrice heard the glass door slam shut hard and heard the click of the lock. She kept edging along the wall, away from the bedroom. The concrete made a right angle and she was in sight of the garage.

She crept on her hands and knees uphill on the rocks toward a door. She turned the knob, relieved to find it unlocked. Inside what appeared to be a storage room, she stepped forward cautiously, but tripped over a coiled hose. A rake fell across her back. She grabbed it to keep it from clattering to the concrete floor.

She could see a door on the other end of the narrow storage area. Again she turned the knob slowly; the door opened to a very large utility room. A door on her right probably led to the garage; a door straight ahead with glass panes probably led to the kitchen.

If she could get into the kitchen, she could call 911. She wouldn't even have to say anything, since Los Alamos had the Enhanced system that would trace the call instantly.

She peeked into the kitchen and gave up on the phone. The whole room was open to the den and foyer, and all the lights were on. She couldn't see Stefan, but she could hear him talking. The front door slammed hard.

She wanted to know what was going on in the foyer, but getting away was her priority. If she could get into the garage, she might be able to get out the far side and make a run for Rick's car. She couldn't risk being seen, though. She had enough motivation to run like a cheetah, but she couldn't outrun a bullet. Recalling how she'd seen Stefan out for his morning run just the day before, she had to admit she probably couldn't outrun Stefan, either.

"Get Cristal and let's get out of here," she heard Stefan

say inside the house.

Patrice edged out of the utility room to the garage in time to see Kent Bolt's Mercedes pull out of the driveway and fishtail in the cul de sac, narrowly missing Larry Dreyfus's parked Jeep as he pulled away like a missile. The door from the house to the utility room opened and Patrice heard Stefan yell, "Cristal! Where the hell are you! We're leaving!" Stefan yelled. She'd missed being found in the utility room by about ten seconds. She crouched behind a stack of cardboard boxes labeled Books.

"She's in the bedroom!" Griegson called. "I'll get her." "No! I have to get my computer anyway. I'll get her. You load the suitcases in your car. I don't have room in the Porsche."

Patrice watched Erik carry a load of suitcases out, set them by the Saturn, and go back for more. While he was in the house, she ran between the Volvo and the Porsche, keeping her head down. She looked inside the Volvo and saw that the keys were in it. She tried the passenger door but it was locked. She checked the back door on the passenger side, opened it, and crawled in.

Griegson came into the dark garage again but before the door closed behind him Stefan yelled something that made Griegson drop his load of suitcases on the ground and run back into the house. Patrice tugged the car door closed tight. She was about to climb over the seat and drive off in the Volvo when the door from the utility room to the garage slammed open and the overhead light came on.

"What the hell is going on!" Stefan yelled. "Where the hell is Cristal?"

"Her car's here," Griegson said stupidly.

"That's what we're going in. I changed my mind; my Porsche would never make it downtown in this storm. We'll leave yours and hers where I parked the rental. Did Cristal leave with Kent?"

Patrice willed herself to contract to the size of a shoebox but it didn't work. She was still a full-sized woman and she was hiding in the back seat of the car Stefan Ellsberg was about to get into. And, to make her life even worse--and more likely to end it--the garage was lit up like a department store with ten shopping days 'til Christmas.

"I'm going to back it out and close up the garage," Stefan said. "She must have gone with Kent. Go take another look in the house," Stefan said. Apparently he then noticed the suitcases sitting out in the snowstorm. "Damn it, you idiot! That's leather out there soaking in the snow!"

"I was about to put them in the trunk when you yelled for me," Griegson said. "I'll put them in now."

"No! Damn it! Give me the keys. You go look for Cristal again."

Patrice could hear Stefan slamming around behind the car, tossing suitcases in the trunk of the Saturn and swearing about the idiot who didn't know leather from cardboard. If only he'd go inside she could get out of the Volvo and run for Rick's Bronco two blocks away. Or climb under the Porsche.

Just then she heard Griegson burst through the door into the garage. "I found her! That Kelsey bitch hit her over the head and locked her in the vault. I heard her banging on the door. Wait a minute; she's coming."

Patrice heard the trunk of the Saturn slam and the two men's voices seemed to diminish. Then the door from the garage to the house slammed, too. She reached for the door handle but the driver's door of the Saturn, parked behind the Porsche, opened, closed, and the engine roared. The headlights came on shining right on the Volvo.

She heard the door of the Saturn open again and heard Griegson swear, muttering angrily about the damn snow. She recognized the sound of someone scraping windows. He was probably standing only a few feet from the Volvo.

She was trapped, and she had no doubt Stefan and company would throw her over the deck without a second thought.

She let go of the door handle and instead felt along the back seat for some kind of release mechanism; the seat was split about sixty-forty. Sitting on the floor in front of the forty percent side and keeping her head down, she fingered the release on the larger side, a plastic button up near the headrest. She tugged hard and the seat folded down.

She tucked herself into a ball and dove through to the trunk, pulling the seat up behind her and locking it in place. In the dark she pulled the gun from one pocket and the bullets from another pocket, and loaded the revolver. A heartbeat later the door to the house opened and banged shut.

"I'm riding with Erik!" Aragon said.

"You're riding with me! Now get in! You've fucked up enough already tonight!" Stefan and Aragon got into the Volvo, a few feet away from Patrice's hiding place. *This one, too, has an eerie resemblance to a coffin*, she thought, with sadness for all she'd miss in life if she died that night. *Mom, William, and Rick. No! Don't think about that!* she told herself sternly. She forced herself to breathe into her hand, making no sound at all.

"That fucking idiot!" Stefan said in English, then what must have been (from his tone of voice) a string of profanity in Russian. He started the car and honked at Griegson to get out of the way. Part way down the driveway he stopped and shut the automatic garage door.

"What happened to Isobel?" Aragon said. "I heard a gunshot."

"Little sister pulled a dramatic scene and threatened to shoot me. All I had to do was kick her hand. She shot a hole in the foyer. Then she and her lover boy had a tragic accident, sort of a lovers' leap."

"Kent said he won't let the paper print anything!" Aragon said. "We could have gotten out of here without all this added trouble!"

"Kent has his head up his ass so far I don't know why you ever listen to him," Stefan barked. "I took care of the paper myself."

Patrice pressed her knees down as hard as she could to keep from rolling. She followed the route in her mind's eye; she recognized the hill back down off North Mesa, then the straight-away by the golf course, up the hill by the Conoco station, and a curve to the left on Diamond Drive.

"Do you have the computer?" Aragon asked suddenly. She sounded like a housewife worrying whether she'd turned off the oven before she'd left.

"Of course I have the computer!" He quickly worked up to another diatribe. "You are such a fool to have let that woman get away!"

She made apologetic sounds in Russian and seemed to calm him down. "What did you mean, you took care of the paper?"

"I mean, if you're standing in the press room in," he paused, "in twenty-one minutes, you're going to be plastered against the ceiling. And guess what happens when a paper has no presses?"

"What about Kent?" she said, alarmed. Patrice found her concern touching, but since Kent never set foot in the press room, and several fine people did, she figured the concern was misplaced.

They went up another slight hill, then made a sudden stop. Patrice figured they were at the light at Trinity Drive. About two minutes later they made a sudden right turn that made her bang her head on the wheel well.

"There's Erik," Aragon said. "Are you sure you have the keys to the rental car?"

"Damn you!" he shrieked, then swore again in Russian. "I told you I have the keys. Just shut your fucking mouth!" The car jerked and Patrice heard the sound of a slap; at the same time she heard Aragon yelp in pain. Remembering how much it had hurt when Aragon had slugged her, Patrice almost felt sorry for her. Almost.

"Now get in the car!" he said. Both doors of the Volvo opened and shut. Patrice heard Stefan lock the doors from outside. So, he took the keys with him. Darn!

She heard him swear at Griegson to hurry with the suitcases. Next she heard the sound of another car engine starting, then moving away.

She waited a full minute before she pushed the back seat down and crawled forward. She looked into the front seat, hoping against hope for a car phone, but--no.

I have to hide in the only luxury sedan in America without a car phone.

She stepped out of the back seat, pain shooting down her legs as the kinks in her circulation system worked their way out. She took a good look around. She stood at the far end of a parking lot in a professional office complex. Everything appeared to be locked and dark. She hiked as fast as she could through the deep snow to Trinity Drive to flag down help.

Fear gripped her, but she felt relief, too. She was alive, and there were still a few square inches of her body that didn't throb with pain. *For the moment, that's good enough for me!*

One of the nice things about a small town, she thought fleetingly, is when someone runs into the street waving his or her arms, someone stops. "Please help me! Someone tried to kill me!" Patrice said to the stunned family in a Dodge Minivan that skidded to a stop in front of her.

"Get in, I'll take you to the police station," the man said. Two little boys moved to the back seat to make room for her in the middle.

"No! There isn't time! Take me to the *Guardian* office, six or seven blocks that way, and I'll call the police from there."

The driver looked doubtful.

"I'm sure the police are looking for me there," she insisted. "It's the best way. Please!" She decided not to mention the possibility of a bomb in the building. She didn't think that would help get him to drive fast toward the office.

In front of the building she jumped out and said, "Go! There could be a bomb here! Don't stop!" The man asked no questions, just peeled out like a racecar driver.

As she had guessed, there were two police cars in front of the *Guardian*. "It's nice to be missed!" she said aloud, almost laughing with relief.

She ran in so out of breath she could hardly speak. "Bomb! Bomb!" she yelled, spotting Lt. Pauling before she saw anyone else. "There's a bomb in the pressroom!"

The call went toward the back of the building like fire up a fuse, and Mark and Dave tumbled into the newsroom from the back.

"What's going on?" Lt. Pauling shouted, just as an explosion sounded, muffled by thick intervening walls.

"Fire!" Marian screamed from the back of the newsroom. "Fire!"

"Everybody out!" Rick yelled as eight or ten people tried to call 911 on all four of the phone lines. Marian streaked past Patrice and straight out the front door yelling "Fire, fire, Omigod, fire!"

"We have a fire at the *Guardian*," Pauling barked into his radio. "Possible explosive device." He turned to the newsroom and yelled at the top of his lungs. "Everybody get out! Now!"

Employees streamed out the front door into the snow. Patrice heard the sirens coming toward them. She turned to find Rick and Luis, but they'd headed toward the fire instead of away from it. The fire engines barreled down Trinity Drive at full throttle, with ear-piercing noise. One of the pressmen, Mark, ran into the street to get their attention. "Around back! Around back! It's in the pressroom! Lots of chemicals," he yelled.

Patrice ran beside them and shrieked to be heard. "Two men are back there." She caught the eye of a search and rescue friend of Rick. "It's Rick and his brother. They're back there!"

Just then she saw Rick hop around the back of the building, no crutches, and hoist himself up onto the fire truck.

Tossing down a hat and coat to Luis, he fed hose out to the others.

Luis steadied the hose as a firefighter screwed it on a hydrant and opened the line. Water shot into the back of the building and the flames diminished for a minute, then came back stronger. There was a second explosion and a wall collapsed. The rush of air into the fire made it shoot a hundred feet into the air. The firemen aimed their hoses precisely on the location of the hottest fire.

The quick response brought the conflagration under control quickly, before the bay full of chemicals caught fire. The flooded floor in the bay was inconvenient, but not impossible to deal with, according to Dave, the press foreman. Along with Mark, he squeezed into the charred area to take a quick look at the presses. They shook their heads and said nothing.

"Patrice!" someone called. "What the hell?"

She lifted her eyes from the scene of the explosion and saw Danny Carter running toward her. Right behind him was Mel Hulle.

"Mel and I have been all over town looking for you!" Danny called. "What happened here?"

"A bomb," she said simply. "Let's go in out of the snow." The bedraggled group of shivering employees filed silently into the newsroom.

Mel Hulle put his hand on Patrice's shoulder. "Are you hurt? We were all worried sick about you when we realized you'd taken off on your own."

All she could do was nod at Mel and accept his awkward hug. She was too shaky to even hug him back.

She walked on what felt like lead soles over to Rick's cubicle and tucked his crutches under her better arm. She took them out the front door and around the side of the building toward the burned pressroom.

Without a word, Rick took the crutches. Holding them aside, he drew Patrice close and buried his face in her hair. She tipped her head back and kissed his wet cheeks, then his lips.

He broke off the kiss with a moan. "Oh, Patrice, Patrice." He kissed her eyes and her hair and held her so close she could scarcely breathe.

"You're shivering," he said. "Let's go inside." On his crutches, he followed her back around the building into the newsroom.

Marian brought Rick a chair and he lowered himself into it slowly. "Are you hurt?" he asked Patrice.

She had to think a moment before answering. "No, nothing serious. I'm...I'm okay now."

"Patrice." Rick put his face in his hands. "I could choke you for worrying us like this. Remind me to do that when my heart stops pounding." Exhausted by his adrenaline rush fighting the fire, he looked around the room. His eyes stopped on his brother. "Luis? Let's go in the office."

Luis helped him up and Rick dropped one crutch, putting his weight on Luis's shoulder.

"I think Lt. Pauling had better come, too," Patrice said. She pulled Rick's other crutch away and let her shoulder take its place. The three of them wobbled slowly toward Kent's office.

"What has three heads but only one brain?" Luis asked.

"I guess you don't expect me to have the answer to that riddle, do you?" she said. "Where's Kent?"

"In jail. He beat you back here and pulled a gun on me. Luis had him on the floor so fast it was a blur. Kent ordered me not to put out a paper tonight, but I don't take orders from soon-to-be-convicted felons."

"He pulled a gun?" she repeated dully. She was having a delayed reaction to her own adrenaline overdose, which she'd conjured up to save her own life, and perhaps the lives of the pressmen.

She started shivering violently from the cold and shock, but managed to tell them what she had seen and heard at Senator Aragon's house.

"I didn't see what kind of car Ellsberg and Aragon and

Griegson left in, but I know it was a rental, and I know they're headed for the airport. That must mean Santa Fe or Albuquerque. No planes can come here in a storm."

"So it was Stefan who left a bomb here? What did he have to gain?" Rick asked.

"Time to get away, out of the country. All he needed was to get rid of our presses and he had a clear shot at a clean getaway. Then I showed up, and Isobel and Larry. Oh my God." She buried her face in her hands and put her head between her knees to conquer the dizziness that overwhelmed her.

"What about Isobel and Larry?" Luis asked. "Did they go there to try and make a deal with Stefan, or what?"

Shaking her head from side to side, she rubbed her quivering hands together to steady them.

"You could use a drink," Rick said. "Sorry we don't keep liquor here even for medicinal purposes."

"What happened to Larry Dreyfus and Isobel?" Luis asked again quietly. He stood close to Patrice and massaged her shoulders.

"They're dead. Stefan threw them both off the deck into the canyon."

Everyone sat in stunned silence.

"What about Kozar?" Rick asked at last. "Did they say anything about him?"

"No. I don't know anything about where he is or what he hoped to gain from this. Oh!" she groped in her pockets. "This is the stuff Cristal Aragon was going to inject me with."

She handed it to Pauling, who looked around Kent's desk for an envelope and put the syringe inside.

There was a knock on the door. "Fire marshal," a voice called. They filed out to the newsroom. Patrice heard the fire marshal say something to Rick about arson, which was no surprise. People sat silent all over the front office, too stunned and exhausted to talk.

Patrice took off her frozen boots and rubbed her toes.

Marian watched her rub her red feet. She left the newsroom briefly and returned with a pair of slippers. Handing them to Patrice, she said, "Gayle in advertising keeps these in a file cabinet for when she works weekends."

Rick shook hands with the fire marshal and assembled all of the staff in the advertising office. They sat on desks and some on the floor. No one sat in a chair.

"The fire marshal says an explosive with a timed detonating device was placed in the press room, probably when the back bay was open for deliveries and pickup of papers by carriers. At the same time, Patrice was thrown into a hidden closet in a house on North Mesa by someone who may have had plans to kill her."

He paused. Worry and exhaustion lined his face. "There's no doubt in my mind it's connected with the story we were hoping, earlier today, to print in a special edition tonight. Anyway, like the police always say at a crime scene, the excitement is over. I want everyone except Patrice, Danny, Dave and Mark to go home immediately. Lock the door behind you."

"I have to make some phone calls," Rick said to Danny and Patrice, with a nod to the pressmen, "then we'll talk. Don't go anywhere. The firefighters will be here for a good long while and the police will be patrolling around the building." He took his crutches from Danny, and limped back to Kent's office, closing the door behind him.

People gathered up their belongings, bundled up in their boots and coats, and quietly filed out the front door.

Marian hugged Patrice as she left. "I'm glad you're all right."

"Maybe I can do something to help," Mel said. "I'll stay."

Luis would stay, too, of course.

The six of them talked in voices hardly more than a whisper about how much worse it could have been, how many chemicals were just beyond the fire line. Dave and Mark told how bad the damage to the presses was. "The explosion brought down the wall on top of the presses," Dave said.

Patrice's shivering got worse. Mel took off his dry coat.

"Here, Patrice, put this on."

She took off her soaking parka and hung it on the coat tree as Pauling walked by on his way out of the building.

"Oh, Lieutenant," she said, "here's something else." She pulled the revolver out of her coat and handed it to him. "It's loaded. I think it belongs to Senator Aragon or Stefan Ellsberg. Here's some more ammunition, too."

"First a syringe, now a gun. Do you have anything else in your pockets I should know about?"

"Just some computer disks I...uh, borrowed. I don't know if there's anything useful on them."

"Let me see," Mel said. She handed him the four disks she'd taken out of Stefan's portable computer. He turned on the monitor closest to him, but nothing happened. "The system's down," he said. "No surprise. I'll go get my laptop out of my car."

Dave, the press foreman, helped Patrice get Mel's coat around her shoulders. "What was Rick saying about someone trying to kill you?"

As she told the men about Aragon and a man named Erik Griegson locking her up and trying to inject her with something, Lt. Pauling listened, too, shaking his head in amazement.

Rick came out, his face grim. He gestured to the two pressmen. "Dave, Mark, come with me please." The three of them went back to the pressroom.

"You should be horsewhipped for going to Aragon's house alone," Luis said. "You know that, don't you?"

"Horsewhipping my battered body would be redundant. Save your strength."

Mel returned, brushing snow off his shoulders, and set up his computer on Patrice's desk. He examined the disks and slipped one in, trying to bring up information. He tried a dozen times, but got nowhere. "Well, the information is apparently encrypted, which comes as no surprise. I'm going to log on to the

Laboratory and get some expert help. This may take a while." He sounded happy to have a challenge at last.

Rick came back with Dave and Mark. The fire chief, the fire marshal and Lt. Pauling were with them.

"Any news on Stefan Ellsberg or Vladimir Kozar?" Danny asked.

"The state police have set up a roadblock the other side of Santa Fe," Pauling said, "and they're watching the airports for Ellsberg and Griegson. The man who calls himself Vladimir Kozar has disappeared, too. The Russians at the Hilltop House all say they have no idea where he went. They haven't seen him since ten a.m., or so they say."

There was a knock at the locked door. They all stood quietly, not knowing if they should open it. Pauling shrugged and went to the door. "Who is it?"

"Sonia Greenway. I have something for Patrice." Pauling opened the door a few inches and looked out.

"I asked her to bring the Ellsberg folder," Patrice said. Pauling opened the door and stood aside so Sonia could come in. Before he closed it he looked out, shading his face from the still falling snow. Then he locked it again.

"Sorry, Sonia," Patrice said. "The last person who said she had something for me had a syringe."

"What?" she said incredulously, shaking snow off her hat.

"Senator Aragon doesn't like visitors. I'll explain later. Could I see the file?"

Sonia had it in a plastic bag for protection against the snow. "Don't lose anything!" she said. "I promised they'd be safe in your care."

"Let's go into the break room," Patrice said to Rick and Danny. Sonia took off her coat and followed them. Patrice spread the photos of Carl and Elizabeth Ellsberg with the Oppenheimers and Elizabeth Ellsberg with baby Stefan on the table. From Rick's desk, Danny got the photos of the Ellsberg family in 1954, the photos presumably hidden by Isobel's mother in her sewing basket. By chance he also set out the pictures of Doyle Silver at the nursing home, the ones Patrice had removed from the bulletin board.

Sonia picked those two up. "When were these taken?" she asked.

"Thanksgiving, at the nursing home in Española. I was especially interested in the balding man. The nurse's aide said he'd visited Mr. Silver several times. Isobel Ellsberg and Larry Dreyfus identified him. It's Erik Griegson. All I knew about him until tonight was that he visited Carl Ellsberg and witnessed the signing of his new will. But tonight I got a lot better acquainted with him."

"This man?" Sonia asked, pointing to the balding man beside Doyle Silver's wheelchair.

"Yes. Erik Griegson."

"His name isn't Griegson, as far as I know," she said. "He's Norman Taggert, the historian from UC Berkeley. I remember him very well from when he signed in at the archives."

Shock registered on Patrice's face. "But you said Professor Taggert had brown, wavy hair," she protested.

"Well, there's no law that says a bald man can't wear a rug," Sonia said. "I'm positive this man is Norman Taggert."

Rick's mouth fell open, as did Patrice's. "Don't move, don't breathe. I'll be right back." He hopped back to his cubicle and picked up the phone. He struggled back to his feet five minutes later with the biggest grin they'd ever seen on his face.

"We're not giving up," Rick yelled from across the newsroom. "This fire is NOT going to stop this special edition."

"Are the presses fixable?" Danny asked.

"No. But we have a plan B. You haven't been here long enough to know this, Patrice, and neither have you, Danny, but this is the second press emergency this paper has been through. A lightning strike about ten years ago shut us down on a Saturday night."

"I remember," Dave said, "I'd just started here then as a

high school intern."

"Then you remember what we did," Rick went on. "We have a reciprocal agreement with the *Santa Fe New Mexican* to use their presses in a dire emergency, and if they were the one with the emergency, they could use ours. That's what we did that night after the lightning hit. It was an ugly paper, since our stuff wasn't a perfect fit, but it was a paper."

"Ugly!" Dave nodded. "You can say that again."

Rick smiled. "I've already called their publisher, and they're expecting us. Getting there in this storm will be an unforgettable adventure, though. So let's take computer disks and hard copy, photos and everything else we need. I can fit five people in my car."

"Oh-oh!" Patrice said, biting her lip.

"What do you mean, 'Oh-oh'? I don't like the sound of that." Rick leaned on a crutch and looked expectantly at Patrice.

"I borrowed your car to go to Senator Aragon's house," she said meekly. "It's, uh, it's still out on the end of North Mesa."

"Well, shoot. My life couldn't be more rich and wonderful!" Rick banged his crutch on the floor in frustration.

"Mel's car is at the Lab," Danny said. "He rode over here in my pickup."

"What have you got?" Rick said to Dave and Mark.

"My wife dropped me off," Mark said. "She needed the car."

"And you know what I drive," Dave said. His old VW Bug probably had one hundred ninety thousand miles on it, and no back seat.

Mel, meanwhile, was oblivious to all of them, lost in the computer disks Patrice brought back in her pocket. "I think you're going to like this!" he called out. "There's information here about offshore bank accounts and documents smuggled by Ellsberg, Senior. The old coot had a long and lucrative career. And some of this looks like a sale of plutonium to somebody, not the government."

Patrice wailed like Earth had when she handcuffed herself to the security fence. "My story!" she said. "The best story of my life is sitting in our collective hands, and we can't get it printed!"

The fire chief and Lt. Pauling exchanged looks, then grinned. "Let's go," Chief McDaniels said. "Load up."

Nine of them, counting McDaniels and Pauling, piled into their two big Chevy Blazers. Mel brought his computer, and Patrice brought the disk on which she'd saved the Ellsberg story before she left for North Mesa. She'd have to update it, but she was a fast typist.

And who can tell it better than I can? I don't even have to interview myself.

All the way to Santa Fe they listened to chatter on police and fire radios about the search for Stefan Ellsberg (a.k.a. Kozar), Kozar (a.k.a. Stefan Ellsberg), and Erik Griegson (a.k.a. Norman Taggert). The rental company cooperated, giving a description of Ellsberg's car and the license number.

It was nearly seven hours later that they made their way up the Main Hill Road, five hundred copies of the four-page paper in each car. The other four thousand would be brought up in the morning.

Patrice fell asleep when they left Santa Fe, her head against Rick's shoulder, but something woke her up. She sat forward and looked out the front of the Blazer. Snow swirled toward them with that familiar--and terrifying--tunnel effect. Suddenly she recognized where they were.

"Please!" she said to Lt. Pauling in the front seat, a catch in her voice. "Please be careful. This is where Rose and I went over the edge."

Chapter 25

Patrice woke up Friday with a paw in her face. Sometime during the night Pirate had whimpered and Patrice let her get under the covers. She heard the phone ring in the bedroom. Rick had considerately turned off the ringer on the kitchen phone to let her sleep.

"What a guy!" she said to Pirate. "No wonder you love him."

Pirate cocked her head and got up like it was the hardest thing in the world to do, then shook her head. Her tags jangled against each other.

Patrice reached up and read the heart-shaped tag. "My name is Pirate. I am lost. Call my dad, R. Romero." Etched just above the point of the heart was Rick's phone number.

Luis came out in a white bathrobe. "Rick's on the phone with Mel. He'll be out in a few minutes. And he said to ask you, where are the keys to his Bronco?"

She had to think a minute, then winced. "In the pocket of the wet ski parka I left hanging on the coat rack at the *Guardian*."

Pirate yawned and Patrice and Luis copied her unintentionally. She walked in a circle on the bed, further tangling the covers, and lay back down with her head away from the hall light.

"You ready for coffee?"

"Yes, please." She heard him grinding beans in the electric

grinder.

"I'm going to take a shower; then I'll have some coffee." She had learned from Rick's experience of how to encase a cast in a plastic bag and delicately take a shower instead of having to take a bath. To Pirate she said, "Save my place, girlfriend."

When she returned, dressed in sweat pants and the sweatshirt with one cuff cut off, the coffee was brewed and Luis had homemade biscuits in the oven. "You're incredible," she said. "Are there any more at home like you?"

"Hey!" Rick said as he hopped into the living room. Balanced on one foot, he removed two blankets from the sofa bed and folded them neatly. "I can cook."

Luis poured coffee for the three of them and said, "Danny and Mel are coming over. I'm going to get dressed. The biscuits need to come out in five minutes."

"Ah," Rick said, leaning over to kiss Patrice. "Alone at last."

Pirate made a whining noise from the bed where she had curled up in the sheets. Then she heard something outside, a car door closing, and sat bolt upright.

"It's probably Mel and Danny," Rick said, hopping to the door. "Oh, good morning, Lieutenant. Come in. We're having coffee, and the biscuits will be ready in a few minutes."

Lt. Pauling came around the corner to the breakfast nook and greeted Patrice. "Good morning. Did you get some sleep?"

"Not enough," she laughed. "You?"

He shrugged. Rick gave him a cup of coffee, took the biscuits out of the oven, and made more coffee while they talked about the weather. The storm, now over, had left behind a little over three feet of snow in town, more in the mountains. Under the blue cloudless sky, the fresh snow was dazzling.

"Did you hear the ski hill will open tomorrow?" Pauling asked. "I think it will be a little thin over by the new chair, but the top has fifty inches."

Mel and Danny arrived just as Luis joined them.

"Any news on Ellsberg/Kozar?" Luis asked Pauling when all of them had their coffee and biscuits.

"That's what I came over to tell all of you. Stefan Ellsberg--I mean the guy who gave the talk at the Laboratory yesterday--and Senator Aragon and Erik Griegson were picked up at a truck stop on I-25. They were stopped by the weather or they might have been out of the country by now. Senator Aragon is being treated with the utmost courtesy as she says she was being held against her will. She claims she's eager to cooperate with the police."

"Does Griegson admit he's really Norman Taggert?" Rick held out his mug for a refill as Luis served a fresh pot.

"Oh, yes. In fact, he insists he's Norman Taggert and that he was kidnapped by the others, that they call him Erik and he ignores them. He keeps digging a deeper hole with all his lies."

"What was he doing masquerading as Griegson?" Rick asked.

"I think I understand," Patrice combed her fingers through her hair. "I think he figured out that Carl Ellsberg and Doyle Silver were part of 'Perseus' a long time ago, and somehow found out about the fortune Ellsberg had managed to salt away. I think that as Griegson he was blackmailing both father and son. By getting Carl to change his will and leave the whole fortune to Stefan, he probably collected a tidy sum. Meanwhile, he was ready the moment he collected his 'fee' to turn them in and make the fortune he figured was just waiting for Professor Taggert, brilliant historian."

"I think you're right," Luis nodded to her. "You were suspicious of Taggert even when you thought he was nothing more than an ambitious historian. I'll admit, with chagrin, I didn't think much of your theory. But since you asked me to, I looked into his travel schedule. And he was definitely here on Sunday, the day Rick's climbing rope was cut and you had a prowler."

"So you think he cut my rope?" Rick raised his eyebrows. "When?"

Luis put his foot on the edge of a chair and retied his running shoe. "Probably while you were having lunch at McDonald's."

"He could have been watching for you near my apartment," Patrice added. "You and I talked on the phone, which was bugged, and you said you were going to bring Pirate to my place."

"But the rope was locked in my car," Rick protested.

Luis gave him a withering look. "Like a locked car door is impenetrable? Oh, please!"

"What about Wednesday afternoon, less than two days ago?" Patrice asked. "I called Taggert's office in Berkeley, and he called me back a few minutes later. He talked about being in sunny California."

This time Luis turned the withering look on Patrice. "Ever heard of call forwarding? Ever heard of brazen lying?"

"Okay, okay, I am properly chagrined." Patrice winked at Rick and turned back to Luis. "But I have another question, oh great Sherlock. Have they figured out how Kozar and Ellsberg switched? And when? And why?"

"I'm glad you asked that question!" Luis said. "I was on the phone with Washington this morning. Last night, while we were busy with the paper in Santa Fe, an intelligence officer from the Laboratory got a call from Comrade Mayor. He wouldn't say where he was at first, but he made it clear he was eager to tell all he knows in exchange for help in regaining his U.S. citizenship. The intelligence officer got another officer out of bed and they met Kozar at his motel in Santa Fe, an old tourist court on Cerrillos Road."

He cleared his throat and went on. "Two FBI special agents got there this morning to begin an extensive debriefing, but what the Bureau has been told so far by the intelligence officers is this: the switch was done when Carl's son--and Isobel's real brother--was about to start school in England. Carl had been very useful to the KGB and to Russian science during the war, but he wanted to retire from the spy business. His handlers had an ideal way to keep him working and keep his mouth shut. They took his son to Moscow and trained him to be a full-blooded Communist, a Party Member so dedicated and committed to the cause he eventually became mayor of Arzamas-16."

"Which made his parents have to deal to keep him safe?" Patrice scratched inside her cast with the handle of a spoon.

Luis nodded. "You've got it. All the time he was growing up, if Carl and Elizabeth wanted him safe, they had to follow orders. Meanwhile, a brilliant young Russian who'd been brought up in a special English-language town the Russians have for spies was substituted for Stefan." He passed the hot biscuits around and set out butter and jam.

He sipped his coffee and went on. "The young Russian, now known as Stefan Ellsberg, continued his education in the best schools in Europe, then college and graduate school at University of California. He worked his way up in the area where science and politics overlap, and was on his way to knife this country in the back big time."

"By working in Russia, right?" Rick yawned broadly and rubbed his eyes.

"Right!" Luis said. "From that State Department position inside the U.S. Embassy in Moscow, with all his special clearance and knowledge of nuclear arsenals, he could make deals with terrorists for weapons grade nuclear materials like you can't imagine in your worst nightmare. Talk about letting the fox guard the henhouse!"

"What about the wicked witch, Senator Aragon?" Patrice asked. "That woman has Freon in her veins. And strong? My so-called 'good arm' still aches."

"She'll cooperate," Luis said. "She's got too much to lose. Let's just say, deals will be made. And you are her witness that she had no part in the murder of Isobel Ellsberg and Larry Dreyfus."

"Don't forget, I'm a witness to the syringe business, too.

Have you found out what was in it?"

"A chemical related to the so-called date rape drug. It wouldn't kill you. But you wouldn't remember what had happened to you," Pauling said.

Patrice nodded. "Nice touch. Did Stefan have the passbooks for the Liechtenstein accounts?" she asked.

"Oh, yes, just like you said he would. They were taken into evidence," Pauling answered.

"Well, that still leaves one enormous unanswered question," Patrice said softly.

Pauling nodded, looking right at Patrice. "It was Taggert who pushed you and Rose off the cliff, but Stefan would have done it if he'd thought of it first and had the opportunity. Rose's quest for truth was a roadblock to the major plans of several vicious, greedy people."

They talked some more, until they wound down from cumulative fatigue, a process that didn't take long, and said good-bye. Luis got a ride with Mel and Danny to pick up Rick's car, leaving Patrice and Rick alone.

For a while they said nothing, each lost in their own thoughts and emotional reaction to the events of the past twelve days. Patrice stared out the window, hypnotized by the prisms of light thrown off by the blinding snow. "Rick," she said with a heavy sigh, "I'd like some time off."

"Time off!" he said. "You've done nothing but lay around for two weeks, and now you want time off?"

"I'd like to spend Christmas in Hawaii. My mom will lend me the money for a ticket. You want to go with me?"

"More than I can possibly express, yes, I want to. But I can't go now. Danny will be gone, Tiffany has decided to find honest work, Carol said she's leaving to go to grad school, and that this time she won't change her mind. Something tells me the paper will be sold again, what with the owner in jail. And now my ace reporter wants to do the one-armed hula in Hawaii, when she has a perfectly good volcano of news erupting right here."

"Well," she said slowly, "if I stay and help you put the *Guardian* back together, will you take me somewhere warm and wonderful when we get our casts off?"

"I, Rick Romero, do solemnly swear to take you, Patrice Kelsey, the woman I love, somewhere warm and wonderful. In fact, come here and sit on my lap, such as it is, and I'll make you feel warm and wonderful this very day."

They kissed, a long, slow kiss, and he was right. She did feel warm and wonderful. Hawaii could wait.